A MIGHTY FORTRESS

Also by LeGrand Cannon
LOOK TO THE MOUNTAIN

A
MIGHTY
FORTRESS

LE GRAND CANNON, JR.

HENRY HOLT AND COMPANY

NEW YORK

Copyright, 1937, by
LE GRAND CANNON, JR.
First published, 1937, by Farrar & Rinehart, Inc.
Published, 1946, by Henry Holt and Company, Inc.

PRINTED IN THE UNITED STATES OF AMERICA

TO

Jeannette Peabody Cannon

[*Chapter 1*]

LEANING FORWARD in his chair, Abel Peele surveyed—
by the good light of the lamp and in the mirror propped
against the Bible on the kitchen table—the side of his face
which he had finished shaving. He noted, as always when
he did this, that it was a good mirror. Pressing the first
three fingers of his left hand against his right cheek, he
drew them slowly downward, feeling the bone beneath—
first the cheekbone and then the jaw—and the skin smooth
under his touch. Smooth, anyway, compared to his fingers.
Well, looked like a fair enough job so far . . . and he
turned to give the razor a few licks on the strop before
starting the other side.

"I suppose," he observed—Minna was back of him, sitting in her rocking chair over by the window—"that the
Reverend would say this was breaking the Sabbath."

It took his wife a moment to answer. Pain happened to
have hold of her just then and she wanted to be sure of
her voice. "Well, if it is, you've broke it pretty regular
every Saturday night since I've known you."

Abel had caught the pause . . . and had guessed closely
at the reason for it. "Yes, sir," he agreed idly, "shaved
every Saturday night since we been married. Five years.
Used to be Wednesdays before. So's I'd look good when
I came to see you."

"I remember."

"Now I got to get slicked up for church, so it's Satur-

1

days. Well, I been regular about it, anyhow. That's a virtue, even in sin."

"You could shave just as regular Friday nights."

"Wouldn't do any good. I'd still have to milk Saturday night. Might's well be hanged for a sheep as a lamb."

Matching proverbs was more than Minna felt up to. The pain was in her back. It was going away now, but it had been worse that time than it had ever been.

Abel turned round to look at her—but he couldn't see her very well because the lamp was too close to his eyes. "What's the matter, Minna?"

"Nothing. Why?"

"Something is. What is it—pain?"

"Crick in my back, I guess. Kind of caught me."

"Going on now?"

"No, it's all right now."

"You sure it ain't—?"

"No, 't's not that kind. I wish 'twas."

He did himself. Anything to get this over with. "Well," he assured her, "don't fret—'nother month, now, 'n' 'twill be."

"I expect."

He turned back to his shaving, biting hard on the formula that after all they were getting just what they'd asked for: they'd prayed for a baby—and now they were going to get one. Maybe Minna had known what all this would be like. But he hadn't. Still, that wasn't the Lord's fault. You'd think a man twenty-seven years old would know enough to find out the price of a thing before he bought it. Well, there was no use trying to back out now. He began to stare at his shaving things, one after another, saying 'that's my razor' and 'that's my water bowl,' trying to get hold of himself. He counted them all over—the

2

wooden dish of soap and the piece of paper with little dabs of lather on it on the stool beside him, his other razor lying on the table, the clean, oily rag for wiping his razor when he'd finished, and last of all his strop, hanging straight down from the small iron hook he'd made for the purpose and set into the table just underneath the edge. Somehow the very neatness of the array—everything handy and in order—shamed him . . . and he managed to put down the confusion in his mind because he must go to work. He reached for the pewter bowl and added some warm water to the drying lather on his face. Then he picked up his razor, and, as he waited for his hand to steady, he reflected wryly that this was another job where it was worse not to finish than it was not to begin.

Clean-shaven, Abel was unique among his New Hampshire neighbors. Fashion, in 1828, demanded whiskers. But Abel, while aware of this, was not interested. And for a beard that would bristle or flow in symbol of his manly strength, he had no need: he stood six feet two in the heavy hose that Minna knit for him, and his thick, narrow shoulders sloped sharply upward to disappear under a great, handsome mane of coal-black hair. He was strong and balanced, and he handled an ax as beautifully as another man might a violin bow. In eight years—since he was nineteen—he had made of the fair-to-middling farm his father'd left him, what was now close to being the best place in New Boston. He could afford to be independent—in shaving or in Sabbath-observance or in anything else. It was a good thing he could, because he would have been anyway.

Minna had begun to rock, adding the *creak*, creak of the chair to the other rhythmic noises in the kitchen— the throb of the katydids that came in from outside, the '*tick*—and tick . . . and *tick*—and tick,' of the clock, and

3

the less rhythmic scrape of Abel's razor. The motion of the chair made her head swim, but she kept on rocking, knowing that Abel was used to the sound of it, hoping that if he heard it he might think she was more comfortable.

Minna was the least mite of a thing. She'd been tow-headed as a child, with two spiky little braids that bobbed up and down behind her sunbonnet and contrasted with the delicate solemnity of her face. Abel had known who she was then, but he was older than she was and he had never really seen her until she was seventeen. By that time the braids were wound severely against her head and the sunbonnet and pinafore had been changed respectively for a very wide-brimmed hat and a stiff white cotton dress. With high boots added. But her face hadn't changed much. Less solemn perhaps, but still delicate and fine, and her eyes the soft blue-gray of powder-smoke.

After they were married, she'd reverted to sunbonnets— except for church—in the summertime, and she couldn't put on an apron without having it look like a pinafore. But she took off her heavy shoes when she was out alone after berries, not in resentment at the shoes' heaviness— all shoes were heavy—but because the dry, hot grass under her toes felt just as it always had.

She couldn't see that she'd get to do much berrying this summer—not blueberries, anyway. They'd all be gone by on the flats by the first of August and she couldn't take a baby on the mountain. The first week in July . . . it was coming nearer and nearer. She looked up at the sky— it was dark now, dark and very deep. But she didn't look away from it.

She said: "We're going to be awful proud, aren't we, Abel?"

Abel was doing the difficult part under his chin. He made a sound of assent, and after a moment said, "There! I guess that'll do," and began to wipe his razor.

" 'Proud'? I am now,—of you, anyhow."

"You needn't be. Three times this week you had to get the breakfast."

"Proud of them, too. Good breakfasts. You'd ought to have tried some."

"Well . . ."—there was no use going into that. "Abel: how soon do you suppose we can take him to church?"

To himself, Abel said, 'Got to get him born first'—but by a miracle of tact what he said aloud was "Soon as you feel like it. They had six of 'em stowed round out in the carriage shed last week."

"Who was watching 'em?"

"Oh, a woman. They swap off. One, one week; another, the next. Has to be somebody that's right to feed 'em."

"I wouldn't like that."

"No, six does seem quite a load. Still, I don't suppose they any one of 'em gets more'n a snack. Just enough to keep 'em quiet."

"I meant I wouldn't like for somebody else to feed mine."

"Well, maybe. That's how they do it, though. I asked Jim Browning. They had theirs there."

"Is she pretty?"

"Oh, I guess. They had it all wrapped up." . . . He was stropping his razor, preparatory to putting it away— *slap*, slap, *slap*, slap—

"Abel—" She'd stopped rocking now.

"Ayuh?"—*slap*, slap . . .

5

"Abel: God's got it all decided—hasn't He?—how it's going to turn out."

Abel sighted along the edge of the blade in the lamp-light—not that he could tell anything that way, especially when the danged thing shook so—and then reached for the oil-rag. "How do you mean," he said, "'. . . going to turn out'?"

"Well . . ."

He knew, all right. "You mean if—if everything's going to be all right afterward?"

"Yes." And then she spoke very calmly: "If the baby is, and if I am."

Abel put down the razor; his forearms rested on the edge of the table, and he was looking at his hands. This was the first time they'd come to talk about that part of it. He'd got to say the right thing. No . . . this was too important: she had a right to what he really thought.

"He could have," he said slowly, "I'll agree to that. He could have decided either way."

Minna said of course He could.

"All right," Abel went on, "and maybe He hasn't de-cided at all."

"They say in church He does—everything, way ahead."

"You asked me," Abel reminded her. "I figure He can decide yes, or no, or not at all. If He's decided at all, what looks to me like the likeliest thing is that He's decided in between yes and no."

"Oh." She half thought he might mean that either the baby or herself would die.

"Like this," Abel was saying carefully: "that every-thing'll be all right—"

Minna had seized on that!

"—only provided that they—us, I mean, you and me—

6

use their brains and do the right thing. And providing there ain't anything else into it that He's figuring on."

"Like what, do you mean?"—resentfully.

"Well, you got to put in something to account for the people that get the short end of the stick when they don't deserve it. That might be us."

Minna knew only too well that it might. It was against that gloomy and unavoidable possibility that she'd asked for assurance.

She said: "Yes, I suppose so."

Abel almost laughed. "That don't seem to help much, does it?" he said. "Well—you asked me, and that's the nearest I can come at it."

Minna didn't tell him that he hadn't come at it at all. She'd forgiven him—and was again peering into the sky. . . . "I wish I knew," she said.

"Well, you won't—not till it's over. That's one thing you *can* be sure of." He put the two razors in their box, and stood up . . . to put the box in its place on the shelf over the fireplace. Then he went over to Minna, and stood beside her chair. He laid his hand softly on her yellow hair.

"You're going to be all right," he said.

As he bent down to her, Minna raised her little face to him. She was smiling. "I'm not afraid," she said. He kissed her, marveling—and told her he guessed it was about time she was going to bed.

After she'd gone, Abel went out through the woodshed to the barn, just to have a look round. It was dark in the barn, and quiet. But not still. Always something going on in a barn. Listen and you'd hear chewing, or a stir and a shifting about somewhere. It was quiet, though. All in

7

order. And he went back into the house, picking up some wood on the way.

He put away the rest of his shaving things, and then thought he'd sit for a minute before going to bed. He settled into his chair—and realized that if he just sat he'd get to worrying. So he lifted the Bible down onto his knees and opened it, turning a few pages until he struck something to his fancy. He read David and Goliath. . . .

He liked that story; he always had. He wondered if the Lord had decided all along that David was going to kill him. . . . No, sir, he didn't believe He had. Take the starch right out of the story, that would. But you take, now, if He'd said to Himself: 'I'll let him kill him, all right—if he can throw straight enough to hit him!'—then you had something. The more you thought about it—he wouldn't want to say this out loud—but the more you thought about it: it'd be a lot more fun for the Lord that way, too. Yes, sir, it would.

All the same, he'd like to know how it was going to turn out. . . .

He stood up suddenly, and blew out the lamp. 'Time to go to bed,' he told himself. And quietly, too,—might be she'd got to sleep already.

He was in bed before she stirred. "Abel, I didn't brush your coat today."

"Oh. Thought you were asleep."

"You'll want to wear it for church tomorrow."

"I can brush it, I guess. You all right?"

"Ayuh. Sleepy."

"Well—good night." If she was sleepy, it was a good sign. He could go to sleep himself on that.

8

MOST PEOPLE SAID it was just a mile from Abel Peele's place to the church. So that, surveyed, it might have proved anywhere from a mile and a quarter to a scant two. Abel himself generally said he guessed it might be a good mile. He was satisfied with the more practical certainty that if he took up his coat off the chair when he heard the church bell pick up to double time, he would, walking comfortably, arrive a safe five minutes after the service had begun. Driving, it took longer. The road was steep, rubbly with stones and crossed by smooth, shelving rock surfaces, so that a man could make better time downhill than a horse. Barring rain or deep snow—when Minna went—they walked; alone, he walked always. Since March, Minna hadn't been at all, being kept home by the welcome dictates of propriety.

It was hot this morning, and no wind—a steamy sort of day, light blue overhead but with the tops of some big, white and gray clouds beginning to show low in the northwest. Thunderstorm later. Abel swung along down the hill, thinking that Reverend would have to put his back into it this morning—there'd be a good many in church thinking about hay. The bell had stopped ringing now, and Abel listened to see if he'd hear the first hymn before he got to the little bridge over Skinner's Brook. He heard it . . . a slow one he didn't like. As he turned into the dooryard of the church, it seemed extra hot. The grass was worn off there, and the sunlight was reflected down from the dry white paint of the building. Over beyond, in the dimness of the carriage shed, he could make out Jim Browning's wife, moving about, trying to get 'em settled down. Well, ought to be another customer for her before long—if everything went well. He put on his coat, buttoned it, and shrugged himself into it as he went up the steps—they needed new treads—and into the vestibule. They were still at work on the first choir-piece, but you didn't have to wait outside for a choir-piece—and he went in.

Abel had always told himself that he was late to church because he didn't like visiting round out in the yard beforehand. Waste of time. But the plain fact of the matter was that he unconsciously enjoyed walking up the aisle when everybody could see him. He was proud of his coat; when Minna went, he was vibrantly proud of Minna; and he was a little proud of being late to church.

The Reverend Mr. Hasketh, darkly perched in his great mahogany chair at the rear of the pulpit, watched young Abel Peele march up the aisle. He saw no sign of humility in Abel's manner, no evidence that he was late in spite of hurry, and not even a hint of apology for his recurrent tardiness. With his head high, Abel opened the door of the Peele pew, entered, and sat down.

In the Lord's House there was, in Mr. Hasketh's view, no middle ground between humility and arrogance. Also in Mr. Hasketh's view, the middle part of the sermon he had chosen for this morning was weak, so weak that the men were liable to get thinking about their hay. As the choir concluded the anthem, the Reverend Mr. Hasketh concluded that the Lord had called his attention to Abel Peele—and he accepted the suggestion in a spirit of earnest gratitude and co-operation which he certainly would not have felt had the hint come from a lesser authority. As a judge of sermons, Mr. Hasketh felt himself practically alone with his Maker.

The service progressed. During certain parts of it, particularly the two anthems, the four hymns, and a long Scripture Reading, Mr. Hasketh got a chance to do a little planning—and even now and again during the forepart of the sermon, which was devoted wholeheartedly to a negative exposition of the divine efficiency as the cause of sinful choices. When the glass showed him that he had finished the first hour, Mr. Hasketh paused. With a fine sense of the dramatic, he reached out and slowly turned the glass, set it down, and watched the tiny cone of sand begin to build up on the bottom. . . .

Abel wondered what was coming next. Suddenly the Reverend swung round—and was pointing his finger straight into Abel's face. "Abel Peele," he said awfully, "you are a sinful man." It was something of a shock.

The next twenty minutes were an earnest, a sincere, and an exceedingly forceful denunciation of Abel Peele and of Abel Peele's conduct. Mr. Hasketh, having identified him both digitally and by name, called him thereafter Child of Satan, Lost Soul, Defiler of the Sabbath, Serpent, and anything else that came happily to mind. He cited the viciousness of Abel's practice of Sunday-milking, and he dwelt at some length on the blasphemous implications of Abel's repeated tardiness at worship. He shook his fist at Abel, he sweat, and he grew hoarse. And although there was no way of telling how much good he was doing Abel, he was pleasantly assured by the rest of the congregation that the Lord had put his finger on just what that sermon needed.

Abel kept his head high throughout it all. Everyone in the church who conveniently could was staring at him. The choir was especially well placed, and even Lizzie Roberts, the soprano, who had had the audience' attention diverted from her during Abel's entrance, could not detect that Abel's expression changed at all.

Not while he was being told to his own stony face that he himself, Abel Peele, was going to writhe in Hell, that white-hot flames would soon be searing his twisting body, and that he was going to scream unheard for mercy through all time to come, did Abel so much as blink an eye. You could see he was listening, though, and he was thinking.

Abel was thinking: 'If God had meant I shouldn't milk on Sunday, He'd have fixed cows so they didn't have to *be* milked on Sunday. I know about cows, and this man doesn't. And the proof of that is that my cows are mostly doing pretty good. But you take *his* cow and she about bursts her bag every Sunday evening—in summer anyhow. Hurts her so bad you can hear her bellering clean up to my place. And each couple of years his cow'll go dry and then the church has to get him a fresh one. I'll admit it's God's will his cows go dry like that. But I say it's more than that. I say it's God trying to teach him that *any* cow has got a right to be milked regular. And the sooner he learns that lesson, the better it'll be for all concerned. God can be patient about it, because a cow every two years don't mean nothing to Him. But it does to us that have to furnish the cows.

'On the other hand, you take preaching, now, and there I got to admit Reverend is good. He knows what he's doing. I don't suppose I ever heard anyone get read out better'n he's doing it right now. He can do some of these people a lot of good. I expect he's *worth* a cow every two years! He's what this town needs, and it's a pleasure to listen to him. All the same, it would probably be a saving

12

thing in the long run if we was to give him milk instead of a cow.'

He'd like to tell Minna when he got home that he'd been read out . . . but you couldn't tell how she'd take it. He'd have to say something about it, though. Some woman be sure to tell her, if he didn't. He wondered how Minna was right this minute. He hadn't quite liked to leave her alone in the house this morning. Getting pretty close to her time. Still, they said if you got by the seventh month, you were generally all right. Minna was delicate, though, and this pain wasn't natural. Might be she'd come ahead of time. He'd thought once or twice this morning there was kind of a queer look to her eyes. Maybe he oughtn't to have left her. But a man had to go to church—and he had a right to expect God wouldn't punish him for *going* to church. He'd be home in another hour, anyhow. If that thunderstorm didn't break—and there wasn't much chance of that in the forenoon—she'd likely be all right.

Reverend, he discovered, had gone on to something else.

Abel resolved that after church he was going to speak to the doctor—even if it was early.

After the benediction, he waited in the aisle for Dr. Craddock so as to get him alone. Doctor told him, well, he'd stop by next week if he got a chance, and not to worry about it. Abel, more or less in apology for speaking to him, told him about the pain. The doctor said, well, now, come to think of it, he was going to be up that way this afternoon—toward suppertime. He'd look in.

When Abel got home he went round to the well to get a drink. He'd take some in to Minna, too. Be colder'n what had stood in the kitchen all morning. . . .

He was lowering the bucket when, above the creak of the sweep, he heard a sound from inside the house.

13

He jerked his head round, and let go the pole. He stood listening . . . the empty bucket came up and jounced. . . . Then he heard the sound again. He didn't say anything, he just made for the door.

He crossed the kitchen to the bedroom door.

Minna was lying on the bed. The baby'd come. That was it, all right—there on the bed. He could see it move. Minna had her eyes closed; she wasn't moving. Abel took hold of the door for a second, and he bit clean through his lip. Then he'd got hold of himself.

He made sure of Minna first. She was alive, only she'd fainted. Good thing she had. He felt the blood from his lip running down his chin. Not enough to amount to much by comparison—but he wiped it off on his sleeve. Certainly no question about that other thing being alive—not so long as it wriggled that way. But it didn't seem right for it to squawk yet. Well, first of all . . . and he got out his knife. No, better get his razor. He stepped into the kitchen, reached the box down off the shelf and opened it. He took out the older of the two razors, trusting it, somehow, better than the new one. Been one of his father's. The blade was worn down narrow, a smooth, dull gray, and it had a good edge on it. Thread, now. Black silk, if it was handy. He looked round for her work basket . . . didn't see it. Maybe it was in the bedroom. No—there it was!—on the floor over by the window—upset. She must have fallen, he thought—and that frightened him. He went over and squatted down on his haunches to search for the right thread. He was fumbling for it, desperately . . . when it occurred to him that Minna'd been breaking the Sabbath, too, sewing. He found the thread instantly after that, stood up, and faced the bedroom. Now, then—

It was easier than he would have thought—he didn't

14

hardly mind it at all. Then he went and got the cover from the kitchen table, rolled the baby into it and set it to one side. He got some water from the well and set to work to bring Minna round. After a while she opened her eyes. He smiled down at her, and he could see she tried to smile back. She even tried to say something.

Abel said: "You're all right. Now don't worry."

She did smile then, and Abel thought maybe there was a chance she was going to be all right. He covered her over with a quilt. There was rum in the kitchen, but there was no use giving her that because she'd only gag on it. He started to put his hand on her head and then, catching sight of his hand, he put it behind him. He said: "I'm going to call someone, Minna. I'll be back in a minute." But she'd closed her eyes again and he couldn't tell whether she really heard him or not.

He went through the kitchen into the woodshed and got down his rifle and the pouch and horn. As he stepped out into the yard, he drew the plug out of the horn with his teeth. He loaded liberally and as fast as he could, tamped home the wadding and fired. Twice more, the same way. Then he reloaded slowly and waited for a minute. He thought maybe the noise might be disturbing to Minna. So he went back in and looked at her. She seemed to be all right. He could see the baby moving. He went out into the yard again, fired, and finished up with two more. He set the rifle in the kitchen when he came in, so that he'd remember to clean it. He was getting low on caps, too. He went in to Minna. She hadn't moved, but she was breathing all right.

He straightened up and looked at the baby. It was a mess. They'd want warm water to wash it with, most likely. He went into the kitchen to get things going.

While he was at it, he heard Thaddeus Blake's horse turn into the yard. He'd figured Thaddeus would probably get there first. Abel laid down the bellows, got up from his knees and went out to meet him. Thaddeus had pretty good sense for a Blake: he'd brought his wife.

He said to Abel: "Your wife?"

And Abel said: "Think it was Injuns?"

Thaddeus always remembered that; afterward he told it about Abel a good many times, and Abel always liked to hear him.

Thaddeus said to his wife: "You go in,"—and she got down and marched right past Abel into the house, without speaking to him. Nor did Abel look at her as she went past.

He said to Thaddeus: "You go for the doctor."

Thaddeus looked a little surprised. "She bad off?"

"I don't know. Go for the doctor."

"Sure, Abel."

Abel turned his horse for him and then went into the kitchen. He heard Minna moan. It hurt him. He thought maybe he'd better pray and he wanted to. He stood there and he sort of looked up. He said in his mind: 'You take care of her. She deserves it better'n most, I guess. I know she does. And so do You. Amen.'

Mrs. Blake appeared in the doorway.

"Abel Peele," she said fiercely, "this is a judgment on you. Suppose she'd died!"

"She ain't, has she?" Abel countered evenly.

"No! And from the looks of it she ain't agoin' to."

"All right. You go back in there and see to her."

Mrs. Blake retired. Pretty soon she called out to know if Abel had that water warm yet. Abel said, no, might be

16

a matter of ten minutes yet. He could hear her sniff—clear out into the kitchen.

Doctor drove in sooner than Abel had expected. Said he'd met Thaddeus Blake down the road a piece. Said he'd heard the shots himself and wondered if that mightn't be it. So, seeing as how Abel had spoke to him after church the way he had, he'd taken the liberty of starting over soon as he'd heard the shots. Mrs. Peele was in the next room? Well, he'd go in.

Abel said: "Go ahead." Craddock had a face like a horse.

When, finally, the doctor came out again, he said to Abel: "Sir, I congratulate you. That's a real fine boy."

"How's Minna?"

"She's doing good, Abel. You done all right."

Abel had always liked Craddock. Hmm . . . boy, eh?

From the day after he was born, it was apparent to Minna at least that the baby looked like his father. All Abel could see was that they both had black hair: in the poor, purple, wizened little face, it was difficult for Abel to detect signs even of humanity. After a month or so, he felt better about it. Then, when Minna pointed out to him that now the baby's eyes were almost as dark as his own, Abel said yes, he'd seen that right along.

Minna was poorly for a while, but she got better. They decided to name the boy Ezekiel, after Abel's brother. Abel said nobody'd ever thought much of his brother Zeke, but he'd kind of liked him. He'd been killed in the war ten or twelve years ago, and even before that, Abel guessed, he'd maybe been kind of wild.

Chapter 3

ALL THROUGH JULY was good growing weather; short spells of hot weather with plenty of rain in between. Grass did well. But milk went down in price, and then butter and then cheese. Conversation after church was gloomy. The trouble, it was bitterly agreed, was the canal. Western hides were coming in so cheap that a New England cow couldn't support herself dead or alive. And look at potatoes: thirty-seven and a half cents a bushel! And corn—why, you couldn't swap corn for sawdust. Look here: supposing a man *should* get a good crop this year—and mind you, that wasn't saying he was *going* to get a good crop—but supposing he *should* get a good crop, just for a change: what *good* was it to him? At these prices, it wouldn't pay him to swing a sickle on it!

Abel had heard it all before, but he couldn't see that it helped him any.

Coming up the hill from church—Minna had thought she might go next week—he stopped in the road to look at his fodder corn. It was the best he'd ever seen it—for this time of year, at any rate. Higher than his head, in some places, and so thick it looked like he'd got a stalk for every kernel he'd sowed. Come to cut it, it was going to run way over what he could silo in his two pits. Be wicked to let all that go to waste. Made you feel sick to think of it—which was one way you knew it was wicked; and that milking on Sunday wasn't. Besides, if every man butchered this fall like they said they were going to, cows might be worth something, come spring. They'd all thought of that, though. And you couldn't go by what a man said when he was talking. When it came time, every last one of them would butcher or not, according to how he felt about it.

What it came down to was this: here was the corn—and you could either feed cows with it, or let it go to waste. He'd feed cows with it. The rest of them could do as they were a mind to.

All the same, it meant digging a new silo-pit. That *was* a job—no getting round it—a big job. It was a big piece of work. And it would take time to do it right. Still, when you got a good silo dug, and lined with good stonework, then you had something. Last as long as you did, anyway—and some after that, too. Yes, sir, quite some time after that. . . .

He wondered who'd have the place then,—who'd be working on it. He hoped it would be somebody who'd know something—somebody who'd say: 'Man had this place in the old days knew how to build a good silo-pit, who*ev*er he was.'

He turned and took a few steps up the hill toward dinner—and then stopped dead in his tracks. The *boy*'d have the farm, wouldn't he!—by gorry, he'd never thought of it up to this minute! And for some time Abel Peele stood there, stock-still, perched on a thank-you-ma'am in the middle of a fine, sunny morning.

He ate a good dinner, and as soon as he'd finished his pie, he went out to have a look round. He'd decided during dinner just where he'd put the pit, but he wanted to look at the place. He paced it off and it came out all right. It would be handy to the barn, which was the main thing, and the drainage would be good. He hoped he wouldn't run into too much rock, but he was pretty certain he wouldn't strike any solid rock. He sat down on the sill of the corncrib to think about it. He figured he

19

could put in some time on it in the early mornings, before the sun got hot, and perhaps another hour or so in the evening before going to bed. That way, it wouldn't interfere so much with his regular work. Ought to take about four to five weeks, depending on what kind of digging he ran into. There wouldn't be any roots, but you couldn't tell about the rocks until you came to them.

As it happened, he didn't come across but one rock that was too big to handle. He dug a hole for that in the bottom of the pit. Then he prized out the rock from the place where it was and it slid down into the hole. Smaller rocks and stones he kept separate from the dirt he took out and he used those to line the sides and bottom of the pit. He found he had more than enough. So he used the extra to build a rim, about a foot and a half high, round the top. He hadn't figured on that in the beginning, but it gave him another three loads of capacity. He used the dirt to hill up round the rim on the outside, and then seeded that with oats, so as to hold it. All in all, it was quite a piece of work. Toward the end, he had to put in some whole days on it, in order to get it done in time.

The last evening he worked on it, he kept at it so long that Minna came out to see what was going on. He'd hoped she would; he hadn't quite liked to call her just to tell her he'd finished something. She came and peered in over the top and exclaimed at how big it was. Abel was afraid she wasn't going to go down inside it—it looked twice as big from the inside.

She asked if she might go down, and he said all right, if she wanted to, but to be careful of the steps. He helped her down. As they stood side by side, looking up, the top of the rim was a good three feet above her head. She stepped over to the wall and ran her hand over the stonework.

She said: "Abel, it's the loveliest silo-pit I ever see. Home, we didn't have one could hold a candle to it."

Abel said, huskily, he guessed it would do all right; it was solid—ought to last for a while, anyway.

Minna laughed. She said it would last as long as either of them did.

Abel couldn't think how to put it. . . . "Longer," he said.

Minna knew what he meant. And she realized for the first time that everything he did, now, on the farm would be done with that in mind. It would seem strange to her at first . . . but Abel would still want her to come look at things—tell him how good they were.

She said: "I got to go in to him."

Abel helped her up the steps and she went into the house. He stayed outside to wash up. It was a hot night—muggy, too. The water felt good on his face. He guessed he'd take his shirt off and give himself a good sluicing. As he was drying his back he saw some heat lightning off to the south. Be hot again tomorrow. It was good and dark now—and the lightning bugs high in the air. The locusts and katydids were going so steady you didn't hear them. He thought he heard the baby cry and when he went in Minna was feeding it. He stood looking down at them for a moment. He was dog-tired, clean through. His head was heavy. It was night. He wanted to go to bed.

Minna looked up. "You go to bed, Abel. You're tired." Then she looked down at the baby, without waiting for Abel to answer.

"Might as well, I guess."

She bent her head slightly over the baby. "We're doing all right," she said.

Abel went off to bed. He was so tired he'd as leave turn in with his boots on. Wouldn't Minna set up a howl! One heel in the jack, he thought to himself: 'What I like about that pit is the stonework. That's going to last.' The boot gave a little at the heel and he drew his foot out of it. Now the other one . . . that always came easier. Felt good to get those things off. He sat down on the bed and stretched and wiggled his toes. 'Lay not up for yourselves treasures on earth . . .' they said. '. . . *for yourselves*,' maybe that was the point. Finally, as he rolled into bed, he thought: '. . . and any fool moth *did* get in there, he wouldn't know what to do with himself. . . .' He closed his eyes. 'Dark now. In six hours it'll be light. . . .'

He was asleep when Minna came to bed—scarcely stirred at all, just moved his arm a little.

[*Chapter 4*]

SOME MONTHS before Zeke was born, Abel had reasoned that now that the ice was broken, she'd probably go right ahead, after this one, and have a lot more. But she didn't.

Minna put it down to the will of God—and was grateful.

Abel, for his part, assumed that the situation was in accordance with the will of God, because, reasonably, everything had to be. It did not disturb that assumption to wonder about some more natural, intimate cause, and he went first of all to that set of related facts which comprised the hour when Zeke was born. They were very

22

clearly in his mind. He concluded that some delicate element within her, something essential to a recurrence of the miracle of conception, had, during the wrenching brutality of that hour, got knocked loose. Well, he was just as glad. If there was anything funny about women having babies, he guessed he'd missed the point to it. One would do him first rate . . . he knew now what he might have to pay for a second.

Zeke was growing into a healthy youngster—and to look more and more like his father. All except his nose. It took time to build a Peele nose, to shape it and to weather it and to give it that authority which would make it an unmistakable and respected Peele nose. For a time Zeke had just a baby's nose, and after that he had a boy's nose. But his hair was his father's smooth, black hair and the frame of him was hard and trim. He was a good-looking boy.

Abel didn't undertake to teach him what work was until he was twelve years old. Except for chores. You could put a boy at chores just as soon as he was big enough to do them. And he didn't have to be so very big, either. Abel himself had swaggered and shouted and whacked the rumps of complacent cows coming up the lane when he was six years old. And when his arms wouldn't reach halfway round a peck measure, he'd had to keep the wood-box filled—not just fill it when he was told to, but see that it was *kept* filled. He could remember now his terror as he tripped over the doorsill and the wood roared and bumped and slithered across the floor. He'd got whipped for that and it had done him good. Taught him to be more careful. And now when young Zeke, all of six years old, would come staggering in the door with an armful of wood and fall, Abel did not cheat the boy out of his lesson: he made him pick it up himself, every stick—and he told him to wipe his nose and that he'd get done a lot quicker if he didn't try to carry too much at one trip.

Up to the time a boy is twelve years old, chores are about all he can do on a farm without getting in the way. A small boy handling a team of horses is a source of pride to his father, but it's a misplaced pride that might better be in the horses. When the boy is twelve, though, if he's ever going to be good for anything, he can be put to work and the work won't have to be done over again by a man.

Abel had been waiting for this time to come. He wanted to see to it that there were things on the farm, as parts of it, that the boy had built himself. Later on, those things would hold him—the boy, that is. He'd feel the pull of them. And he would not lie uneasy at night, itched by a temptation to go away from them and try something else.

On Zeke's twelfth birthday, Abel gave him a job of work to do. He gave him a man to work with him and the oxen. He set him to building a stone wall.

Including woodland, Abel had three hundred and forty acres now and three to five men on the place the year round. More in summer. He was getting ahead. Some others weren't. Thaddeus Blake was doing all right, but Jim Browning had pulled out—gone to Indiana. Said his land had run out. Abel's land didn't run out. His farm was better now than when he'd started. There was no special trick to it: every so often he'd let a field rest—though some said that that was more than he did for the men who worked for him. Still, he got good men and some of the best ones stayed. For about a year and a half now he'd had a big black man on the place named Joe. He was a powerful man in a slow, easy sort of way; give him the right kind of work and he could swing into it twelve or fourteen hours at a stretch—and the same thing the next day. Abel counted up once that Joe had hoed four miles of corn between sunup and sundown. He told him so . . . and Joe said he was sorry, but he'd done the best he could. For a while, at first, Abel tried to teach him to handle an ax, but big Joe never could get the knack of it. He could strike fair and of course deep, but it was only luck when he took out a nice chip. He never seemed to have any notion at all what the grain was going to do to his ax. Abel thought he'd better stop him while Joe's feet were still on his legs.

But when Abel came to pick a man to work with young Zeke on the wall, he picked Joe.

It was a hot day when they started and it kept getting hotter. Joe and the boy were working some distance from the house, down over a rise. The field was lying fallow that summer and Zeke knew his father would have it plowed under after they'd got the rocks out. Zeke guessed his father thought that building a stone wall was the easiest thing to do with the rocks. If his father'd had to build the wall himself, he'd have seen that dragging the rocks to the edge of the field and dumping them into the woods would have been about ten times easier. But it was not likely to help things any to tell him so.

First of all, they took down the old shad-fencing and piled it up for wood. They got that done before dinner. Zeke had had in mind to go swimming that afternoon, but it didn't work out that way, because after dinner his father went out with them to set up the sighting stakes. That took up the best part of the afternoon and then his father hung around after that to see them get started on digging the trench for the footing stones. They had to get down below the frost line and Joe didn't even know what a frost line was. He had to be shown. By the time Zeke did get a chance to go swimming, along in the evening, it didn't seem worth it to go alone. He decided he might as well go to bed.

Day after day, for a week, Joe was digging that trench. And all that time Zeke was hauling stones. Four kinds: ones he could just roll onto the stoneboat by hand, ones he had to use the bar to get them out of the ground with, ones that he had to dig away from around them and use the bar too, and a fourth class, rocks so big that he had to leave them for Joe, the oxen and a chain. Eligibility for this fourth class varied with the time of day. When he'd got the stoneboat loaded, he'd ride on it to the edge of the trench where he'd dump the rocks. The oxen had far and away the easiest job of all. Most of the time they stood.

Toward noontime, one morning, Zeke went off to fetch some water. Joe didn't notice he'd forgotten to take the gourds with him, and when Zeke came back for them Joe was working with his shirt off. Zeke caught sight of some long gray scars running slantwise across Joe's back. He asked Joe what they were. Joe put on his shirt and was slow about answering, but finally Zeke got it out of him that they were where a lion had scratched him when he was sleeping out one night in the jungle in Africa. Zeke wanted to sit right down and have the whole story. But Joe wouldn't talk about it; he said it was bad luck to talk about those kind of marks. Zeke wouldn't let up on him; he'd seen some smaller scars, fainter, running crisscross of the others, and he asked Joe if that was the same lion. Joe said it was the same *kind* of lion, only a different time. Zeke said he'd have thought that after a while Joe would have learnt not to sleep out in the jungle. And Joe said he *had* learnt. And then he tried to talk about something else so

26

that Zeke wouldn't ask him any more questions. Zeke stuck to him; he wanted to know why some of the marks went one way and some went the other way. Joe said that the second time it had been a left-handed lion. Then he swung round and he picked Zeke up and held him right straight out in front of him—straight out—and Zeke didn't so much as dare wriggle. He didn't know what Joe was going to do with him. Joe said he mustn't never let on to nobody about seeing those marks, and he'd got to swear his oath. Zeke promised, all right. Because Joe said if he *was* to let on, the lions were liable to haunt big Joe and they might come in the night some time and take him away—whoosh!—like that! When he said "whoosh!" he swung Zeke clean up over his head and shook him. Zeke looked down and saw his big pink mouth. He was so scared that when Joe set him down he ran off a ways, and Joe had to talk to him to get him to come back. But later on, he got to figuring. Daytimes, he thought it might be fun to see if the lions really would come for Joe. Nights, he thought it wouldn't.

There wasn't any excitement all the rest of the time, except one day Joe knocked over a middling-sized wood-chuck with a stone.

Zeke was getting pretty sick of hauling rocks. He had an idea his mother was kind of sorry for him, too; she acted a little that way. His father didn't, though. His father wasn't sorry for him a bit. Mealtimes, his father joked him a good deal—more than usual and worse jokes.

He bashed his fingers and he stubbed his toes. It kept getting hotter all the time. He noticed for the first time in his life that Joe smelled bad when he got too close to him. Then his head began to ache whenever he bent over, and soon after that it ached all the time. Finally, he saw what he was up against: his father was trying to see if he'd quit.

One afternoon he had to go into the woods to be sick. He didn't tell Joe because he was ashamed of it, and because Joe'd tell his mother and she'd make him take oil. That night they had pork and greens for supper. His father helped him, and when Zeke got the pannikin in front of him, he didn't think he could get down a mouthful and stay at the table. But, if he didn't eat them, it would be kind of a signal to his father that he'd won. He ate them, somehow, but it made him sweat a good deal while he was doing it.

Next day, in the morning, his father showed up to see how they were getting on. Zeke tried not to speak to him. He'd found out at supper that he hated his father and was doubtful if he ever would speak to him—he'd probably be leaving home anyhow as soon as he got this wall finished, although he might die instead.

His father stood and watched them awhile, and Joe said: "Comin' good, Mr. Peele! Comin' good!"—and his father said, "Yes, looks all right," and pretty soon he went away.

Later, it came on to rain. It felt good.

When Zeke went to bed that night there were only three days between him and the finish. . . . He spent them in bed, having the yellow jaundice.

He'd lie there and all he could see was that field and the wall. The wall would go up and down, wavy. When he'd open his eyes, the room would move, too. His father came in sometimes to speak to him and he'd never known his father to seem so big and so strong. It made him feel worse just to think how strong his father was. He wished his father'd get sick sometime, himself. Then he'd come in and stand by the foot of his father's bed. That would show him.

Tad Blake and Henry Stevens came by one day to see if he could go swimming. He heard his mother talking to them at the door. They went away. He didn't suppose he'd ever be well enough to go swimming and he cried for a while. His father came in later and sat down on the foot of the bed. It made the covers tight over Zeke's legs so he couldn't move them. His father said he had a present for him. Zeke knew his father could get anything in the world for a present for him if he wanted to—and if he put his mind to it. He could buy him a gun if he wanted to. It turned out to be a piece of paper. His father explained he was giving him that field—to own. This was the paper to prove it. He said he was probably the only boy round who owned a field that was his all to himself and always would be. He held out the paper for Zeke to see his name on it.

Zeke tried to look at the paper, but he couldn't, because he was about to cry. He couldn't help it. His father stood up and Zeke turned over in bed, away from him.

Zeke felt terribly. He wished his father'd go away. He wanted some water, too.

His father kept on standing there and then Zeke heard him go over to the door. He stopped there and turned round and then he said: "You want some more water, son?"

Zeke said, "No, thank you, pa," and as soon as his father had gone away he wished he'd come back, or his mother would, or Joe, or somebody.

He was a lot better the next day. He ate a whole custard and it made his stomach feel fine, although he was still hungry. When his father came in to see him again, they laughed and joked and had a great time together. Zeke knew his father was a wonderful man. And he didn't care, now, that his father had beaten him about the wall. He even told his father about wanting a gun. And his father said, well, now, he'd had in mind to pay him something for the work he'd done on that wall, and he wouldn't be surprised if maybe that wouldn't just about cover it.

It was cool that evening, and Zeke fell asleep early hearing his mother and father talking in the kitchen. When he woke up again, it was dark and everything was still and he could see moonlight coming through the window onto the wall. He thought he'd like to get up and look out, so he rolled over onto his stomach and slid out feet first, pushing down on the bed with his hands and then taking his weight off it gradually as he stood up, so it wouldn't creak. He got over to the window and slid it back as easy as he could and put his head out. He looked around, first, and then looked down—Joe!—sitting with his back up against the house and his legs straight out in front of him and his head kind of drooped down on his chest. Sound asleep, Joe was, propped up against the house in the moonlight. Zeke had been scared when he saw him, and now he wanted to laugh. He wanted to wake Joe up—he could almost reach the top of his head—and talk to him . . . only they'd hear him if he did that. He stayed there awhile and then he drew back into the room, shut the window and went back to bed. You know, it was kind of nice having Joe there. And Joe was just the kind of person to think of that, too.

[Chapter 5]

ZEKE WAS SITTING in church. Church wasn't so bad—
long as you sat up straight, you could think about anything
you wanted to. He'd been in church every Sunday since
he could remember—and some before that—and he'd found
out how to handle it. He'd been looking forward to this
morning. He was going to think about running away to
go to sea. Be fifteen next month, and it was high time he
was doing something about it.

He set himself to look the minister plumb in the face.
He could do that for a while and pretty soon he wouldn't
be hearing a sound out of him. Then he was free to
think. . . .

It wasn't so much the sea part of it that was going to
be fun—although it would be fun being called 'Captain
Peele, sir,' and bossing everybody around—the real fun
would be when you went ashore and strolled up and down
the streets and all the people looked at you. A Yankee
skipper—say, about eighteen—would be quite a sight in
some of those places . . . like London and China and . . .
and New York, and those places. And now and again he'd
come home and bring his mother a lot of presents and sit
up in the evening and talk with his father.

Old Hasketh was getting ready to give out the notices.
Zeke generally listened to those—sometime there might be
some news in them. Old Hasketh certainly looked like a
turkey buzzard, a black one—about to starve to death. He
was giving out now about the revival meeting three weeks
off. They all knew about that! Zeke had known about it
for a month or more. And old Hasketh stood up there and
made as though it were a big piece of news. . . . At that

31

he left out the important part, which was that the man who was coming to run the whole show was going to stay at their house.

Abel, when the matter of a revival week had first come up in meeting, had been against it. Hasketh had spoken next. He was disappointed, he said; he'd been counting on the visiting divine's staying at Brother Peele's place. That had put Abel in a tight place. He didn't approve of the revival meeting and he'd said he didn't, and he wasn't going to change. All the same, a visitor as entertaining and traveled as a revivalist preacher was not an opportunity lightly to be let go. So Abel spoke again and said that even though he himself was against the revival meeting, still, if the church wanted to have one, that was up to them—and he'd be glad to entertain the Reverend Watling to the best of his ability. That woman of Tad Blake's put in that perhaps the Reverend Watling might prefer to be in a house where the Lord's work was not opposed. Abel said perhaps he might—that was up to the church. It was voted to have him stay at Abel's. Everyone wanted to make the best impression possible on the Reverend Watling, and Abel Peele had the house and the farm to do it.

Mr. Watling showed up on a Saturday, as he had said he would in a letter, and he got there just about in good time for dinner. Zeke had been keeping an eye out for him all morning. He was around the yard when the man drove in. Zeke liked him as soon as he saw him. He drove a fine-looking black mare—drove her well—and he had a big, black hat pushed back on his head. He said, "Good morning," to Zeke and smiled—not "Hello, there, sonny," or "young man," or anything like that—just good morning, same as he would to anyone, easy and pleasant. Zeke liked him. She *was* a fine-looking mare! Not like the old bone-bag that Hasketh perched up behind looking like he was waiting to eat her soon as she died. Zeke took the mare's head and she stood for him nicely. She was sweated some from the hill and there was old sweat on her from earlier in the morning. The man must have stopped down in the village.

"You'd be Mr. Peele's son."

"Yes, sir."

"Zeke, isn't it?"

"Yes, sir."

"My name's Watling."

"Yes, sir, I know it is."

He got down and stretched and grinned at Zeke. Zeke grinned back. He was glad the man was going to be there a week. He'd get to see him a lot. And because he'd been the first one to see him, before his mother and father had, the man sort of belonged to him.

Zeke's mother came out of the house. She had on her best apron. Reverend Watling stepped over and made a low bow to her. Zeke couldn't tell whether his mother would like that or whether she'd think it was too fancy. When his mother up and dropped him a curtsy back again, Zeke nearly let go of the mare. He'd never seen her do *that* before! They said some things back and forth to each other and then Zeke's mother said to Zeke for him to put the Reverend's horse up and bring in his bag. Zeke didn't know what bag she was talking about and he didn't know which he was supposed to do first. But he wasn't going to ask. The man said, "Here, I'll take the bag," and he came over and lifted it out of the back as easy and light as Joe could have done. He said to Zeke: "Tell your man not to water her till she's cooled out, will you? She's tender that way—more'n you'd think."

Zeke said: "Yes, sir, I'll see to it."

Zeke led her down to the barn. There wouldn't be one of the men there now. He'd unhitch her and sponge out her mouth and then rub her down himself. And not a drop of water would she get till he was through. He looked back toward the house. They'd gone in. My, she was a pretty horse! He patted her neck. She seemed to take to it. He wished somebody could see him.

Abel came in to dinner and found the Reverend Watling sitting in the kitchen talking to Minna. The Reverend got up when Abel came in and they shook hands and Abel inquired what sort of trip he'd had—he'd come up from Worcester. Watling said he'd had a good trip, taken him just two days. Abel liked his face. It was quiet and pleasant. He was well dressed, too. Had on a good frock coat and a white linen shirt and had his boots all shined up like a sailor's hat.

Minna went and called Zeke and then she put the dinner on and they sat down. Reverend Watling asked the blessing, which was short—not over two or three minutes. When they straightened up, Abel noticed that Zeke had slicked his hair down with water. He hadn't a doubt he'd brushed it with the currycomb, but it would be mean to say anything and it would only distress his mother. He asked Watling how things had looked on his way up, and was told what crops appeared to be doing well and just how well, and what crops weren't. The man had kept his eyes open, Abel found, and he'd known what to look for. He could tell about it, too. The conversation ran about that way all through dinner: Abel asking questions and the Reverend Watling giving him good answers to them. Abel could see he was a capable man. He'd probably take two or three hundred dollars out of the church before the week was out, but it wasn't as though he couldn't earn the money any other way.

Minna scarcely said anything. She'd been worried about her dinner . . . but from the way the Reverend tucked it away, it seemed safe to say that *he* was satisfied with it, anyhow. She'd feel more comfortable, though, when they'd got past the pie. She'd never been very good at pie.

Toward the end of the meal, Mr. Watling had some talk with Zeke about the mare. He told him where she'd come from and how she'd been bred. Zeke said he supposed a mare like that must be worth an awful lot of money. His mother started to say something to Zeke, but the man went right ahead talking before she could get it out. He said, well, he couldn't say really just what she had stood him in money, because he'd come by her in a trade. He said it was funny how many people always seemed to want to swap horses with a preacher. He said it slow and as though he were thinking about it, and Zeke was surprised when his father laughed right out. Once his father'd got started, Mr. Watling laughed, too. His father said maybe they couldn't tell a preacher from a minister. And Mr. Watling said, either that or they couldn't tell a preacher from a horse-trader. And his father said, well, you mustn't expect too much of them.

After dinner Mr. Watling said he'd got to go down into the village to talk to the minister—make some plans about the meeting tonight. He asked Zeke's mother what time they had supper—but his father spoke up and said generally six o'clock, but he guessed on account of the meeting they'd better have it earlier tonight, say half past five—how would that do? Mr. Watling said fine! he'd be on deck. But he warned Zeke's mother he never ate much before a meeting and not to tempt him too strong.

35

Zeke's proprietary feeling toward the man had so strengthened and developed by the time they'd got into the church that night that he seemed to himself to be wholly on Mr. Watling's side of the fence. He was not a part of the audience at all, nor would anything that Mr. Watling might say be addressed to him. He was there to watch his friend, Mr. Watling, work at whatever it was he did and he felt sure that Mr. Watling was going to be good at it. If only the people would *see* that he was!

Zeke sat between his father, who was in his regular place filling up the end of the pew next the door, and his mother, who had on her shiny black dress. Zeke never liked her to wear that dress—it made her hair look so light, and her face sort of bright and separate from the rest of her. He liked her in the kind of dress she wore at home; it made her look more the same all over.

Old Hasketh had to get up and talk awhile first and then they sang a couple of hymns and then Mr. Watling began. Zeke saw that everyone—and the church was full—was paying attention. He took it to be a good sign. Although he didn't like it that Mr. Watling was content to get off to such a slow start—not even waving his arms. He just seemed to be going along easy, not talking any louder than he had at supper. But they were listening to him, and they were watching him,—Zeke seemed to be the only person who was looking round.

All of a sudden, Mr. Watling had somehow started them into a hymn. That was a new dodge! And they sang it, too—best Zeke had ever heard. Four verses, and in the last one they sang like billy-o! Mr. Watling took a step forward just as the noise died away and he held out both hands to them and started talking again just as gentle as before, but his voice was stronger and had more pull to it.

Some of the people were leaning forward toward him. Zeke began to feel easier, more confident. There was another hymn, almost shouting this time, and again Mr. Watling stepped forward and picked them up at the end of it and swung them along without a break. He was getting warmed up to it. Zeke saw him loosen his collar—but he didn't believe anyone else saw it—and he wanted to call out to him that he was going great.

"Amen . . ." somebody said—over across the church. It had a funny sound. It went right through Zeke, made him afraid. Mr. Watling was going right on, stronger than ever, moving from side to side now, and he'd stand still and stretch his arms straight up in the air and tip his head back, with the light from the lamps making his face look as though he were a different man. A woman called out "Amen and Amen!" and Zeke could hear someone behind him crying. It didn't seem to be the same church as it was on Sundays.

Mr. Watling leaned out toward the people and held his hands out to them. He'd brought his voice way down low, so that he seemed to be speaking to each one of them separately, and yet it filled the church until it was the only thing in it—except his face. Zeke couldn't hear what he was saying, but he knew what he wanted: he wanted him to come up there—and so he'd go. He started to get up— and then he saw that his father was in the way.

His father was too big to climb over. Zeke stopped. He didn't know what to do and he felt queer. Then his father turned round to him and smiled, friendly and comfortable, and his face the same as always. Zeke watched his father's face for a minute, and then he felt good, and the queerness gone out of him. He hitched back into his seat.

There wasn't much to it after that. Milly Clarke went

up the aisle looking kind of bug-eyed and weaving around some, but Mr. Watling didn't do anything to her when she got there. He could see she didn't amount to much. She was pale and skinny and had been converted half a dozen times already. Nobody wasted a hallelujah on her. A few more went up after she did, but Zeke could see Mr. Watling had eased off. After all, he had a week to go and there wasn't any sense in trying to convert everybody the first night. They wound up with some more singing and then Mr. Watling was very polite and stepped aside to let old Hasketh come forward and finish it off with a prayer—just as though *he* amounted to something!

Zeke noticed that there hadn't been any collection. He spoke to his father about it, coming out. "Won't fire till he's in range," his father said.

During the week, Zeke went every night. Daytimes, he'd get to ride around with Mr. Watling, here and there, wherever Mr. Watling had to go. Zeke knew the roads and the short cuts. And when Mr. Watling was inside, Zeke would keep the flies off the mare and talk to her. Her name was Sheba. Mr. Watling said it wasn't *his* choice, she'd been named that when he got her. But Zeke thought it was a fine name for her, all the same. Three times, Mr. Watling let him drive her.

All through the week, he knew he'd never had such a good time in his life. After he'd get to bed it would be a long time before he'd go to sleep, what with hearing the meeting still going in his head and thinking about the stories Mr. Watling had told him during the day.

People said the meetings were first rate. Church full every night and more and more people going up the aisle every time. Milly Clarke got converted fresh every night. Zeke's father laughed about it and said, poor Milly! maybe she was entitled to it, at that. But his mother didn't think it was funny. Zeke didn't see what was funny about it, either. He felt it wasn't very respectful toward Mr. Watling.

The next to last night was the first time they had a collection. Mr. Watling took it up himself. He used a big, round, pewter platter instead of one of the little cloth bags on a stick that they had on Sundays. He'd got to know a good many of the people now and he spoke to them as he went round and thanked them for what they put in. Some people didn't put anything in, probably because they didn't have any money with them. But Mr. Watling said he thanked them just the same.

The last night was the big night. They had an extra amount of singing and it was fine, loud singing with lots of swing to it, because by now everybody was feeling worked up, this being the last night and they could let themselves go. Before Mr. Watling had hardly got started, the 'Amens' and the 'Hallelujahs' began to crop out all over the church. Milly Clarke started off on her regular trip looking more bug-eyed than ever, and then when she was halfway up, she fell down in a kind of fit and three or four of the men carried her out.

Right in the middle of it, Mr. Watling said he wanted everybody to come up front and get his blessing, single file beginning with the front pews on his left—now then, Mr. Peters, you lead the way. Mr. Peters started up and Mrs. Peters after him, and then old Mrs. Greene, all bent over, who was Jimmy Peters' grandmother, and then the pew back of them. The big platter was on a little table right next to Mr. Watling and Mr. Peters put some money in it. Zeke couldn't tell how much, but you could hear it clink. Mrs. Peters took a pin off her dress and put that in.

Zeke couldn't see what the old lady did, but she did something. And Mr. Watling blessed them. Everybody went up. And everybody put something in the platter. Then Mr. Watling would bless them. It came turn for the Peeles' pew. Zeke stood up and so did his mother. But his father sat still. His father looked up at Zeke and said, "I'm not going. You can go if you want to," and he opened the door of the pew and pulled his legs in under him to make room for Zeke to get by. Zeke didn't know what to do. His father said: "It's all right. It's up to you." Zeke looked up where Mr. Watling was and said: "I—I guess I better go." He didn't look at his father again, he just went. He was most of the way there when he found his mother hadn't come with him. He wanted to go back then, but there were so many people behind him, he couldn't. He went ahead. When he got up to the platter, he didn't have anything to put in. So he put in his knife. Then he was opposite Mr. Watling. Mr. Watling was just bringing his hands down after blessing the man in front of Zeke. He saw who Zeke was and his face changed all of a sudden to what it was like at home. He said, "Hello, Zeke; thanks for coming up," and he held out his hand and shook hands with him. Next thing Zeke knew he was on his way back to his own pew. He felt happy. His father made room for him and he sat down.

Driving home, Zeke couldn't make up his mind whether to speak to his father about it or not. He'd been wanting to for several days, but he hadn't been able to get the right chance. He was sure it would be best to speak to his father when he was alone and now that meant he wouldn't get a chance to do it until tomorrow morning, because he'd have to go to bed as soon as they got home, and his father and Mr. Watling would be sitting up talking. Tomorrow morning was the time—first thing.

He was up early, and when his father came down to the barn before breakfast, Zeke was waiting for him. He didn't know how to begin and so he stood around and waited. He hoped his father might say something that would give him a start. But his father just went right ahead, going from place to place, doing the things he had to do. Zeke followed him 'round.

Finally his father said: "You got your chores done?"

"Yes, sir."

"Up early."

"Yes, sir."

"Well—what's on your mind?"

Zeke was in it now. "Do you think I could get a job with Mr. Watling?"

"I thought likely. You said anything to him about it?"

"No, sir."

"Talked to your mother?"

"No, sir."

"What'd you have in mind to do for him, son?"

"Anything. Look out for Sheba—keep the buggy shined up—drive him round—anything he'd let me."

"No preaching for a while, I suppose."

"No, sir."

"You want to leave here, do you?"

"No, sir. I figured just for the summer."

"Set on it, are you?"

"I'd like to, father. I'm fifteen."

"Yes. So they tell me. Well, I don't know as I can compete. You didn't figure he'd *pay* you, did you?"

"I thought maybe it could be—well, like an apprentice."

"Thought you said just for the summer."

"Well, you know—I mean: I thought it could be like an apprentice while I was working for him."

"Yes, I know. You run along now. I got to finish up here."

Zeke wanted to say, "Well, can I?"—but his father turned and went into the barn after something and Zeke thought he'd better go away. It must be still quite a long time to breakfast . . . he guessed he'd go down and look at his field. He had it to oats this year, and they were up as high as any around. Joe said higher.

Minna came out to the barn after some eggs and found Abel sitting on the bench by the harness pegs, doing nothing.

"Abel! You sick?"

"No. Why?"

"Well . . ."

"I got to think *some*times, haven't I? He wants to go with Watling."

For a moment her face seemed to harden—she sounded accusing: "You going to let him?"

"I been thinking about it, yes."

She turned away and looked out the door. "He won't come back," she said quietly.

"In the fall," Abel said.

"But—what if he gets sick?"

"He won't. He's sound as a dollar."

"He was sick a while ago," she said desperately.

"Three years," Abel reminded her.

"Where is he now?"

"Gone down to look at his oats. He'll be back."

Minna didn't say anything for a long time.

Finally Abel said: "It's no more than fair, Minna,—I figure."

42

Minna turned round then. She came toward Abel; she was trying to smile. "Well, if you've figured," she said, "there's no use of *me* talking."

"Not a mite," he agreed cheerfully. "Set down—you've got time enough for your eggs—I want to tell you."

"All right—" she sat down on a little stool. "Abel! He's no more than a baby! You *know* that!"

Abel was not to be deflected. "It's like this," he said. "I want him to stay here. It's a good farm and, far as I know, if a man's good for anything, farming's the best thing there is."

Minna nodded mournfully. Abel always had to begin with things she knew anyway. Then, when she agreed with those, he thought she had to agree with the rest of it.

"But farming's the only thing I do know," he went on. "As I see it, I got no right to tell him it's the best thing when I never tried the others."

"He'll come back wanting to be a preacher," Minna said.

"There's worse things than a preacher—a good one, anyhow."

"But, Abel, all the things—everything you've done on the place—since he was born—"

"Sure," Abel nodded, "I know. Oak slats in the corncrib, 'stead of chestnut—so's they'd last. I know. And every stone went into that silo-pit—just right, so's it'd last. Last longer'n we would, we said. I been thinking about that. *Why* did I want it to last so? For him? Well, partly. That wasn't the whole of it, though. Here's the main reason: I wanted those things to last because I'd worked on 'em. My own sweat dripped off my chin into the mortar in that silo; and I danged near nailed my thumb into that corncrib, too, if I remember. They'll last, all right. I saw to that. Because someday he might be using them—after I was gone. He might be working with a gang of men. Maybe he'd say to 'em: 'Pile her in, boys! My father built that silo-pit, and she's a good one!' You know—" it was hard for him to say this, even to Minna—"you know—I'd be alive, too, then—in a way, sort of."

Minna saw a smile draw down the corners of his mouth.

". . . be some satisfaction," he added, "even if I *was* in Hell."

She was not greatly enlightened. "But why do you want him to go away?"

Abel had really supposed he'd made it clear. "Because," he said, "it wasn't for his sake I wanted him to stay. It was for mine."

In that case, there was only one answer. "I guess he'll go, then."

"Ayuh." Abel stood up. "Well, I got to go to work." He wished Minna'd say something—make it easier. He couldn't just walk out of the barn and leave her sitting there. . . .

[*Chapter 6*]

AT ELEVEN O'CLOCK Joe let go her head and she danced out of the yard and Zeke swung her into the road. He couldn't wave good-by, but he turned his head and grinned at them and saw his mother wave her apron. The mare saw it, too—and they went drumming up the road as if she'd been hitched into a sulky.

As soon as she'd quieted down some, Zeke pulled out his watch to see what time it was. It was really his father's

44

watch. That is, it had been. Zeke wasn't quite sure just whose it was now. His father had held it out to him while his mother was doing up his things. He'd said: "Here, take this along with you. You may need it to tell you when it's time to come home." Zeke had taken the watch into his hand and was looking at it—and then his father had gone out of the room.

They had a great summer. Eight meetings altogether, each one a week long, and traveling in between. Every week Zeke would send a letter home. He'd tell in it where they'd be the next week and then, as soon as they got there, he'd go first of all to the post office. Every single time there was at least one letter for him. Sometimes two from his mother.

One week they didn't have any meeting. Mr. Watling said he'd been dickering with a church in Bellows Falls for that week, but the thing hung fire so long that when it finally fell through it was too late to get anything else. Zeke was worried about it. But Mr. Watling didn't seem to mind a bit. He said he wouldn't take less than sixty per cent from Baptists if he never saved another soul in his life. He'd go back to horse doctoring sooner than split fifty-fifty! It took all the dignity out of it—put you right on a level with the minister—and a Baptist minister, at that! He meant it, too. He bought some bottles and mixed up a batch of medicine and he made up some pills and he shined up some tools he kept in a box under the seat and all that next week they stopped at every place they came to along the road and Mr. Watling would inquire if any of the stock happened to be ailing and if there was anything he could do to help out. About one place out of five they'd let him have a go at it, after he'd explained there

45

was no charge except in case of a cure. When he got through, he'd give them an address where to send the money—providing it turned out to be a cure.

Zeke asked him how he knew the people would ever *send* the money. Mr. Watling said: "How often do you have a horse or a cow sick on your place?"

"I don't know . . . I suppose about every week."

"How often do they die?"

"Well, not more'n a couple of times a year, I guess."

"Ninety per cent of 'em get well. So if two-thirds of these people send the money, there's my sixty per cent. And no harm done to the animals any more than there would have been to the Baptists. Maybe some good, even. You can't tell . . ."

Most of the time that week they had a horse of one kind or another on a lead out behind. But Mr. Watling never traded Sheba. He said that when he traded her, it'd be some place where they had *horses*.

Zeke was driving most of the time now. Mr. Watling would sit over in the other corner with his feet up on the dashboard and sing or tell stories or just sit, according to how he felt.

One morning he said: "Zeke, you ought to learn Greek. Some say Latin comes first, I know. But I'm not so sure. Listen to this: . . ."

Zeke listened. It sounded funny, all right, but only at first. When Mr. Watling really got his voice to working, there didn't anything sound funny—not unless he wanted it to. After that they had a Greek lesson every day. Sometimes an hour, sometimes longer if it was raining and they had to drive slow.

The week they were in Pittsfield, Zeke asked as usual where to tell his mother to write to him. Mr. Watling said he didn't know—he'd just have to let it go this week. And when they drove out of Pittsfield, Mr. Watling wouldn't say where they were going. They headed east, and they kept traveling. Nights, they put up at houses. When the people asked Mr. Watling where he was headed for, he'd say he was going down East. When they were out on the road, Mr. Watling either sang or kept quiet. No talking. And nobody said anything about Greek. Zeke knew they were getting nearer home all the while and he thought maybe that was where they were headed. He let the mare go her own pace and they covered forty-two miles in one day. Although the maples had begun to turn a week ago, the roads weren't muddied up with frost yet. It was good going. There was a fine sort of brightness to the air and the sunshine really seemed to mean something. They had three days of this and then it came on to rain. They piled right into it just the same—Mr. Watling driving now. And how he could drive!

There was half the morning gone and Zeke was beginning to get hungry when he saw a barn he thought he'd seen before. He wasn't sure though, because there wasn't anything special about it he could remember back to; it just made him feel that way. Then they splashed full tilt over a crossroad and he caught a glimpse of a sign that said NEW BOSTON ☞ —they were going home. Now he knew the road, all right—he'd ought to have known it way back there. Probably it looked different in the rain. Pretty soon he knew everything he saw. Everything. He could even tell what was coming next. They were getting nearer and nearer. He forgot all about Mr. Watling—he was thinking what it would be like to be home again.

Mr. Watling said, "Know where you are?"

Zeke said, "Yes, *sir!*" without turning round. They

47

were passing Henry Williams' house. Nobody in the windows. New well sweep. He didn't see Henry anywhere.

The marker went by where his father's land began. All this they were passing now was his father's land. They'd been away a long time. He wouldn't know just what to say to his father. He was grown up now, and his father'd see it.

But as soon as he saw them—his mother came out into the yard with her apron over her head and his father after her—he was so glad to be there he didn't think how he did feel.

His father said, "Well, son!" and stood there looking at him jump down and then his mother took him and said something and then said: "You get into the house now out of this rain!" Zeke ran in. His mother followed in after him. When he looked at her now, it made him feel that it was her he was looking at, instead of the way it usually was when he looked at her just because she'd spoken to him or to hear what she'd said.

His father came in in a minute, carrying Zeke's bundle. He said, "You wanted these, did you?" and set them down in the corner.

Zeke said: "Yes, sir. Thank you. I—I got to go see to the horse now."

"You'll have to hurry."

Zeke got out the door—and the yard was empty. He saw that the barn door was shut. They'd gone.

He came back into the house and looked at his father and then at his mother.

His father said: "He asked me to tell you good-by for him. He was in a hurry."

"Yes. But—"

"It's all right, son. He said he'd write you a letter. And he says you done first rate."

Zeke didn't understand. He felt kind of gone. And he wasn't as hungry when he got his dinner as he'd thought he was going to be. But when he'd tasted it, he realized the trouble had been he'd forgotten how good things were at home—he'd been away so long. His mother wanted him to tell them all about what had happened, but he found it was hard to do. He wanted to hear what had happened at home. And then, while they were telling it, he'd find he was thinking about things that had happened while he was away.

When dinner was finished, Zeke said he was going down to the barn to look for Joe. His father was fishing in his pocket and he brought out something and said: "Your friend, Mr. Watling, asked me to give you this." He handed it to Zeke.

It was a knife. It was the best knife Zeke had ever seen.

His father was saying: ". . . said if you figured a knife was bad luck when it was a gift, you could call it a trade."

Zeke was turning it over in his hand. He couldn't think what Mr. Watling could mean about it's being a trade. But he was glad to be home! He looked up and said: "Well, I guess I'll go down and see Joe."

And his father said: "All right. He'll be waiting for you."

His mother called after him to put on his reefer.

Zeke shouted, "It's all right, ma," and ran.

Abel grinned. "Well, he seems to be back, all right."

"Yes."

"Don't seem to have done him much harm."

"He looks three years older, Abel."

49

"Well . . ."

"Abel: why did he go away like that—Mr. Watling?"

Abel tipped his chair back, slowly, balancing with his fingers on the edge of the table. Then he looked up, straight at Minna. "Said he had to go to town."

" 'Town'? But—why didn't he—what town?"

"I don't know." Abel stood up; he walked over to the window and looked out. "Boston, I guess."

"But—I mean—was that all he said?"

"M, hm."

Finally Minna said: " 'D you pay him?"

"Tried to. He wouldn't take it."

"Oh."

"Said he'd enjoyed having the boy with him: take it as a favor if I'd figure the boy had been his guest. Maybe he'd come again sometime. He said 'Good-by, Mr. Peele, —and thank you.' " Abel turned away from the window. "Then he went," he added.

Abel got his hat and went out to go down to the barn.

It was raw and chilly coming out of the warm kitchen. Well, the boy was home safe and sound. Abel turned his face up to the rain; it felt good. Abel couldn't help but smile—Watling, out there in the yard a few minutes ago, after he'd said good-by; last thing he said was: "Come on, Sheba, you damned old three-legged skate, you and me are going to town!" Abel chuckled. Watling had promised him he wouldn't touch it so long as the boy was with him. He guessed he hadn't.

[Chapter 7]

FOR SOME TIME Zeke had thought it likely that when he
grew up he'd be a preacher. He guessed he knew about all
that was necessary now about the business. All he'd need
would be the voice and to practice some with his arms
and moving round and then some things to say. Mr. Watling, of course, had so much knowledge laid up that he
never had to think of what to say. He just drew on this
and that as he happened to for hours on end and kept it
up the next night and right on through the week. Although the next week, starting fresh, he'd go back and use
some of the same things over again. A good many of these
stand-bys Zeke was pretty easy with, himself. Toward the
end of the summer, he'd tried it out once or twice with
his father's watch and had found he could keep going
on Repent-ye-for-the-kingdom-of-heaven-is-at-hand for a
little better than fifteen minutes without having to stop
once. His throat had ached some and he was a little dizzy
when he finished; he realized he was a long way yet from
being up to Mr. Watling's stint. But what he *had* done had
been all right. It was just a question of being able to keep
it up.

The Saturday after he got home he took Joe down into
the woods and tried it out on him. Joe sat quiet on a log,
chewing on a birch twig all the time, and looking at him.
It made Zeke kind of uneasy at first. Joe didn't seem to
get the idea and Zeke thought maybe because Joe was
colored he'd never been to a meeting and so he didn't
know how to act. But he couldn't stop in the middle to
tell him about it, and so he just went right ahead, same
as he'd seen Mr. Watling do a hundred times and before

long he was going pretty good. He began to wish Mr. Watling could happen by and see him; it would make Mr. Watling feel proud. He even went Mr. Watling one better, putting in a few words of Greek. In a minute or two now it would start to work on Joe . . . and that *would* be something!

But Joe never budged. He just sat there, chewing slow, and now and again he'd scratch or slap at a bug or something and that was all. Zeke felt himself beginning to run down. He said a couple of things over again that he'd already said near the beginning and then he couldn't think of anything more, so he just had to quit. He turned his back on Joe and went over and leaned up against a tree and waited for Joe to say something. Joe'd *have* to say *some*thing.

Joe said that was fine preaching. Certainly was fine preaching. Said he expected that was about the finest preaching ever he heard in his life.

Zeke said: "What the hell do you know about preaching?"

Joe said that was all right, he knew about preaching. Been first class all the way.

"No, it wasn't," Zeke said, "and you know it. What's the use of putting it on? You never got stirred up a bit." He remembered now that he'd planned to bless Joe at the finish—it made him ashamed to remember it.

Joe said, well, now, maybe he *hadn't* been *power*fully stirred up. But he was a hard man to preach to. He always had been a hard man to preach to. He didn't suppose even a colored preacher could do much with him—not single-handed, anyway. He told Zeke that the way he'd always found it, it didn't come at you right straight from the preacher—not with him, anyway. It kind of got into you

52

from the other ones. They'd get all stirred up and get to shouting out and everybody swaying round and the singing and all that . . . and the Spirit of the Lord'd rise up in you strong! You *couldn't* hold that back, and away you'd go! Louder'n the rest of 'em! Hallelujah an' Amen! Whoopee! Lord have mercy on my soul! He said that was the way it was with him, anyway.

Zeke couldn't take much comfort in it. He said, no, if he'd been as good as he'd thought he was, he could have started Joe off. He said he guessed maybe he wasn't cut out for a preacher, after all.

Joe said, well, maybe that was so.

Zeke didn't like him for that. He'd wanted him to say *sure* he was cut out for a preacher!

Joe scratched his head and said, well, now, farming wasn't so bad—if you'd got a good farm to do it on—and good help—help that knew the place.

Zeke came over and sat down. He said, no, he didn't know as he'd like farming. He'd thought some of being a sea captain—when he was younger.

No, sir! Not for him! Joe said. He'd had enough sea! —'n cap'n, too! That is, he'd heard about 'em, you understand. Never seen it! Never been near to it! . . . never been even *close* to it! . . . and now he'd got to go back to work.

Joe stood up. "You come to think it over," he said, "farming ain' so bad."

Zeke was lying on his back, his head on the log, looking away up through the branches. . . . "Nope," he said, "I'm going to be a preacher."

"All right—all right . . ." Zeke could hear Joe for a long time moving off through the woods.

Then he didn't hear him any more.

Zeke stayed where he was, looking up through the trees, through the branches. It was a high, old maple—most of the leaves gone now and the sky easy to see. It was a warm day and no wind down here in the woods. High up, it looked as though the clouds were stuck right onto the sky and the sky still—but with the branches moving across it . . . moving slow and even . . .

He said it again—"I'm going to be a preacher"—and he listened to the sound of his saying it. That made it true now. He'd said it out loud. He was going to be a preacher. No more wondering—because he knew. It was so. He practically was a preacher right now, because all the rest of his life, from now on, would be all the same thing. Still, the very first part of being a preacher was a little different from the rest, because in the first part you had to do some work getting ready. He'd have to get at that right away. Probably the best way would be to read the whole Bible—and when he'd come to parts Mr. Watling used, he could learn them. That would be a good thing to do this winter. He'd get hold of a Greek book somehow, too, and learn some more Greek this winter. And he might learn Hebrew. Mr. Watling knew Hebrew. Zeke had never heard him talk it, but he knew Mr. Watling could have, if there'd been anybody to talk it to. Read all of the Bible and learn a good deal of it, get to be pretty good at Greek—so you could swing it around some—and learn Hebrew. That would probably be enough to keep him going this winter. He could see about next spring later on.

The cold was beginning to come up from the ground and he got up and started back for the house. He'd have to tell his father about this, some time or other—and that wouldn't be so easy. His father was probably still counting on his staying on the farm, same as he always had been.

He'd never told his father he wouldn't. And his father wouldn't like it now when he did tell him—because he'd think that Zeke felt the farm wasn't good enough for him. Maybe if his father was to see him reading the Bible enough, his father would get on to it by himself, gradually, and it wouldn't hurt him so much. That way, he might not have to tell him at all. Still, it would be kind of uneasy waiting for it to come out. Or he could tell his mother and let her tell his father. That would be like what he used to do. But it wouldn't be quite the way it ought to be, now that he was grown up. Well, if he was going to tell him, he might as well tell him and get it over with. He supposed he could go find him now and tell him. Or perhaps it would be better tonight. Maybe the best thing would be to try reading the Bible, just for tonight, and see if anything happened. It wasn't really putting it off, because if nothing happened he could tell him tomorrow night.

But after supper his father took the Bible. Zeke just kind of fiddled. He didn't know what to do with himself. There didn't seem to be much to do at home after supper, when all summer there'd been the meetings. Finally his mother went to bed, early. Zeke stayed up. He could now, long as he wanted to. It was quiet in the kitchen after his mother had gone—too quiet. Zeke thought he'd go out and walk round some. He was just going to, when his father shut the book. Zeke thought probably his father was going to go down to the barn now to have a look round. He always did that before he went to bed.

His father said: "Well, son, you had a good summer."

Zeke happened to be standing over by the door. He turned and looked at his father. "Yes, sir."

"What's next?"

Zeke's mouth went dry. " 'What's next?' "

His father nodded and said easily: "Yes. That's the idea."

"Well—I kind of thought you wanted me to—to stay here on the farm."

"M, hmm."

"Isn't—isn't that—what you wanted me to do?"

"Maybe. It was, anyhow—one time. What do *you* want to do?"

"Be a preacher," Zeke said before he knew it—and then he was looking his father square in the eye—and neither of them looked away.

Finally his father said: "Come here, Zeke."

Zeke went over to him. His father'd stood up. He took hold of Zeke's arm, just below the shoulder.

"Be a good one."

Abel said that. But it was Zeke's father who, turning away, said: "—I got to go down to the barn now—see to some things. You want to come?"

Zeke went with him and they talked all the time—about things in the barn.

[*Chapter 8*]

ABEL PACKED HIM OFF to Andover just as soon as he could get a letter back from them saying that it was all right for the boy to come. Zeke hadn't thought it would be as quick as that and when he found he was going the day after tomorrow, he seemed to keep thinking of things that would have made it nice if he'd been going to stay home that winter. But he didn't dream he could back out now, and when he thought of what it would be like if he *did* back out, he didn't want to.

Zeke stayed three years at Andover. The first summer vacation he was at home, but the second summer he made a month's trip with Mr. Watling. They were mostly villages this time, back in the hills. Revival meetings were dying out. They weren't the thing any more. Zeke had expected, when he started, to go for all summer, but at the end of a month he thought he'd better be getting back. Mr. Watling had changed a good deal since two years ago. He drank, for one thing, and on top of that he seemed to expect Zeke to take more or less care of the horse.

What Zeke had come for was to get a chance to preach. And Mr. Watling, according to agreement, gave him a chance—every night. But he always made Zeke speak first and he only allowed him fifteen minutes. Then after Zeke had broken the ice, so to speak, but before he'd had time really to get any results that would show, Mr. Watling would cough loudly and Zeke would have to go into his peroration. Then Watling would come forward, and in practically no time at all—as a result of Zeke's spade work—the congregation would loosen up. It was anything but fair treatment, and Zeke resented it. There was not one of his classmates, he was certain, who would have stood for it for a minute.

He was minded to think a good many times how much the congregations in these backwoods towns reminded him of Joe—that day he'd tried to preach to Joe down in the woods. His preaching had certainly changed since then! His voice was good now and his gestures were all carefully thought out. Also, he had something to say. Still, it troubled him that he wasn't able, for some reason, to get it across more effectively.

57

He'd been thinking about it as they were driving along one day and out of a long silence he said to Watling: "What's the matter with my preaching?"

"You've been to Andover," Watling said, "suppose you tell me what's the matter with mine."

Zeke had never said anything to Watling about the way he drank. Hadn't known quite what to say. But this was his chance. "Nothing," he said, "—now," and he kept looking straight ahead, wondering how Watling would take it.

"All right," Mr. Watling answered, "you're right. And I'll be equally honest with you. And what's more, I trust you'll benefit from my advice as much as I might from yours. Now, then. Look here: when you stand up there, what are you thinking about?"

"What I've got to say. Naturally."

"No, you're not. You're thinking how lucky these poor hayshakers are to get a look at the Andover Theological Seminary. Listen, Zeke: they don't give a damn about the Andover Theological Seminary. Neither do I. I was there two years as a student—short of a month. Look it up when you get back, if you want to. Maybe they'll tell you what I was fired for. But the point is this: forget about yourself and forget about the Andover Theological Seminary. What you want to do is to think about those people. Then maybe you can make *them* forget about *them*selves. *That's what they've come for, Zeke!* When you can give it to 'em, you'll be a preacher. And even if you're going to be a minister and preach every Sunday from the same pulpit into the same faces,—every one of 'em in the same pew, week after week,—well, you remember it then, too. People will pay high to forget themselves. I ought to know."

Zeke did look it up after he got back. The name was there all right. And Watling, T., had had a good record. There in red ink, at the end of it, was written: "Expelled." He shut the book and handed it back to the Registrar— and went out. He wished he hadn't come in.

Three weeks before he graduated, he was offered a job as one of two assistant pastors at the Twelfth Congregational Church in Boston. It was a big church and the Reverend Dr. Somers was said to be an old man. Zeke took it— at four hundred dollars a year—and wrote to his father that he had done so.

[Chapter 9]

BOSTON as Zeke walked further and further into it—the railroad station now lost somewhere behind him—seemed a big city. But more noticeably it was dirty—and it was fearfully hot. There was an unpleasant smell to it. It had rained in the night and the mud and filth in the streets steamed up and stank—hurriedly drying out so that it could blow about as dust. He found, in time, the Twelfth Congregational Church, hunted up the sexton and said that he was Mr. Peele. The sexton was not convinced. But as he couldn't offer any evidence in rebuttal, he contented himself with telling Zeke that Mr. Somers was out of town. Zeke asked when Dr. Somers would be back and the sexton said he didn't know when Mr. Somers would be back. Zeke thanked him and was about to leave. The sexton asked him if he'd picked out a place to board. Zeke said: "Why?"

The sexton said, well, he didn't know, but he thought maybe his wife might consider it. Zeke said thanks, he guessed he'd look around. The sexton said all right, that it was a big city and he'd probably find some place they'd take him; he didn't know as his wife really wanted to take a boarder anyhow.

After a long morning's search, Zeke finally took the room that he stood in. It was a little longer than he was—say, six feet and a half—and the woman assured him there was plenty of room in the hall for his trunk and never no fear about keeping it locked. Two dollars and seventy-five cents a week with breakfast and supper as good as he'd find anywhere and better than most. She'd take a week now, if it was agreeable to him. Zeke paid her and she disappeared. He went out and found a carter who went after his trunk with him and brought it back for twenty cents. Zeke carried it up himself. He thought it might make the room look a little better if it had something in it, so he got out his books. He had sixteen of them altogether, various sizes. About the only place they'd go was under the bed, so he put them there. Then he went out to get his dinner. He decided the safest thing to do was buy what he wanted in a store. He got a quarter of a pound of crackers and some cheese and a couple of pickles and carried them back to the Common and ate them sitting under a tree. It was the pleasantest spot he'd found all day and he stayed most of the afternoon.

He bought a postcard on the way home and wrote to his mother, saying he'd arrived safely and had engaged a fine room. He hadn't seen Dr. Somers as yet, but he expected to see him tomorrow. He was well and he hoped they were, too, and how was Joe? He addressed it to Mrs. Abel Peele, New Boston, New Hampshire. He supposed it would get there sometime tomorrow. Either his father would find it in the post office, or else Mr. Blake would bring it along with him and stop by with it as he was coming up the hill. They'd get it sometime after supper. It was probably cool and pleasant there now. Well, they'd be glad to hear from him—know he was all right.

After supper at the boardinghouse—there was no one he could ever like and as far as he could see the meal seemed to fit with the people—he went upstairs to his room and lay down on the bed. There wasn't much else you could do in that room. The pillow was musty and so he lay on his back, looking up at the ceiling. Tomorrow he'd see Dr. Somers. You couldn't really expect things to start before then. . . .

Nine o'clock in the morning he was shown into Dr. Somers' study. The Doctor was a little man, white hair and beard, and determinedly in the best of health. Zeke felt certain that the Doctor had enjoyed, as a matter of course, a very excellent breakfast. He even took Zeke entirely for granted—not asking him so much as a single question. He began straight off to explain to Zeke—he called him 'Peele'—his duties, listing them, perhaps, rather than explaining them. And Zeke nodded and said, "Yes—yes, I understand," and "Surely," and "Oh, yes! of course," and waited for the really important part which was what the Doctor would have to say about preaching.

The list of routine duties ended with: ". . . and you will be expected to take Prayer Meeting on such Tuesdays during July and August as Mr. Graveson does not find it convenient to be present." The Doctor placed the tips of his fingers together, bent his head forward so as to peer at Zeke over his glasses, and said nothing.

Zeke said: "Thank you."

"Yes. You will find Mr. Graveson in the office."

When Zeke got out into the hall, he looked round for someone to tell him where he would find the office. No one appeared. He took his hat off the table and went out. As he closed the heavy, stained-glass door behind him, he resolved that never, if he could help it, would he go into that house again. Not even if they were to invite him to supper.

He found out from a policeman where the office was and, on his arrival there, Dr. Somers was proven to have been mistaken. Mr. Graveson, so the woman told him, would not be in today.

Zeke said: "Well—er, my name is Peele. You see—"

"Yes . . . ?"

"That is, I'm—well, I'm supposed to work here."

The woman shook her head. "Oh," she said, "you'll have to see Mr. Graveson about that. I wouldn't know about that. He'll be back tomorrow."

Zeke had had just about all he could stand. And he didn't like the woman's looks, either. Someone, he judged, had given her the job because they were sorry for her. Well, he wasn't sorry for her. He said: "Look here: my name is Ezekiel Peele. I've been hired as assistant pastor of this church."

The woman seemed absolutely terrified then. Her mouth hung open. She was going to scream, probably. Zeke felt pretty sure he was as good as back on the farm already. Then the door opened and Mr. Graveson came in. Zeke knew it was Mr. Graveson as soon as he heard him:

"Ah! *Here* we are! Mr. *Peele*, isn't it? Yes, yes! Of course. Well, well. That's fine! Mr. Peele. Thought you might be here. What's the matter with you, Miss Beacham? You look sick."

Mr. Graveson didn't look sick, anyway. He looked like a bull.

Miss Beacham opened and closed her mouth and her head went up and down. "This—this is Mr. Peele," she said.

"Certainly it's Mr. Peele!" Graveson agreed. "Assistant Pastor of the Twelfth Congregational Church. Mr. Ezekiel Peele, isn't it? Come in, Mr. Peele. Come in and sit down."

Zeke followed him into his office.

Graveson, it instantly appeared, was an old Andover man himself. But all that was behind him. Impatiently he accorded Zeke the few moments of reminiscence which the situation demanded, and then plunged lustily into the invigorating waters of the present, thrashing about in a perfect welter of Opportunities. The whole of Boston was just one great tumbling, seething, beckoning expanse of Opportunities as far as Mr. Graveson's excellent eye could see. Vice? said Mr. Graveson enthusiastically. Why, there was enough vice along Water Street alone—just one side of Water Street!—to afford a man Opportunity for the rest of his life. And drunkenness? You couldn't ask for a finer place for drunkenness than Boston—*any*where in Boston—the market, the wharves, the Common—everywhere. The challenge of drunkenness in Boston was enough to make a man exult. Mr. Graveson did exult. He himself had obtained thirteen pledges in a single week last spring without going a step out of his way. And every one of them a real drunkard, too!—not a child or an old woman in the lot. Thir*teen* in a single *week*, mind you! Why, if a man really wanted to do the Lord's work, he could keep busy around here twenty-five hours a day. Not that he meant by that that he believed in *over*doing it. Not for a minute. He didn't want his young friend to get *that*

63

idea. Good health, Mr. Graveson said, was paramount. No man could render to his Master the service that he owed Him if he didn't feel good. Mr. Graveson made it a point to take a long walk every day of his life and at night he slept with a window open—generally. He hadn't had a chill *or* a fever in over three years! *Neither one!* And, moreover, he was in and out of sickrooms, where you never knew *what* was the matter with them, a dozen times a day.

Well, now! About the work! Mr. Graveson's brow furrowed and his lips drew together. He was considering the advisability of saying something. Suddenly he rose, went over and closed the door, and came back and sat down. "Dr. Somers," he said, "—and you may as well know it first as last—is—well, he's an old man."

Zeke said, well, yes, he supposed he was.

"Ah!" said Mr. Graveson, "a *fine* old man, I agree with you, but—well, *you* understand—an old man. The fact of the matter is, Peele: Somers likes to preach."

"So do I."

Mr. Graveson realized that he hadn't really looked at the boy yet . . . a thin face, already lined, but the color boyish, the mouth set and the dark eyes steady—so steady that Mr. Graveson didn't have time for any more details, except the high-bridged nose and that black, black head of hair. All external evidence to the contrary, Mr. Graveson decided that young Peele was joking. Just a boy, Mr. Graveson reminded himself, but—well, somehow Mr. Graveson preferred that he *should* be joking. So Mr. Graveson laughed resolutely and, to bolster it up some, slapped his thigh. "Very good!" he said. "Very good indeed!" . . . and he was pleased to see young stone-face's mouth unbend at the corners and to have him blink his eyes.

"You do like a joke, don't you?" said Mr. Graveson. "Yes, yes, of course. Well, er—ahem, so do I!" . . . but Peele still sat unmoved and easy in his chair, one long leg hung across the other and his arms folded; he appeared to prefer his own jokes. Mr. Graveson was not much disappointed—it was, he'd found, a universal failing. He said: "Ha, ha! You and I ought to get along well together. But, to get back to the work. Somers, as I say, likes to preach. And to give him his due, I verily believe, my young friend, that he is convinced—*convinced*—that something is accomplished by it. For the *work of the church*, Peele, it leaves you and myself. I am frank to say that *I* am the *minister* of this church. Dr. Somers is the preacher. Peele—" Mr. Graveson rose and stretched forth his large and chunky hand—"I *wel*come you to the ministry of the Twelfth Congregational Church."

Peele got out of his chair . . . and finding Mr. Graveson's hand still waiting, placed his own in it.

"*Shoul*der *to shoul*der," said Mr. Graveson, jerking the arm for emphasis, "you and I will do the work of Our Lord Jesus Christ in Boston! Eh, Peele?" He looked him in the eye.

"All right."

Mr. Graveson let go the hand and turned away. "Now then," he said, becoming very businesslike, "what time is it?" He drew out a gold watch and clicked it open. "Let's see. We-ell . . . just about make it." He snapped shut the watch. "I've got a funeral to attend to at eleven. No family, so I won't take you along. You stay here and let Miss Beacham show you the lay of the land. You'll soon get to know the ropes, I'm sure. See you later, friend." He stepped to the door, flung it open, and strode into the outer office.

Zeke heard him address Miss Beacham. "I may not be in till tomorrow. If you're behind on those notices—as I daresay you are—I've told Peele to help you . . . 'By" . . . and the door crashed. Whoever was to be buried, Zeke felt sure, would be buried thoroughly and on time. As for himself, he was left confronted with the thought of facing Miss Beacham.

By the end of August, Zeke's handwriting had improved materially. As had also the facility with which he took the midweek prayer meeting. Tuesday evenings, for a limitless variety of reasons, had been regularly inconvenient for Mr. Graveson. Zeke didn't mind. The Tuesday Evening Meeting had a twenty-minute address in it, which for him, at any rate, was the bright spot of the week. He was accomplishing a vast number of parish calls, too—explaining always how sorry Dr. Somers was not to be able to get there—and he had already acquired quite a familiarity with certain aspects of poverty and disease which he had not known before existed. From the church-membership list, those in the higher brackets as to contribution had been knowingly culled out. That was Dr. Somers' little list, and most regularly did Dr. Somers wait upon them. The middle class of contributors were Mr. Graveson's flock—they were well tended, too. Zeke drew the rest. A good many of them were not contributors at all. These did not trouble him. But there were some who should not have been contributors, who were. There wasn't much Zeke could say to them. It had never occurred to Zeke that the giving of twenty-five cents a year to a church—to the maintenance of Somers and of Graveson, among other things—could constitute, for the giver, a sustaining joy. But it did. He saw these people.

The Twelfth Congregational Church, its second assistant pastor soon became aware, was not in any sense a fashionable church. It was big, yes—close to two thousand members by Miss Beacham's list—but even Zeke could see that they lacked style. There wasn't one really famous name among them—that is, no one he could write home as having met and have it mean anything. The Unitarians had the names. But Zeke, out of a loyalty he did not understand, developed a reiterated satisfaction in that fact. A satisfaction which, in time, was genuine.

He was lonely, of course, during those first few months. True, Dr. Somers now experienced no difficulty in recalling his name, but it seemed unlikely they would ever be boon companions. Graveson, Zeke neither hated nor disliked. He had never come across anyone whom it was possible to regard so objectively as it was Graveson. Zeke even got used to Miss Beacham and could tolerate her presence in the room on a cool day, providing she didn't speak. Friends, though, he had none. He liked some of the deacons, and some of them he didn't like. Some of them, he thought, liked him. But they were older men, bankers and storekeepers and what not, and as they had no need of young Peele in their lives outside the church, they assumed, if they ever thought of it, that young Peele had no need of them. A minister, too, does complicate things socially.

It was Deacon MacIntosh, whom Zeke liked least of the entire Board, who first asked him to his home for dinner. Zeke accepted, realizing that his opinion of the man had been founded on incomplete evidence.

The MacIntosh family, when he looked them up, were

67

down in the records as consisting of the Deacon and the Deacon's niece. Zeke had an idea he'd been introduced to the niece some time or other—after prayer meeting or sometime—but he was blessed if he could remember what she looked like or anything about her.

Making his way across a windy Common, bound for the MacIntosh address, he concluded that it was just as well. If he couldn't remember her, it must mean that there was nothing very bad about her, anyhow. And after the food he'd been living on for the past four months, it would take far worse than an average young woman to spoil his enjoyment of any change at all. He was wearing his new frock coat, too.

After two inquiries and a wrong turning, he found the house. It was not Louisburg Square, by any means, nor even Beacon Street, but it was certainly a far happier locality than any to which his association with the church had called him heretofore. He pulled the bell and was let in by a mulatto girl. She looked him over with one swift, easy glance and became indifferently polite. She put his scarf over her arm and held his hat for him to put his gloves into it. Zeke noticed—it seemed an odd thing—that she was strenuously perfumed. She showed him to the door of the drawing room, and without a word, bowed him in. The Deacon came forward to welcome him.

Deacon MacIntosh was a stout, heavy-set man with a droopy face, and his thick dome of a head was bald halfway back. He looked to have been a strong man in his day. But his face was sallow now and his voice husky and the whites of his eyes not nearly so white as Mr. Graveson's. Still, he carried his weight well and, with the Deacon's shoulders, it was impossible for a man to look dumpy.

When he spoke to Zeke it was as a completely self-satisfied host in his own house: said he was glad he'd come and invited him up to the fire to warm himself. Zeke could see it was something of an effort for him to be polite—but, at any rate, he was making the effort.

His niece, the Deacon said, would be down in a minute—and he sat down, with a grunt.

Zeke, standing before the fire, spread his coattails, rocked gently on his heels and remarked that he was probably a little early.

"Mr. Peele," inquired the Deacon, "what is your position on slavery?"

"Slavery, sir?"

"Slavery. What is your position?"

Zeke hadn't any. "Slavery," he repeated, "well, you see, sir,—politics, I'm afraid, are not quite in my line."

"Church used to *run* politics, didn't it?"

"Yes, I know, sir. That isn't true nowadays, is it?"

"No. Nothing's true nowadays."

"You are a shipping man, I believe, sir, are you not?"

"Yes. Used to be. Don't know what I am now. Nobody does."

"You know, I always wanted to go into shipping when I was a boy."

The Deacon looked him over. "Too late now?"

"Well—" Zeke laughed—"there isn't much demand for chaplains in the merchant service, is there?"

"No demand for anything. Business gone to the devil. Why, rum— How old are you?"

"Eighteen."

"You wouldn't remember. Why, I've known as many as twelve cargoes of rum to clear the Port of Boston in a single day! You see anything like that nowadays? I don't, anyhow."

69

"No, I—I guess that's true." Zeke was not hopeful of the conversation. The state of the rum trade was an item he knew even less about than slavery. Perhaps he'd better try slavery again. "We have a black man on the place at home," he said. "I suppose he may have been a slave once—though I never knew for certain."

"How'd you come by him?"

"Why, I don't know. I suppose he just turned up there one day and Father took him on."

"And said nothing, eh? By God—oh! there's m' niece." The Deacon craned his neck round, but did not attempt to get up.

Zeke saw that he'd never met her. She was too thin to be a hopeful augury of the meal to come, but otherwise she was probably all right enough—a bit sallow.

"Viola," said the Deacon, "this is Mr. Peele. Mr. Peele, this is my niece, Viola."

Zeke bowed. "I am indeed honored, Miss MacIntosh." He could tell he'd made a mistake.

"Blair!" ejaculated the Deacon, "m' sister."

"I beg your pardon—Miss Blair."

Miss Blair's laugh of reassurance was high and fluttery.

Zeke thought: she does look like his daughter, all the same.

The girl had turned to her uncle. "Have you—have you had a good day?"

"No," said Mr. MacIntosh.

"The *Queen Titania* get in, did she?"

"She did."

"Did she—er—have a good voyage?"

"Well, if you call having to jettison her cargo—every last one of 'em!—four hundred miles east of Barbados a good voyage, then she had a good voyage. That's Gowan's story, anyway."

She looked at him a moment—and then returned to her uncle's guest. "I know so little about business. Tell me, Mr. Peele, when do you preach?"

Zeke said, well, he wasn't preaching at all just now. He had been, though, during the summer . . . only it was in the evening.

"Oh, yes—prayer meeting."

"Yes," he admitted. Preaching, though—no matter what she thought.

The Deacon discovered then that the maid was standing in the doorway of the room. He grunted, "Dinner," and got to his feet.

Zeke—partly because she had been right in her estimate of prayer meeting—offered her his arm. It would be the first time he'd ever taken a lady in to dinner. He thought she seemed pleased to have him do it, and it went off all right. He was grateful to her because it did go off all right.

Dinner, commencing with a strange soup and a sweet wine—a Madeira, so he discovered before he'd had to speak of it—was, on the whole, a good deal more than he had dared to hope for. And when the conversation lagged— or even when it disappeared entirely—he did not let it trouble him in the least. He ate. It was what he had come for.

The Deacon drank a glass of brandy with his dessert and when he had finished some business behind his napkin, he pushed back his chair and stood up. Zeke escorted Miss Blair toward the drawing room . . . but the Deacon deserted them en route and went into the library.

Zeke asked her if she played the piano. She said that she did—a little. And asked him if he would care to sing.

Zeke didn't want to sing. He wanted to sit down and stretch his legs out . . . and that, only a little to his own surprise, was what he did.

She played, it seemed to him, pretty well. Her back was to him now, and with his eyes half closed he found the situation thoroughly supportable. Miss Blair, whatever her lack of interest in preaching, was neither sick nor poor. And, compared with Miss Beacham . . . He stretched his long legs still further and settled even more comfortably into his chair. What a meal! What a meal! It would be pleasant, now, to run over it in his mind, dish by dish. . . .

When she stopped playing, he roused himself somehow to civility. Boston, he said, was a hot place in summer, wasn't it? Miss Blair, this being autumn, said, why—why, yes. Zeke said it had seemed so to him, anyway. Miss Blair said, well, possibly it was. She asked him if he played piquet. Zeke said he didn't know as he did. He asked her if by any chance she were fond of Greek. Miss Blair failed to state—merely looked troubled for a moment. She then offered the fact that she had had her photograph done lately and perhaps Mr. Peele might be amused to see it. Zeke said he'd be glad to. But Miss Blair remembered then that the photograph was in the library. Zeke offered to get it for her, but she cut him off by starting in to play again.

Zeke managed to dispose of seven minutes with an anecdote and Miss Blair, repeating her opening number on the piano, laid low another twelve. Zeke asked her to play it a third time. She played it. And he told another anecdote. Taking alternate whacks at it, they beat the evening to a lingering death.

There was no clock in the room and Zeke could not maneuver to his watch. Dawn or the Deacon, he felt, might appear at any moment. He rose to go. He told Miss

Blair he had had a delightful evening and she said she was glad he had. He asked her to convey his apologies to Deacon MacIntosh. She said she would do so, but the shoe, she thought, was on the other foot. Zeke said not at all, not at all, he understood perfectly. Miss Blair said good night.

Once around the corner, he got out his watch, and bending to catch the light from an area window, saw that it was close on to ten o'clock.

He was back again within the week. He had a selective memory, and after the first four or five days, had been able to see no barriers at all between his appetite and the prospect of a good, sound tea at the MacIntoshes'. Fruit cake, in all probability, and quite possibly cold meat. And his mother had written him, in her very first letter when he had come to Boston, always to call promptly upon those who had had him in to supper.

Miss Blair, upon his second arrival, was caught flatfooted in the hall. It was on her suggestion that they went to walk; it would, she remarked, give them an appetite for tea. Zeke said, yes, that was true, and set forth with her to adorn the rose.

They enjoyed the walk, both of them. Miss Blair saw— by the face of each lady whom they met—that her escort was really quite good-looking. While Zeke, side by side with her, and the walk to carry them along, found her not at all difficult to talk to. The further they got from the house, the brighter she seemed to become. And, dressed for the street, she was very far from being a disgrace to any second assistant pastor. They covered a mile or so and returned for tea. No meat, as it turned out, but the cakes were excellent. Zeke ate them all. The mulatto maid waited upon them with the same smooth, unspeaking insolence that Zeke had noticed before. But he felt much more at

73

home now and was only a little irked by it. He had as much right to be here as anyone and would come again when he chose.

He did—often. But he left the fact of his letters home. This was because, when he had first met the MacIntoshes, he had described them. His description of the Deacon still held. And even now, he was quite well aware, Miss Blair was not perhaps precisely the sort of person that his father and mother would be apt to take to. But that was merely because his father and mother, living always in a small village, had never happened to know anyone just like the MacIntoshes.

Although Zeke was often at the MacIntosh home when the Deacon was out, there did occur evenings when the Deacon was there and Zeke was not. On such occasions the family life of the MacIntoshes reverted to its accustomed atmosphere of absolute conversational freedom. The Deacon, on a Peele-less evening in March—some six months after Zeke's first visit—had followed his niece into the drawing room. It was a departure from custom which, she felt, called for comment.

"What's the matter with you?" she asked him. "Getting wakeful?"

He lowered himself into a chair, accepted his brandy and coffee from the maid, and waited until she had left the room.

"Well . . . ?" she prompted him.

"Take your time," said the Deacon and took a gulp of brandy. He wiped his mouth. "I got an idea," he told her. "Think you can keep your mouth shut?"

"If it suits me."

"I guess it will."

"What's on your mind?"

"Somers is sick," the Deacon said, and had a swallow, "going to die."

"Well, that's very interesting—for him, anyway. When?"

"I don't know exactly. Sometime."

Miss Blair, standing against a corner of the mantelpiece, merely waited.

"And I've got half a mind," said the Deacon, mulling it over, "to put Peele into his job."

Miss Blair's comment was slow in coming.

"What of it?"

The Deacon looked into his glass. "I want you to marry him."

She stood perfectly still, watching him. "Why?" she asked.

"Oh—I don't know . . ."

"I think I do. 'Guardian and uncle of the wife of the Pastor of the Twelfth Congregational Church.' Yes, you could keep on with the 'shipping business' at that rate for quite a while. I don't believe anybody'd suspect you."

It was a tribute which touched the Deacon deeply. "You know," gazing into the future, "I don't believe they would."

Miss Blair said coldly, "You know how old he is?"

"Peele? Nineteen—come June."

"Young, for a pastor."

"Only for a church as big as this one," defended the Deacon. "Other churches have 'em. Hell! Back in the country they take 'em right out of this school he went to. You don't need any experience to be a minister."

"No, I suppose not. It's not like the shipping business, is it?"

"Not a bit! Not a bit! And besides," he expounded, "look here: what's more, it'd be a matter of three—four years before he had to *be* a minister! He could have

75

whiskers a foot long by that time—maybe. Somers has got to die first, hasn't he? That's liable to take him a year. And don't worry he'll resign! Somers'd die in the pulpit before he'd resign. Say he lives a year. All right. Then they got to argue and bicker and fight for two or three years trying to agree on a new one. They got to send men around all over to listen to prospects, too. And the church pays their traveling expenses. So *that* lasts quite a while. How do they end up? Everybody on the Committee with a candidate that nobody else wants. And about then the rest of the church begins to get uneasy and starts asking 'em why in the hell they can't make up their mind. All right, fine! Right there is where I trot young Peele into the pulpit some morning and turn him loose to preach."

Miss Blair had been improving the time by leaving her post beside the mantel, selecting a chair and sitting down in it. "How do you know he *can* preach?" she asked.

"Ah! I've *heard* him."

"*You?* When?"

"I been to prayer meeting."

"Oh." Her eyebrows rose, and fell again. "Prayed, did you?"

"Cer'nly I prayed! Prayed for five minutes." A trifle resentfully, he filled his glass.

"Oh, I see. You mean standing up and out loud."

"Sure. How would I pray?"

"Standing up and out loud."

For a moment the Deacon suspected an insult; but, a nice judge of his own condition, he preferred just now to speak on matters he had thought out before. "He's got form," he adjudged, "he's got good form. All he needs is to get his back into it."

"I see."

76

"He's smooth as the devil, right now—just as smooth and as pretty as you'd want to ask for. He looks good, too. He's got a nice hand on the wheel and he knows all the tricks. Only thing he needs is to get some fire under his tail!"

"A word from you might light him up," she suggested.

"Wouldn't do any good." The Deacon shook his head. "No—wouldn't do any good. For it to do any good, he's got to do it on his own account. Sincerity is essential,"— any man who could say 'sincerity is essential' had a long ways to go yet, and happily the Deacon swallowed forward. As he set down his glass: "He'd ought to preach on something that means something to him."

"Cold ham, for instance."

The Deacon hadn't heard her. He wiped his mouth, and settled back in his chair, and then folded his hands across his stomach. "Now I had in mind for him 'Slavery.'"

"You're getting confused, uncle. It's Mr. Peele who's going to preach."

"Oh, I admit it don't mean anything to him now. But it could be made to."

"What feeling he has got," she pointed out, "is 'Free.' At least I think it is. I'd like to see you try to change him."

"Stubborn, is he?" said the Deacon, as though something pleased.

"A little," she admitted. "I don't know—it might be that he's honest. *You* know, uncle,—'honest.'"

"Oh, I know! Sure. I think he is myself."

"Well, then!"—a little disgustedly.

But the Deacon smiled with the happiest of satisfaction. He leaned forward and spoke with a sort of delighted scorn. "He's going to *preach* 'Free,' you numskull! What

77

did you think? He's going to preach anti-slavery to beat hell! He's going to preach '*Abolition*'!"

"Perhaps I've been mistaken—you *are* in the slave trade, aren't you?"

"Listen," he said, unchecked: "I'll be as safe behind that feller—" and he swung his upraised hand in a reassuring arc— "I'll be as safe behind him, as if he was a stone wall!"

"You've got to make him pastor first."

"Easy!"—and again the gesture with his hand. "This is a Congregational church, isn't it? Sure! So all hands get the same vote! All right. And I happen to know that Peele is solid with 'em. Solid! Not, I don't mean, with the ones that sit up in church to show their hats off. They don't even know him! Nor I don't mean he's solid with the heavy givers that old Somers goes around and kisses their foot all the time. Hell, they never heard of Peele. The ones Peele stands in with is the old women with shawls over their heads. Nobody else counts them, because they don't come to church. But Peele knows 'em; he goes round and calls on 'em. And the sick ones, too. And all the poor families— all over the place. Why, when it comes time to elect a new minister you're going to see people at that meeting there didn't anybody except Peele and the list in the office know was alive. And every one of 'em a bona fide member of the church and fully entitled to vote. Why, 'easy'? It's as good as done. Peele's done most of the work—only he don't know it yet. One sermon—then the meeting—and he's in. You leave it to me."

She seemed to be thinking it over.

"Well, what do you say?" he asked.

"I say: 'No.' "

He leaned forward in his chair. "*You* say 'no'! You'll do as you're told!"

78

"Will I?" she said serenely. "Don't forget I know quite a lot about the shipping business."

It brought him, ugly and quivering, half out of his chair—reaching toward her.

She said quietly: "Sit down, father."

He poised a moment—and then sat down, whatever menace there had been, gone out of him. His jowls were wobbling and he was uglier in appearance than he had been before.

"That's better," she approved. "Have a little brandy."

He had a glassful—spilling comparatively little.

"Now, then," she said, "if I should marry Peele, there's just one thing I want to know: do we get a separate house to live in?"

"God!" said the Deacon. "Him around here? I'll see you get a place to live, all right!"

[*Chapter 10*]

ZEKE WAS STANDING, one March evening, in the now familiar drawing room of the house she lived in, and that her uncle lived in, too. The room was ill-lit—Miss Blair not being at the piano, but seated instead before the slow diminishing of an old fire in the grate. He had his back to her; he had wandered over to a window and he had taken the heavy brocaded curtain in his fingers and was twisting it, nervously and idly—drawing it a little aside and then looking out against the darkness. He knew what he was going to do, and he knew why he was going to do it. He was going to ask this woman to marry him. And he wasn't going to question himself again as to whether or not he loved her. He was not proud that he was going to ask her to marry him. But he was going to do it. Because his life ahead had a bleakness of aspect and an unchangeability about it that he could stand no longer. He had said, back along, that he would become a preacher. And he would. From that he could never turn aside until it had been done. But because of the grayness of the near days that had passed and the same grayness of the days to come, he had got to have change and excitement and uncertainty from somewhere—and most of all he had got to have some excitement. He had decided to ask her to marry him—and when his words had stopped there would fall a time in between the sound of those words . . . and the sound of the words that would be her answer. He was curious as to how he would feel during that time. All his life, probably, would depend upon her answer. And he would not even know, hearing the answer, whether the decision had been for good or ill. But it would have been made, and the effect of it would be over all his lifetime. It would have been made—even while he was standing there listening for it.

He supposed neither of them had spoken for some time. Impelled to it, he said suddenly: "Will you marry me?"

He felt, then, spent—dulled, and there came to him no excitement at all.

Miss Blair, who knew how long it had been since either of them had spoken, answered, for once, hard upon the point. She asked Zeke if he really wanted her.

And Zeke, not at all strangely—since he was a man grown—found suddenly that he did. He said, "Yes, I do."

There was a great silence in the room.
She said: "Yes—I will."

Zeke had scarcely a qualm over the prospect of confronting the Deacon with the news that he, the Deacon, was getting a pretty good husband for his niece. He tackled him in the drawing room the following evening, before Viola had come down.

The dominant note in the Deacon's response was one of pure surprise. He said, "Well, well!" a great many times and when it became impossible to say it again, he suddenly produced quite a good speech on how near and dear Miss Blair had always been to him, how she seemed to him, he must say, hardly more than a child—but that, of course, was only because he was getting old—and that if he had to lose her to anyone, he was proud and happy to lose her to a minister of the Christian gospel and a man connected with the Twelfth Congregational Church. He then suggested, in the unmistakable tone of a man who feels that he has earned it, that they have a drink.

Zeke didn't want a drink, and he didn't particularly care about drinking with Deacon MacIntosh, but he knew that when a man sets out to get married, he has to make some concessions, and so he consented.

The Deacon proposed, "The Bride!" He sucked in his drink, and Zeke, having downed his, set down his glass— more or less dusting off his hands and feeling as though that job were done, at any rate. He reminded himself that his wife would be the man's niece, thank God, and not his daughter. Viola was a good sort and they would be very happy together and it was certainly going to be very interesting.

Zeke wrote to his family.

The reply came from his father. It said nothing at all about Zeke's being young, nor was there any question anywhere in it as to how he proposed to support a wife on his present salary. Zeke had his defense ready for each of those points, and was left with them on his hands.

His father said that they were both of them glad that this happiness had come to Zeke, and that he was sure Zeke had considered the responsibility that went with it. He said he would like to come to Boston to pay his respects to the young lady and to call on her uncle, but that things were pretty busy on the farm right now and he did not feel that he ought to leave it. He suggested to Zeke that if Dr. Somers could spare him for a day or two, he bring the young lady home with him for a short visit. They would be glad to see both of them.

Zeke told Viola he thought they'd better go.

When they arrived, Zeke knew what had happened before he'd walked in the door. He knew it as the four of them stood there in the yard—after the greeting and waiting for someone to make the move to go into the house. He knew it as his mother put her arms round his neck and he could feel the pressure of her hands against his shoulders. He'd known it all along, anyway. But now there was no avoiding the fact of it: he had hurt them, hurt them both—and they had resolved, because they both loved him, that they would never let him see that he had hurt them.

He and Viola stayed until the early morning of the third day, and in all of that time he did not see any excuse to change this certainty.

It was a long trip back to Boston. And he looked forward during the latter part of it to leaving Viola at her uncle's house and going alone back to his room. Viola tried to be enthusiastic about his mother and father. This annoyed Zeke, because he knew that she had never even seen them. But that, he knew, was not a thing that he could explain to her.

He left her at her uncle's house. . . .

[Chapter 11]

WHEN SHE WAS a little girl, June, in Viola's mind, had been the month in which she would be married. Deacon MacIntosh couldn't think of any reason why he should object to June. And Zeke said he thought June would be fine. June, then, it would be. A Thursday, Miss Blair thought, and finally chose the twenty-fourth. Thursday, the twenty-fourth of June, 1847. Not a native, she realized that when one wants June in Boston, it is advisable to wait until pretty close on to July. She was also influenced by the fact that if she waited until the twenty-fourth, her husband would then be a sound and thorough and uncriticizable nineteen years of age, whereas, on either of the first two Thursdays, she would be marrying a boy of eighteen. Still, as her uncle pointed out to her, there were plenty of skippers in the China trade not a day over twenty and first mates two or three years younger than that. If a Salem boy could take a sloop to China when he was twenty, why shouldn't a Christian minister get married at nineteen? And Miss Blair said she was sure *she* couldn't think of any reason.

Zeke was now spending an allotted four evenings a week in the presence of Viola, whom he was soon to marry. And Miss Blair was spending four evenings in the presence of assured respectability. She was no more than mildly disappointed to discover that, as an aphrodisiac, respectability did not seem to affect her as much as it might. On those occasions when Zeke tried to make love to her, she was not helpful.

Zeke was busy all through the spring, past the point of being merely overworked. Dr. Somers' health was failing, and Mr. Graveson had moved up into the higher-donation brackets of the parish calling list. Mr. Graveson was now calling, as he said himself, on people who demanded forethought and tact, and—as he also said himself—he was finding it something of a strain. Consequently, every time he succeeded to one of Dr. Somers' former customers, Mr. Graveson felt justified in dropping, say, five of the least productive names from his own list. These fell to Zeke, and Zeke had about all he could swing to. Graveson even turned over to him an odd funeral or two during the rush period in March and April. There was no fee attached to funerals, but Graveson assured him that there was nothing like a good presence at a funeral to put a man in line for weddings later on. Zeke rather counted on a wedding or two in May, as he was virtually without any money at all and he doubted that a walking trip would have much appeal for Viola as a wedding tour. He did get three weddings during May, at that, but unfortunately in each instance the groom was so much worse off financially than he was himself that it was impossible for Zeke to accept the fee.

With his own wedding five weeks off, he was down to six dollars and forty cents. But there were two paydays falling within that period, and the Deacon was giving Viola a small house and the things to go in it. Zeke figured he'd get through all right, if he was careful. He drove a bargain with his landlady by which he ceased to take his meals with her and he tried to break himself of the habit of eating breakfast. The Deacon was driven to observe that love, so far as he could see, had not cut into the young man's appetite at all.

Ten days before the wedding, Zeke had a letter from his father enclosing fifty dollars. His father wrote that he thought it might be it would come in handy. Zeke knew where fifty dollars came from on a farm: it came from a lot of places, saved up, a little from this crop and still less from that. He hadn't had any idea his father would send him anything, nor could he see any reason why he should. He wrote and thanked him—and the fifty dollars was often in his mind.

Later that same week the Deacon spoke to him on the same subject: "If you're short of money, my boy, don't hesitate to call on me. I know how it is for a young man at a time like this: you want to make a good showing. Clothes—present for the bride—lot of expense for a wedding trip. You let me help you out. You're not marrying a poor man's daughter, eh? You knew that, I guess. And you'll want to keep your end up. Only natural. Say a couple of hundred. The groom ought to get *some* present, eh? I can afford it. Even if I did put up for the house and things. Say a couple of hundred. You're marrying MacIntosh's niece, boy. Been like a daughter to me. You want to make a show! I'll give you a check before you leave."

For some reason the boy appeared uncomfortable. Well, thought the Deacon, perhaps it was just as well. "Come, come!" he said. "You don't need to be stiffnecked about it. You know you need it. Take it! I can afford it. After all, it comes out of the shipping business easier'n it does out of a farm."

Zeke hung on hard, repeating to himself: 'I asked her, and I won't go back on her.'

"I'm all right," he said. "People don't expect much from a minister, you know."

Graveson was to marry them. Zeke himself would rather have been married by a Catholic priest or by the Devil himself. But there was no way out of it, of course. There was, however, one compensating factor: he would take quite some satisfaction in handing to Graveson a white envelope containing the fee. He hadn't been able to think of just what to say when he did it—but he'd think of something.

Zeke's father and mother came to the wedding. As they had written they would, they went straight to the church, arriving there at a quarter before three. The wedding was at three. Zeke met them in the vestibule. They told him to hurry along or he'd be late. Zeke said he'd see them at the house afterward. But his father—looking taller than ever and untouched by the excitement—said he guessed they'd better start along home after the service, they'd get as far as Reading before dark. Zeke felt relieved: it would save having to explain the Deacon to his father. Then his mother kissed him and his father shook hands with him.

Zeke still stood there—very thin, very tall, and the color showing over his cheekbones. He had on the same frock coat he'd bought to come to Boston, but with a white cravat. His mother saw how much he looked like his father —but pale, as though he were not eating enough. She tried to tell herself it was only the excitement.

Zeke had said: "How's . . . how's Joe?"

His father said: "Joe's all right, son. You get along, now. You'll be late."

Zeke said he had lots of time. "You're sitting up front. Aren't you?"

Abel said: "Seats all the same price?"

And Zeke laughed, in a way, and said he guessed they were. He said: "Let me take you up."

His mother protested, but Zeke took her by the arm and led them up the center aisle. He enjoyed doing that. He opened the door of the pew and showed them in. His father said: "Come and see us when you get settled." Zeke couldn't say anything. He walked down the aisle, suddenly conscious that he was not much moved by the wedding to come. Now that—well, now that it had begun, it seemed pretty simple, made up of unimportant steps one after another and no special climax anywhere. He thought of Viola then—and when he did, he felt sorry for her.

He went round to the vestry and Graveson was there getting into his gown. Zeke fished the envelope out of his pocket and handed it to him. "Here's your fee," he said.

Graveson refused it. "Professional etiquette," he advised.

The first thing Viola said to him when they came out into the air was: Zeke! Why *did* you take your mother up the aisle that way? *You* weren't supposed to do *that!*"

"Why not?"

"Oh, well, never mind."

After they'd got into the carriage, she said: "Well, we're married now. Are you glad? I am."

Zeke said, certainly he was glad. He had the same feeling he'd had under the tree that day when he'd decided he was going to be a preacher—of his life stretched out ahead of him, set, fixed between two straight limits narrowing with perspective into the time ahead. He was married now. Each time he made a decision, the limits moved closer together, straighter, more rigid. There would be no change affecting them. He would go ahead between them—year after year.

[Chapter 12]

THE DEACON, bent upon creating within the bosom of Viola's husband the pure, white flame of antislavery zeal, perceived that there were almost an embarrassing number of sources from which to obtain the fire. It occurred to him that the easiest way would be to send him on a trip with Gowan. The Deacon chuckled at the idea. Strong men sailed in the *Winnie Lou*—or whatever Gowan had painted on her behind this time; a handsome young parson out of the New Hampshire hills would most probably lose his mind. And *wouldn't* there be hell to pay if Gowan should tell him who owned her! No . . . an entertaining thought, but not practical. The Deacon passed it up.

Let's see . . . just at the moment there were a half dozen or more prominent, blabber-mouthed rascals running about Boston shouting Abolition at the tops of their lungs. Some of them preachers, too. If the thing were catching, Zeke might be infected by one of them. Parker, Chalmers, Burleigh, that doctor—what was his name?—Bowditch, Higginson—they all had it—bad. Maybe they could inspire a minister; thank God, they didn't seem to be having much luck with more responsible citizens! Still, they'd been at it for some time now, and for all Peele had ever said to *him*, at any rate, the boy didn't even know they were there. No, it had got to be something more personal. He'd have to think up something. There was no hurry. Old Somers looked to be good for several months yet. Take plenty of time and think of something good.

The Deacon took plenty of time—six months of it, in fact,—and it paid: he thought of something very good indeed. He was alone in the library when it came to him, having a peculiarly quiet hour after dinner. It was late in January, and he was enjoying the wise, seasonal preventive of a long, hot drink. Wait now! he said suddenly to himself, wait now!—how about that nigger on the boy's father's farm? How about *him*, eh? From what he'd gathered, the boy thought a good deal of him. Sure—why, there was that time the boy told about when the nigger'd sat under his window all night, when Zeke was sick or something, to keep the spirits away. What the hell was his name?—'Joe.' That's right: 'Joe'—and a runaway, sure as guns. 'Joe!' Yes, sir, Joe looked like just the ticket. You take old Joe, and this Fugitive Slave Law—if they'd ever pass the damn thing—and young Peele, and mix 'em all up together, and if young Peele didn't come out of it an Abolitionist, the Deacon would eat his shirt. Why, you let this Fugitive Slave Law clamp into dear, kind old Joe, and, my God, you wouldn't be able to *hold* Peele! He'd preach Abolition until he was bald.

The Deacon settled back to a blissful appreciation of his own brains. 'What that idea has got,' he told himself, 'is handiness. There it is, laying right there like a tool. When you want it—pick it up and use it. *I* thought up that idea. I set myself at it, and I thought it up. Now that's what I call *thinking*. Gowan, the skunk, couldn't think up an idea like that from now till Judgment. All he's good for is to bounce around on the ocean with a boatful of niggers and get himself shot at. If I was to cut him to twenty dollars a month, it'd be more'n he's worth. What any business depends on is the man who does the thinking. That's me. I done a good job of thinking tonight and so now I don't have to think any more till tomorrow.'

He had a long drink on that, and then leaned his head way back and breathed pleasantly through his mouth—as relaxed and happy and contented a man as there was anywhere in Boston.

Dr. Somers waned with commendable steadiness throughout the next eighteen months. And through all this period of decline not one of his Board of Deacons showed more loyalty in the regularity of his calls at the parsonage door than did Deacon MacIntosh—the man, perhaps, from whom such devotion might least have been expected. As Dr. Somers' body failed, so, too, did his mind; he had queer ideas and strange irascibilities. His nurse, naming for the third time in a month the name of MacIntosh in the list of callers, was troubled to hear the old man pipe something about MacIntosh being a fat vulture, and he wondered what he was hungry for.

Dr. Somers died not long after—and the Deacon decided it was time to get busy.

He began by expressing opinions in a Deacons' Meeting anent the type of man they ought to get to succeed Somers. Deacon MacIntosh opposed—on principle—the calling of too young a man. He realized, of course, that that was more or less the tendency in the church today, but he felt that in these peculiarly troublesome times, with doctrinal disputes on every hand, the church—any church!—needed a man of mature judgment and experience at the wheel.

That was, he said, all he had to say—but he felt, he said, very strongly about it.

The Senior Deacon, subsequently appointing A Committee To Consider Candidates, seemed to recall that MacIntosh had shown some interest in the matter, hadn't he?—sometime or other?—and put him on the Committee.

MacIntosh, it proved, was a man who got things done. He produced a candidate inside of six weeks, recommended him strongly, and the man was invited to preach a sample sermon. But no one seemed to like him at all. Nothing to do with his sermon, of course,—except that during the preaching of it he seemed to have a distressing amount of trouble with his teeth. It was agreed that that was not Deacon MacIntosh's fault, but—well, really, you couldn't have a man in the pulpit of the Twelfth Congregational Church week after week who was going to have trouble keeping his teeth in. Deacon MacIntosh pointed out that probably the church could get the teeth fixed—but no one seemed very much interested.

Each Sunday there was a new, unhappy face in the pulpit of the Twelfth Congregational Church, and each Sunday there was more space in the pews. Somehow, the knowledge that he was on trial, never seemed to bring out the best in a candidate. A committeeman would sit unnoticed in a rear pew of a church in Springfield and hear a tremendous sermon. And then the very selfsame preacher would shamble to the front of the pulpit of the Twelfth and proceed to shame his sponsor with a sermon that would have disqualified a man to teach the Infant Class. Every week, some committeeman would say: 'He's a different man in his own church, I assure you!' But the following week, when it was that man's turn to be assured, he'd be skeptical. Polite, of course,—but skeptical. A rather intense dislike of each other developed among the members of the Committee, and their joint deliberations became anything but smooth. The Chairman of the Committee on Finances sent word to the meeting of September 3, 1850, that during the last twelve months collections had been cut in half. This produced a long silence and a motion to adjourn. Deacon MacIntosh seconded the motion. When a committee of deacons said nothing for over a minute, it meant they were going to do something. Well, so was he!—and he hurried home to write a letter.

[Chapter 13]

IT WAS THREE YEARS and a long summer since they had been married. "Come and see us after you've gotten settled," his father'd said. And Zeke had gone. Twice. Viola had not gone with him. He'd had to go in the winter— Graveson taking the summer jaunts—and each time she had not been well enough to make the trip. Since Somers had died, Zeke hadn't been home at all. Well, Graveson was back now, and he was going.

He told Viola that they had put it off long enough: he'd got to take a trip home to see his family. And he asked her if she cared to go with him.

"Do you want me to?" From her tone she might have thought the fact was either way.

But Zeke used it to accuse himself: first, of not wanting her to go with him and, second, of having failed to pretend he did. Guilty, he knew, on both counts. It didn't make it any easier to reply.

"Just as you like," he said. "I don't want to force my family on you."

"Well—" She checked herself. "Perhaps I'd better stay here. You go ahead, Zeke. They'll be glad to see you."

"Well . . . it would be kind of a long trip for you."

"O-o-oh, I don't know . . . I think I could stand it."

"Come along, then."

"No, I'll stay here. But don't tell them vaguely that I didn't feel like traveling just now. You've already disappointed them twice that way. Just tell them your wife's uncle had delirium tremens, and she thought she'd better stay home. You go ahead, Zeke. You'll have a good time."

"Well, I thought I'd go Monday. I'll be back Thursday. You don't mind, do you? You'll be all right."

"Yes, I think so."

"Then why do you object to my going?"

"But I don't."

"Well, you didn't seem very enthusiastic about it."

Mrs. Peele had had to give up saying "My God!" when she had married. She felt the deprivation keenly at times. "Oh, go!" she said. "Heavens! Go now, if you want to. And stay a month."

Zeke said he didn't want to stay a month. He ought not to take four days even.

Mrs. Peele made no comment.

Zeke, interpreting this as a peculiarly sarcastic aspersion on his indispensability to the Twelfth Congregational Church, made no comment either. As soon as he felt that he could control his voice, he said that he had to go out and make some calls.

Mrs. Peele reminded him to take his key.

He made no calls. He walked instead out along the west side of the River, mostly in darkness, and covered eight

93

or nine miles. But he was home again in less than two hours.

There was a light in her room upstairs. He went into the living room and sat in front of the fire, what there was left of it, and finally went to bed. He could see from the hall upstairs that she'd put her light out. He supposed she must have heard him come in.

Zeke got there late Monday afternoon—not much more than in time for supper. They were glad to see him and he was intensely glad to be there. He had no trouble explaining why Viola hadn't come, because they didn't demand any explanation. It seemed odd to Zeke to realize that they both recognized that he had a life of his own now and that they recognized his right to talk about it or not as he chose. It made him want to talk about it, in a way. But that was the last thing he could do. If he owed it to Viola to pretend he was happy, he certainly owed it about ten times as much to his father and mother. And he paid off the obligation well. At the moment, he *was* happy.

After supper he followed his father round the chores, saw what he could of new things near the house. With his father, he projected a more complete inspection in the morning. As they were going down the line of stalls in the new barn, he caught himself thinking once or twice what it would be like if he were to show his father round his own workings. . . .

'That one there, father? You don't remember her, do you? That's old Mrs. Welland. It's the dropsy makes her look that way. Oh, no, it's not fatal. I get in here to see her every couple of weeks; she doesn't change much—do you, Mrs. Welland? I say, *do* you, Mrs. Welland. You *don't change much, do* you! . . . What's that? You want me to pray with you? . . . Yes! Surely! . . . If you'll excuse me, father, I'll pray with her for a minute or two.

I—er, I generally kneel here by this chair. Yes, I know it looks a little ridiculous to you, but we can't help that. This is my job. . . . "Our Father in Heaven, grant us, we ask Thee . . ." How do I know whether it does her any good? Ah! It so happens that I don't believe it does her—that it does her dropsy, at any rate—a bit of good. Shall I tell her that, father? Or perhaps you'd like to tell her. . . . Good-by, Mrs. Welland. Nice to have seen you. I'll be in again before long. . . . My, the air smells good out here in the street! I tell you, father, the way to appreciate the air in the Boston streets is to go into some of the houses. Like Mrs. Welland's, for instance. We've got five more like Mrs. Welland's, and then we can go home. Two of the five more are a little worse than Mrs. Welland's, but the other three aren't so bad. After that we can go home. Viola'll be there, father! Oh, Viola's certain to be there! Viola's my wife.'

They came out of the barn—into the clear, dark stillness of the early evening. Zeke looked up at the sky. Not a roof against it—only trees. It was clear—and dark. . . .

He stumbled.

"That's the silo-pit," his father observed, "don't fall into it."

In the morning they started out to have a good look all round the place. About a half mile from the house, down in a hollow, there was a wet, swampy place, with alders round it and full of wobbly grass hummocks and purple flags. Probably the best soil anywhere on the farm, his father said, if it was drained properly and plowed and then left to lie for a year. He'd been thinking about it for some time and he'd decided to set Joe at it. He was going to put him at it this morning. They'd stop there first.

95

They picked Joe up at the new barn and the three of them set out for the swamp—Zeke and his father ahead and Joe a step or two behind. Joe was carrying a mattock and a spade and also a heavy knife, like a machete, to use on the alders. Any other man would have used an ax, but Joe was handier with a knife. Joe didn't talk much, because, with Zeke grown up now and the boy's father being there too, it wasn't up to Joe to talk. All the same, you didn't have to take more than one look at Joe's face to tell that he was glad to have the boy home. It made it a big day for Joe.

When they got to the swamp, Zeke watched his father while he showed Joe exactly where he wanted the trenches. Joe'd be there all day. He'd brought his dinner with him, so he wouldn't have to walk clear back to the house at noon. When his father had made sure Joe understood, they went off and left him at it.

They came to Zeke's field. Zeke said: "Is this still mine?"

And his father said: "You've got a deed to it, haven't you?"

"Gosh, I was sick that day!" He didn't know where the deed was now; he was ashamed of that. "That's a good wall Joe built, isn't it?"

His father said, yes, it was a good wall . . . then they went on. By eleven o'clock, Zeke had begun to get pretty hungry. It was still an hour to dinner. They were getting back nearer the house now, although they weren't able to see it yet because they were down over the other side of the rise. His father noticed a piece of fence that he said ought be attended to now before it got any worse and he asked Zeke if he'd go up to the barn and get the auger for him.

Zeke said, certainly,—thinking he'd go up to the house,

too, and get a few cookies out of the jar to stay him till dinnertime.

As he came into the yard, there was a man standing there waiting for someone—looked as though he might be most anything. There was a dirty horse and a dirty buggy out by the gate, but the man, now that Zeke got closer to him, seemed to be dirtier than either of them. He was small and droop-shouldered, with a scraggly mustache, and tobacco juice in the seams of his chin. Zeke wondered if he hadn't better get rid of him for his father. "Good morning," he said.

The man didn't seem to wake up as he would if he were selling something. Zeke didn't know what his errand could be.

"You Mr. Peele?"

"I'm one of them. What's on your mind?"

"Gramp's my name. United States deputy marshal."

Probably the man had been sent to his father for assistance of some kind. "I see."

"Got a warrant here," said Mr. Gramp, "made out for a nigger works for you. Name's Joe."

Zeke didn't understand. He exclaimed simply: "Joe?"

"Joe," said the marshal. "Here—" he drew the document from his pocket. "Take a look at it. I been waiting here most of the morning."

Zeke took it and read it through. It was a warrant, all right—as far as he could tell. It called for the arrest of one black man, now passing under the name of 'Joe.' There was a description of 'Joe,' too, and there also appeared the name: 'Abel Peele, landowner, of the Town of New Boston . . .' There wasn't much use trying to argue that it was meant for some other Joe, somewhere else. Nor in denying the fact of Joe. Joe was down there in the swamp, alone,—singing, probably, while he worked. What could Joe have done to be arrested for? Nothing! And yet he, Zeke, was all there was to keep this filthy individual from arresting him.

"What's he done," Zeke asked, "—or what do you claim he's done?"

"Don't know as he's done anything," said Marshal Gramp, "—except run away from them as owned him. That's enough, ain't it?"

"Nobody owns him!" Zeke blazed. "He's been here since before I was born!"

The marshal nodded and looked Zeke up and down. "Yes, sir—that's a long time, all right." He spat. "All the same, there was somebody *did* own him, and I guess now they aim to get him back. Well, all I got to do is arrest him and take him back to Manchester. If you don't mind my asking: where is he?"

If there'd been a clean place on him to take hold of, Zeke would have picked him up and thrown him out of the yard. The rise of his own anger frightened him. "You wait here a minute," he said, "I'll step in the house and see if they know."

The marshal, speaking in a safe tone toward Zeke's back, said, "Well, if you can get anything out of her, sonny, you go ahead."

His mother was standing in the kitchen. "What's the trouble, Zeke? What's he want?"

"I'm not sure there is any trouble—yet. Just let me think what to do, will you?"

"Who is he? He was so dirty, I wouldn't ask him."

"Name's Gramp, he says."

"No Gramps round here that I know of. Where's he come from?"

"Manchester. Please, mother, let me think—"

"You wouldn't have to think, if you didn't know something's wrong. What is he? What's he want? Said he wanted to see your father, but I didn't want to leave the house to go tell him."

Solitary meditation was out of the question. "He's come after Joe," Zeke said.

"Joe!?"

"Claims Joe's a fugitive slave."

"Well, what if he was? Twenty years, Joe's been here."

"I know. I told him. He wants to arrest him."

" 'Ar*rest* him'! Zeke Peele, you go right out and tell that man to get off the place! Tell him he'd better get before your father sees him, too!"

"I know, mother. He's got a warrant with him."

" 'Warrant'?" Mrs. Peele exclaimed in disgust. "What's a warrant! This is your father's farm, ain't it?"

"Yes, of course, mother, but—"

"Well, then!"

"It's the law, mother! It isn't him, it's the law! You can't chase the law out of your yard just because you don't happen to like it, you know. Now, please, mother—let me try to think what to do!"

"You get him out of here before your father gets back, or there'll be trouble."

Zeke wondered what she'd call the present state of affairs. Well, fortunately, Joe was safe out of the way—for the time being, anyhow. Zeke went over and sat down beside the table.

There was a knock on the door.

"What's he want now!" Zeke said. "I thought I left him outside."

His mother had turned toward the door, but Zeke went

99

past her and opened it. It was Joe. A few paces behind Joe was the marshal, both his expression and his pose—one hand was thrust inside his coat—indicative of complete satisfaction and triumph. He was chewing hard.

Joe brought the information that there was a man out here wanted to see Mr. Peele.

Zeke said: "Come in, Joe. Come in here." He turned and went back into the room and sat down again beside the table.

Joe had stepped wonderingly through the door.

"Shut the door," Zeke told him. "Come over here, Joe, and listen to me. Now you've got to do just exactly as I tell you, do you understand?"

Joe said, yessuh, and hurried on to explain that he'd come up to grind his knife, he'd got a big knick in it. He exhibited it in proof.

Zeke said: "Yes, yes, all right. Now listen, Joe: something has happened, do you see?"

"Sump'n bad?" Joe's head thrust forward—and his hand tightened on the knife.

"No," Zeke said, "not very. And I'm going to help you all I can. It'll come out all right. But you're in trouble and—"

"Me . . . ?" said Joe. They'd come after him!—and the skin on his back crawled and his eyes rolled up their whites and the muscles in the backs of his legs tightened.

He swung for the door and jumped—and he thought of the man outside only as being between himself and the woods. His fist struck the door just above the latch and the door popped open. He was through it and out into the sunlight—just as Zeke shouted "Joe!" and leaped after him from his chair.

Mr. Gramp was a prudent man whose experience as a

100

United States deputy marshal ran back over a period of three days. As the nigger had loomed round the corner of the barn, Mr. Gramp, marking the tremendous size of him, had slid his hand—prudently—inside his coat. And when Mr. Gramp had seen the size of the knife Joe was carrying, Mr. Gramp's forefinger had slipped—prudently—round the trigger. It had stayed there, a little sweaty, while Joe was in the house.

He shot him—before his feet had touched the ground. But he didn't stop him. Joe kept going. He got clear across the yard before he pitched onto his face.

He was dead when Zeke got to him.

Mr. Gramp, walking prudently to his buggy, got in, and drove away.

Zeke was down on one knee. He'd raised Joe up and was holding him, the way a man does, in the crook of his thigh. Joe was dead. Zeke reached down and took the knife out of Joe's hand and tossed it away. It occurred to him that if he'd thought to make Joe put down that knife before he started talking to him, Joe might be alive now—instead of being dead.

He turned to see where the man was. . . . He'd gone. Zeke was glad he had. Joe was dead now. Joe had changed so quickly from being alive to being dead!

Abel went down to see the First Selectman right after dinner. The First Selectman was a tough old specimen, old enough to have thought, fifty years ago, that Abel's father was too young to get married. Jabez Nickerson. He wasn't much bigger than a grasshopper now and he generally raked instead of pitching.

Old Jabez had just finished his dinner as the Peeles stepped into his kitchen. He looked at Abel and then at the boy and told them to come into the parlor. Abel called him Jabez, but Zeke naturally addressed him as Mr. Nickerson.

When they were seated and Abel had answered that his wife was well, Abel told what had happened.

Jabez said: "That's the trouble with these damn ca't'idges. A man can shoot 'fore he's got to take time to think 'bout it."

Abel said it might be. He asked the old man if he'd care to come up to his place and have a look round. Jabez said, no, he didn't know as that'd do any good; he asked to see the warrant.

Abel said; "Zeke—" and Zeke handed over the warrant. Jabez read it.

"Seems to be a good enough warrant," he admitted. "You know who this Gramp is, Abel. Father was Dudley Gramp. Come from round Nashua."

Abel said maybe he had heard of them.

"None of 'em any good," Jabez said. "Still, if your man came for him with a knife, I don't know as there's much we can do about it."

"He didn't go for him!" Zeke put in. "Joe was just scared and trying to run!"

"You told that to this Gramp, did you?—while your man was goin' for him?"

Zeke's face grew a little paler than it had been.

Jabez handed the warrant to Abel. "Main thing to do with this, Abel, as I see it, is to not have any fuss about it. You know how 'tis, some of these boys round here see a chance to start something, no telling what might happen. First thing they'd want to do, be t' raise a regiment and march to Manchester."

Abel didn't say anything.

" 'F you want my opinion, some of them Abolition hotheads more'n likely put Gramp up to this just to see if they *could* start something. They didn't figure on the shooting. But then your man got scared, and this Gramp got scared, and that's what happened. Way it looks to me, anyhow."

Abel said that was about the way he figured it.

"Well—" the First Selectman of the Town of New Boston concluded: "I guess that's about all *I* can do. You going to have a funeral?"

"In the forenoon," Abel said, "eleven o'clock."

"Mm, hm. Small, eh?"

"Yes. Just us—and the other men on the place."

"Well," said Jabez, "if it should happen somebody *should* hear about it meantime and ask me about it, I'll remember the funeral is eleven o'clock."

Abel said, yes. Well—he'd go along back.

"Say—" it occurred to Jabez to inquire, "you wouldn't have any idea who *did* start it, would you?"

Abel said, no, he wouldn't.

"Politics." Jabez nodded as though Abel had confirmed his opinion.

"Maybe," Abel said; "account for most anything, sometimes."

"Yes. That's true. Well—too bad he had that knife." He spoke to Zeke: "How's things in Boston? You like it?"

"All right."

Mr. Nickerson said: "Married, ain't you?"

Zeke said he was.

" 'S a good thing," Mr. Nickerson approved.

Abel said good-by, and Mr. Nickerson, following them out through the kitchen, was forced to say good-by, too.

Zeke and his father were crossing the dooryard—"Too

bad to have this kind of a thing happen when you're home on a visit," Jabez called.

Abel said, yes, it was.

They had the funeral next morning just as they'd planned to. They buried Joe in the cemetery—in a lot Abel had bought ten years before and that they hadn't had any use for up to this time. Actually, it couldn't really be called a funeral, because there was no one there except the family and the rest of the men who worked on the place and Walter Holmes, the sexton, who'd dug the grave and who acted as undertaker. Zeke handled the service—which was very brief. By pretending to himself that he was somewhere else, he got through two passages from the Bible, but when he got into the Twenty-third Psalm his voice went back on him, so that he just about managed to finish out the psalm. He let the rest of it go. And everyone was glad he did. Both Abel and Minna had felt that they ought to have the funeral more out of deference to Zeke's position as a minister than as a tribute to Joe. They'd been fond of Joe, but it didn't seem as though now a funeral would do him much good.

The rest of them drove back to the farm and went to work and worked hard—harder than usual. Except Zeke. Zeke said he guessed he'd walk home.

He noticed a new plank set into the bridge over the brook, and going up the hill, he kept seeing things he knew—a place washed out under the downside of a great, flat stone, and then, sooner than he'd expected it, the dry, rotten birch stump, jutting out from the high bank on the left. There was less bark on it now—it would be hard to make it so frightening at night.

He wasn't grieving for Joe now and he knew he wouldn't be. He knew perfectly well that when he got back to Boston, where Joe had never been a part of his life, there'd be no occasion for him even to miss him. All the same, he was going to need something with which to meet the knowledge that it was his fault Joe had been killed. He went over the source of that knowledge: the man had shot Joe in self-defense, because, for all he could see, Joe was coming at him with a knife. And Joe wouldn't have had the knife if he'd been told in the first place to put it down. It was so simple you could see right away that there was no escape from it.

Zeke hadn't said anything to his father about it's being his fault. He'd wanted to, but what was the use? He knew himself it was his fault, so what was the use running to his father, bellowing: 'It was my fault! It was my fault!' to get his father to say, 'No, it wasn't,'—and a chance, too, his father might not say it. His mother would, though, and he'd know that she believed it. But that wouldn't change the fact of it any.

He wished he didn't have to go back to the house now— and go into the yard. He'd just as soon go back to Boston. But his visit wasn't up till tomorrow morning. He'd stick it out.

He got back to Boston late next night.

When Viola came down in the morning, she asked him about his trip and he told her what had happened. He told it to her flatly, every detail exactly as he remembered it, exactly as it had happened. He wasn't looking at her as he talked. He'd tell her the whole thing—and then he'd wait to see whether she saw that it was his fault Joe had been killed. He'd be able to tell, all right.

Viola, seeing his face and hearing his voice, didn't interrupt. At the point where Joe was shot, she didn't make a sound. When Zeke had finished, she didn't say anything. Viola knew where this game had started.

Zeke realized, from her silence, that she saw plainly that it had been his fault and that she was trying to think of something else to say. He hated her for that.

"And your uncle," he said, "he's been well? Busy, I'm sure. Remember me to him,—if he drops in to see you today." Zeke got up and left the room—a bitter self-sufficiency in his manner intended to repulse any pretense on her part that she felt inclined to answer him.

Viola remained at the breakfast table, making her way from just plain fright to terror. She was in this thing. And if Zeke ever found it out . . .

Viola decided she didn't want much breakfast—just some coffee.

Deacon MacIntosh dropped in late that afternoon. His niece opened the door to him, and the Deacon, being in the best of spirits, said: "Well, my dear!"

"Husband home?" he asked, as he put down his hat . . . and leaned his cane against the table in the front hall. He strolled into the living room, not in the least disconcerted, merely wondering what had got into her now. He had come for a report on how Zeke had taken the little incident in the New Boston barnyard. The Deacon knew, of course, what had happened in the barnyard, but the important thing was how the boy had taken it. It was that which would determine whether or not young Peele was now ready for the pulpit.

She followed him into the room.

The Deacon had seated himself and his gloved hands rested comfortably on the arms of his chair. He had walked slowly and his stomach rose and fell only a little more rapidly than usual.

"Didn't he get home yet?" he inquired.

"Last night."

"Well, er, he's—he's not in now, is he?"

"No."

"Why'n't yuh si' down?" The Deacon didn't quite like the way she looked—just standing there. She'd often expressed hatred of him and scorn, too. But verbally, usually, and as though she enjoyed doing it. He wished she'd say something.

"Say what you've got to say," she told him wearily, "—and get out."

The Deacon felt better. This was more like herself.

"What you got in the house?" he said. "Anything? I had a long walk."

"Nothing."

"That's a fine way to talk! I paid for this house, didn't I? At least I ought to be able to get a drink in it!"

"What did you come for?"

"I came to see you. Came to see if he'd got home. Came to ask what kind of a trip he had."

"You ought to know."

"So *that's* it, eh? Now look here, young woman, you can't accuse me of that! Pure accident, that was. And self-defense. I didn't have any more to do with that than—than you did."

"Well, that's enough—for me."

"Come, come!" said the Deacon. "You don't like having him killed, do you? All right—neither do I. I'll admit it isn't what I'd planned at all. But there's no need for you to be upset about it, because it isn't going to make any difference one way or the other. It may speed things up a

107

little, but that's all. And so much to the good if it does. The church is ready any time. It's only a question of if he is. That's what I came to find out. Now, then: how did he take it, eh? That's what I want to know, how did he take it? Stir him up any? It ought to, you know. It ought to."

"Yes," she said slowly, "it stirred him up."

"Of course it did! I was certain of it. He'll preach, all right! You leave it to me!"

"I wish I could. He was fond of that man."

"Of who? The nigger? Sure he was! That's what'll stir him up."

"And he's kind of stunned by it right now. He knows it happened—and that's about all."

"Good God!" said the Deacon, "that's all I *want* him to know!"

"Yes. But, you see, when he does wake up, he's going to begin to wonder where all this started from . . . and then he's going to start in to find out."

"To *try* to find out."

"You don't know him. He'll never quit. Never. And when he does find out—"

"All right, what then? Suppose he does. It was all legal, wasn't it? We did our duty, didn't we? We did just what the law tells us. And we did it in spite of it was going to hurt our own family! That's Christian, that is. That's what they teach you in church. I'm a deacon, ain't I? I guess I ought to know!"

"And when he does find out," she repeated, "what happens to me?"

"Nothing."

" 'Nothing'? I'll tell you what happens to me: back to 'Uncle'!"

The Deacon warded it off. "Not at all!" he said. "Not at all! Why, he'd respect you for it, Vi! You don't understand 'em. They're *like* that."

"Try to get this through your head," she said quietly: "I hate you. Do you understand?"

"Yes, yes, but never mind about it now. I want to talk about *this* business."

"I'm coming to it. I hate you and you know why—so there's no need to go over all that part of it again."

"I've explained 'all that part of it,' as you call it, to you a great many times. Your mother—"

"*Shut up!*"

The Deacon did. Bad humor she was in this morning. Well, better let her blaze up and get it over with.

She chose not to blaze. She stood there—shaking a little and her face working—but saying nothing.

The Deacon found it discomforting.

When she could, she spoke—turning away from him: "Get out, will you?"—quietly.

He sat where he was.

She walked toward the piano . . . and the Deacon thought she was going to bump into it. She put out her hand to it—stood there—and her voice came dull and flat. "I don't think I could go back," she said. "I don't know what else I could do, but—I don't think I could go back."

This was beyond the Deacon's understanding. Tactfully, he said nothing.

She faced round to him now. "You don't see what you've done, do you?"

"Well, I—I guess I don't see it the way you do."

"I lived in your house because it was the only way I could eat. Quite a price—but as long as I was willing to pay it, you had to do your part, thanks to Gowan. And then

Zeke Peele turned up. He wanted food, too. And I fed him. So when it occurred to him that it might be exciting to get married—he asked me. I married him. I married him, all right! Because it was the only chance I had to get out of the house you were in!

"It worked. There've been four or five days in a row when you haven't come into this place at all. In time, people might have thought of me as being his wife, instead of as your—well, niece. Maybe *I* could have, even. Sounds a little far-fetched, I know—but it might have been that way—after a while. Even the chance of it was worth living for."

The Deacon made no sign, one way or the other. This general topic of their relationship was one he'd never had any luck with.

"You can't see what that meant to me, can you?—just the possibility of being tied up with someone other than you—with anyone! I know he doesn't love me. Do you suppose that matters to me? It doesn't. It doesn't matter to me that I don't love him. The only thing that I care about is being away from you. I'm not even sorry for Zeke. I didn't cheat him. He cheated himself. He knows it now. He's known it for some time. He's very decent about it. He even goes so far as to pretend he *doesn't* know it. I can't very well ask for more than that, can I?"

The Deacon was finding it difficult now to follow her. "Come, come!" he said, "you ought to be very happy."

"I am. Because the other side of the picture is living with you. I'm very happy. I want things to stay just as they are. It may not sound like an ideal married life, but it's good enough for Viola. Plenty! Why couldn't you leave it alone? Why did you have to go and kill a man?"

"But I didn't, I tell you!"—it wasn't often the Deacon had a chance to protest his innocence so genuinely.

"Who did, then? You wanted to stir Zeke up, didn't you? Well, he's stirred up, all right. You've done nicely. And he'll stay stirred up, right straight up until he finds out who did it. I don't expect he'll calm down much, even then. Oh, don't worry! He won't hurt you. You'll be safe enough. You can sit right there with your fat hands folded over your belly and match your sense of duty with any-body's! It's me I'm thinking about! Me! What happens to me! I was in on it, too. I helped. I knew what was going on. Do you think his sense of duty is going to keep him tied up to me when he finds that out? Like hell it is! 'Back to your uncle, Viola! Back to Deacon MacIntosh—right back where you came from in the first place!' " Her voice had risen to a scream.

She slumped now and had to hold to the piano for support, arms outstretched on either side, and her head swaying a little—still staring at him.

The Deacon figured she was about through. He spoke in a tone of comfortable superiority. "If you can tell me just this one thing," he said, "I'll agree there's something to worry about: how's he going to find out?"

She didn't hear him, she didn't know that he'd spoken—although she was looking right at him. She drooped still further, sagged, almost as though she were about to col-lapse. She'd burnt herself out now. Pretty soon, he thought, she'd be able to talk sense. Women were certainly trying sometimes! Well, patience was the only way.

" 'Uncle'!" she said thickly, and her head moved slowly up and down. "Maybe I could come back, if you were. I'd hate you, of course. But you wouldn't be part of me. You wouldn't be all through me—so that at night I dig at my body with my fingernails! That's kind of silly, isn't it? You'd think that after ten years I'd get used to knowing you were my father."

"You mustn't feel that way about it," said the Deacon. "What do you eat your meals for? That's where your body comes from."

She turned from him—and let go of the piano; she was making her way out of the room.

He realized they hadn't got anywhere. "Wait a minute!" he called. "I came here to find out how he took it. D' he say anything to you? About how he felt, I mean?"

In the doorway, she faced round to him. "At breakfast," she said; "'. . . and your uncle? How has he been? Busy, I'm sure. Remember me to him if he drops in to see you today.'"

"He said that?"

"Yes. He said that."

"Was that all?"

"Yes."

"Hmph! Well, be damned! You're sure that was all?"

"Yes."

"Polite bugger, anyway," said the Deacon, "isn't he?"

. . . but she was already on her way toward the stairs.

The Deacon got himself out of his chair and followed her out into the hall. She was standing at the foot of the stairs, one hand on the newel post, looking straight ahead. The Deacon recognized the pose. He himself, tired, had often stood at the foot of the stairs, just waiting until he should have a mind to tackle them.

He said he'd got to go along.

Her lips moved as she said what looked to be 'all right.' She was still waiting for strength to get herself upstairs.

It suddenly dawned on the Deacon what might be the

matter with her—and he was swept by a wave of tenderness. Well, he *would* be damned! Why, sure! That must be it! This last year or so, somehow, he hadn't thought about it.

"You run along upstairs," he told her, "and take a nap."

His tone startled her so that she looked at him.

He smiled at her—thickly, to be sure, because of the structure of his face—but with benign intent.

"You'll feel better as time goes on," he assured her. "You take a good rest. And don't worry about anything you said to me. I understand how it is when you're upset. And my feelings weren't hurt at all."

Her expression didn't change a particle. She faced the stairs again and started, slowly, to go up.

The Deacon said again that he must go along. And he put on his hat, picked up his cane and went. "What the hell!" he said cheerfully, down the steps. "Now *there's* something to have a drink on!"

Viola, reaching her room, lay down. She'd known what he meant—but the vision of his face, smiling, had been too much for her. She lay there a long time. . . . But supposing it *had* been so? Supposing that sometime it should be so? Then Zeke would have to keep her, wouldn't he? He would, then. He'd have to.

Zeke had been at his work all day. It had been easy not to go home for supper. Half the time he didn't, anyway. But it was getting later now, and not many real excuses left. Past nine—and he left the office of the Twelfth Congregational Church to walk home.

It was like him, now, not wanting to go home, to take the direct route—not far, a mile perhaps, and in three years he'd come to know it as well as ever he'd known the long hill road up from the village. Knew it too well—for what his mind needed tonight. There was no diversion. Automatically, he picked his way round each familiar mudhole, stepped on the firm places in the crosswalk planks and, without thinking about it, swerved aside at a place where for the past six weeks nature had been gradually disposing of a cat.

He waved, as he passed his little window, to a cobbler, and the man answered as he always did, seizing the hammer in his left hand after the downstroke so as to wave his right and smiling delightedly with his dark eyes—his mouth pouched out with tacks. Two parishioners in a single block, each placed for a summer evening on the steps, spoke to the tall Reverend as he passed . . . and were answered agreeably and by name. Zeke knew none of this. He was thinking: 'It was my fault—my fault because I was stupid. Joe, frightened. And I said to him that I would help him. Joe, running across the yard—but perhaps he didn't know that, shot through the heart, they said—and then falling on his face, dead. I did that to him. I can't tell him that it was my fault. I can't tell him anything now. All there is for me is to remember it. I had my chance. "Put down the knife, Joe." That was all. And I didn't say it. That's why he's dead now. That's why he was dead then, when I lifted him up. I know it. And everyone else knows it. But they won't say it. No one will say it to me. But they'll be saying it among themselves all the same. After a while, they'll get tired of it and not say it. They won't even think of it—except when they see me. Then they'll think of it— and they'll be hurried, as I come towards them, to think of something to say.'

He turned a corner in the ripe smell of a saloon and went two blocks over on a side sreet, with the houses set back further and small elms along the gutter. And turned again onto the Avenue, which was wider.

After the next crossing, and seeing the white marble flags dim to gray stone, he raised his head to look at the Unitarian church. He'd done that and enjoyed it ever since the day Somers had said that even the outside of that edifice was slimy with transcendentalism. In the daytime, it always appeared particularly fresh. The church was lighted now and full and Zeke saw for the first time the long line of carriages, and groups, here and there, of coachmen, who'd climbed down to talk. There wasn't the atmosphere of a wedding and yet there was more feel of excitement than there would have been for a service. He wondered what was going on—and had an impulse to go in and see. . . .

He hesitated a moment and then went toward the steps, through the few people who were standing there, and on into the vestibule. Then over to a door at the far side and went in. The place was packed, but there was room to stand at the rear of the church.

He could see before he'd heard a word that whoever was preaching had the crowd with him.

He didn't know who the man was. Never seen him before, he was pretty sure. Tall man, bald, and preaching without a gown. A layman—but he was good. You could tell that, all right. Funny—you could tell it same as you could with a horse—by a lot of things, but you saw them all at once and didn't try to separate them out. He asked the man next to him who it was and he thought the man whispered 'Harrison,'—but he didn't like to ask again. Well, he'd listen. . . .

It was an hour and forty minutes later when Zeke came out. Deacon MacIntosh should have been there to see him.

The Deacon had wanted slavery to mean something personal to Zeke. The rest of the people had been listening to Mr. Garrison giving a lecture—superb or execrable, according to the taste of the listener—on Slavery.

Zeke had been listening to someone telling him that it was Slavery that had killed Joe. Slavery was so great, so tremendous and huge and overpowering, that it dwarfed the marshal and it dwarfed Zeke and made them tiny and impotent. Slavery had done it. Slavery had killed Joe. Zeke, insignificant in the menace of that great evil, had been powerless. It was Slavery that had done it.

Walking along Brimmer Street in the lateness of the evening, hungry and with his mind whipped to sensitiveness by an hour's thought, Zeke walked lightly—because a great weight had been taken from his shoulders. He should have been feeling, he knew, a certain gratitude toward the institution that had done that. He knew he ought to feel that way . . . but he didn't. He saw that here was a good chance, perhaps the only chance he would ever have, to get rid of the knowledge that he himself had killed Joe. He could shift the responsibility to Slavery now, and get rid of it. For good. He tried it. . . . But it wouldn't work. It *looked* like a good formula. But Slavery refused to take the burden. Slavery remained grim and horrible and big beyond any personal concern of Zeke's. Slavery didn't even answer, saying: You did it, Zeke, not I. Slavery ignored him.

And for that reason, suddenly and passionately and through all his spirit and through all his body—in his upraised face and down through his arms into his clenched fists—Zeke hated Slavery.

Zeke had never hated anything before.

He was not himself when he reached home. He opened

the door, his hand shaking a little at the lock, and he went upstairs without putting out the light in the living room.

"Zeke . . . ?"

He turned his head and saw that her door stood open. She must have called him, he thought,—and he went toward the door and went in.

[Chapter 14]

SHEBA—Mr. Watling had never yet traded her—was quite willing to turn in at the gate. It had been a long pull up the hill and she'd tackled it with more enthusiasm than good judgment—and then been too proud to admit it. Her flanks were going hard as he threw the reins over the dashboard and climbed down.

Mr. Watling had not gone out of his way to call at the Peeles', because for the next four weeks he had no special way to go out of. Revival meetings were few and far between. Mr. Watling had divided his time about evenly this past winter between drinking and horse doctoring— with a certain amount of overlapping which benefited neither pursuit. Today, though, he was in pretty good shape. It had taken four days of abstemiousness to put him there and a day to paint the buggy. The Peeles, he hoped, would see no change in him.

Minna came out to welcome him.

She looked about the same, anyhow . . . and Mr. Watling's bow, they both were aware, had lost nothing of its effectiveness.

She said Abel was just coming up now, he'd been down

117

to see about a new garden, where the swamp used to be; he was figuring, she said, on putting some celery in there.

Mr. Watling couldn't think what celery was selling for now, but he said he thought it was a fine idea.

Abel appeared, and when he was yet twenty yards away, Mr. Watling wished he'd known better than to come. There was going to be a lot of difference between them—and Peele would see it.

Abel did see it, but it didn't in any way affect the fact that he was very glad Watling had come.

Abel came up and grinned and stuck out his hand and said: "What'd *you* come for . . . trade that mare?"

And Mr. Watling said: "I came in hopes I'd be invited to dinner."

"Ask Minna. She's got charge of the commissary."

Right then and there, Mr. Watling felt as though he'd like to stay a month. Peele looked the same, she looked the same. It forced him to think of himself as being the same, too.

Abel said he'd take the horse and Mr. Watling could go round and wash up.

"Where's Joe?" Mr. Watling asked. "He'll take her, won't he?"

The pause was so slight that only a person knowing Abel—and having a quick, sensitive ear—would have noticed it.

"He's not here," Abel said, laying his hand on the mare as he went toward her head.

Mr. Watling said: "Oh,"—and to Minna: "You're quite sure I may stay to dinner, Mrs. Peele?" . . . and was confirmed in his guess that something was wrong. He went off to wash up, wondering what it was.

After dinner Abel took him down to the new cow barn.

118

"About Joe—" Abel said, sitting down on a milking stool. Mr. Watling selected a piece of chewing-timothy.

Abel told him the story, and when he'd finished, Mr. Watling was still chewing the same piece of timothy.

Finally Mr. Watling spat, sniffed once or twice, and said: "Who was it?"

Abel stretched his legs and leaned back against the stall post. "I'd kind of like to know."

"Mmmmm," Mr. Watling said, "no idea, eh?"

"No."

"Funny."

"Maybe," said Abel. "You didn't happen to be planning to be up round Manchester this next month or so, did you?"

"I had thought something of it," said Mr. Watling, "just this last minute or two."

"Need any money?" Abel inquired.

"Yes. But if I had any, I'd drink it."

"You sure of that, are you?"

"There's precedent for it."

"And some the other way."

"I did keep sober that summer, that's true. But if I remember correctly, we had a very wet fall."

"Well, suit yourself about the money. I just didn't want you to be to any expense on my account."

"I shan't be. Well—" Mr. Watling stood up. "I'll go see if Sheba's got her dinner down yet. Don't suppose you gave her anything but straw, did you?"

"Little sawdust," said Abel. "What's your hurry?"

"Got a long drive this afternoon." Mr. Watling stretched his long arms and yawned luxuriously. "Huh!" he concluded, flapping them to his sides. "Yes, sir, got a long drive this afternoon. Got to be in Manchester, New Hampshire, tomorrow night. Nice place, Manchester. Ever been there?"

"Not to my knowledge."

"Delightful place. Charming people. Family named Gramp lives there. Ever hear of the Gramps?"

"No," said Abel, "don't know as I have."

"Neither have I," said Mr. Watling. "I hope to, though. I might even say I expect to." He leaned against the doorway, gazing speculatively into space. "I've got a feeling that about the third day Dr. Watling is in Manchester, one of the Gramps is going to send for him to come look at a sick horse."

"You're sure he's *got* a horse," Abel said.

"He will have—and a sick one. You know," Mr. Watling sat down again, "I don't suppose you realize what a hard life a horse doctor—a conscientious horse doctor—has got."

"No-o-o," Abel agreed thoughtfully, "I don't suppose I do."

"He has, though," Watling said. "Sits up all night, sometimes, and the man that owns the horse has to sit up, too. And if the doctor happens to have a bottle of whisky along—why, half the time, the man owns the horse'll drink the whole thing and the poor doctor won't even get a swallow. Just has to sit there and listen to the man talk."

"Must be terrible," Abel said.

"It is!"

"Terrible whisky, I mean."

Watling laughed—and stood up. "God, I'd like to stay here awhile!"

"Any time," Abel assured him.

Watling said over his shoulder, "Say good-by to Mrs.

Peele for me, will you?" and started across to the barn where Sheba was.

Abel watched him go . . . and then went up to the house to tell Minna he was leaving.

[Chapter 15]

DEACON MACINTOSH had a dislike of leaving anything to chance. On the Tuesday following his call on Viola, and before committing himself to attend prayer meeting, he first took pains to ascertain that this was Peele's week to run it. He then arranged to have himself driven to the church and lingered after the services to offer Zeke a lift to his home. He waylaid him at the rear of the church, after the last parishioner had gone.

Zeke said, thanks, he guessed he'd walk.

For the very briefest instant, the Deacon was about to say, well, in that case, he'd walk along with him. But he thought better of it. "I see," he said, "well—glad to see you're home, anyway. I don't know that I've seen you since you got back. Good trip, was it?—er, that is, I mean to say, you found your parents well, did you?"

Zeke looked down at him sullenly. "Seemed to be."

"Rather a trying experience you had," the Deacon said in sympathy. "Viola told me."

"Oh, did she? Yes, it was—rather."

"Yes," said the Deacon, "unfortunate. Very unfortunate." He seemed to have all night to stand there and talk. "You know, I've thought all along that law was a mistake.

121

I must confess, that since it is incorporated, however, as a part of the legal structure of our country, I feel that it should be obeyed. Like any other law. Ah, me! Slavery is a big question! Isn't it!"

"If you don't mind," Zeke said, "I'd rather not talk about it."

"Why, of course! Of course not! I understand—painful to you. That's natural. Still, as time goes on, I'm afraid you may find it difficult not to say *some*thing."

"I expect to find it exceedingly difficult," Zeke said.

This was a little too indirect for Deacon MacIntosh. "You, er—"

"I mean that if I ever get a chance to *preach* in that pulpit—" he jerked his head toward it, but without taking his eyes off the Deacon, "I hope to preach you the damnedest Abolition sermon that's ever been preached in Boston."

"Well!" said the Deacon. "Well!"—either the boy talked so you couldn't understand him, or else he took your breath away. "Well," he said again, "there's been some pretty good ones preached."

"I know that."

"Dear me! I'd no idea you felt as strongly about it."

"I didn't—until lately."

"Yes, yes. The new convert—ah, yes, yes. How does Viola feel about it?"

"About what? Slavery?"

"About your preaching Abolition."

"What difference does that make? I haven't asked her."

"I feel that you should, my boy. I really do. A husband and wife, you know—"

"Slavery doesn't mean anything to her. Nothing at all! It does to me. And when I get my chance, I'm going to say what it *does* mean to me in spite of you, or Viola, or—or anyone else. I'll say it if it costs me my job!"

"I admire your spirit!"

"I daresay. Well—excuse me for going off half-cocked. Was there anything you wanted? I've got to speak to Mr. Partridge." Mr. Partridge was the sexton, working his way down the center aisle, straightening up the hymn books.

"No, no,—nothing," said the Deacon. "Good night."

Zeke said, "Good night, sir," and turned away.

"Oh, er—my boy!" the Deacon called after him and—as Zeke turned round and said "What?" the Deacon beckoned him to come closer.

Zeke stood still.

Once again, the Deacon thought better of it. Some other time would do as well for the congratulations. "Never mind," he said, "never mind!" and, with a cheery little wave, he turned and marched out. " 'Polite,' eh?" he said to himself when he had settled into his carriage. "Polite, hell! By God, his wife's a treat compared to that boy!"

But once home and settled comfortably with an aid to thought, he was able to view Zeke's impoliteness with that cool, dispassionate detachment so helpful in penetrating the disguise of any blessing. The boy was irritable, on edge. A good sign and a sure one. "He looks to me," the Deacon pronounced, "ready to go."

. . . and on Sunday, Mr. Graveson took, he said, a peculiar pleasure in announcing that the sermon, the following week, would be preached by the Reverend Ezekiel Peele.

Chapter 16

ARRIVING EARLY at the church, Deacon MacIntosh graciously accepted a congratulation or two on the honor that was his, and went vastly up the broad aisle to his pew. The boy was not yet in the pulpit, but shortly Viola arrived at the pew door, and the Deacon rose and stepped out into the aisle to permit her to enter—a most polite gesture, however necessary. Again he settled into his corner. It was five minutes to eleven. . . .

The Deacon had his eye trained on the little door at the side of the pulpit. Zeke appeared in it, stepped out into the church, and swung the door to behind him. He was very pale, and his gown flowed out at either side as he went rapidly to the pulpit stairs and climbed to his place. The Deacon lost sight of him then. It was a high pulpit and deep, with a solid railing round it like a battlement, and the minister's chair was right back against the wall. The minister, seated, could be seen from the side aisles of the church, but not from the center aisle. The Deacon, unfortunately at the moment, sat on the center aisle—but *he* could be seen from anywhere.

He experienced, now, a momentary fear lest the boy collapse like all the other candidates and make a holy show of himself. But, he remembered, the boy didn't know that he *was* a candidate—so that part was all right. "How's he feeling?" he whispered hoarsely to Viola.

Viola turned and looked at him, and then looked away. "All right, I guess."

A swift survey of the congregation showed it to be of about average size—just about what it had been lately, or maybe a little bit better than that . . . and as he faced

124

forward he saw that Zeke had come to the front of the pulpit. The organist was tapering off. . . .

Zeke waited for his silence . . . nervous, the Deacon could see, drawn, and very white—but he knew where he was! He'd go the route!—and Deacon MacIntosh, with what sporting instincts he had, honestly wished him well.

Viola was startled by his voice. It was hard and clear—in no way recognizable as his own. But he had control of it; it didn't break, anyway. And he certainly was handsome! After some of the scarecrows who'd flapped and croaked in that pulpit, he looked like a god. Suddenly she was very proud of him—so proud that for an instant she dreaded the approach of the sermon, and then, with a rush, she could scarcely wait for it. He'd show them!—and in his own right. He was free and clear of her uncle—wholly free of some little part her uncle had had in his being up there—tall and thin and beyond the reach of any of them. But he was hers!—and even if he had forgotten that, it did not matter now.

Zeke got through the long list of chores—hymns and notices and Scripture Lesson and even the long prayer—without the sensitive feelers of his consciousness reaching out five feet beyond the pulpit rail. The congregation were there, he knew, but he did not want yet really to see them. He had himself to work on first. Get set, get quieted down—get ready. . . .

Well, this was it . . . and he rose and came forward, stood there, and looked down and out over the pews with people in them. They wouldn't focus. But he could see that there was someone coming up the aisle, alone, toward the front of the church. He said to himself: 'I'll watch that man coming up the aisle, and when he straightens himself out and looks as he ought to—I'll be ready to go.'

The man came nearer, blurred still, but nearer. In an instant he was clear—Watling!

Mr. Watling looked up at Zeke and smiled and said something with his lips. Zeke smiled back at him. And he knew that he was ready. He looked out over his people, seeing them clearly now, and glad that they were there. He felt easy and comfortable. He was not alone. Watling would understand all through it . . . and no matter how it came out.

. . . he closed the Bible, after finishing his text, and laid it to one side, and beside it he laid his watch. 'It may help to remind you when it's time to come home,' he thought and he began to preach.

There was in Zeke's mind at this moment no thought that he hated Slavery. He had not any emotion concerning Slavery at all. He was thinking that he must *rouse these people* to hate Slavery—and the sundry aspects and elements of Slavery were so many tools to that end. Even Joe's death.

As a workman, he went to work—in the sight of the man who had taught him. And from one minute to the next he watched his own progress just as clearly and as accurately as a man building with tools watches his progress, as a man building a wall, as a carpenter,—without any frenzy. When a man shifted in his pew, he saw it and he read it. He watched their faces, and he read them.

A quiet start, relaxing them, drawing them to him with his voice—and then testing them with a little shock. Not too much—keep them off the defensive—and then another shock, harder. He moved them that time. And so he worked his way along.

He had them with him now, he could carry them, easily.

And he let into himself a little of his own passion—and he passed it on to them, gave it forth in his voice and in his words—and saw that it had been the thing to do. And a little more—he had store enough of it! Think now of Joe!— and his own passion stirred in him, sure and strong and proud. Preach? He'd preach to them! He'd show them what he had seen—and with him they would feel what he had felt. Come! . . . Come! . . . and he swung them forward with him with no check from them nor in himself. They were his audience, and he knew them.

. . . it had passed. Gently and surely, almost with tenderness, he led them back. Not all the way—but enough so that they might part. He stopped speaking—and in the stillness looked down on them a moment, and turned away.

[*Chapter 17*]

"AND THAT," said the gentleman sitting behind Mr. Watling, "ends his connection with *this* church!"

Mr. Watling was pleased. As he'd entered the pew, he'd noticed the man: a solid, marble pillar of the church, cold and well polished—in very expensive soft, gray trousers. What pleased Mr. Watling was to have him say exactly what Mr. Watling had expected him to. But the girl with him . . . Mr. Watling reached for a hymnbook, and out of the corner of his eye, watched her as she answered.

"Does it?"—and her eyes narrowed ever so little.

Her also Mr. Watling had noticed when he came in— noticed the set of her head, and the soft, fine chestnut color of her hair. 'Does it?' Ah! Now if only Hymn No. 186

could be '. . . by schisms rent asunder'! . . . He was leaf-
ing through the book. Well, Zeke was going to have the
girl with him, anyway. But they'd be outnumbered. You
didn't see a girl like that once in a year, but the man you
could match in any bank in Boston. Oh, yes, 186 was *Ein
Feste Burg;* he should have remembered. Well, there was
good singing in it . . . and the organist approved of it,
too. Never any use forcing hymns on an organist; they
always had the last word.

Mr. Watling stood up, thinking that Old Four-Per-Cent
would probably do some stolid violence to the bass. He
himself was going to take the tenor. He wondered about
her. . . .

She—could—sing! She had an alto that gave Mr. Watling
goose flesh just for the joy of it. He laid into the tenor,
and never gave a thought to Zeke all through the hymn.
Nor to the girl's father, who, as a matter of fact, had
stonily refused to sing at all. Sing in the presence of people
who'd listen to a sermon like that? Not he!

Mr. Watling, the hymn over, and watching Zeke as he
stretched forth his long arms in the lonely, quiet earnestness of the benediction, thought: 'I can't tell him today.'

He was slow in leaving the pew, thinking to say a word
to Zeke as he came down the aisle. The girl was slow, too—
looking for something she said had slipped down behind
the cushion in the pew . . . but she got no help from her
father.

Zeke was coming along now and the man stepped stiffly
from the pew into the aisle perhaps ten feet in front of
him. Zeke, Watling saw, had not even begun to recover.
It would be a mercy to the boy not to have to speak to
anyone. Watling watched Zeke recognize the man and

step toward him, saying somehow or other: "Good morning, Mr. Cameron."

And Mr. Cameron, the fine sunlight shining on his polished cheek, looked the boy up and down . . . and turned away.

It made Mr. Watling a little sick—but it was Zeke's fight, not his.

The girl stepped down from the doorway of the pew, gently, gracefully—the gray silk of her dress, and the sharp, small black of her gloves against her hands. "Mr. Peele—I'm Eleanor Cameron. That was the finest sermon I ever heard,"—and perceiving that Mr. Peele had heard her, she left him before there was need for him to answer.

Mr. Watling moved into the aisle, and Zeke, turning toward him, improvised a smile.

Watling grinned. "It was all right, boy," and he nodded, looking Zeke in the eye. "I was proud of you."

Zeke wasn't up to answering.

The Reverend Mr. Watling took him by the arm, hard. "The hell with all of them," he said quietly. "Come on! You can break down later when you're alone. It's more polite."

Mr. Watling had to move aside then, to make room for some other people—for a thin, sallow young woman to say to the boy honestly: "Zeke, it was wonderful!" . . . and Mr. Watling thought: 'Oh, so it's you, eh?' Zeke was trying to show that he'd got hold of himself: "Was it? I'm glad you liked it,"—coolly. Hurt her, all right, Watling could see. But what mattered was a suspicion that Zeke had known before he said it that it was going to hurt her. That made a pretty picture, didn't it!

This must be MacIntosh wheeling into position. What a beauty you are! "Quite a sermon, my boy, quite a sermon.

Quite a sermon. But I'll stand behind you! Don't worry!"

"Thank you, sir,"—unworried, anyhow. Then Zeke was remembering him: "Oh, er—Mr. Watling—"

And Mr. Watling, amused by the delicacy with which he had been waiting for this, stepped forward to be introduced. Zeke said professionally, "I'd like to introduce you to Mrs. Peele—" and both Zeke and Mr. Watling thought suddenly of the boy's mother. Zeke said, "—Mrs. Ezekiel Peele. Viola, this is Mr. Watling."

Well, she was the boy's wife: Mr. Watling, gallantly tempering it only enough to suit the interior of a church, bowed. He was wondering, as he did so, what it was that she was afraid of.

"Mr. Peele has often spoken of you," she said. "It was nice of you to come this morning."

"He was my only pupil," Watling confided easily, "I had to come."

Zeke had recognized the Deacon: "Deacon MacIntosh, Mr. Watling."

Deacon MacIntosh said, "Sir," with enormous dignity, and inclined his head; Mr. Watling, very cheerfully, said, "Deacon MacIntosh," and inclined his. Mr. Watling thought he'd never seen anyone so engagingly vulnerable as the Deacon.

By precedent, it was Zeke's duty after the service to go clad in his gown out into the vestibule, and there be alert in remembering names, hearty in handshaking, and bend attentively to what each face was trying to say. Viola knew this, so did the Deacon, and so did Mr. Watling. They moved down the aisle now—toward it.

At the rear of the church, where the minister was generally waylaid by the more importunate and forced to fight his way out to his post in the vestibule, there were now perhaps a dozen men. . . . Zeke's squad passed unimpeded.

They were in the vestibule now—in a space oddly cleared at the doorway from the center aisle. Watling and Viola turned round to the two following them. The Deacon glared to the right and to the left, and was very much upset.

Zeke looked round the vestibule. One side of it was filled with people who had been talking. So was the other. They weren't talking now—any of them. The people on his right were looking at him with sympathy, a sort of pathetic sympathy. They were wondering what he'd do now. Zeke didn't know himself. He hadn't thought as far as this moment.

The people on his left were not looking at him. Zeke saw who they were. Cameron ought to be there. Zeke looked for him, but the Camerons had gone home. These people, as they turned from one to another, or as a woman put up a hand to her hat, would glance at him. Zeke could see that he was distasteful to them. Some of the men hated him, apparently. But these things did not reach into him. They were phenomena connected only with those people. Within himself, Zeke felt a quiet bewilderment and an ominous, beginning disappointment. They had not understood. Neither had he. He had misread them while he preached—thinking of himself, he had been. An old fault—someone had told him of it before. Some of these people were hating him now. They ought not to do that. He'd wanted them to hate Slavery, not to hate him. Something had gone wrong. They hadn't understood.

He turned back to the three confronting him. "Guess it's time for dinner," he said, "I'll go take off this gown."

The robing room was round back of the pulpit. He went up the aisle steadily, with his head up, finding it not

131

difficult to avoid thinking—and finally in through the door, into the small room, and was alone. His teeth were shut hard. He took off his gown and hung it up on the peg. He must get out of here, quickly. He stepped toward the door and stopped, shutting his eyes for an instant as though to brace himself. He shouldn't have done that—but it was too late now. In the darkness, he said: 'Oh, God, I want to go home!' He opened his eyes then, sniffed once, and remarked aloud, "*That* was silly." Then he went out into the church.

Mr. Watling had come home with them for dinner. So had the Deacon. And the Deacon, all through the meal, had been puzzled as to how on earth young Peele had ever managed to pick up such a poised and worldly and generally finished gentleman for a friend. Under the circumstances, Deacon MacIntosh felt that it devolved upon himself to show this man Watling just what sort of family young Peele had married into. The Deacon showed him—with anecdote and flourish, with innuendo and with hearty, if sometimes single, laughter. Brandy did not appear either with dessert or after it. But a man of the Deacon's resource was equal even to that emergency. He called loudly for it, thus making the brandy shortage appear an oversight rather than ignorance.

They left the dining room and went into the living room—the Deacon nobly brushing aside some small thought of a nap. Watling, a moment ago, had introduced the subject of restaurants in New Orleans.

Viola, the Deacon rather hoped, would leave them now, but Watling thoughtlessly restrained her with some needlessly polite questions about the china bibelots in the cabinet.

There was a moment's hesitation over the allotting of

furniture. The Deacon took a strong line, however, and with no maneuvering at all was in possession of the large combination rocker; an ordinary man might have slipped about on the horsehair, but the Deacon wedged in comfortably. Mr. Watling had gracefully cornered Mrs. Peele on the sofa. Zeke sat on the high footstool before the grate. The Deacon was about to suggest to Watling that they resume in the matter of restaurants.

"Zeke," said Mr. Watling, "your father's looking very well."

"Oh—you've been there? You didn't tell me."

"Yes—two weeks ago. Your mother, too. Seemed very well. You and I are older—and perhaps Sheba. But they're not."

Viola thought: 'Why didn't he tell him before?'

But the Deacon understood perfectly, and almost laughed aloud at the neatness of it. That ought to show the boy what his parents amounted to! Sheba must be the hired girl. He wondered what she was like.

Zeke said: "You—you must have been there just after I was."

"Yes." There was a little silence. "I always liked Joe," Watling said.

Viola thought of ways to get out of the room. It was coming now! This man knew—and he was going to tell Zeke!

" 'Joe'?" said the Deacon helpfully. "I guess I don't know Joe. Who was he?"

" 'Joe'?" repeated Mr. Watling, "—friend of Zeke's."

The Deacon scarcely hesitated. "Oh, er, yes—yes. I do recall now," he said. "He was that colored feller. The one they—er—"

"Yes," said Mr. Watling.

Viola said: "I'm afraid, Mr. Watling, Mr. Peele finds that—a little difficult to talk about."

Mr. Watling understood instantly: he said he was sorry, that he should have known. "Mrs. Peele," his tone fresh and pleasant, "I'd been hoping all through luncheon that you'd play something for us. Sunday, I know. But if you play as I think you must, *no* one could object!"

"Play?" said Viola pitifully. "Yes—if you like."

She started to get up from the sofa, and Watling rose and bowed her to the piano.

Her arms ached, and although her hands were damp, her fingers, inside, were dry and stiff. She had begun to play. . . .

Zeke knew the piece well, although he hadn't heard it much of late. He recollected the first time he had listened to it. He wished to high heaven she would stop.

Viola, in the course of playing, remembered, too. She went on defiantly to finish it. After the last note, she couldn't hear the stillness in the room.

"Zeke," Watling said quietly—and when Zeke was looking at him: "That sheriff that went after Joe was sent by Deacon MacIntosh."

Zeke heard the words separately, one at a time. When he had put them together he believed them. He turned before he had had time for any emotion, to the Deacon.

The Deacon still had his hands folded over his stomach. He was gazing at the ceiling.

"Did you?" Zeke said.

The Deacon shifted his position. "Well . . . of course I had hoped to tell you myself, but—"

Zeke had stood up. He was coming toward the Deacon. "But what?"

The Deacon looked up at him. "But now Mr. Watling's told you," he said hastily.

Zeke stood still.

The Deacon hoped to God Viola'd keep her trap shut for a few minutes and give him a chance to work this out. Watling wasn't likely to do anything until he'd seen how things were going. What *was* his game, anyhow!

"Go on," Zeke said, "clear out!" . . . "My dear boy!" the Deacon protested very humorously. Zeke came a step closer. "Shut up, and get out," he said. He looked a foot taller than he had. Viola, behind him, was advancing from the piano. The Deacon's hands took hold of the chair arms, and his head drew in a little. "This isn't your house!" he said. "It's hers! You can't do anything to me here!"—and he saw Zeke turn from him to Viola. With a little thrill the Deacon realized that MacIntosh was a pretty good man in an emergency. Viola, God damn it, looked as though she were in a dream.

Zeke said to his wife: "Were you in this?"

"Yes."

Zeke, they could see, was about to call her something. The Deacon felt a quick, delightful sense of victory. It was pleasant to see the cloth thus humbled, to see young Peele—proud and six-feet-two—standing up in his own living room, his head bent forward, calling his wife names.

But young Peele had turned away. . . .

Mr. Watling shifted on the sofa.

Viola said: "What are you going to do with me?"

Zeke answered her casually—much as though it had been a question at the end of breakfast. "Why, nothing," he said.

Viola realized that he had done it in that instant. She called after him, now while she could: "Zeke—"

"Yes?"

It was too late, he'd gone. She said quietly, "You'll continue to live here, I suppose?" Live with her? After this? It seemed to amuse him. "It's very kind of you."

What he would say next was to Viola inevitable. She could hear it more plainly now than she did the next moment when he was saying it—"You can go back to your uncle."

Mr. Watling, watching her, had got up swiftly from the sofa. The girl looked as though she were going to fall— and Zeke looked as though he'd let her.

She didn't fall.

Mr. Watling said: "I apologize to all of you. Mrs. Peele—" He led her easily to the sofa and saw her seated. There was no use trying to get Zeke into a chair. Mr. Watling took a corner of the sofa. The Deacon, he could see, was not going to say a word until he had to.

"I'm afraid I owe all of you an explanation," Mr. Watling offered frankly. He had leaned forward and was looking at his hands. No one took him up. There was a touch of embarrassment in Mr. Watling's tone as he went on. "You see—" he spoke to no one of them directly—"the fact is, that that particular bit of information—that the Deacon had sent the sheriff after Joe, I mean—well, if you'll forgive my trying to justify myself: it didn't seem to me to be mine to keep. As far as Zeke and I were concerned, it belonged to Zeke. So I—er, well, I thought I'd better turn it over to him." He raised his head and spoke directly to the Deacon. "After I'd met you, Deacon, I thought I'd be a little happier about it, so to speak, if I were to do it in your presence."

The Deacon had had time to select his attitude. "Why,

136

certainly," he agreed, "of course. Only thing you could do."

"Thank you," said Mr. Watling earnestly. He stood up, and he smiled pleasantly upon the Deacon. "I don't want to hurry you, but perhaps you'd—er, care to join me."

There were two things the Deacon wanted: to get out of this place, and a drink. And he'd got to find out how much this fool Watling knew. In reply to Mr. Watling's suggestion, the Deacon said, yes, he guessed he'd better get along himself.

While the Deacon was getting out of his chair, Mr. Watling attended to Zeke. He handed him a card. "I'll be there for a day or two. Come and see me." Zeke took the card mechanically. "Yes," he said.

Mr. Watling went over to Viola. He bowed and said very softly, "Good-by, Mrs. Peele,"—and then went alongside the Deacon, made fast, and with a sort of casual ease, towed him from the room.

It was some time later, when Zeke, still standing there, laid Mr. Watling's card down on the table. He walked over to a window, and looked out into their fenced back yard. It had a small, worn pear tree in it, and a thin elm.

"Zeke—"

"Yes . . . ?"

"I want to stay."

"I don't see as it's much use, do you?" He was still looking out into the yard. He'd never tried to grow anything in that yard. It had seemed ridiculous, in a way. And besides that, the yard had originated with the Deacon. Well, he could have them back now—house and yard. Zeke felt a little sorry for the yard and house. They'd never done anyone any harm.

"Nothing's any different—if you'll only believe me."

"I believe you all right—as far as that goes."

"I didn't know he'd ever heard of Joe, Zeke."

"Oh. I asked you if you were in it, and you said yes." He didn't want to turn and face her. It was easier this way. Just a moment before, looking out into the yard, he had seen clearly, as a fact, that all that part of his life was over. Viola and her uncle and everything about them would be gone now. From now on, there would be left himself alone, preaching. He had seen that ahead. But as he let himself be drawn into talking and into listening to her talk, it became less real.

"I said yes because it seemed to be true," she said—not to him particularly, but recalling what had happened. "I didn't even want to say anything else. You stood over me and looked so terrible and said 'Were you in this?' and I said 'yes.' " She went on: "I want to tell you the rest of it. I'm not pleading. I just want to tell you."

Zeke knew she wasn't pleading. The situation was bigger than either of them. It wasn't a case for decision on his part to which he could be influenced by argument. She knew that. 'Just himself alone, preaching'—an odd little vision, but one that he had seen clearly. Then it had dimmed, and receded, and now was almost gone.

"I knew what he'd planned to do," Viola said. "He'd told me—a long time ago. Nothing to do with Joe. And it didn't—well, it looked differently then."

Zeke wasn't altogether sure what she was talking about. But it didn't trouble him much. He said, "Why?"

There was no interest in his voice. It solidified her certainty that there was no longer anything she could lose. She was going back. It had been for fear of being sent back that she had been carrying the weight of these things she couldn't tell. Now that she was going back anyway, she could get rid of them. It wouldn't matter much now, perhaps—but she'd always wanted to, and now that she could, she might as well.

"He told me about it before—" she knew there was some reason why she couldn't say 'before you asked me to marry you,' so she said: "—long before we were married. He had a scheme to make you pastor of the church. That was all I knew then. It didn't seem the way it does now—his planning about you. I'd begun almost to forget about it. Then this happened about Joe. It happened because of his plan. But I couldn't tell you that. And he didn't plan to have Joe killed. Just to arrest him. So that you'd be 'stirred up,' he said—and preach better." There was more to it than that. But it was a separate part— the why of his having been moved to do all this: so that behind Zeke he could trade safely in slaves. That was separate. She'd told him one part. For a moment, she could rest.

Zeke was speaking. "I rather liked that sermon," he had said. "So it was his, was it? I suppose I ought to have known there was something funny about it."

She said nothing. She had not been waiting for what he would say. She had been realizing, while he spoke, the approach of the moment when she for some reason would be telling him that she was her father's daughter. About her father and her mother. She didn't know why she would be telling this. While she was doing it, she wouldn't know. Soon, now, she would be saying the words. The excitement of it had begun to take hold of her. When it was over, she would be going back. There were just those two things ahead of her. There was no reason for there being anything else.

Zeke turned away from the window. In motion, she had

to look at him—the deep lines in his face, his hair black, and the hurt presence of his eyes, whether she looked at them or not. All this was the outside of Zeke. He had been her husband. And his long coat hanging loosely from his shoulders. That was the way he looked.

He picked up a white card from the table, examined it for a while, and put it in his pocket. He was walking across the room, toward the hearth. "We'll have to find some place to live," he said.

For one instant she saw what she must do: tell him now. And in a few minutes they'd be starting fresh, on a clean foundation. Zeke wouldn't turn on her—not now—saying terribly that she had lied to him. Zeke had sat down on the high footstool, his back to her, bent; he was looking into the empty grate. She could tell him now—but if she found that she had lost, then it would be all over. Never again any chance. Always, her whole life ahead, in her father's house. She knew, then, that she wasn't going to tell him.

Zeke said: "The joke's on your uncle, in a way—if there is any. It didn't look to me after service as though that sermon was likely to make me pastor of anything."

"It was a good sermon, Zeke."

"It *felt* like a good sermon—while I was preaching it. You can't tell, though. Well—anyhow—it's gone now."

This, she felt certain, was all he meant to say about it.

They sat silent for some time. "If they'd asked Joe," he said, "he'd probably have done it."

"How do you mean?" She knew what he meant: if they'd said, 'Joe, will you die so that Zeke can become a great preacher?' Joe—well, Joe'd have done it.

"He'd have done it for Father, I expect," Zeke said. "Died, I mean."

Viola couldn't say anything, and be sure of herself. All this belonged to Zeke; she was afraid to intrude. She waited until she thought he'd gone on to something else. Then she said: "Where did you want to live, Zeke?"

"He even had to cheat Joe," Zeke said. Then: "What did you say?"

"Did you have some place in mind you wanted to live?"

"What . . . ? Oh. No, I don't think so. Anywhere. It doesn't matter. Anywhere but here. He paid for this place, you know."

"Would you like me to look for a place?"

"Yes—if it's cheap enough. Rent, I guess. I don't know just what we'd buy with. We may be lucky if we have anything to rent with."

'We,' he had said—twice. "All right," she agreed.

Zeke was talking into the empty grate again. "I didn't used to hate him—just because he was evil. I didn't even hate him because of what happened to Joe. It sounds funny, but—well, you see Joe came out of it better than he did."

She thought she understood, but she was afraid to say so. He'd have completed that part in his mind and wouldn't like to be called back to it.

"That sermon was the one thing that ever really belonged to me. I'd done it myself. It was a pretty good sermon, too. I know that. I'd thought I could take a certain amount of satisfaction in it—well—always, I guess. That's gone now. It seems like quite a lot to have been cheated of."

"It's still a good sermon, Zeke."

"Is it? You know, it's too bad, in a way, that it wasn't someone more intelligent than your uncle. He must have missed seeing just how funny I really was this morning. Well—that's that." He stood up, took out his watch and opened it. "The Primrose Knitting and Literary Society," he announced, "will be addressed this afternoon by our beloved assistant pastor, the Reverend Ezekiel Peele." He clicked the watch shut. "—beloved of himself, at any rate," he added under his breath. "I'll be back for supper."

Viola watched him cross the room toward the front hall. She was not much moved to say, "Wait, Zeke. I want to tell you something."

[Chapter 18]

GOING UP THE HILL from the village, Mr. Watling leaned forward on the buggy seat much as a man does in the saddle. It was no reflection on Sheba's knees to have an eye out for a stumble on that road, even going uphill. Loose stones on shelving rock. He'd think Abel would get after the town about it.

He wondered how he was going to explain things to Abel.

He pulled up when they were almost there, so that Sheba, the old fraud, could trot into the yard looking brisk and fresh. It was close on to suppertime, though, and she was restless and didn't want to stand. So Mr. Watling said, "All right, go ahead," and they sailed in at the gate with a gratifying flourish.

He wasn't sure anyone was watching until after they'd stopped. Abel stepped out of the barn then, and coming across the yard said, "Give you five dollars for her."

Mr. Watling sat where he was. "I'd give her to you for nothing if I thought you could drive her."

Abel said, "Hello, girl," and took her head. "Minna's gone visiting," he said to Watling. "She said for you to stay till she got back," and added: "She wants to hear about the boy."

"He's all right." Mr. Watling climbed down. "Mrs. Peele well?"

"First rate. Her father's laid up. She'll be back tomorrow, I expect."

"You got my letter."

"The one from Manchester," Abel said.

"Yes. I didn't write you from Boston."

"How is he?"

"Zeke?" Mr. Watling was getting out his bag. "His health's fine."

Abel called a boy up from the barn to take the horse.

They walked toward the house, Mr. Watling carrying his bag.

"I told Zeke it was MacIntosh," Mr. Watling said.

Abel looked straight ahead for a moment. "Seemed best, did it?"

"I can't claim that it did. I told him more or less on impulse."

It had been Abel's province to say whether or not to tell Zeke. Abel said: "Well—that's all right. I wasn't there, so I don't know."

"It wasn't up to me, I know. You want to hear about it now—or after supper?"

"It'll keep, I guess. You better wash up and we'll go in and eat. We got a woman here, cooking. Only trouble is, she can't cook. She makes Minna feel easier about going away."

Mr. Watling set his bag down on the bench outside the

door. He looked up at Abel. "I'd like to get this straightened out now," he said.

Abel grinned. "I didn't seem so annoyed as all that, did I?"

Mr. Watling grinned, too.

Abel put his head in the door and shouted: "Mrs. Tarbell!"

Mr. Watling heard a thin, high voice say: "What is it?"

"Deaf," Abel explained, in an aside.

"I see."

Abel roared into the kitchen: "You go ahead and feed the men when it's time. I'll be late to supper."

Mrs. Tarbell's voice said: "Time now, ain't it?"

Abel said, "All right," and withdrew. "Minna'll be back tomorrow," he explained. "You come with me, and I'll show you some good apples."

Mr. Watling was thinking of what he had to say. They set off toward the nearest orchard. "Good year for apples," Abel remarked, "—so far."

"That uncle of Zeke's wife," said Mr. Watling, "comes pretty close to being the worst I ever saw."

"I never talked to him. Got a glimpse of him the day Zeke was married. You may be right."

"I am."

"What did he do it for?"

"Well, I took a little stroll with him Sunday afternoon. Block or two—long as I could stand it. Seems his game was to have Joe arrested. That was all, and stop there. He figured that would stir Zeke up enough so that Zeke would preach on Slavery with some conviction. On the strength of a good, rousing sermon from Zeke, MacIntosh had an idea he could land Zeke the job as pastor of the church."

" 'T wouldn't seem a little far-fetched to you, would it?"

"Not very. MacIntosh's business isn't any too brisk. He'd like to see a good salary coming into the family."

" 'Shipping,' Zeke said."

"That's right. And if we get a war, there won't be much of it."

"Preaching on Slavery won't help to stave off a war."

"You flatter my profession if you think it'll bring it on."

Some other time, maybe, they could go into that. "You said you told Zeke," Abel reminded him.

"Yes. I went home with them after church. So did the Deacon. After about an hour and a half, it seemed as though anything that might blow Zeke loose from his uncle-in-law was worth trying. So I told him. Right there."

"She there, too?"

Mr. Watling indicated that she was.

"What did Zeke do?"

"Asked her if she was in it along with her uncle."

Abel thought for a while. "I don't know—" he said; "when you use dynamite, it's a good thing to know where the break's going to come."

It was a good deal less than Mr. Watling had said to himself a great many times since then. He answered truthfully: "It didn't seem to matter, then."

"That's Zeke's business." Over and over, ever since Zeke's first letter that had mentioned her, he had had to remind himself of that. He reverted to Zeke's question. "Was she?"

"Well—" this was a part that was going to be very difficult to make clear—"she said 'yes.' "

Abel's lips set and he turned his head slowly away. "Makes it nice," he said.

"I think she's honest," Mr. Watling said.

When Abel returned to the conversation, it was with a new subject—"How'd Zeke do preaching?"

"I'd like to make you understand," Mr. Watling said slowly, "just how well he did do."

"I could try," Abel said dryly. "He's my son." Mr. Watling didn't answer right away, and Abel, trying to make it sound more or less offhand, said, "Was he good?"

"He was better than that."

"You mean he—" Abel turned to watch Watling's face— "he was real good?"

Mr. Watling had stopped in his walk. He looked up squarely at Abel. "I mean he meant what he was saying." Abel said, "Oh." "And besides that—" Watling said as he resumed his walk—"he can preach."

Abel broke a twig he was carrying in his hand. He threw it away. "His mother thinks a lot of that boy," he said.

They'd swung back toward the house. "Hope you like ham," Abel said. "That's about all this female can cook. Minna'll be back tomorrow, though."

"Yes. So you said."

Abel cocked an eye at him. "How've you been?"

"I've been fine!" said Mr. Watling.

[*Chapter 19*]

THE DEACON didn't like the neighborhood at all. A slum was one thing. And a respectable neighborhood was another. This, financially speaking, was in between. Why Viola should have wanted to move in the first place was

146

a mystery to him. A boy had brought the keys round to his house, and a note: 'These are the keys to the house. We have moved,'—and signed 'Viola Peele.' The Deacon, with their new address obtained from the church office, was on his way to find out what it was all about. 'Second door from the corner,' Graveson had said coldly. 'They're upstairs. Third floor, I believe; Peele didn't say.'

The Deacon found the street door open, went in, and began to climb. The steps were steep. He didn't look up until he was almost at the top. When he did, directly in front of him, across the bare floor of a narrow hallway, Viola was standing in a doorway looking down at him. The Deacon, on top of being out of breath, was startled. He stood there, three steps from the top.

"Zeke will be home shortly," she told him, her voice flat and distant, "I think you'd better not be standing there when he comes." She went back inside the door, closed it . . . and the Deacon distinctly heard it locked.

He had a fatherly impulse to climb up and go across to that door and rap on it—to hammer on it! But, he remembered suddenly, and for no reason, that he was three stories high above the street, and that even the street was in an unfamiliar neighborhood. It gave him an odd, panicky feeling—and he turned and scuttled downstairs and out into the air.

Viola, he reflected on the way home in a cab, was a little like himself—high-strung. But she had no brains. How he himself could have begotten—even under the circumstances—a daughter quite so brainless as Viola was beyond him. You never knew what she was going to do! Must be from her mother. Her mother had been difficult enough . . . Deacon MacIntosh sought for something pleasanter to which to turn his thoughts.

147

When he reached home, he went directly to the library. The door stood open, which surprised him—and there was a man in there. Gowan, for God's sake! The Deacon had recognized him in spite of a brand-new, dark-brown Vandyke—Gowan having worn a spade beard last time, and chin whiskers before that. But he could never disguise his hands. You could spot them clear across a room. He had the longest, whitest hands that ever were on a man.

Captain Gowan was sitting comfortably in a high-backed chair, reading a newspaper and smoking a cigar. He said, "Hello, Mac," into his newspaper as the Deacon, without answering, went round behind his great desk and sat down in his armchair.

"What did you want to come here for?" the Deacon accused him.

Captain Gowan folded the paper and laid it beside his chair. "To make a report to the owners."

"I told you not to come here." And then the Deacon saw a disquieting thought. "My God," he said, "what are you doing here anyway! You weren't reported. Where's your ship?"

"You didn't want me to bring it with me, did you?"— and then he nodded. "But you're quite right, at that. We haven't any ship."

Minor catastrophes made the Deacon angry, but under a major blow he merely shrank. He shrank now, back into his chair. "What happened?" he said weakly. There was a suggestion of a whimper in his tone, which the Captain chose to ignore.

"You may recall that some three years ago I had occasion to jettison a cargo?—east of Barbados?"

The Deacon recalled. Thirty-one thousand dollars, that had cost him.

"Same man," said the Captain succinctly. As, in truth, it had been. Only this time, that same man had been willing to buy both the ship and the cargo.

The Captain now departed from the truth without saying good-by, although it was doubtful when they would meet again. "I preferred not to have him board me this time," he explained. "On the last occasion he commented rather pointedly on a peculiar odor in the hold. Said a smell wasn't much use as evidence in court—as I think I told you—but that the next time he wouldn't bother with a court."

MacIntosh, he could see, was not going to interrupt. "When it became apparent that we were being overhauled, I—er, disposed of the cargo, and a few moments later the ship took fire. We abandoned her. An explosion occurred on board, and she sank. She sank beautifully, Mac, if I do say so. You'll find on the manifest—if you ever see it—a consignment of heavy machinery from Birmingham which accounts for it.

"Well, they picked us up, of course. Captain Brookins was rather surly, it seemed to me. He remarked that since I'd burned up even the smell, he wouldn't be able to hang me."

The Deacon had lost seventy-one thousand dollars.

Captain Gowan, observing the effect on him, rose and went to the small cabinet, and got him a drink.

The Deacon's eyes were still wandering a little when he was able to say: "They'll sweat it out of the crew."

Captain Gowan was patient. "The crew," he explained, "were not armed. They went down with the ship. Heroes, to a man. Only the two mates and myself were picked up." He watched the Deacon for a while. "And my mates, Deacon MacIntosh, don't sweat."

The Deacon did, cold.

Gowan regarded him with a clinical tolerance. "The trouble with you, Mac, is that you have been weakened by too frequent exposure to the doctrine of Retribution. Now I can positively assure you that the punishment for quite a large number of murders is no worse than that for one. You were guilty of your first—indirectly, I admit—some time ago. That was the time for you to worry. They can't hang you twelve times for twelve murders, you know. Once you've committed one murder, you get the other eleven free. That ought to appeal to you, Mac."

It didn't seem to. The mottled condition of the Deacon's face failed to clear up. He attempted to pour himself a glass of brandy . . . while the Captain politely looked the other way.

"You go to church too much," Gowan continued helpfully. "You know as well as I do that the United States Government can't do anything to you about those eleven extra murders. One murder, one hanging. Their imagination stops there. Unfortunately, yours doesn't. You get to thinking about God, I'm afraid. A man needs a very strong character to think about God, Mac. You aren't up to it."

The Deacon couldn't summon the strength to tell him to go away.

"I would suggest," said the Captain with penetrating coldness, "that for the time being you concentrate on the United States Government. How much money have you?"

The Deacon could only stare and shake his head.

"Come, come! Your house is clear, isn't it?"

The Deacon's head continued to shake—but more as with a beginning palsy than in a negative.

"Of course it is," Gowan assured him. "My guess is that,

if you had to, you could still raise a hundred thousand dollars." . . . That brought him!

"No! No!" he said.

"Now, then," said the Captain—he had put down his cigar—"with a hundred thousand dollars we could buy a really decent ship. Not a barge, you understand, but a ship. Something with sails on it. I give you my word, I was really more embarrassed by that last tub than I was by her contents. This time, Mac, I'm going to have a *ship* under me. She's going to be rigged properly, she's going to have decent canvas, and she's going to mount better guns—inch for inch, and pound for pound—than they've got in any Navy that wants to chase us. You can put the money you've never put into insurance into guns. I prefer them to underwriters' men, myself." He sat back. "Well—how does it appeal to you?"

Apparently not at all.

Gowan said: "You're afraid you'll lose, aren't you? Look here: every time we've lost in the past, it's been for just one reason. Lack of proper equipment. With that defect remedied, the venture becomes a good bet. Not a safe bet, but one at reasonable odds. One I can conscientiously recommend to you. And in which, of course, I shall participate. You don't risk anything that I don't. What do you say, Mac? One last whirl—clean up, and get out. I'm going to retire after this, and look for something with some excitement in it."

The Deacon had found his voice at last. "Go away," he said; "leave me alone."

"The reason I mentioned the United States Government," said the Captain, "is this: if your past should happen to catch up with you sometime, there's just one thing that could keep a rope away from your neck. That's money. Money for lawyers—money for politicians—money for every last person who could do you any good. You've got to have *lots* of money, Mac. And to get it, you've *got* to gamble!"

The Deacon's instinct was still that of a man who prefers to cower behind a small tree rather than cross the open to a larger.

The Captain stood up—and the Deacon's eyes followed him as he rose.

Standing easily, the Captain looked down across the desk at him. "Mac: we've been in this together since we started." He spoke very slowly: "You're not going to desert me now. Because—"

The Deacon fought off the main point. "No! No!"

"Because if you do," continued the Captain—and he injected the faintest note of whimsicality—"I'll tell on you."

The Deacon stared for a moment, and then his great head commenced to fall. It had been a long time coming to the Deacon, but he had seen, through all that time, that someday it would come. His head collapsed onto his arm, and he wept—rather unpleasantly and not exactly like a child.

The Captain went back to his chair, sat down, and picked up his paper. He read through an uninteresting item concerning a new bridge over the Charles, and commenced another. The Deacon had quieted down.

"Write me a check, will you?" said the Captain, still reading. "I'm afraid I ought to go."

The Deacon raised up some. His arm slid across the desk, and his hand flopped to the upper drawer.

"On top of the desk, isn't it—the checkbook? And payable, if you don't mind—" the Captain yawned—"to bearer."

Chapter 20

"I THINK," Mr. Cameron had remarked to a member of A Committee To Consider Candidates, "that it would be as well for you to recommend *some*one as soon as possible. Leaving the matter open will only result in a repetition of the sort of thing that happened last Sunday."

The Committee Member had agreed.

"And furthermore see to it that the new man, whoever he is, is free to choose his own assistants. Although Graveson, I think, does very well."

And again the Committee Member had agreed. This was on Tuesday. Subsequently, the Committee had agreed also; Deacon MacIntosh—rather tactfully, they thought—having remained away. MacIntosh, whatever else one might say about him, was at least free of any taint of nepotism. And, as a matter of fact, poor MacIntosh was probably just as embarrassed about last Sunday as anyone. No one had seen him, since.

On Thursday, Miss Beacham—with Zeke's assistance—succeeded in sending out the notices of a Special Meeting of The Society to be held a week later.

Technically, it would be a meeting of the Twelfth Congregational Society of Boston, Incorporated. But anyone who was a member of the Twelfth Congregational Church was entitled to vote at a meeting of the Society. In purely secular matters, such as the holding of property, the incurring of a debt, or the calling of a minister, the Church invariably did business as the Society. It made it, so Mr. Graveson was glad to explain when asked, 'more legal.'

The Deacon received his notice, and read it. He would

not attend. Since Gowan's call, he had preferred not to go outside the house. He had sent for his bankers that next morning, and had arranged to meet the check he had given Gowan, and after that he had stayed in the library, swiftly developing his capacity for worry and drinking even more brandy than he knew was good for him. For all he knew— or could do about it—Gowan now had the money in his pocket and had disappeared forever. And the fact that this was precisely what he would have done himself, had he been in Gowan's shoes, did not induce to philosophic calm. Gowan now had him at his mercy. And the Captain's mercy, by his own account, offered small grounds for hope. Still . . . he'd always come back before, hadn't he? He had. But before—and the Deacon shuddered—there had been something for him to come back for.

When he tried to forget Gowan, he'd find he was think-ing about Watling. And that didn't help much either. The last thing Watling had said to him—and he'd said it so damn cheerfully, too—had been: 'I'll not lose track of you.'

No, he wasn't going to the meeting. He wasn't going to go anywhere. He was going to stay right here in the library. It was a small room and he could see all of it from his chair. He'd stay right here . . . and in the morn-ing he'd waken in his bed. But not, he dared to hope, during the night.

Miss Cameron received her notice, too. At breakfast. She mentioned it to her father just as he was about to comment unfavorably on the fish. Mr. Cameron said, yes, he'd told 'em to call it.

"Oh, did you? Why, father?"

"You were in church Sunday, weren't you?" He probed

viciously here and there about his plate. "You heard the same sermon I did, didn't you? *Some*thing had to be done, didn't it? This fish is stale."

Miss Cameron said she'd speak to the cook about it. "What do they do at the meeting? I've never been."

"You ought to. You've got a vote."

"What *do* they do?"

"Vote! Elect a new minister. The Committee brings in its recommendation and the church votes to call him."

"What if they don't?"

"What if they don't what? Why don't we have sausage any more?"

"We'll have it tomorrow if you like. What if they don't vote to call him, I mean."

"The kind in cakes. What else would they do? That's what the Committee's for, isn't it?—to pick someone out and recommend him. They've been at it a year and a half."

"I think I'll go. It might be fun."

"Nothing but routine. Wouldn't interest you. Tell her to bring me some more coffee, will you?"

"She's coming now. I think I'll nominate Mr. Peele. Could I do that?"

Mr. Cameron said, "My God, Eleanor, this is breakfast!" and picked up the paper.

"Sorry," she said coolly.

He read for a while, and then suddenly put it down.

"The reason I called the meeting," he said, "was to get rid of Peele!"

"Oh. I didn't know that."

"Well, I did." He opened the paper again, and from behind it muttered: "Sorry if I've been rude."

"Not at all," she assured him, "but I really do think I'll have to go to the meeting."

"Go ahead, then," said Mr. Cameron, who had become interested in an advertisement of women's corsets.

[Chapter 21]

STANDING IN THE VESTIBULE, the sexton had already counted twenty-two people going in, and it was still fifteen minutes before the hour. Be a big meeting. Old Mrs. Groark, now, she hadn't been to a meeting in three years. Mrs. Nevins was with her—she was another one of those Primroses. Nevins had got killed on the railroad. All these people coming now were on foot. No carriages until just on to the hour—and most of them after that. You'd think it was winter, now, you would, and the early ones coming in to get warm.

Mr. Cameron, with carriage and daughter, arrived on the dot. Both outside on the steps and inside in the vestibule, Mr. Cameron saw evidences of a good turnout. That was gratifying. The church was a stabilizing force in the community. The more people, the more force. The community needed stabilizing. With Eleanor on his arm, he entered the center door—and saw to his amazement that the place was nearly a third full! He didn't understand it. Ordinarily, the first half dozen pews on either side of the aisle accommodated a routine church meeting. But this was carrying things a little too far. Something must be up!

Mr. Cameron never liked having something up, more especially when he didn't know what it was. He shoved

Eleanor into the nearest pew and went back to the vestibule to investigate. He found his friend, the Committee Member, there.

"What's up?" Mr. Cameron demanded. "Why are they all here?"

The Committee Member said he'd been wondering about that himself; it did seem a good many.

Mr. Cameron said something was up, and the Committee Member had another look around and said it certainly looked that way.

Mr. Cameron said it most certainly did. They stopped talking to watch a very old woman being brought through the front door by a thin-faced young woman. The old woman was mumbling something, but the young woman seemed to be used to it and eased her along with a sort of resigned, unflinching determination. They passed into the church, and Mr. Cameron said, "Who the devil's that?"

The Committee Member said he didn't know, it must be some member of the church.

"Good Lord!" said Mr. Cameron disgustedly, "you'd think it was Christmas. Wallace isn't here yet, is he?"

"Wallace? I don't think I've seen him . . ." Wallace was Chairman of the Committee.

Mr. Cameron said, "Well, we can't stand here—" and went purposefully to the front door and out onto the steps, where he looked this way and that. As though as a reward for this vivid piece of action, he was permitted to descry Wallace, head bent, making his way toward him across the sidewalk.

Mr. Cameron went down to meet him. "Look here, Wallace—" he said.

Mr. Wallace had almost thought of a nice touch to add to his Report.

"There are too many people in there," Mr. Cameron announced.

"Too many people?"

"Yes. Not the right kind—the kind you'd expect. I don't understand it. You know—all the people who don't come to church. They're here for something, of course, or they wouldn't have come. All of them. Something's up."

Mr. Wallace said, "Well . . ."

Mr. Cameron had a vague idea of telling Wallace not to make his Report at all. He said, "Wait, now—I've got it. No—no, I haven't, either." That, he had foreseen, would only leave the meeting open to whatever onslaught was impending.

"I'm afraid I ought to be going in," Mr. Wallace suggested. "I've got a Report to make."

A group of young people passed them, going in. Mr. Cameron's head turned on his collar as he watched them go. "I don't like this business at all," he said.

Mr. Wallace said, "Well—" and turned to follow the young people who had come to hear him make his Report. He had it in his pocket.

It left Mr. Cameron alone on the sidewalk. He told himself that if anything did happen it certainly was not his fault—and went in himself.

Eleanor, he saw, had moved. Fiercely angry with her, Mr. Cameron stalked up the aisle and sat in a pew all by himself.

After a time, Mr. Graveson rose and faced them. He was standing on a raised space below and in front of the pulpit. He cleared his throat, exerted the full force of his presence, cleared his throat again, and waited. The conversation died down. "It is not my place to convene this meeting," Mr. Graveson said, "but someone has to stand up in front to get things started, and I happen to be the tallest." It was not successful. Still smiling, he said: "Shall I lead us in prayer?"

He led them. The Clerk of the Church, Mr. Robinson, writhed quietly throughout the petition because, according to the By-Laws which the Clerk knew by heart, the prayer was supposed to come later on.

When everyone had straightened up again, Mr. Graveson addressed them once more. "I think perhaps it might be in order—I'm not a parliamentarian, perhaps, like our good friend Mr. Robinson here—but I think it might be in order for me to read to you now the notice, which you have all received, calling this meeting together. That's right, isn't it, Mr. Clerk?"

To Mr. Robinson's single knowledge, it was not right. But Mr. Graveson had already begun to read with great clarity and force. ". . . together with such other business as may properly come before said meeting," he finished. Mr. Robinson had drafted the notice himself, and ordinarily would have enjoyed hearing it read. But duty would require him to insist that it be read again—at the proper time—and people would laugh at him because he did insist.

"I believe the next thing, is it not, Mr. Clerk—" Mr. Graveson reserved a measure of independence by not looking at him—"is to proceed to the election of a moderator. I am prepared—er, that is to say: will someone nominate someone to act as moderator . . . ?"

No one did, and Mr. Graveson added, ". . . as moderator."

Someone had been lately reminded of Mr. Robinson in some way, and said rather suddenly, "Mr. Robinson." Mr. Graveson, plunging delightedly into a crescendo of assured routine, finally pronounced Mr. Robinson elected, and invited him to take his place.

Mr. Robinson did so. He was seen to be a spare man, with a parchment skin and coldly neat in his appearance. He formally called the meeting to order. But his courage failed him then, and he found he could not ask Mr. Graveson to lead them in prayer. He did, however, resolutely read aloud the notice. And those who realized what was happening looked at Mr. Graveson, whom they found to be making a splendid effort to appear amused.

Mr. Robinson, Moderator, then said he would be glad to hear the report of the Committee.

Mr. Wallace stood up in a front pew, and with his back to the meeting, drew a considerable document from his pocket and began to read. The preamble, he had felt, was undeniably witty, but he unfortunately left out a line, and no one could hear him anyway. With a continued lack of response from those he still believed to be his audience, a sickening disappointment began to settle on Mr. Wallace, and he finished his last paragraph with hatred for mankind in his heart and his pulse beating in his ears. He sat down.

The Committee had now recommended to the Society that it call the Reverend Mr. Tidman to be pastor of the Twelfth Congregational Church. There were four members of the Committee present, and each one of them was uncomfortable, remembering the Reverend Tidman as the one who had had trouble with his teeth. Consequently they said nothing. The rest of the meeting couldn't remember Mr. Tidman at all, and so they said nothing. Mr. Robinson said, "Are there any remarks?" . . . and Mr. Cameron wiped the palm of his hand along his thigh.

"Mr. Moderator—" Eleanor Cameron, in an exceptionally good light, was standing in the end of one of the front pews over toward the side.

Mr. Robinson said, "Miss Cameron."

"Well, the fact is," she said, "that I don't seem to recall the Reverend Mr. Tidman. Would the Chairman be good enough to tell us what he looked like?" The request was obviously one approved by the meeting as a whole.

Mr. Robinson had never had any great fondness for Mr. Wallace, and he took a certain pleasure, now, in saying: "Mr. Wallace . . . ?"

Mr. Wallace stood up and attempted to unfold the report which he had been miserably crumpling in his hands. Miss Cameron courteously remained standing. Mr. Wallace located a paragraph. He read out the date on which the Reverend Tidman had preached to them, and also the text. As he was in the process of sitting down he said hopelessly that he'd thought it had been a very good sermon.

Mr. Robinson turned to Miss Cameron, who said, "Thank you," to Mr. Wallace. She asked Mr. Robinson whether she were still eligible under "Remarks," and Mr. Robinson said, yes, she was. She addressed the meeting: "I should like to suggest that you call the Reverend Ezekiel Peele as pastor of this church." She smiled on two hundred people individually in less than a second, thanked Mr. Robinson, and sat down.

Mr. Robinson knew a crisis when he saw one, and he stared it uncompromisingly in the face.

There was a buzz—two or three men said, "Mr. Moderator—" . . . and there was a murmur.

But for Mr. Cameron, mercifully alone in a back pew, the crisis had already passed. Mr. Cameron's daughter had risen to address a public meeting. And had Mr. Cameron suddenly come upon her strolling professionally along

Water Street, Mr. Cameron would have felt much the same as he did now.

"Are there any further remarks?" said Mr. Robinson, and his voice was cracked and hard.

Everyone who had just said "Mr. Moderator," said it again.

Mr. Robinson made a careful selection, and recognized him.

"So far as I know," the man said, "this church has never voted other than to accept the report of any committee."

"Time they did!" piped someone. Mr. Robinson's man looked a resentful appeal at the Moderator, and then *he* sat down.

Allegiance to accuracy demanded of the Clerk of the Church that he tell them what he knew. "In 1801," he recited, "the Society rejected the recommendation of the Committee on the Care of Property that the church be painted. The vote was 42 to 3." It was the sort of feat the regulars had learned to expect from Robinson, and they smiled knowingly. "Our membership at the time"—it had amused the Clerk to look it up—"included three house painters."

It was a joke anyone could understand, and they laughed. They laughed, in Mr. Robinson's sincere estimation, out of proportion to the provocation. He banged pre-emptorily on the little table before him. "Are there any further remarks?"

The moment was still one of relaxation; the meeting as a whole being inclined to let Robinson say something more,—which might be even funnier. Mr. Robinson called for a motion.

Mr. Cameron, in the back pew, was now discovered to be standing. "I move," he said—and Robinson dispensed with recognition—"that the Reverend Dr. Tidman be called as pastor of this church."

No one had ever thought of Cameron as an old man, but they did now.

Into the quiet of the church, Mr. Robinson repeated the motion . . . the people turned but slowly away from Mr. Cameron.

Mr. Robinson called for a rising vote; those in favor would please stand. Here and there, dazedly almost—as though they had been told to stand and would obey—people stood up. All Mr. Cameron's friends stood up, and the old lady who mumbled, seeing a general move to stand, began to stand up herself. Husbands arose, and with them wives to match.

Unseen, an irrepressible called: "Peeles, sit down!"

People looked round—first to the voice and then at one another. A few who were already up, sat down, and some who were halfway up, oscillated for a moment, and then collapsed. There was no more motion.

It was hard to tell—those who are standing appearing more numerous than they are—just what the situation was. Only a few attempted it, and those furtively. Mr. Robinson had his eye on them, and was counting. "You may be seated."

The rows were leveled off again.

"Contrary minds!" . . . and they came up with a rush, outnumbering the first crop two to one.

"It is a vote!" called Mr. Robinson.

There was confusion and noise, each one saying something to his neighbor, and then saying it a little louder to be heard. Mr. Robinson said the things that he had to say, asked if there were any further business, and with a remarkably keen ear picked out from somewhere a motion to adjourn. He professed to hear, also, the seconding and a vote. It was over.

The better dressed half of the meeting was already in the aisles, but among the others there was uncertainty. These lingered, some in the pews, some standing in the aisles. They tended, very slowly and hesitantly, to converge on Mr. Robinson.

A small boy stepped forward. Mr. Robinson saw him as say, twelve, probably polite, and noticed that he smelled of strong soap and underwear. Mr. Robinson said, "What is it, sonny?"

"Yes, sir. They said about slips for the coal."

And the people moved in closer, so they could hear.

"They said what?" said Mr. Robinson.

"About slips for the coal. We heard they was goin' t' give us slips out—for the coal."

There was a nodding of heads then, and a good many said: "That's right!"

Mr. Robinson could see all this, and knew that he had to answer through the boy. "Coal?" he said. "I—really I don't know anything about it. . . . I'm sorry." And then told him what he did know: "Coal is supposed to be under the Deacons' Poor Fund Committee."

The boy's expression did not change at all. He was waiting for yes or no.

Mr. Robinson said that he was sorry, and humorously, that there was no coal here. He said kindly that he was sure it must be a mistake.

"They ain't gon' to?"

"No."

The boy nodded then, and turned away.

Mr. Robinson, without looking at them, left the platform

164

and went down the side aisle. He met the sexton who, from a distance, had had an eye on what was going on.

Mr. Robinson said: "Well, Partridge—"

"What'd they want?"

"Slips for coal, apparently. There must have been a mistake."

"Aaah, they get ideas. Tell 'em to go home." And Mr. Partridge moved up the aisle to attend to them himself.

[Chapter 22]

WHEN ZEKE CAME into the office next morning, Miss Beacham beamed at him with a doughy smile, and Zeke decided not to try to account for it. He said good morning to her, and assuming that she said good morning to him, went on toward his desk in the corner. Graveson appeared forcefully in the door of his own office. He roared, "Well!"—and stood there, rubbing his hands and beaming hardly.

Zeke looked at him and laughed. "You look cheerful," he said; "who's dead?"

Long ago Mr. Graveson had succeeded in completely ignoring things like that. It was a fact, now, that he didn't even hear them. "How's the new pastor?" he said, that being what he'd planned to say.

Zeke said, "Oh," and went to his desk. "Tidman, eh? I couldn't go last night." He sat down. "Our neighbors down the hall were having a fight,"—picking up the top letter. " 'Blessed are the peacemakers,'—maybe. You should have been there, Graveson; I didn't have any pledge with

165

me." The letter was from the American Board. "How did the meeting go off?"

It had dawned on Miss Beacham that Mr. Peele didn't know what had happened. She said in a blurred squawk to Mr. Graveson: "He doesn't know!"

"Do you mean to tell me," said Mr. Graveson from his diaphragm, "that you don't know?"

"Know what?" Zeke was reading the letter—and talked at the same time. "I know that whoever the new pastor is, he's going to choose his own assistants. So . . . you'd better be planning . . . to take him out to dinner."

"Mr. Peele!"—from Miss Beacham—"*you* are!"

If there was one thing he hated worse than the woman's voice, it was to look at her. He could see himself taking Tidman home to supper. . . . And Viola cook it! And afterward they could entertain Mr. Tidman with a good fight next door. That would be great. "I'm afraid not," he said absently. Work. Always—that was the remedy.

"*You're* the new pastor!" Miss Beacham squealed.

Zeke looked up—and from her to Graveson. He saw that they believed it . . . and he did, then, himself.

I am pastor of the Twelfth Congregational Church.

. . . a half hour later, he wrote a note to Viola and sent it home by messenger. He had signed it, because he liked his name, 'E. Peele.'

[*Chapter 23*]

DR. SOMERS' RESIDENCE had been owned by Dr. Somers. And allowance for the fact that the church was thus saved the expense of a parsonage had been made in Dr. Somers' salary. The amount of the allowance, so the Doctor had noticed, had been almost equal to what he paid in taxes and insurance. But the Deacons said among themselves, why, if Somers chose to live in a house of that sort, that was up to him. Privately, as individuals, they felt that the church lost nothing by this evidence that their principal employee was in good shape financially.

Now, when it came to paying for that evidence, they fell back upon more spiritual ground. And as someone pointed out, Somers had habitually turned back nearly a third of his salary into the church anyway, so that there was really no need for regarding even the amount of the allowance made to him as being in any way a precedent.

The Chairman of the Investment Committee had in mind an entirely suitable dwelling—after all, Peele was really very young!—on which the Society held a first mortgage that had been for some time in arrears. It was agreed to be an admirable selection. The necessary steps were complied with, and in the third week of December the Reverend and Mrs. Peele moved in. They hadn't much to move—but it was a good deal more than the box of books Zeke had jammed under the bed that first hot night he'd slept in Boston. Although, thriftily, the books were still part of it.

Viola seemed to be delighted with the place. She found there was not a store in Boston, not a really good store, at any rate, that didn't allow at least some discount to a minister's wife. When, for instance, she'd get Zeke to agree that it was all right to buy a chair, the discount would be enough so that she'd get a small table too.

Viola did pretty well by the living room. She achieved two cabinets of china bibelots, which was just twice as satisfactory as one.

In the flat, they had occupied the same bedroom—there being but the one—and Zeke had made no comment on it either way. Nor did he now, when Viola first referred to the other bedroom as the guest room. He'd have called it the spare room himself—and when he had occasion to refer to it, he did.

He liked the house. It was his own. Not that he'd paid for it, or that it stood in his name. But he'd earned the right to live in it—which came to about the same thing.

Viola could have done with a little less considerateness from the ladies of the church who appeared determined that the Peeles be given a great plenty of time to get themselves settled before being disturbed by callers. With a couple of carriages at the curb, and three or four callers in the living room, and Zeke somewhere from home being pastor of the Twelfth Congregational Church—but liable to walk rather gloriously into the living room at any moment—Viola would have felt quite happily secure. She didn't like being alone. While two draymen were bringing in the sagging roll of a new carpet, their strong presence was enough to put aside the knowledge that all this was still shakily founded. No incident could get rid of that knowledge for her, but almost any incident helped to put it aside. Callers would have put it further aside, and waiting carriages still further. Until with a multiplication of such evidences, all crowded closely together, filling the day and the immediate outlook, she would have felt that a foundation might not be so very necessary, after all. The new structure would probably stand of itself. And after a while—when it had stood of itself—she would be enough satisfied of its ability to go on doing so, so that everything would be all right. If she could be solidly, unbrokenly, over a long enough period of time, Mrs. Peele-the-wife-of-the-Pastor . . . why, she would in time become so truly just that, that nothing could be done about it.

But that was not to be accomplished by sitting around wondering how soon something was going to happen. If she sat around too much, she was given to hearing the heavy, unsteady feet coming up the stairs, and to seeing his head, low between his shoulders, loom up across the bare floor of the narrow hall. Viola saw herself, now, for a sensible person. And so she kept busy. But it would have been easier, in the late afternoon when darkness came early and inevitably, and Zeke would not be home until a long way into the evening, to have some callers in, filling the living room with clatter and the bright noise of tea. And addressing her, over and over, as Mrs. Peele.

The first week in February, Miss Eleanor Cameron came.

Viola didn't see the carriage, because in the room the lamps were lighted and the curtains had been drawn. But when Miss Eleanor Cameron came into a room, no one gave any thought to the carriage question.

It was too hot in the Peeles' living room, and Eleanor gave the maid her coat. . . . The silk in it crackled as she took it off, and the fur stood sharp and fresh, but had been warm against her cheek. She said she was sorry to come so late.

Before they had sat down, Viola had seen that this was what she herself never could become.

Miss Cameron handled the conversation, and Viola grew proud to have her here and she wanted Zeke to come home and see what was in their living room. She expected, then, that he would come . . . and before long she heard him open the front door, and close it. He came into the room.

Zeke didn't seem to realize what had happened. He spoke

to Viola first, and then spoke pleasantly enough to Miss Cameron. He appeared glad to see her, but no more glad than he had expected to be to see her or anyone else—and he asked about his tea.

Viola saw him very objectively, with the skin on his face cold from having been outdoors, and his boots big, and his voice not yet dropped to what it would be when he had been in the house a little longer. She started to explain that Miss Cameron had said that she had had tea before she came, and that she herself—but Zeke had turned to Miss Cameron. "It was brave of you to come here, wasn't it?" cheerfully. "I'm afraid your father—well—" and his face had become serious—"he's so sincere about it. I hurt him, I'm afraid."

"I'm afraid you did. I want you to speak at an Abolition meeting. Will you?"

Zeke thought about it. "No."

Viola saw it all distinctly, but it had no reality.

Miss Cameron, as though she understood perfectly, said, "Oh, I'm sorry. Well, I'll tell them then. I told Mr. Chalmers I thought I could get you, and he seemed very grateful—not to you, to me. He'll be cross, now, I suppose. But it doesn't matter."

"Not a bit."

"Why don't you want to?"

Zeke looked up at her. There was a good chance, he thought, she might understand. "Because I do want to."

She smiled a little. "Then I shan't try to persuade you. Mrs. Peele: for futility, I give you an attempt to persuade a Puritan to do what he wants to do."

Viola said: "I guess you're right."

Miss Cameron permitted a little pause, and Zeke, his

eyes narrowed very slightly, said, "What did you want me to speak about?"

She was earnest. She said thoughtfully: "I should like to hear you preach again the same sermon that you preached on Slavery—in church—in October. I spoke to you about it at the time. You may remember."

Zeke stood up, forgetting more or less the present scene and that his wife was there and so on. He went over by the fireplace, trying to think. He turned, then, and faced them, feeling the mantelpiece against his shoulder blades. "I'll have to give you an analogy." He hadn't it thought out, of course, but he'd got to be saying something. "Suppose a painter had done—well, a picture that meant a good deal to him. I suppose there's more or less goes on while you're painting a picture, isn't there? I don't know. Anyhow, he wouldn't care much about painting it again—the same picture. Would he? Even though you asked him to." He was beginning to be embarrassed. It was all right to say things like that—perhaps—if you were understood. Otherwise, shut up.

"Yes," she said thoughtfully, "you're quite right."

"Do you see what I mean?"

"Yes. I do. I'm thinking about musicians. It's a much better analogy, I think."

Zeke laughed. Already the absolute clearness of his first aversion had blurred. He couldn't see two things at once as clearly as he had seen that. He was looking at Miss Cameron—her head bent forward just a little, but in a moment it would lift.

"You will do it, won't you?" she said, looking up—and not even noticing that he'd been looking at her, because all her life whoever was there generally had been.

Zeke shook his head. "I'm afraid not." He'd thought of

a dozen reasons now, all of them small and concrete, matter-of-fact, reasons Miss Beacham would consider perfect. "I do enjoy being asked, though."

She said dryly that that was flattering.

It made him angry. He hadn't meant it that way—at least not until after he had said it. "When is Mr. Chalmers' meeting?"

"On Thursday, the twentieth."

"Whereabouts?"

"At the church, I believe—his church."

Zeke took out his little morocco notebook. There was something written in it for the twentieth—some penciled duty or other—he couldn't quite make out in this light just what it was. Probably not in the evening, anyway. He closed the book. "All right. I'll be there"; and with that done, he could say: "I suppose there'll be rioting, won't there? Stones through the windows, and so on?"

"Hymnbooks tossed into the chandelier."

"And shouts from the audience? 'Traitor!' 'Blasphemer!'?"

"Not at all! Huzzahs."

"Huzzahs?"

"It's an invitation meeting. You have to be next thing to an anarchist to get in at all."

"Then I'm not supposed to convert anyone to the Cause?"

"Heavens, no!"

"Oh. I see." So this was what his sermon had come to. He put the notebook away. Probably they'd cheer. After all, what was he fussing about? Watling did the same thing, didn't he? Earned his living by it. "Eight o'clock, you say?"

"Eight o'clock. And if I didn't feel you were mistaken

about the artistic integrity part of it, I wouldn't let you do it."

"That's very kind of you," he said. "I shan't worry about it, I assure you."

She stood up and turned to Mrs. Peele. "It's been so nice to see you. And thank you for letting him come. Anyone who preaches as he does is sort of public property, don't you think?"

Viola had risen too.

"You'll come and see me soon, won't you!" said Miss Cameron. "Father's out during the day, so you won't have to worry about his being rude to you. As a matter of fact, I'm a parishioner, am I not? So it's your duty to come." She said simply to Zeke: "Good-by. And thank you."

Zeke saw her to the hall and held her coat for her. It was notably lighter when he held it out than he'd have thought to look at it. And when he'd opened the front door for her, he could see, stirred by the light from it, the footman throwing the rug off and starting to clamber down from the box. She went past Zeke swiftly and called "Good night!" over her shoulder.

He came back into the room.

"I forgot about your tea," Viola said. "Do you still want it?"

Zeke said, no, he guessed it was pretty near suppertime. Anyway, he'd got to do some work. "She's quite a lady, isn't she?"

"She's beautiful, Zeke."

"Yes, I suppose she is." He stood again with his back to the mantelpiece, over toward the end—it was too hot right in front of the fire. "It seems funny to have a footman in front of the house. Watling would have been entertained,

173

if he'd driven up in the buggy. I used to be his footman. I wish he'd come here sometime. I'd like to see him."

"Was her father with her that day in church?"

"Yes. Cameron? Yes. Wouldn't speak to me because I'd preached Anti. And now his daughter comes round and wants me to speak at an Abolition meeting. You know, I don't believe that woman's any more an Abolitionist than I am."

"You do believe in Abolition, don't you?"

"I believe that slavery ought to be abolished, yes. But that doesn't make me an Abolitionist. An Abolitionist doesn't believe anything else. They haven't got time to."

"Why did you tell her you'd speak, if you didn't want to?"

"I don't know . . . well, I do know too, in a way." He knew exactly why. Aloud, he said: "She was so gosh-dinged sure of herself, sitting there that way, that I just thought I'd show her that one little Abolition meeting one way or the other didn't mean much to me. I'd like to do something for Chalmers, too. He's a good man."

"She proposed your name to the meeting, didn't she? . . . that night they voted to call you?"

"Great Scott, that's right!" Zeke laughed. "I'd forgotten about that. Graveson told me. Said he'd heard she did it just out of spite for her father. You can count on Graveson, every time. At that, I wouldn't be surprised if she did. I haven't seen her since then. I suppose I ought to have thanked her. Well—I ought to go and do some work." He pushed himself away from the fireplace. "Call me when supper's ready, will you?"

Viola said as he was crossing the room: "Do you have to go out tonight?"

"Oh, yes! I don't know just what for, because I haven't

looked it up, but there'll be something. You know—" he said, stopping by the piano and poking a long finger, bent backward, against one key, "ever since this church was founded, it's been sprouting committees. They never die —never! And they all bloom at night—or at five o'clock in the afternoon. I used to have supper at five o'clock." He struck the key one shrill, treble blow, and went out of the room.

Viola, after a bit, went over and stirred the fire. She wondered what sort of work he was doing. Something with papers, probably. Sitting at his desk, writing. She'd always thought of a minister as in the pulpit, or as being spoken of by people. When she'd first thought of Zeke as a Pastor, instead of as an assistant, it had been in those two ways. She'd thought mostly of the things they'd say about him. They'd say some of these things—praise and little phrases—when they came to call on her. Miss Cameron— had been very beautiful. Zeke had seen it. And had felt it. It was that that had made him talk so much after she'd gone. He was working now, sitting at his desk, his forehead in one hand, and writing. She wouldn't understand what he was writing if he told her.

[Chapter 24]

CHALMERS' CHURCH was not so large as the Twelfth— neither its membership nor its building. Zeke, sitting on the low platform with four or five other men, realized that he was going to miss his pulpit, miss the massive shelter of its mahogany battlements, and miss, too, the feeling that it gave him to look down on his audience spread out below him—spread a little thin, perhaps, of late, but that was a condition that would correct itself. It was a condition left over from having the church so long without a leader.

He leaned toward Chalmers who was next to him. "I suppose I get credit for an exchange on this . . ."

Chalmers' drawn face smiled briefly. "When you have an Abolition meeting at the Twelfth, I'll be glad to address it."

The thought of an Abolition meeting at the Twelfth made Zeke realize how far from home he was, and he began to take stock prudently of his surroundings. He didn't like the chandelier hung so low over the center aisle. All right at a morning service, but with it lighted you couldn't see anyone in the rear pews. "Aim for the back seats," Watling used to say. He couldn't tell about the acoustics, but except for the effect of the chandelier, they ought to be all right—no galleries along the sides, or pillars, and only a small gallery at the rear.

It certainly was going to be a meeting, though, and not a service. There was no hush at all. The people coming in talked all the way up the aisle and after they'd sat down. Someone must be giving out handbills at the door—they all had them, and a few had dropped them in the aisle. The ushers weren't bothering to pick them up. No one seemed to pay any attention to the ushers, anyway. People came wandering up the aisle—sat where they wanted to—turned round to talk with someone three pews away, and if they felt like it got up and changed their seats. There was laughter occasionally, and—yes, sir, he saw a man eating something.

It was going to be hard to get hold of them. He was glad he didn't have to pull them together and get them quiet to begin with. That was Chalmers' job. Chalmers was going to introduce him. 'Just a word or two,' Chalmers had said, '—unless there's something particular you wanted me to say?' And Zeke had said, 'Oh, no. I'm afraid there's not much for you to say.' Chalmers, a good deal on his mind, of course, had let it go at that.

The place was about half full—not much better than that. It was now probably twelve minutes past the hour. The number of people coming in had slowed down. Suddenly Chalmers raised his head, got up, and went ungainly to the forward center of the platform. He had not a table or anything beside him. He was a taller man even than Zeke was. He looked bitterly tired.

Chalmers stood there . . . while one person quieted another.

He said: "Let us pray:"—and with his head raised asked his prayer. Most of it, Zeke thought, was very well suited to the occasion. He wondered whether Miss Cameron had come in—he hadn't seen her. Chalmers finished abruptly, and Zeke slowly sat upright. He hoped they were going to have some business first, he should have asked about that. And then he hoped they wouldn't. He was ready now, all ready. The sooner, the better.

Chalmers had a slow voice, with a bite to it. "We are to be addressed this evening by the Reverend Ezekiel Peele."

Zeke's muscles contracted. He shuddered—and to cover it, shifted in his chair. He looked up then, and saw that Chalmers had turned to him—was expecting him to come forward. The surprise straightened him out. He stood up, and as he went forward nodded to Chalmers without seeing him, and took his place. He got a good easy grip on the floor with his feet, and he saw the people clearly. This wasn't going to be hard.

He gave them the text—the good, familiar text . . . and as he did so, he knew that he was doing it well. He could see the whole sermon ahead of him if he would look, every word as he had written it—and hear each phrase as it would sound.

He saw that he was getting his response. He loved the sermon. It was right to do this.

And he could do it better now, because he was not at all afraid. This was the second time. There was nothing ahead unknown. He was able to think of the place in the sermon where he was now, and get the most out of it that he could—knowing the rest would be there safely when he got to it.

It was an exciting business—watching them, watching them, bringing them along—and feeling them stir and answer. . . . He was changing no words, but he was timing his pauses this trip, using what he had—the things that were in the sermon—better than he had done before. Much better. He could see it in every face. He was preaching now. This was preaching. . . .

He found that he had lost some of the perfection of his detachment. He had not meant that it should be so—this was just a speech—but he was going along with them now. He had to, to keep up with them. Or he would fall so far behind that they would see it. They would be angry, then, because he was cheating them. He let himself go then—not perfectly, because he found that was not possible. . . .

They had gone suddenly beyond his control. He saw dimly a man rise in place and apparently shout, but he scarcely heard him. And more men.

. . . this was the climax of the sermon, he couldn't hold

178

back now . . . he knew that—and suddenly he gloried in it. And he let them have it for all that he was worth.

He could hear them roar as they stood up.

Zeke stood there. The sound was terrible. They were cheering. He could have laughed at it—but he didn't want to cry. There was more to the sermon—a quiet part to end with. Not much chance of throwing anything quiet into that mob. There was a bearded man standing on one of the seats shouting, his fist held over his head.

Zeke saw that it was rather a disgusting mess. He turned back to Chalmers. Chalmers was coming forward . . . and he went past Zeke as though Zeke hadn't been there.

The intensity of the racket rose as Chalmers reached the center of the platform. No hymnbooks sailed into the chandelier, but they might as well have. Zeke retreated to the vicinity of his chair, but he expressed his sense of responsibility for having caused all this, by hesitantly continuing to stand.

They were cheering Chalmers now, because he was the obvious focus of attention—there in the center of the platform. He made no acknowledgment to them that Zeke could see, nor was he making any effort to quiet them. He showed no impatience to be heard. He waited, indifferent apparently as to whether he waited two minutes or an hour. Zeke finally sat down. The man on his right leaned over to him so as to make himself heard. Zeke was ready for some praise, and ready to deprecate it in his answer. "He's always got hold of the reins," the man said. Zeke smiled, and nodded. He looked toward Chalmers. No change there, but the bedlam was lessening. It dropped suddenly to almost nothing. Chalmers waited so long to speak that it was almost embarrassing.

"I wish it were possible to free slaves by shouting," he said.

"Fight!" someone called, and there was another cheer, solid but brief.

"It's easy to cry 'fight!'" Chalmers said, "and it's not so very difficult to mean it."

"We mean it,"—but there was no cheer this time.

"I respect your enthusiasm," he went on. "I respect Mr. Peele's ability to evoke it. That particular type of enthusiasm is effective up to two hundred yards. With more of the windows open, it might be heard three blocks. But shout your loudest, my friends—I doubt that you'll be heard above the bids spoken before a single auction block."

Zeke realized, then, that the insult had not been intended. It was merely a part of Chalmers' way of building on what Zeke had done already.

"Scream and shriek," Chalmers was saying, "and a thousand miles away the man with a blacksnake whip upraised will only strike again. He cannot hear you. And if he could—he's used to screams. Yell all together—all of you— yell now!—and you'll not be heard above the groans and prayers that at this moment are coming up through the sleek decks of a pretty slaver, three weeks out from Africa and with fifty thousand dollars in her hold!"

"You can cry 'fight!' from now till doomsday!—and never free one solitary slave. Because you are not ready."

There were no cheers this time.

"Oh, yes," he said wearily, "you mean 'fight.' You're all of you in earnest. I know that. Well—fight whom? The government of the Commonwealth of Massachusetts, to begin with. To say nothing of the City of Boston. And also, may I remind you: the government of the United

States of America. That happens to be treason at the moment. *Fight now and you hang!* That's all there is to that."

They were surly.

"If you insist on being hanged—all right. Perhaps that is your privilege, and I ought not to interfere. But don't think for one minute that with your lives you will have bought anything for Abolition. Later on, it may be, there will come opportunity to make a better bargain.

"I hate Slavery, as you do. And I love you—each one of you—who is sincere. That is why I speak to you as I do now. Lay down your lives—yes. But see that you get something in exchange. To exact that something in exchange, we must be stronger than we are now. And in order to *be* stronger, we have got to have money, we have got to have organization, and we have got to have time. These are prosaic things, I know; because I mention them some of you will call me a coward."

"I do!" a man did—from the balcony.

There were a few grudging smiles, but there was no laughter.

Then patiently, and with some skill, Chalmers recited to them the things for which money was needed. He exhorted them to bide their time, to work, and get ready.

He came back to his chair.

A collection was then taken up, and while that was going on, someone improved the time by reading notices: pamphlets were obtainable from So-and-so and should be distributed, there would be a meeting on the following Thursday at eight o'clock, and a letter had been received from Mr. Parker who was abroad. The letter was read—and Chalmers sat through all of it with his legs stretched out in front of him, staring morosely at his boots. The man had run out of notices, and he left his audience and came back to ask Chalmers if there were anything more. Chalmers glanced up, and then looking at his boots again, said, "No,"—and the man went back to tell the audience that that was all. The audience had assumed that to be the case and had begun to go home. The atmosphere now was not much different from what it had been when they were coming in. Zeke thought it was the strangest anticlimax he had ever seen. He stood up to go.

Chalmers said: "Sit down, will you? I owe you some explanation."

Zeke said politely, "Not at all," and sat down still more politely on the edge of his chair. The other men on the platform were standing round talking, getting ready to go home.

"This is the first meeting you've attended, isn't it?"

Zeke said it was.

"I'd heard about your sermon, and I wanted them to hear it. I want more of them to hear it. Will you speak again?"

Zeke said he'd be glad to do what he could, of course.

"They can't hate Slavery enough. You can do that for them. It's a great contribution."

"Well—"

"But they aren't ready yet for more than that. That's why I arranged the program tonight back-end-to. Most of these people are my congregation." He turned to Zeke. "Good night," he said, "and thank you."

Zeke assured him that it had been a privilege to come here . . . but Chalmers was staring at his boots again.

The other men who had been on the platform had either left or were now leaving two at a time, talking to each other. Zeke walked all the way down the aisle behind a pair of them but they apparently didn't know he was there, or at any rate didn't turn round.

The crowd had not lingered outside the church. It was good and cold, but black and clear overhead, and he turned up his collar to walk home.

He went along briskly for a while, and the air felt good in his throat. There was something he wanted to say to himself. He said it, finally. He said: "Well, they cheered, anyway." After he'd said it, it was easy for him to decide that that ended it.

Viola was still up when he came in. "Well!" he said, "still up? Thought you'd have gone to bed."

" 'Bed'? No . . . You're home early, aren't you? It's just struck ten."

"Oh. I thought it was later than that."

"How did the meeting go?"

"All right, I guess."

"What's the matter? Didn't they like it?"

"Seemed to—they cheered, anyway."

"Cheered? Really, Zeke? Why, that's wonderful! I never heard of anyone cheering a sermon before!"

"Neither did I."

"Didn't you want them to? I don't understand."

"Don't you? Well, I do. And that's all that's necessary." He recollected that he had intimated something to Chalmers about being available again sometime. Well, never mind. He could cross that bridge when he came to it. Maybe Chalmers wouldn't ask him.

[Chapter 25]

On a December Friday a little after three, Zeke went into his study to put together his sermon for Sunday. It would not be difficult. He'd preached a good many sermons to these people. Just about a year of them. Well, he must think about the sermon. So he put his feet up to think. Sunday would be December seventh—wouldn't it? There'd be snow at home, perhaps, or maybe not. Just a dusting of it, to whiten the light gray-green color that the short grass has when it's frozen. And it would show white in the road ruts, but the crests of the ruts bare, a dry brown, the frost in them in some way taking out the red color that they had other times. If it was cold, the first snow would be that way. But if it happened to come when it wasn't so cold, you got a layer of it, spread thin, and the ruts showing through. Enough to track a dog with, but when you got out of school at noontime it was gone . . . with a half inch of mud left, most places, and the ground hard underneath. December seventh. Christmas was getting close. Sometimes there was no snow till after Christmas. He'd preached to them about Christmas last year, and Somers had every year—but no matter. Still, there was a sermon on Christmas Sunday to be reckoned with. If he used Christmas now, he'd have to find something else for Christmas Sunday. On the other hand, Christmas was a pretty obvious topic for a sermon on Christmas Sunday. He had a right to expect something more original from himself than that. And they had, too, he supposed. Besides, they'd be tired of Christmas by that time. Be better to give them Christmas now while they had an appetite for it. There was a lot of scope in Christmas. A familiar ground, and a

184

wide one. Near the beginning there was a good five minutes of atmosphere that you could do with one hand behind
your back. Especially to city people. The first snow in the
country . . . white in the road ruts, and the crests of the
ruts bare, dry brown. The point to that phrase was
'crests.' It was funny the way those things came to you.
He'd never thought while he was looking at the top of a
rut that it looked anything like a wave. It did though.
Well, he'd get at it. . . .

He pulled up to his desk. There was no grinding urgency
about it, after all, because this was only Friday afternoon. A man with all of Saturday safely between himself
and the pulpit has got time to do himself justice on the
words. He's got time to carve the phrases, and even to
whittle them if he wants to . . .

. . . and if after two hours he's whittled a good many
phrases—each one of them down through three or four
different meanings until there was not enough left of them
but to throw away—well, he can throw them away. And
he can resolutely square himself to lay down the broad,
directing outlines of the sermon as a whole. Once that's
been done, it's simple. Nor need the thought be too disturbing that in this last two hours he has accomplished
nothing. And that Saturday, perhaps, is not so clear as he
had told himself. It is always possible to get up two hours
earlier on Sunday morning. A good, solid, tangible resolu-
tion to get up two hours earlier on Sunday morning can
be almost as productive of self-respect as the mere fact of
two hours' work accomplished.

The maid knocked on the door, and Zeke recognized
the impossibility of a man's getting any work done when
there were constant interruptions.

The maid had knocked because Mr. Wislon was outside

waiting in the hall. Mr. Wislon was a square, heavy man, given to a thoughtful, slow-spoken accuracy. He was Chairman of the Committee on Finances, and had been for a long time. Zeke told her to show him in. Not a penny was paid by the church but what Wislon, at least formally, approved of it.

Mr. Wislon said he had come to talk about the finances of the church.

Zeke put aside his sermon on Christmas.

"We have to present a budget, as you know, the first of January." Wislon was sitting in the deep, comfortable chair, but he had not resigned himself to it. "Just at the moment, we're paying out more than we're taking in. I wondered if you could see any reason for anticipating that the income of the church will be increased next year."

Zeke said well, no . . . he didn't know that he could. Unless it would be that the improvement in business over what it had been, say, two years ago, might be reflected in the contributions.

"Well, I don't know. Sometimes, hard times are better for a church than good times."

Zeke said agreeably that in his experience no time was a good time for a church, really. It was like a farm.

The parallel did not appeal to Mr. Wislon. "At the time you became pastor," he said, "our income had dropped to about half what it had been under Somers."

Zeke pointed out that no church could prosper without a leader.

"Since then," Wislon said, "it's dropped still further. Call it momentum, if you want to. I don't suppose you can expect a tendency that's been going on for two years to turn round and go the other way overnight. All the same—there we are."

"Yes, it's—it's distressing."

" 'Tis to me. I'm kind of attached to this church, in a way."

"I don't know what the church would do without you, Mr. Wislon, I'm sure."

"Run into debt, probably. You don't mind if I'm frank, do you?"

"Perhaps you don't realize how difficult it is for a minister to get frankness from the members of his congregation."

"Mmm. Well, as I was going to say, about half our income comes from endowment. That part of it's increasing—for the reason you just pointed out. The other half comes from contributions. And that half of it's falling off a good deal faster than the other half is going up. I don't suppose it's any secret to you that when you were made pastor there were a good many people'd rather have had somebody else. It's always that way, and you're not to blame. But it happens this time that the ones who'd rather have had somebody else are the ones who've done most of the giving. In amount, I mean. And some of those have stopped giving. I'm just explaining this to you, so you'll understand."

Zeke said he understood.

"I don't think you do. I'm not asking you to resign. Don't get that idea."

The best Zeke could do was to make an effort to relinquish the idea—but he made the effort willingly.

"It happens," Wislon said, "that I don't agree with you on Slavery. But I do feel that the very worst thing you could do for the church right now would be to quit."

With agreement between them on that point, Zeke felt

there was a good chance of harmony in the rest of the discussion.

"We'll get that money back somehow," Wislon assured himself, "or we'll do without it. But for the time being, I guess, we've got to do without it. Can you get along with only one assistant?"

Zeke's impulse was to say that he'd cheerfully do all the work himself . . . now that he found he wasn't fired. But Wislon wouldn't respect him for that. "I can, yes," he said.

Implication, Wislon enjoyed—but not inference. "How do you mean?"

"The question is whether the church can."

"Oh."

"It would make very little difference in my work," Zeke told him, thinking as he went along, "whether there were two assistants or one. The pastor has his work to do; the assistants have theirs. They're separate jobs, you see. I know, because I've done both. An assistant doesn't preach; the pastor doesn't address envelopes. What you're really asking me is whether the church can get along with fewer envelopes."

Mr. Wislon was considerably surprised.

Zeke, on the other hand, was astonished. He'd never talked like this to anyone. "So far as assistants are concerned"—and how easy it was!—"a church gets just about what it pays for. Seldom any more than that. If it can afford the work of two assistants, all right. But if it can't—well, it will have to get along with one. Won't it? Quite frankly, I cannot do the work of an assistant, and at the same time do justice to my own job."

Wislon appeared to be trying to rearrange his approach.

"Graveson and I used to handle the work all right

188

while we were both assistants. But there are certain types of work which I did then, which Graveson is not fitted to do—and I haven't the time to do now. Work among the poor of the church. I can't do that now, much as I'd like to. Because I haven't the time. It's not a matter of unwillingness. It takes time to write sermons! And you can't write a sermon while you're listening to some old woman telling you about the pain in her back."

"No," Mr. Wislon admitted, "I suppose not. I never wrote any. Would it be your suggestion," he asked, "that we—er, replace Mr. Graveson with someone of—er, perhaps more general ability?"

"Not necessarily—no."

"What would you recommend?"

"I'd prefer not to recommend anything. I don't think it's a matter for me to decide."

"The new pastor was supposed to be at liberty to call his own assistant—or assistants, it was then."

"Yes, so I understood. And I expected to lose my job by it. But the point is that they're not 'his' assistants. They work for the church. The same as the pastor does. And it's a mistaken courtesy to make the pastor responsible for selecting them."

Mr. Wislon's mustache wiggled, and he rubbed it.

"I hope I make myself clear," Zeke said earnestly.

"Oh, yes! Quite."

"The pastor is the spiritual leader of the congregation," Zeke enlarged. "Mainly—or ideally, rather—he exercises that leadership in the pulpit on Sundays. In practice, as we both know, he has a thousand and one other things to do. But ideally, the administrative work, if we can call it that—" Mr. Wislon nodded to indicate that they could—"should properly be done by the assistants. Certainly it was under Dr. Somers."

Mr. Wislon said, yes, he guessed that had been so, all right. Still, when Somers had been there, he'd brought in enough money so that they could afford to have two assistants. They couldn't—now.

Zeke said he understood perfectly. But what *he* was trying to bring out was that whether the church had one assistant or two—or who they were to be—was, as he saw it, entirely up to the church.

Mr. Wislon said it was a question of what they could afford.

Having made his position clear—and as forcefully as he had—Zeke could now say for Wislon what Wislon had been trying to say all along. "Naturally," he admitted, "if there's to be only one assistant, you can count on me to turn to and help out all I can."

Mr. Wislon smiled. "I had counted on that."

And Zeke smiled in acknowledgment. "Thank you." It was time to change the tone of the conversation. "A congregation," he confided humorously, "always sees a sermon as representing no more than the time it takes to preach it."

"Or to listen to it, some of them."

"Perhaps that's not always the congregation's fault," Zeke said.

Mr. Wislon said nothing.

"I'd like nothing better than to be free to do all the parish calling that I did before. And more besides. But where's the time to come from? Before you came in, I'd been working two hours, solidly, for Sunday. And there's a whole lot more to be done yet, I can tell you."

Mr. Wislon said he wouldn't detain him any longer.

Zeke said not at all!—he was glad to see him any time. After all, it was the welfare of the church they were both working for, wasn't it? And Mr. Wislon said, yes, he guessed it was.

After he'd gone, Zeke came back to his desk. There was the temptation, of course, to sit thinking about the conversation for a minute or two. But he put that aside. The afternoon was too far gone. He took a sheet of the satisfyingly white—not yellow—paper that the church paid for and squared himself for work. He'd start fresh. Never mind any of the things he'd thought before, because if they were any good, he'd think of them again.

Christmas. Now, then, what about Christmas? What could he give them about Christmas? You couldn't just retell the story. And you couldn't improve on it. But if he read it to them, simply, just as it was . . . well, they wouldn't see why he'd done it. Besides, the Scripture Lesson would use that up, anyway. He'd got to preach to them. That's what they were paying him for—and once each week he'd got to stand up and prove to them that he was earning it. Wislon hadn't said they were dissatisfied in any way. Contributions were going down . . . but that was just a few people, upset about the Slavery sermon. What on earth did Slavery have to do with giving money to the church? Nothing. They knew that. The point was, they didn't like to give money, and so any excuse to stop giving it was welcome. He'd enjoy telling them that. After all, why wasn't a sermon on Christmas a good time to talk of giving? It wouldn't do for a whole sermon, perhaps, but there was a place for it. It would help. Well . . . back to the sermon.

The maid knocked at the door again—to tell him it was

191

time for dinner. Zeke said: "All right." . . . Whatever those appointments were for tomorrow, they'd have to be canceled. His duty was to preach.

[Chapter 26]

SITTING BEFORE A GOOD FIRE in Mr. Cameron's library, a man might oppose Mr. Cameron, but he was bound to do so respectfully. The ceiling of the room was high and noticeably Adam; Mr. Cameron was tall, and in the texture of his baldness—polished but not shiny—there was the essence of respectability. Mr. Cameron's tail coat fitted him and clothed him as naturally as the bookshelves did the walls, and the fine quality of broadcloth in his coat was just as quietly assertive as was the preponderance of good leather on the shelves. The carpet in the room was deep, and the brass about the fireplace was rubbed each day, and the white bear rug before the dustless black tiles of the hearth was a sound cream color, something this side of meerschaum. The cigars which Mr. Cameron furnished were better than excellent. Mr. Wislon was not a man peculiarly susceptible to these influences, but no man could be immune. Mr. Wislon was glad that he had come.

And somewhere in the background there was the little point that he was present by invitation, written. He'd had a note from Cameron asking him to come to Cameron's home on Wednesday, eight o'clock, for the purpose—honestly set down and thus dispersing any smell of plot—of discussing certain matters touching on the welfare of the Twelfth Congregational Church. There would be two or three others, the note explained, and Mr. Cameron was counting on his presence.

The others hadn't shown up, and Mr. Cameron and Mr. Wislon had been discussing now for ten or fifteen minutes. "In effect," Mr. Cameron said, "he holds office during good behavior."

Mr. Wislon said he supposed that was so. Still, a year did seem a little short.

"It's more than a year. If we'd adhered strictly to the letter of the agreement—assuming that there'd been an agreement—his good behavior wouldn't have kept him in five minutes."

"Well, of course," Mr. Wislon answered, the influence of the room becoming less strong the more he thought and talked, "we have to remember that the privilege of defining 'good behavior' rests with the church as a whole. They mightn't all feel the same way you do." He didn't himself.

"Not for the same reasons, perhaps. But as far as action is concerned, they will. Look here—turn it around: call it the privilege of defining bad behavior."

"Well . . ."

"Take the man's absolute preoccupation with overthrowing the United States Government. That's bad behavior, isn't it? Do you realize, Mr. Wislon, that our young friend Peele, by actual count, has spoken at eight—eight, I tell you!—Abolition meetings within the period of the last sixty days?"

Mr. Wislon said he hadn't realized it, no.

"Well, he has! I've made it my business to keep track."

"It does seem a good many. You been to any?"

"Good Lord! I wouldn't be found dead in one—and I probably would be if I went. There are some things I *can't* stand. Here—let me have your glass."

"No, thank you. I've been wondering—do you suppose Abolition really means so much to the average person? The people in church, I mean—all classes?"

"No!—ridiculous. Nine-tenths of them are in it just for the excitement. Nonetheless, they're damn dangerous. And don't you forget it!"

"May be." Mr. Wislon was not hurried. "But I can't say I altogether agree with you about their lack of sincerity. Old—"

"All right," Mr. Cameron interrupted, "look at my daughter."

Once or twice on his way to the house, Mr. Wislon had entertained a mild but pleasant hope of doing just that.

"You may not have known it," said Mr. Cameron with a certain courage, "but up to two months ago *she* was an Abolitionist. My own daughter, mind you! How would you like that?"

Mr. Wislon said he had heard something about it.

"I don't doubt you did! Everyone did. I had all I could do to keep it out of the papers. And where is she now?"

'Couldn't say,' thought Mr. Wislon. 'Liable to come in any minute, if I had my way.'

"Visiting her aunt in Winston-Salem. Having a beautiful time—riding, balls, dinners—having a lovely time. Calls them 'darkies.' Mrs. Cameron's sister."

"Oh," said Mr. Wislon. "We shipped a nice order to Winston-Salem . . . just last week." The Wislon firm made woodenware.

"How's their credit?"

"Mmwell . . ."

"Exactly. Well, as I was saying, about Peele: as far as I'm concerned, these repeated—these *repeated* attempts of Peele's to stir up trouble are bad behavior enough for me.

I opposed calling him in the first place, as you know, after that sermon. And I'm in favor of getting rid of him now."

"I know. But this is a Congregational church."

"I'm aware of that. Who *did* call Peele?"

"Majority of a meeting."

" 'Majority-of-the-meeting' hell! The poor of the church called him. Why they ever came to the meeting, I don't know. It wouldn't surprise me if that were some of Peele's work, too. *Why* did they? Because Peele's name meant just one thing to those people. Peele was the man who gave them money."

"Well, they liked him, too. Peele's done a lot for some of those people—in the past."

"Of *course* they liked him! Peele had been paymaster for the Church Poor Fund. Did they stop to think *whose* money it was he'd been giving them? Not they! I doubt if Peele ever did. Why, he didn't know what money was until he was made pastor. A farm boy—never had a cent. That's one reason he's so dangerous. He's got absolutely no sense of responsibility, I tell you! Father sells meat and so on to one of the hotels here. That's a fine background for a successor to Somers—isn't it?"

"It's all right if it's good meat."

"It's excellent, I'm told," Mr. Cameron said coldly. "But to get back to the point: what's the situation now with regard to those same people?"

"The poor of the church? Some of them are hungry."

"Ah! Why?"

"Well, hell!—" the influence of the room completely dissipated—"because they don't get enough to eat, I suppose. Same reason you or I'd be hungry, if we were poor."

"Fundamentally," said Mr. Cameron, happy to concede so small a point, "you're quite right. Actually, the answer is Peele. Young Mr. Peele—the Pastor. By going around blatting about Abolition to every bunch of yawping fools who'd pretend to listen to him—young Mr. Peele has succeeded in alienating everyone from the church who used to give to the church the money that the church gave to the poor."

"Well, some of them, I guess."

"Look at your figures!"

"Yes, I know. I have."

"Now, then: is it fair to those people to allow Peele to remain?"

"I don't know; it would seem to me it might still be possible to give to the poor—even if you don't like Peele."

Mr. Cameron disposed of that by saying: "Let's be practical."

"What do you want to do?" Mr. Wislon asked.

"Get rid of Peele. The sooner, the better."

"'Soon' enough. Little over a year. I never heard of a pastor staying less than that."

"He was a mistake in the first place."

"May be. But he didn't make the mistake."

"He just *is* a mistake! And his wife, too. She's terrible."

"I don't know her so well."

"I don't either, but I've seen her in church often enough."

"She doesn't look very strong, does she? You seen MacIntosh lately?"

"No. I'm afraid he's pretty far gone."

"He must be, I'm afraid. I stopped by there the other day, but that girl of his just shook her head."

Mr. Cameron had a nice distaste for gossip. "I take it, then, that you prefer not to act with me in this matter."

"I don't know what you want to do."

"Get rid of Peele."

"How?"

"Only one way that I know: call a meeting and put it to a vote."

"Well, you don't need me to do that."

"Fortunately."

"I'm sorry, Mr. Cameron. But I kind of like him. He's young yet."

"Well, I'd prefer not to have him aged at the expense of the Twelfth Congregational Church."

"Oh, I can see your point. He's expensive, all right—right now."

"He hasn't got a friend in the church. Not one. The poor hate him because they think he's neglected them."

"Yes, I know. He has."

"They're sensitive to that sort of thing, you know. It isn't just the money. They think that he's had his head turned."

"So do I. It'll turn back."

"I trust so. Most earnestly. But in the meantime he's not going to be allowed to complete the ruin of this church. Not while I'm a member."

"When's your meeting?"

"Just as soon as I can get the names together to call it."

Mr. Wislon got up. "Who you going to get in his place?"

"I don't know."

"Tidman?"

"I don't know, I'm sure. Someone—*anyone*."

"Well . . . thank you for asking me to come here. Sorry I can't help you out."

"So am I—very. By the way, you haven't been bringing us in much paper at the bank lately. I hope it's not going elsewhere."

"Don't worry. We're still customers. We're trying to go kind of easy on paper right now. If we don't want to sell 'em on open account, we try to get cash, or else not sell 'em."

"Winston-Salem didn't pay cash."

"No, but I put in the prices on the order."

"That doesn't lessen the risk any. Someday you fellows are going to learn that."

"I suppose so. Same day that you learn not to judge a bond issue by the size of the discount you get."

Mr. Cameron laughed. "Come in again," he said. "I've enjoyed seeing you. Good night, Wislon."

Trudging home against the wind, Mr. Wislon reflected that it took all kinds to make a world. Or a church, too, for that matter. Cameron had the skids under young Peele, all right. And there was not much anybody could do about it. Matter of fact, it might be a good thing for the church—provided they got somebody good in his place. Oh, well, he guessed the church'd keep going somehow. He was sorry for Peele, though. Man turned out of a church after only a little over a year wasn't going to find it easy to get a job somewhere else.

[*Chapter 27*]

SOMEONE HAD KNOCKED, and Zeke, without altering his unfocused gaze toward the litter on his desk, said "Come in." It didn't matter who it was. They'd bring nothing that would affect him. The study door opened, and after it had opened, he looked up. It seemed to be Watling. As

198

soon as he was sure that it was Watling, Zeke's face broke into a grin—something it hadn't done, not of its own accord, at any rate, in weeks. He tilted back his chair. "Well!" he said. "Where'd you come from?"

"Working?"

"No. Come in, will you? Gosh, I'm glad to see you!"

"Maryland," Mr. Watling said, which was where he had come from. He put his big black hat—a fairly recent one—on a corner of the desk, and sat down in the deep chair. Zeke watched him delightedly, not thinking to get up and shake hands.

Mr. Watling hung one leg over the arm of the chair, and settled well down and comfortably. . . .

"I hear you've been fired," he said.

"Oh, yes. Some time ago."

Each man's tone attempted to rate the event as about equal to the loss of a really good dog.

"How's Mrs. Peele?" Watling asked.

"Seems to be all right," Zeke said. "Very well. You look all right."

"I had a pretty good winter. I like to eat in Maryland."

Zeke wanted to ask him if he'd given up drinking; he looked almost as though he might have. "Sheba?" he said.

"Fat," Watling answered, getting out a toothpick. "Going to make her wear stays pretty soon. What do you hear from your father and mother?"

"They're well. Had a letter last week. Corn's in, but it's been pretty wet."

"Mm. Everywhere, I guess."

"Everywhere?"

"Oh, come! Contrast isn't as marked as that, is it? Tell me, Zeke: when did all this happen?"

"End of February. Six weeks ago tomorrow."

"Any reason?"

"Too much Abolition, I guess. Man named Cameron engineered it. They've given me till June."

"Cameron . . ." Watling said, "let's see . . . I remember him."

"Do you? I didn't think you'd met him."

"I didn't; that's one reason I remember him so well. He was in church that day I was here. Sat behind me. Had his daughter with him."

"Oh, I guess I do remember. Yes. Why, Cameron's all right. I don't blame him."

"What does he blame you for? Not the Abolition Movement?"

"Worse than that—money. Or the absence of it."

"What!" The quickness of Watling's disbelief made it funny.

Zeke laughed. "No, not that. You won't have to bail me out. No . . . it was just that the donors quit donating because I was an Abolitionist."

"Oh." Mr. Watling turned away. "They'll do it—every time! *Any* excuse! He had you there, Zeke."

"Didn't he! So did the beneficiaries—the former beneficiaries. Twelve people, by the Clerk's count, voted to have me retained."

"You there?"

"At the meeting? No, I wasn't. I was lecturing that night—at an Abolition meeting."

Mr. Watling was not one to be appalled by poetic justice. "Well," he said, "that makes a nice coincidence to think about. Cameron time it for that?"

"Couldn't help it, I guess. I was lecturing most nights."

Mr. Watling wondered how he'd managed to amass

twelve votes. "You got quite a name out of it, anyhow. I heard about you even down where I was."

"Must have been complimentary—in Maryland."

"Oh, I don't know . . . you, and Garrison, and the Devil, and Parker . . . they lump you all more or less together. You still at it?"

"No. I—" He had to start again. "I lost my taste for it."

Mr. Watling heard that by Zeke's reckoning they were getting close to the part that mattered. He said gently: "What were you giving 'em, Zeke?"

"My sermon."

"That one I heard?"

"Yes."

Mr. Watling began to understand.

Zeke got up from his chair, and in a step or two—the room was very small—was facing the window.

Mr. Watling glanced at the boy's profile . . . and looked away.

"Over and over," Zeke said, "so as to hear them cheer. When they cheered, it meant I could preach. I saw through that pretty soon. It wasn't preaching—stirring them up to yell and make fools of themselves."

Mr. Watling was thinking that there was a great deal to be said for the Roman Catholic practice of confession. He tried to tell himself that every so often.

Zeke said: "It sounds funny now, but—I loved that sermon once."

"What sounds funny," Watling asked, "the sermon?"

"I wish it did"—ruefully.

Well, the boy wasn't weeping into his beer, at any rate. "Why shouldn't you have? It was a good sermon—when I heard it."

"I still thought a good deal of it, I guess—even after I

found out I'd been jobbed into writing it. That didn't affect the sermon itself any. I believed it when I did write it."

Mr. Watling wondered how many weeks of arguing had gone into that attitude. "How is my old friend, anyway?"

"MacIntosh? Been drunk for six months."

"He has my respect."

"Give it to his liver." Zeke turned away from the window, and came back toward the desk.

He stood there, rubbing one finger along the edge of the desk. "If I'd let it be then—been all right. I knew that, too. But I had to go to work and trot it out again." He turned suddenly on Watling. "You try it!" he pleaded for understanding. "You don't know what it does to you!—being able to do that to an audience."

"Don't I?" Watling answered. "Well, maybe not. My mind's usually on the collection. It's a preoccupation which disposes to a very healthy degree of disinterest. Now sit down, will you? It's my turn" . . . and then Mr. Watling considerately left him to himself and began scratching a fleck of dried mud from a trouser leg.

Zeke, after a moment, sat down.

"There's one point," Watling continued, "that you've overlooked." He was still working at the mudspot. "And that is, that this power you have over audiences—fascinating as it may seem to you—doesn't exist. You ever try speaking at Cameron's club? They'd have thrown you out in the gutter."

Zeke didn't answer.

"Zeke, these audiences of yours knew before they left home they were going to cheer. All you had to do was give 'em the signal. When you'd wave this prize sermon of yours at 'em, then they knew it was time to let loose. And so they did. You shouldn't have let 'em fool you. What did you *do* it for, Zeke!—anyway. You *must* have known that!"

"I don't know . . ."

"Well, why *did* you? I'm curious. I'd like to know."

"So would I—now."

"You do. Why'd you quit?"

"I told you. I said I lost my taste for it."

"Why?"

"I don't know."

"Listen here, boy: if I've got to listen to your confession, you're going to confess. Otherwise, no absolution. That's what you're looking for, isn't it?"

"I don't think so."

"I do."

"Anything else you'd like to talk about?"

"No. Why did you quit?"

"Leave me alone, will you? I can look out for myself. I'd never have wanted to preach, if it hadn't been for you."

"You never have preached. Why did you quit?"

"Because I got a good, clear look at what I was doing."

"Somebody show it to you?"

"No."

"Well, that's something."

"That sermon was the only good job I'd ever done. Then when I preached it without believing it—well, then there wasn't much left of it after that—was there? What there had been—before, I mean, I'd gone and swapped for this feeling I got out of their damned cheering. When I got round to weighing it up, it didn't look as though I'd made much of a trade."

"Lately, this was?"

"Well—few weeks ago."

"Less than six? Since they fired you, I mean?"

"I guess it was. Anyhow: it looked as though I'd been cheated. Oh, I know: I'd done it myself—but that didn't make it any pleasanter."

"No, it doesn't," Mr. Watling agreed.

"Well, I had to take it out on somebody, so I took it out on the ones doing the cheering. A good many nights. I stood up there and used every trick I knew just to talk that crowd into a frenzy so I could stand back and laugh at them. Well . . ." and he sniffed—"that's that."

Mr. Watling sat motionless in his chair. Finally he said, "Zeke, I never thought you'd be such a fool."

"No," Zeke said truthfully, "neither did I."

Mr. Watling remained thoughtful. "How much they been paying you here?" he asked.

"Thirty-five hundred."

"You got anything else in sight?"

"Not a thing."

Watling appeared to muse; his leg, dangling over the chair arm, swung back and forth. He stood up suddenly. "I've got to go along."

"Salary runs till June," Zeke reminded him. "We still eat. Better stay, hadn't you?"

"No—like to," and he shook his head.

"We'd like to have you . . ." Zeke stood up, too.

"No, I can't." Mr. Watling picked up his hat. "I may see your father next week. I'm going by that way."

"You're lucky. Wish I were going with you."

"You'd better stay on the job, I should think, while you've got it to stay on."

Zeke said: "Thanks. If you see Father, tell him we're doing all right, will you? Everything's fine."

"He know you've been fired?"

"Certainly."

"Well—maybe I will. Good-by, Zeke." He held out his hand. "Good luck."

Zeke shook hands with him. "Good-by, sir."

Watling gave him an odd look, and turned and went out. Zeke thought he seemed not to want to be escorted to the door, so he stayed where he was. When he'd heard the front door close, he went out into the hall so that he could look out the window and see whether Sheba really was as fat as Watling had said.

[Chapter 28]

IT WAS VIOLA'S SUGGESTION that if they were to move out of the parsonage before June, the church might be willing to pay them something for the use of it.

Zeke was more impressed by the impracticability of the suggestion than by its sacrificial character. The church wouldn't save anything, he said, because, until it got a new minister, it wouldn't have any use for the parsonage. Besides that, they themselves would be out the expense of two movings—one now, and again when he got a new church. If she wanted to save money, why didn't she let the maid go? He doubted they'd be doing much entertaining during the next two months.

So Viola let her go.

Whatever else Mr. Watling's call had done for Zeke it

had at least made it seem natural that he should go out and look for a job. Up till now, he'd merely listened—the ethics of his profession entitling him to refrain from any more positive method. He had not even gone so far as to make sure that anyone knew that he was listening.

He had three churches in mind. Old Dr. Prestwick, in Worcester, he knew, was going to retire in the fall. That was a good church, and then there was Johnson in Cambridge, who was in pretty much the same boat that he was himself. There was also Carrick's old church in New Haven, its pulpit occupied temporarily since Carrick's death by a man who had been two years ahead of Zeke at Andover. The New Haven church was said to be liberal in more ways than one, and was admittedly looking for the right man. If they found him, they were ready to pay for him.

Zeke wrote to all three of them—to the ministers, that is—on the same day. Each one he invited to exchange with him. It was a perfectly dignified thing to do, and entirely customary. Except for Prestwick, the others stood to gain as much by it as he did himself.

The reply from Welch, in New Haven, came within a week. Welch wrote that he had no dates open until fall.

Zeke had not expected that all three of them would accept. There were still two good, solid chances left. . . .

After a long week, he stood in his study opening Prestwick's letter . . . three wandering pages. They said no.

He was not surprised. From the beginning Prestwick had been the least likely of the three. But it made him a little ashamed, and yet grateful at the same time, to have Prestwick decline on the score of his age and the resulting difficulty of the trip in from Worcester.

Johnson sent back Zeke's own letter, and had scrawled across a corner of it, 'Leaving for Sandusky, Ohio, on Tuesday. Why didn't you speak sooner?'

All three of those chances were gone now. It would not be possible to use them again in his thinking.

It had also got to be the end of April. Whenever he went out, he argued defensively against each sign of spring. They were further south here than they were at home—it was not as late as the tree buds indicated. Why, time and again, in Boston, he'd seen days as warm as this right in the middle of winter. And just last week there had been snow. Summer was a long way away yet. Crocuses meant nothing—they came up the first week in March, and especially under the warm shelter of a brick house. And the daffodils, sold out of pushcarts in the streets, had been shipped up from the South somewhere.

Wislon came in to see him one afternoon, when it was reassuringly raw and cold.

After a minimum of preliminaries, he said that he didn't know what Zeke's plans might be for the future, but one way and another he'd happened to run across some things that he thought Zeke ought to know about.

Zeke tried not to appear too excited. He said: "Well, I—that's fine! What are they?"

Wislon said, well, he didn't know how 'fine' they were; he'd had to go round to some other churches lately, and he'd—well, he'd sort of sounded them out, so to speak, seeing if they were looking for someone.

'Didn't know how "fine" they were'! Zeke thought. Well, he'd judge of that! "Were they?" he said happily. Wislon said some of them were looking for a man. "But I thought you ought to know you're not on the list."

Zeke didn't quite understand at first. Wislon explained,

then, that most of these people—well, all of them, for that matter—seemed to think they'd rather have someone who'd not been quite so much mixed up with outside affairs.

Zeke understood quite clearly. But he found he couldn't say to Wislon that he'd forsworn Abolition less than two months ago, for reasons of his own, and that if only someone would hire him, he'd promise to be a good boy from now on.

So he thanked Wislon for coming—said a minister's hands were pretty well tied when it came to looking for a job, and he was grateful to Wislon for letting him know how things stood.

Wislon accepted his thanks, said he hoped everything would turn out all right, and left.

Zeke didn't tell Viola about it, because he wanted to get it straightened out in his own mind first. It didn't take him long: if he were blacklisted in the ministry, he'd have to do something else.

Even now, he thought, he probably wouldn't say anything to Viola. Not just yet. Because he didn't want to have Viola intimate that there was a lack of divine justice somewhere—that a man who had served God as strenuously as he had was entitled to better treatment in return. Zeke wasn't conscious of any temptation to feel that way about it himself, and he thought he'd rather not discuss the matter. The whole thing seemed very practical at the moment, and worldly and unemotional, and he wanted to keep it that way. He was up against the same problem that confronted other men—get a job, or go hungry—and he rather enjoyed knowing that that was so.

He decided to try some schoolmasters to begin with—having in mind his Greek.

He went to see four of them, two of whom he knew,

and the second two, he was pretty certain, would know of him. He found he could have saved time by calling on the last man first. The other three had been uniformly well-staffed in Greek, but this last man admitted that he was not. He also said that if he were to hire an Abolitionist to teach Greek, he'd lose half his enrollment.

Zeke said he wasn't so sure that in this instance he'd be hiring an Abolitionist.

The Headmaster said that that might be true but, like a good many other truths, it would not be apparent to parents—nor to trustees. He was very sorry about it, and he didn't wish to appear cynical about Education. Also, he was afraid he'd have to excuse himself now, as he had to teach a class.

Zeke, on his long walk home, noticed that the elms were pretty well leafed out. Well, elms or no elms, the calendar said it was only the tenth of May. And they had some money saved up. Not much, but it was something. The first of June, too, was really no more than a theoretical dead line. And once that was crossed, he'd be free and have more time to look for something.

He had all summer, as it turned out. And each day, he had all day.

[Chapter 29]

THEY WERE LIVING NOW in the same place from which they'd moved to go to the parsonage—except that now they had two rooms instead of three. One room was the bedroom, and the other room had to be everything else. But the couple down the hall had moved in the meantime, and the Pisanelli family who'd replaced them were cheerful even to the point of an accordion.

Zeke spent a good many days just walking about. He kept away from the Common, because crossing the Common he had to walk briskly, as though he had an appointment. You never could tell who was looking at you as you were crossing the Common. But along the water front he could go slowly, if he dodged the drays, and occasionally men said "Good day" to him, and two or three times had shrewdly called him "Father." It was a clean, tough place, along the water front with plenty to look at, and if they obviously didn't need a minister, still, it had never occurred to them that they could need one, and so there was nothing in the least personal about their not wanting him. Often he wouldn't do anything about dinner, and when it was getting along late in the afternoon—perhaps somewhere near five o'clock—he'd walk home. Viola never asked him how the day had gone. He felt that she might have been less blatantly tactful about it, but he was not in a position to complain.

The evenings were the worst time. Viola, proud, presumably, in the possession of work, would at last finish her aggravating preoccupation with the dishes, and would come and sit down in the chair on the other side of the table. She'd take up her mending then, or knitting, neither of which was work, actually—merely an attribute of women. Zeke would keep on with reading the paper—going from item to item, hoping for something that would hold his mind.

He knew that each evening was a plain, barefaced opportunity to do some studying, to salt down for future use some of the reading he had so long protested he didn't have time for. An opportunity, even, to get two or three sermons laid up ahead.

But reasonably, on the face of things, he would never have any use for two or three sermons. And he couldn't enjoy the ludicrous picture of himself bent solemnly over the table on a hot, gummy night, desperately building a little sermon he would never preach. But the time was there—night after night confronting him—and the only way to get rid of it was to do something about it. If he could only have admitted: 'I have no duty to use an hour that no one will pay me for,' it would have been all right. Or if he could have said, 'I shall never preach again'—which was certainly a safe enough prediction!—*that* would have taken care of it. But he couldn't bring himself to say that. And so the hours continued to loom up as opportunities—and he continued to twist and turn and try to get away from them, knowing that he was doing just that, but unable—in the hot nights and with the accordion going down the hall—to do anything else.

When the end of August had come very close to him, he knew, one evening, that he had stood it as long as he could. Tomorrow morning—early—he would go to see Chalmers.

He had fought this off all summer, but he was licked now, and he might as well give in. He would offer to sell Chalmers both the sermon and his preaching of it.

That was the last step down. Once he had taken it, he would feel better. He would have nothing left to be afraid of . . . because he'd be at the bottom of the pit then, on a firm, dead level. He'd be a new person, having shucked off all self-respect, and he'd be able to move about and compete freely with other men. Most men were unhampered by self-respect, and were happier because of it. And if Chalmers should turn him down—well, that wouldn't matter either, because it would be natural and easy, once he had tried to sell the sermon, to take money any way he could get it. He could stand at the tail of a cart, then, and sell patent medicines, and it wouldn't touch him in any way. If he should get a job in a barroom, he'd be glad of it, and he'd take a flawless and proper pride in the fact that he was scoring ten dollars weekly against the world. Just as any barman was entitled to be proud of it. Once he had lost, everything gained would be clear gain. It was even possible that whatever Viola would think of him would not matter, either.

He would go to see Chalmers in the morning.

He ate very little breakfast—partly because there wasn't much—and started downstairs. When he came out into the street, he could feel that it was going to be viciously hot before the day was over. Twenty minutes of nine—he still had his watch anyway—and Chalmers probably in his office right now. He was excited about what he was going to do—and he was glad that he was going to do it. But he walked slowly so as to be cool when he got there. What he was going to do seemed tremendously important, possibly more important than it really was. It was a turning point, though. He knew that; it was not an illusion. When it was over he would have come out on the other side.

There was not much of the freshness of morning left in the streets . . . but he remembered that nine o'clock even in the city is nearer to noon than it is to daybreak. He thought of his father and mother, momentarily, and they seemed more like other people than they ever had. Without examining it, he recognized this item as the first sign of his independence—the independence that he was heading for by walking toward Chalmers' office. If he should think about God—which he was pretty sure he could avoid—no doubt the same phenomenon would hold there . . . that is, God would look to him more as God looked to other people. It was only three blocks to Chalmers' office now.

They told him to go right in.

Chalmers appeared about as he used to, as soon as Zeke had remembered that Chalmers had used to look like this. He told Zeke to sit down.

Zeke wondered if Chalmers would have asked him to sit down if he'd thought he was selling hymnbooks.

"What are you doing now?" Chalmers asked him.

"Looking for a job"—and he watched Chalmers accept it as information, nothing else.

"How did you come to leave the Twelfth?" Chalmers asked peculiarly.

Zeke knew that he'd got to hurry—Chalmers was aware that the answer was a fact and that Zeke knew what it was. He fumbled for something to say which would fit onto what he was here for. "Why did I leave . . . ?"

Chalmers was looking at him, waiting.

There didn't seem to be a thing he could lay his hands on except the truth, and so he picked that up and offered it: "Because I didn't do the work."

Chalmers accepted that, too. "What did you want to see me about?"

The words presented themselves before Zeke: 'You aren't paying lecturers, are you?' . . . but he didn't like the looks of them, somehow, and rejected them. He said with some disinterest: "Well, I did have in mind to ask if you were paying lecturers, but I guess I've changed my mind about that." He supposed Chalmers would understand; it seemed clear enough. And it was disposed of.

Freshly concerned, he said pleasantly: "How's your work going?"

"Oh, pretty well. We do what we can." He laughed. "You don't lose anything by changing your mind, though —I haven't got a cent."

Zeke couldn't see just what that had to do with it. He'd just told Chalmers that he didn't want to sell him the sermon. He was surprised that Chalmers should revert to it.

It suddenly occurred to Zeke that he was sitting here beside Chalmers' desk without any reason for being here. It embarrassed him . . . and the thought of pretending that he'd dropped in just for a chat embarrassed him still more.

He laughed, unsuccessfully, and stood up. "Hope I haven't disturbed you," he said. "You know it's going to be hot today."

Chalmers was turning a pen in his fingers. He said "yes," absently. "If I hear of a church, Peele, I'll let you know." He hadn't looked up.

Zeke said good-by, and was leaving.

Chalmers called, "Wait a minute—" and then, "Miss Bates!"

Zeke turned round and looked at him, but Chalmers, having called, was waiting for her to appear. Zeke stood aside for her to come through the doorway. She was dressed precisely as Miss Beacham always had been but she was smaller than Miss Beacham, and she was alive.

Chalmers said: "Somebody was in here yesterday said something about a church somewhere. Do you remember?"

"No . . ." She tried to remember, but no longer than was required by the fact that Chalmers was her employer. "You were in Providence yesterday, Mr. Chalmers."

"Oh, that's true."

214

"No, I don't remember, Mr. Chalmers,"—and after a decent pause: "Mr. Peters is here."

"Who is?—Peters? Oh—well, tell him to come in. Peters, eh? I want to see him."

"Yes, sir."

"Good-by, Peele. Come in again."

Zeke said good-by, and went out.

When he had gone fifty feet up the street, he couldn't understand why he was so cheerful. He was, though! He felt exceedingly cheerful in his stomach. And yet never in his life—if you stopped to think about it—had he been through a more footless proceeding than that was. Go in there to sell Chalmers the sermon—change his mind about it . . . and come out again. Poor old Chalmers must have thought he was crazy; that is, if he thought about him at all. Chalmers had forgotten about him before he was out the door. He wondered whether Chalmers really had heard of a church. He might have—or he might not. You couldn't tell. He liked Chalmers, and admired him. Of course the real reason he hadn't been able to say that to Chalmers about the lecturing was that it would have seemed as though he were crawling on his hands and knees right down there beside the desk . . . and with Chalmers, a little puzzled and disgusted, peering down at him. It would always seem that way. So he didn't have *that* to worry about any more. But he did want something to eat!

He had seventeen cents in his pocket—he knew without counting—and out of it he was going to buy something to eat. After a pleasant moment of high, selective thought, the answer was revealed to him. What he must have was a good, crisp, fresh—from deep down in the barrel—dill pickle. There was a grocery store ahead, and he would turn in there, and from the very heart of that whole grocery store he'd pluck out the one thing that he wanted. Come to think of it, it was about the right time of the year for them, too.

He went straight home, when he had finished it, and going up the stairs he still felt cheerful. He was going to suggest to Viola that they do something—take a walk, maybe, or something like that. He hadn't been very cheerful lately, and now that he was, he'd like to do something for her out of it.

He said, "Viola?" as he opened the door.

She was standing in the center of the room; she'd been crying.

"What's the matter?" he said, and looked round the room but saw only that she'd been lying on the bed. She must have stood up, hearing him coming up the stairs.

He looked at her again, and thought that something new must have happened.

Viola said: "I'm sorry—I didn't think you'd be back so soon."

"Well, I'm—I'm glad I am. What's wrong?"

"Nothing. Did you have any luck with Chalmers?"

" 'Chalmers'?"—he'd forgotten he'd told her he was going. "No. Tell me: what's the matter?"

She didn't speak for a moment, but he was sure, while he was waiting, that she was going to tell him.

Her face was perfectly still. "We're going to have a baby."

Zeke didn't even try to think of something to say. He turned away and took a few steps across the room. Finally, he said a little thing, unimportant, that he could say— "You sure?"

"Perfectly. So is the doctor."

" 'Doctor'?" Zeke swung round. "You're—you're all right, aren't you?"

Viola'd sat down in her chair beside the table. "Yes, apparently." She looked up at him. "Does it matter much to you?"

"Does what?"

"This."

"Our having a baby?" Zeke said.

"Yes. Why—was there something else on your mind?"

"No. Of course it matters."

"So I see. I'm sorry you're angry. I was afraid you would be, but—well, there we are."

Zeke was up, walking round the room again. "This isn't much of a place for it," he said.

Viola shrugged her shoulders, and said: "Well—"

"When's it going to be?"

"March."

Zeke thought of March. "This place'll be worse in winter than it is in summer."

"Oh, you'll have something by then, Zeke."

"Maybe. I guess I'll have to. Sooner than that. You don't care what, do you?"

"Only for your sake."

"We've got to have something coming in—even to stay here."

"We don't owe anything."

"What's that got to do with it?"

"Well, if the worst came to the worst, we might borrow something."

Zeke turned slowly to look at her.

She held her ground. "Well . . . couldn't we?"

217

"From whom?"

"I don't know . . . I'm sure. But—well, people do, don't they?"

"Yes, they do. From whom?"

"Well . . ." Against an expression such as Zeke's face had taken on, it was difficult to say anything.

His lips were thin. "You haven't tried it so far, have you?" he accused her slowly.

"I don't know what you mean."

"I mean: have you tried to borrow money from your uncle—up till now?"

"I'm not trying to now."

"Have you?"

"No."

Zeke turned away then. He put his hand up over his eyes. "I'm sorry," he said. He dropped his hand. Raising his head, he shook it, and sniffed once at the same time. "Well—" he said, summing up, "not much use sitting round here. I guess I'd better go out and look for something."

He had to pass her in order to get to the door. He hesitated.

Viola, looking up at him, came near to smiling. "Good luck," she said.

Zeke grinned, ruefully. "Thanks." He picked up his hat from the corner of the table. Still with the same smile, he nodded to her. "Same to you." He put his hand on her shoulder as he passed. She was poorly—he couldn't help but feel it. It was up to him now, all right.

At the door, he again hesitated. "You'll be all right?"

"I think so."

There was a tremulousness in her voice that he tried not to hear.

When the door had shut, Viola cried for quite a while. She'd never felt so happy as this in her life.

Toward noontime, a letter came for Zeke. One of the Pisanelli children brought it to the door. It was one of the three or four older ones—she always had a feeling his name was Dominic, for some reason, and yet she knew it wasn't. He was very polite, smiled and handed the letter to her and bowed, and went away just quickly enough so as not to appear to be waiting for anything. The younger ones always stood and gaped at her.

The letter had been forwarded from the church office— which meant that it was not from someone he'd seen lately. It had been mailed from somewhere in Connecticut . . . she couldn't make out just where. Nor was there any seal marked in the wax. But it was plainly a letter that amounted to something. The handwriting looked that way. And the whole thing had a completeness about it.

She put it up on the shelf. When Zeke came home, not having found anything, she could give it to him the first thing. It would take care of those first few minutes that were the hardest.

He was late coming home—the time had passed six o'clock. From his step, she knew that today had been like the other days—except that this morning, when he had gone out, he had expected that he would find something.

She managed to be across the room with her back to the door when he came in. "There's a letter for you on the shelf there, Zeke." She turned toward him as she spoke. Zeke was reaching for the letter. He'd needed that; he hadn't been able to say that he'd failed again.

"Watling," he said, ripping it open.

It seemed to take him some time to read it. Viola

watched him . . . but she couldn't understand what his expression meant. There was not much light where he was standing, and she couldn't see him very clearly. But she could see enough to know that now was not just the time for her to suggest that he take the letter over by the window.

. . . it might be that it had bad news in it about his family, she hadn't thought of that. Still, even a man like Watling wouldn't have waited to mail it until he got down into Connecticut.

The skin over his cheeks twitched, and she could see his hand shake.

He'd finished reading it. His arm dropped to his side . . . and with his head up, and trying to control his face, he was walking stiffly into the other room.

"Church," he told her.

[Chapter 30]

MR. WATLING'S LETTER—soon worn soft and furry at the creases—stated merely that he had been talking with some people about a church at Halleck's Bridge, over in the northwestern part of Connecticut, and inasmuch as they seemed to be looking for someone, he'd suggested to them that they get in touch with Zeke. It was a small church, he said, ". . . smaller, I should think, than any we hit when you were with me. From what I gather, though, it's in pretty fair shape. They said they'd write to you, and I think they will."

There was no reason, of course, why the letter from

Halleck's Bridge shouldn't come in the next mail. Or it might not come for two or three days. It might even be a week. And when it should come, and he held the envelope in his hands, he would not know then but what inside it said . . . that they were not going to ask him to come out there, after all.

If Watling had said they'd write, they'd write. After four days he was down to reminding himself of that most of the time.

When it did come, it was instantly apparent, as he unfolded the letter and saw the face of it, that they were asking him to come out there and preach to them as a candidate.

He was soon reading the details. They were plain and accurate; they were the things that he wanted to know. September 26th or October 10th, they suggested—which meant, of course, that they had somebody lined up for the week in between. He would have to pay his own railway fare, both ways, but he would be under no expense after he got there. They would pay him five dollars for preaching, which was the same as they paid for a supply, and they wouldn't expect the sermon to run much over an hour.

They added that it was a small church, membership one hundred and sixty-two. From this he instinctively calculated an annual salary of four hundred to, say, four hundred and twenty dollars, half cash at best, plus his wood. The attendance, providing the twenty-sixth was a good day, would be in the neighborhood of seventy-five. Three-fifths women, two-fifths men, and throw in the children.

There was one more sentence. "There is no need to wear a gown unless you have a mind to."

In a few minutes, he had sat down to write his

sermon. He'd give the man who was going to be there on October 10th something to shoot at, anyway.

But Viola reminded him that he'd better write to them first and say that he was coming. So he did that instead.

And at the end of three weeks he had started that sermon at least once each day, and sometimes twice, and he had worked on it practically all the time—except one day when he took a walk and stopped in at the public library to look at a map. It was a bad minute—but Halleck's Bridge *was* there, even though obscured by the fact that the C in Connecticut covered most of the Halleck's. He'd also been into the railroad station two or three times, but, with some self-restraint, had contented himself with inquiries and timetables. There was no use putting out the money for his ticket ahead of time, because you never could tell what might come up. He had an idea, too, that Viola might like to go with him to buy the ticket.

In trying to produce a sermon, he had used, one after another, every approach he knew. Each one, as he began, promised strongly and hopefully. But always the promise was only to start with, and then it would thin out, and disappear. And finally there would be first the impulse and then the reasoned inclination to push aside what he had done and start fresh. And so the same thing all over again.

The time that remained was melting away, and he began to be frightened. He had been over every one of his old sermons to see whether there was any chance of reworking one of them, or if there might be parts of some of them that he could use. There was nothing. Generally they were embarrassing, and a good paragraph here and there had its roots too deep in the context for it to live if it were taken out.

He remembered one day Watling's old advice—about trying to make them forget themselves—and he tried to start from there. But he found it was lifeless, and he very soon gave it up. He'd been up that alley once. Once was enough.

Another time he sat thinking of what the congregation would be like, how they'd look—close in before him in the tiny church. He tried to think of what they'd be wanting in the way of a sermon, and of how he could give it to them. But he could not hold a fixed idea of them, nor even begin to satisfy them. And anyhow, they would not be, on Sunday morning, as he had seen them in the evenings of the weeks with Watling. What *did* they want? Well, fundamentally, of course they wanted to be told that they'd go to Heaven when they died. Unhappily he had no promises that he could hand out.

There were ten days left now.

What did he know?—really know, that is. What had he learned himself, beyond the possibility of its ever being taken from him, that he might preach on? He couldn't think of anything—that he could preach on. What *had* he learned? Well, he'd learned this much: he'd learned that if you didn't do the work you got fired . . . and if he didn't get this sermon written pretty quick, he wouldn't stand much chance even of getting a job to be fired from.

He picked out a text then—without benefit of revelation—and wrote a sermon.

It took him the best part of a week, and when he'd finished it, that was the principal feeling he had about it: that he'd finished it. It was too short, for one thing; it wouldn't preach over forty-five minutes. It would be an easy thing to piece it out, with illustration and restatement, but he thought he wouldn't do that. They could take it the way it was. It was a fair enough sermon. Sometimes he thought so, anyway. Sometimes he didn't. Well, it was all he had.

[Chapter 31]

ON THE TRAIN, he was surprised at the length of time it took to get clear of the city. They'd been going for some time now, and although these were farms, they were not real farms, not country. These were truck farms—gardens, more than farms. And yet they'd been traveling half an hour. He unbuttoned his coat, and dug in after his watch . . . which said flatly that it was exactly twelve minutes since the train had left the station. He put the watch back. At that rate, it was going to be a long day.

A drop of oil from the lamp overhead missed his knee by a few inches, and he hitched over, closer to the window. Soot he could brush off, but if he came home with an oilspot on his trousers, Viola would want to know whether he'd picked it up on the way there or coming home. She'd spent half the night on his clothes, mending in places that would never show anyway, and brushing terribly. More especially, his coat. Well, it was a good coat. It was as good a coat as there was anywhere in the car—and the tails of it he had carefully parted when he had sat down.

All day ahead of him . . . six hours unbroken to reach Pittsfield, and there get off and wait two hours and twenty minutes for the Housatonic train which would go south to Beemansville. It would be after six o'clock when he'd get to Beemansville—just about sundown. And then ten miles by stage over to Halleck's Bridge. It looked like ten miles on the map, but not much more than that. He guessed it was safe to figure fifty cents for the stage fare.

The important thing about this trip—sitting here in the train with his bag beside him and the country going by outside—the important thing about himself, here among these people, was that he was making this trip because he had to. He'd been sent for, and he was going. He was a preacher, and he was going out to Halleck's Bridge, in Connecticut, to preach as a candidate. He'd be preaching tomorrow morning. And with a slight motion, not at all noticeable—just a lowering of his right shoulder—he could feel his sermon safely in the inside pocket of his coat. His ticket, both ways, was in his waistcoat, and against his thigh he could feel the pressure of his purse whenever he thought about it. All day ahead of him . . .

The land was flat here, cleared long ago, and it didn't look as though it had ever been very rocky. Those must be celery ditches, way over. It was a long time since he'd had breakfast. Viola had put him up a lunch, but he knew what was in it, so there was no excuse to look. He'd figured to put off eating until after he'd left Springfield. That would be one o'clock.

The natural thing to think about, given this time to think, was what the people would be like where he was going—the man in whose house he'd stay tonight, and the people tomorrow. But he'd thought about that a good deal, and always arrived at the same picture—which was certain to be wrong when he got there. The temptation, stronger now, was to skip over the crisis and to think about what things would be like after he'd got the job. Not even 'if'— after. There was something about the joggling and swaying of the train, or the country sliding past outside, or the general unreality of things—or unaccustomedness, rather, thank Heaven, it was all real!—which induced to forgetfulness that it *was* a temptation. He could slide so easily into thinking that things would be thus and so *after* they'd called him. And forget the 'if.' At that, daydreaming was all right if you recognized it as daydreaming and if it didn't interfere with your work. Right now, there was nothing whatsoever that he even ought to be doing. There was no use going over the sermon—he knew the sound of every word in it. Except there was that one place . . . and he got it out of his pocket, and found the place, and looked at it—and it looked all right, and it sounded better than he had thought it did. He raised his head, and with the sermon still on his knee, he turned toward the window and said the part over again, once or twice. No, it sounded all right—he couldn't see any way to improve it. . . . Man out there plowing—it was early for that. And now nothing but woods. . . . When he got home, he'd say to Viola, 'Yes, it seemed to go all right. You can't tell, though. All we can do now is wait till we hear from them.'

And later on they'd get the letter.

And still later—when she was getting things ready—he'd say to her: 'I think you'll like the parsonage. I only saw it from the outside, of course. But it looked all right. It's a white house, set close to the road.'

At Springfield, when he got out to walk up and down, it was a fine day, and sunny, and the wind still out of the west. The brakeman told him they'd probably be there twenty minutes to half an hour. So he decided he'd eat his dinner out of doors. He went back into the train and got the parcel and brought it out with him, and he drew himself up onto a baggage truck and set the parcel beside him. Viola had put him up a good lunch. He was thinking, as he bit through the meat, that there was a chance it might be another good day tomorrow.

Funny thing—it was a lunch till you got round to eating it, and from then on it was your dinner. Except to a man like Cameron maybe, who probably ate his dinner at night and who saw all language only as a plain, dull surface without any background or mystery.

He'd like some water now, but he didn't know where he'd get any. He guessed he'd let the tea do him.

The waiting time at Pittsfield was heavy and impenetrable when he tackled it, and the things near by that he could see became too soon familiar.

There was a train of two cars over on another track, and he wondered if that was the one. After a while he'd ask, if someone came by. The sky was beginning to get white now, and a weathervane on top of a feed store showed the wind was working round into the north. If it kept on into the northeast, it would rain. Well, the regulars would be in church, anyway. And in a small church, they were the ones who counted.

The two cars were his train, and when he got into it, he was affronted. It was old and dirty, and it smelled. The other one had smelled, too, but as a train should. This was different. And instead of four lamps overhead, there were only two. He put his bag up in the rack this time, and before he sat down he had a look into the seams of the upholstery. He couldn't see anything moving, but he wasn't sure, even then, because the light wasn't good. It was an hour and ten minutes to Beemansville.

They got there, right on the dot.

He was the only passenger out on the platform as they slowed down, and before the train had stopped, he'd seen what was certainly the Halleck's Bridge stage waiting backed up to the platform.

He stepped smartly across the platform toward the stage. The door at the back hung open, but there was no one inside, and he went round front, thinking that the driver was no doubt prudently at the horses' heads. But the horses, an overworked team of bays, one of them bigger than the other, stood with their heads down and the hitch-rope hanging slack to an old sash-weight lying in the road. Zeke went back and stepped up onto the platform again. Up ahead by the engine, there were a dozen or so men, and a few boys. He waited, where he was. As the train pulled out, he had an eye on the two bays, but the driver, wherever he was, was justified in his absence: neither of them batted an ear.

A man came along the platform—small, thin-faced, and with a straight-sided, black cap. He nodded to Zeke—as he would have done to any stranger—and said, "How'd do."

Zeke answered in kind.

The man stopped now. "You goin' t' the Bridge?"

"Hope to," Zeke said, offering no more than he received.

The man nodded very slightly. "You be the Reverend?"

"I am."

"Well, guess we might's well go, then." He set off around the station, and Zeke followed, carrying his bag.

They'd sent for him!—which raised his spirits unbelievably—and he was in fifty cents.

Coming round the corner of the building, he saw that he'd been on the wrong side. Here were half a dozen vehicles—and at the end of the row, a little removed, a big, ugly, hammer-headed gray, hitched into a light buckboard. There was a small boy holding him, coming off the ground every time the gray raised his head, and cursing manfully. Zeke's man headed for the buckboard. He came up on the near side, and the boy, seeing him, shut his lips.

The man turned half round and held out his hand for Zeke's bag. Zeke gave it to him, and he swung it neatly in, in front of the seat, and pushed it across to his own side. He climbed in, took up the reins, said, "You! Get over!" to the horse, and when that had been accomplished, indicated to Zeke that it was his turn to come aboard.

Zeke got in, the boy was flung clear, and with the lines tight and straight, they shot out of the yard and curved nicely into the road.

Zeke didn't say a word all through the village, but he would have given his eyeteeth to change places with the little man at his right, to have had those reins in his hands.

There was a long hill outside the village, and the gray showed signs of settling down to work.

The man spoke to Zeke. "Pleased to meet you," he said. "My name is Meeker."

Zeke said: "Pleased to meet you. Peele is my name."

"They told me. Boston, you come from."

Zeke wasn't certain whether he meant his birthplace or the start of his journey. "Yes," he said.

"Quite a place."

Zeke said it was.

Mr. Meeker said that he had a nephew resident in Boston, named Roberts. But even when Mr. Meeker added hopefully that his nephew worked for a leather concern, Zeke was unable to recall meeting him. He was aware that this was a revealing shortcoming on his part, but Mr. Meeker was kind enough not to comment.

There was no further conversation until they reached

229

the top of the hill—and saw an even longer hill ahead. Zeke, speaking of the horse, said: "He can go."

"He can go," Mr. Meeker acknowledged. "He can eat, too, the—well, he can eat."

Zeke was used to that, long ago. It no longer made him feel shut out.

"You tell *me*, now," said Mr. Meeker easily, "how old is he?"

Sixteen, Zeke thought, if he's a day. "Am I buying or selling?"

"You're telling me how old he is," Mr. Meeker said positively.

"You own him?"

"I ain't stole him."

"Eight."

Mr. Meeker's delight was concealed with the greatest difficulty. "Eighteen hundred and forty-nine, that horse was foaled," he announced, "on the seventeenth day of April."

Twelve years? He was nearer twenty.

"Eleven years," Mr. Meeker reckoned it, "and I ought to know, because I was there myself."

"Gracious! You weren't alone, I hope?"

"All alone, sir!"

"Too bad," Zeke said. "You should have had witnesses."

Mr. Meeker turned slowly to look at him—and again faced forward. "You said Boston," he reproached him.

Zeke decided it was better not to explain. "Mr. Meeker—"

"Reverend."

"I don't suppose you'd want to let me drive him, would you? It's a long time since I drove a horse."

Mr. Meeker pulled up without a word, handed the reins

to Zeke, and jumped down. Zeke moved over. Mr. Meeker came round and climbed in on the other side. For fifteen minutes Zeke was perfectly happy.

Then he realized that Mr. Meeker was trying to convey to him, discreetly, that Mr. Meeker was uneasy. So he pulled up—to the gray's distaste—and handed over the reins. "Thanks," he said, and, as Mr. Meeker had done, climbed down, went round, and climbed in.

They started up.

"I didn't want to say anything," Mr. Meeker remarked earnestly, "but I didn't know if you'd know—you being a stranger."

Zeke didn't know.

"Now, me," said Mr. Meeker, "I'd understand. But there's some of them—you know how it is—Saturday night and more p'tic'ly your being a preacher—well, they wouldn't like it. Seeing you driving. Don't matter with me so much, because I don't go to church. Say! You didn't get your supper, did you?"

"Oh, yes, I ate."

"You ate on the steam cars?"

"I had a lunch."

"That ain't anything! Here—" Mr. Meeker fished blindly under the seat, and came up with a paper bag. "They're good any time."

There were doughnuts in it—cold, shrunken with time, and hard. Zeke bit a chunk out of one and settled back.

"Now you take breakfast—" Mr. Meeker was saying. "There's some likes to fry up a steak. Some like ham. Pie is good. All them things is good. But the trouble with them things is they digest on you. But you take doughnuts now— plenty of doughnuts!—and you eat *them* for breakfast—

231

and you can feel 'em settin' there and a-nourishin' ye and a nourishin' ye . . . all—day—long."

Zeke said, yes, that was right. He leaned back and looked up at the sky. It was dark in the east now, and the hills showed black. The wind had gone down with the sun. He could feel the quietness that was beyond the reach of the noise of the buckboard.

Mr. Meeker didn't encourage reverie. Slow off the mark, conversationally, he more than made up for it in the stretch. Coming down the hill into the Bridge, he was disposing of as many as three and four topics between thank-you-ma'ams.

Zeke interrupted two or three times in an attempt to find out what the 'Eliot White'—on whom he was to be quartered—might be like. Correspondence had disclosed merely the fact that he was senior deacon. As a personal description, it left a good deal to the imagination.

But he couldn't get anything out of Meeker, either. White, Mr. Meeker said, was a fine man—and he cited an incident of a generation ago which seemed partially—and not favorably—to illuminate the character of Mr. White's younger brother, Luke White.

Zeke asked Mr. Meeker if Mr. Eliot White were a farmer. And Mr. Meeker said, well, yes, he supposed he was, in a way, if you could call anybody a farmer nowadays, the way the things were around here. Now take turnips, for instance: he didn't suppose he'd seen a turnip in the last ten years that was what you could really call a turnip.

Mr. White have a family? Oh, sure, said Mr. Meeker, he had a family, all right. But what did that amount to? A man raised up a family, and the first thing he knew they all went away on him. And no sooner were *they* out of the house, than his relations begun to move in. And just about an even thing who'd get there first—them or his wife's.

They came up a short rise—and there was the street before them: the houses lighted and close together, the street wide, and tops of the elms high and indistinct in the darkness.

Mr. Meeker swung to the right and pulled up at the gate in a low, white fence.

"This is it," he said, and turning to Zeke: "That'll be fifty cents—if it's agreeable to you."

Zeke said, yes, that was all right. How much was it on the stage?

"Same thing," said Mr. Meeker, "fifty cents."

Zeke got down into the street, paid him, and Mr. Meeker handed him out his bag.

Mr. Meeker said: "Good night, Reverend. Enjoyed your company."

"Good night, Mr. Meeker. May see you again."

"Maybe," said Mr. Meeker, "—can't tell"—and the buckboard pulled out suddenly from between Zeke and the gate.

Zeke, faced toward the house, said, "Well—here we go"—and went in through the gate.

While he was closing the gate behind him, the front door opened, and a man—square and heavy-set in the light—said pleasantly, "Good evening, Reverend . . ."

"Good evening, sir."

Zeke shifted his bag to his left hand as the man came down the step and forward to meet him.

"Well, I see you got here."

"Oh, yes. You're Mr. White?"

"Yes. How do you do?" They shook hands. Zeke liked his voice, and he liked the feel of his hand—hard and cool,

233

as an older man's is apt to be. As they went side by side toward the door, Zeke could make out that Mr. White had a short beard and seemed to be solidly well dressed.

"You didn't come over by stage," White said.

"No," Zeke told him, "Mr. Meeker saw me first. We made a quick trip, though."

"How much?" inquired Mr. White.

"Fifty cents."

"Oh. Same as the stage. It varies, reason I asked. Jamie . . . come get the Reverend's bag."

A small boy sidled shyly through the door and held out his hand gingerly for the bag.

"This is Mr. Peele," White said, and still looking at the boy, he said to Zeke: "My grandson."

Zeke said: "How do you do?"

Speech, however, was not within Jamie's reach at the moment and to his relief he was handed the bag. He stood aside for them to go in.

As Zeke moved in front of Mr. White to go in the door, his concern for the impression he was making, himself, dropped away—for an instant—and he was free for an awareness of the new elements surrounding him. His nostrils spread, his eyes took in all that he could see, and his step was careful. He did not know that this was so, but for the rest of his life if he were ever to meet again the same odor that there was then and there in the narrow hallway of Deacon White's home in Halleck's Bridge, he would see again that hallway. It might be that he would see it suddenly sometime, and not know why—but that would be the reason. He would see the wide, black-painted floor boards, ridged here and there, and slippery under the oval rug with a wrinkle in it. He would see the half-circle of mahogany table against the wall, thin-legged and dan-

234

gerous, with a cream-colored china ornament on it. The hall was wider where he stood, with a door at his left, and at his left in front of him the stairs went up. There was the thick and gilded frame, more than a yard high and leaning outward, which would have in it always, whether he saw it now or not, a dark engraving of a battle. And the odor, the smell, that would make him see these things again was specific and unique. It would continue to be there, of course, right along. But coming in from outdoors, he was eligible to appreciate it. It was clean and sharp, but softer than sandalwood, and it was to be smelled not so much in the nose as in the lower reaches of the throat. It was pure—one odor—for all that it was made up of wool and wood-smoke, and a thousand contributions from all over the house and from the kitchen. There was not quite too much of it, and he had scant time to think of it now. He would not recollect it until he should be reminded of it.

White said: "Let me take your hat"—and Zeke gave it to him—"and come in." White hung up the hat, alone, on a peg of the rack against the wall. The family's things, Zeke guessed, were elsewhere.

"Or perhaps"—and in White's face, turned pleasantly to Zeke, there was absolute considerateness—"you'd rather go and wash up. You've had a long trip."

Zeke spread his hands instinctively and glanced at them. "I guess perhaps I'd better."

"Surely."

The door Zeke had noticed was to the spare room, and Deacon White came back to it and opened it. The lamp inside was already lighted and turned down. Jamie, hanging onto the bag, was waiting by the front door for orders. "Take it in, Jamie," White told him.

Zeke remembered, and suddenly, "Well, I don't know—" he said hesitantly, "that train—"

"We always do," White assured him, and taking the bag from Jamie held it before him and examined it, turning it over. "No—not one," he reported, "it's all right—" and passed it over to Zeke. "We'll be in the sitting room. Come on, Jamie." He collared him, and closed the door.

Zeke turned up the lamp, looked round the room, saw that the curtains were drawn, and with an enjoyable furtiveness went over and tested the bed, pressing it down once or twice with his hand. It was a superb bed!—if he could sleep anywhere tonight. He took off his coat, opened his bag, and got out a pair of clean cuffs. Crossing the room to the washstand, he tried to put out of his mind the rhythmic 'I-want-this-job,' that kept beating there, over and over. He wondered who'd be in the sitting room. Mrs. White, probably, whom the chances were he was going to like, and maybe four or five others. Well, the others he'd have to take as he found them.

Lifting the full, heavy pitcher from the bowl, he carefully poured in the first water—thinking that White was someone he could count on, and with a quick grin at his own failure to guess even close to any picture of what White had turned out to be. He'd thought of him, for no reason, as being thin and tall.

With his sleeves turned up, he thrust his hands slowly, backs up, down into the water. . . . It was warm—it was hot, almost! And it sent some kind of feeling up his arms, and down the backs of his legs. His eyes half closed, and he stood there a moment, and his lower lip turned in as he bit down on it.

236

He had one look round the sitting room before they saw him. Mrs. White, yes—another woman, a young man—and some children. White saw him, and stood up. . . . Zeke was presented.

Mrs. White was an ample woman with good wrinkles at her eyes, and she was reasonably glad to see him. The other woman—not so glad. "My sister-in-law," White said, "Miss Donaldson." And the young man—to whom something had happened lately from which he hadn't yet recovered—was White's son. He spoke to Zeke automatically—but doing the best he could. The children—Jamie and two girls, one older than the other—were young White's children. The girls curtsied, after their training, and Zeke, seeing out of the corner of his eye young White turn away, knew that the man's wife—whom young White had watched teaching them to curtsy—had died recently.

White said, "Sit here, Mr. Peele," and moved a square armchair for him.

Zeke sat down. When he leaned back, the back of the chair wasn't where it should have been, and his hands clutched convulsively at the arms of the chair. He eased back then, and felt the reassuring firmness against his shoulder blades. Involuntarily, he glanced over his shoulder and caught a glimpse of the upper corner of the chair back.

The old gentleman had seen, and was enjoying the fact that he understood. "It's the seats on the cars," he explained. "The backs are perpendicular. As soon as you try to lean back in something else you feel as though you were falling backwards."

"It is that way, isn't it?" Zeke said, and laughed—and everyone else laughed, except young White who, Zeke saw, was trying to, and would have liked to say something.

Jamie brightened suddenly and said: "I been on the cars." And his older sister said: "Jamie, you hush!"

Mrs. White inquired calmly: "Papa, did you ask Mr. Peele if he'd had his supper?"

"Oh, yes, I had." Zeke said hurriedly, "I did have. Thank you."

"Meeker bring you over?" she asked.

"Yes—Mr. Meeker and the gray. We had quite a ride." He was surprised, having had a vision of all of them sitting round watching him eat, to have turned the invitation so easily.

"I expect he tried his doughnuts on you." She looked at him suspiciously. "*That* wasn't what you had for supper . . ."

"Well, they were—they were dessert."

Mrs. White was preparing to get up. "I thought likely," she said. "You haven't had a thing. Now just you wait a minute—"

Zeke said desperately that he'd had his supper at Pittsfield, that he really couldn't eat if he tried; he pleaded with her, and finally he had her quieted, though not convinced. She retreated to a minimum of a glass of milk and some cookies, and seemed determined not to yield further.

"Maybe he doesn't want to eat," said her husband.

Mrs. White turned on him. "A minister?" she said, and settled back, ruffled but satisfied.

"Grandma, it's eight o'clock—" the older of the two girls speaking with the loftiest indifference but keeping an eye on Jamie.

It was a form of treason that Jamie had become inured to. He pretended not to have heard her.

"Eight o'clock?" said Mrs. White.

"Yes, grandma"—piously, from the girl.

"Jamie," said his grandmother, "eight o'clock."

Jamie stirred.

"You know what we said," she reminded him.

"You said I could stay up to see what he looked like."

His older sister said: "Well, you've seen, haven't you?" And his younger sister said: "You even brought in his bag!"

Miss Donaldson said helpfully: "Come, Jamie. I'll go up with you."

Jamie ignored the offer. He had one shot left in his locker, but he fired it hopelessly. "Pa ain't said I had to."

'Pa,' Zeke saw, was working his hands nervously. "Well, I—"

"Jamie." That was Grandpa—and Jamie never even looked in his direction. He went dutifully to his grandmother and said good night. Then to his grandfather—and to his father, who said, "Good night, son," and kissed him. The boy came over to Zeke and stood squarely in front of him. "Good night, Mr. Peele."

Zeke said, "Good night, Jamie," and after Jamie had examined Mr. Peele's face with a mild interest, he ran from the room.

Zeke said to young White, "How old is he?" and was not sure he had been heard.

Then White said: "Eight."

"Not till the tenth of October," put in the older girl.

"What of it?"—from the stairs.

"Go to bed," his grandfather called—and they could hear him do the rest of the stairs and go down the hall.

There was a general air of settling back after a crisis, but no one said anything.

Young White rose suddenly, said that he had to go up the street, and left. Zeke stood up too as he went out, but White paid no attention to him.

239

When Zeke had sat down again, the old gentleman said thoughtfully: "Tell me, Mr. Peele, how do you find sentiment in Boston?—politically, I mean. Things seem to you to be about the same?"

Zeke welcomed it. He had never had occasion to look very closely at more than one phase of political sentiment in Boston, but since June no one had read the papers more thoroughly than he had . . . or at any rate more completely. He found, as he talked, that he was far better posted than he had realized. And with a name or two here and there—resurrected from chance introductions of last winter—he gave a good and intimate account. He had done little talking for the last three months, but he talked now—and well.

Mr. White had access to the same newspapers that Zeke had. They got along very well.

The two little girls stuck it out for about forty minutes, and Miss Donaldson went when they did.

The clock struck ten during a pause. Mrs. White, who had not spoken for some time, said, well, *she* was going to bed. "You men can stay up and talk if you want to. Good night, Mr. Peele."

White said he guessed they'd better all go; Mr. Peele had had a long trip.

[Chapter 32]

ZEKE HAD BEEN IN BED an hour. He'd been over most of the things he'd said during the evening to Deacon White, and he'd preached a good many random selections from

240

tomorrow's sermon, some of them several times. He'd re-hearsed his train journey, he'd conversed with Mr. Meeker, and he'd done some driving. It had been a long day—and it gave promise of being an even longer night. He'd won-dered a few times about young White—whether that were really the matter with him, that his wife had died—and he'd felt sharply sorry for him. He'd wondered if he him-self would be as tragic-looking as that if Viola died. He thought very likely he would be. More so, probably. And then quite consciously as an antidote, he thought about Jamie. He liked Jamie. Although he'd never been quite as young as that himself, and Jamie had light hair.

. . . he wakened, gratified to discover that he'd been asleep, worried for a while about the sermon . . . and was asleep again.

Sometime during the night he heard a man say, "Yes, father," and realized that just before it he'd heard the words, "All right, son," . . . but quiet and kindly, and no responsibility of his, and he let himself confidently back into sleep.

There was a great noise of a cow wanting to be milked that wakened him in the morning, but he kept his eyes shut, and before he'd opened them he had it figured out and knew where he was. It was light in the room, but not yet sunup, and rather than give in and reach for his watch, he tried to go back to sleep. He'd almost make it—and then the cow would let loose again. She seemed to be just outside his window. It would be an abiding pleasure, all his life, if he could have the privilege of shooting her. They had noises in Boston, but no cows.

When he looked at his watch, it showed twelve minutes past six. He tried to imagine what the street would be when he saw it by daylight . . . and whether you could see the church from the house.

Pretty soon he got up.

It was a fine, bright morning. He went to the window that was at the side of the house to see the cow. She was not directly under the window—she was not in the yard—but there was *a* cow, so far away as to make it impossible that she could be *the* cow, standing sidewise to the fence two hundred yards down off in the distance. She seemed peculiarly small and inoffensive. The sky was blue and fresh—but you couldn't tell what it would do in the next hour. The next door neighbors' house, partly hidden by evergreens, was brown and rather run down. It must be their cow.

Barefoot, he crossed the floor—cold between rugs—to the other window, and at the side drew the curtain enough to see out toward the street. The white fence was there, low, and the gate, but nearer the house than he had thought, and the elms that he had seen last night were now distinctly just plain elms. Over across the street was a white house which looked to be smaller than this one he was in. And next to it a brick house, with green trim, hard and high and narrow. Down the street he could make out two more houses, and because of the angle, no more than the out-buildings of the third. No church.

The land appeared to drop away back of the houses, and beyond was a steep hill, too steep ever to have warranted trying to clear it. The sun had come no more than halfway down it. He was looking west. An odd maple here and there had turned—well up the hill where it was dry. Down there in the hollow there must be a stream of some sort—probably the river that the 'Bridge' was for.

He turned back into the room, and because of a sudden

surge of excitement, decided to get dressed to allay it. He'd have to shave with cold water, though—and that being a further abnormality wouldn't help to put down the excitement any.

Someone was moving round upstairs now, which was a relief. He tried not to hurry—but he cut himself because of the cold water, and for a dread minute thought he was going to have a time of it to make it stop bleeding.

He was dressed, finally. After a short debate with himself, he realized that he couldn't stay in the room any longer. It was nearly seven o'clock, after all, and certainly he wouldn't wake anyone up. He approached the door . . . but then decided he'd better not. They might think it was odd if they saw him wandering around out in the yard before breakfast. He might try reading his Bible . . . and decided against that. He wasn't just in the mood for reading the Bible. He didn't seem to be in any specific mood that he could account for. One minute he'd be enjoying the idea of breakfast—and the next minute he'd realize that he wasn't hungry. He walked up and down, the palms of his hands cold and sweaty. He wished Jamie would come in and talk to him. He'd like to talk to Jamie—nothing on Jamie's mind!

And phrase after phrase of the sermon appearing on the inside of his forehead and demanding to be spoken.

Eight minutes past seven. Not getting along very fast. Almost three and a half hours to churchtime. All right, what of it! He was Zeke Peele, wasn't he? And he was a preacher. He'd preach to them!—any time.

A noise at the door—startled, he stood perfectly still, listening . . . then a knock.

Zeke swallowed, dry, and he said: ". . . Yes?"

"Mr. White told me to tell you it was time to get up and

243

I brought you some hot water and I'll set it down outside the door here and you can come get it."

He'd never heard the voice before—must be the hired girl.

"Thank you."

"Oh, that's all right. Glad to do it. He said it was to shave with."

"Yes—thank you . . . very much."

"You're welcome, I'm sure. Good-by."

When he was certain that it was safe, he opened the door no wider than was necessary, hurriedly drew in the pitcher, shut the door, and with his back to it stood there holding the pitcher. No one had seen him. Rather pleased at having thought of it: he went over and poured most of the hot water into the slop jar. There was just about room for it. They'd never know the difference.

Twenty minutes later, which seemed liberal enough, he was none the less the first one into the sitting room. Miss Donaldson followed, suddenly and silently, but Zeke was impeccably examining the view from the window, and for some time they took turns in enlarging on each other's comments on the weather. The younger daughter came next, and handily defeated all efforts to make her talk. Then White, his beard shining in readiness for church, and his trousers and shoes contrasting noticeably with his worn and comfortable coat—which he would put off in favor of the proper one when it was time to leave the house. Zeke felt that White had slept well and that he liked Sunday. It made Zeke feel more apart from them. Mrs. White arrived—amazingly serene—and Miss Donaldson volunteered to go on a hunt for Jamie. White showed Zeke various things that could be seen from the window, and Zeke found it impossible to be interested in any of them. His voice, as he exclaimed politely over each one, was not quite his own.

Jamie was brought in dirty, and his older sister—now some minutes late and having nicely timed her arrival so that it would be covered by Jamie's—was discovered to be in the room. White told the younger girl to speak to Hattie . . . and as soon as Hattie had come in very fresh from the kitchen, they were ready for prayers.

They stood in a row, with Hattie on one end of the row gazing across the room in cheerful satisfaction of her curiosity as to every detail of the Reverend's appearance. Jamie was prudently placed between his grandmother and Miss Donaldson. Then Zeke, and then the two little girls.

White stood facing them, opening his Bible to the place marked in it where he had finished last week.

No one had mentioned young White, and no one was going to.

"Where's Pa?" Jamie asked.

Miss Donaldson said: "He didn't get up yet, because he's not feeling well."

"Is he sick again?"

"He has a headache," Miss Donaldson told him. "He'll be here later on."

White waited quietly and apparently unmoved until this was finished. While he was waiting, Zeke realized that young White had come home drunk last night, and that the two voices heard in the night had been those of the old gentleman and his son.

"Second Chronicles, thirty-one," White read without looking up. Zeke tried to think whether there was anything in the chapter which would be unfortunate under the circumstances—because he was sure White would go right ahead, anyway—but he didn't think there was.

White finished the last verse. "May God bless to us the reading of His word. Mr. Peele, I'll ask you to say a prayer."

Zeke, in his place, offered a short prayer, and they joined him in the Lord's Prayer.

He looked up to see White smiling on his family.

"Well," said the old gentleman, "let's have some breakfast" . . . and Jamie had shot into the dining room like a young cat rushing a tree.

With his breakfast in front of him, Zeke's attitude toward it became unwavering: he didn't want any. Still, that had nothing to do with his having to eat it. And so he ate—each mouthful jamming up against the one before and pushing it on down. There had been a time, he could remember, when he had liked sausage . . . but it was only by the purest and most detached of reasoning that he was able to argue that that time would ever come again. As for fried hominy, the outlook was dark clear to the outermost reaches of time. Happily, the Whites were not of Mr. Meeker's persuasion as to doughnuts—and as he screwed his napkin into the ring, his heart, although compressed, had left in it a little thankfulness.

An hour and forty minutes stood between him and the church.

Jamie, scrubbed, polished, buttoned, inspected, and financed, was sent off to Sunday school, lagging a few paces behind his sisters.

When there was half an hour remaining, Zeke retired to his room. Now was the time for prayer . . . but he couldn't come at it. He stood looking out the window, seeing each unimportant detail of the landscape with arresting clearness, but unable to think. He could only feel. And not even that with his body, which had gone back on him and in any motion he asked of it was unreliable. But with his mind he could feel: that this business was up to him . . . sink or swim, however it came out. God—looking upon him at this moment—certainly knew him well enough by now to realize that this attitude was no violation of humility. Help—yes, he stood in need of it. Never a man more. And for any that was vouchsafed to him, he would be grateful. But this was his job to do—and it lay not far ahead of him. In a few minutes he would be permitted to walk toward it . . . and when he had come up with it, he would—before God, he would do the best he could. He asked for help then, suddenly and without words.

The bell—two strokes . . . the bell had started—and with a grim smile he turned away from the window.

He picked up a hairbrush from the bureau, and he slung it across the room at the pillow on the bed. It was a sizable mark, and he expected, as he threw, to hit it. He did—fairly near the center. And he left it there and started for the door. He was glad he'd had sense enough to pick out a good-sized target. If he'd missed, he'd have had to look for another omen.

Miss Donaldson was in the sitting room—every stitch and wrinkle of her as 'ready for church' as if she had been a symbol.

Zeke said: "Well, Miss Donaldson, I guess we're the only ones ready, eh?" It seemed to please her for some reason, and for a rapid ten minutes he entertained Miss Donaldson, and Miss Donaldson entertained him. They were almost cronies when White came in, and Miss Donaldson became a dependent relative. Mrs. White from the front hall said, "Well, *I'm* ready," and White said, "Good for you, mother."

. . . and they had started toward it.

Just past the end of the fence—Miss Donaldson and Mrs. White being the front rank, and Zeke and Mr. White walking behind them—Zeke's left hand insistently felt empty. He looked at it, and then said, "Oh! I've come off without my Bible . . . you go ahead, I'll catch up to you,"—and before Mrs. White and Miss Donaldson should turn round and have to be explained to, he was loping back to the house. He'd have liked to put his hand on the gatepost and clear the gate—but they were probably watching him, and he slowed down to a walk. He went up the step soberly, with his head down, and in the door.

Young White had come two-thirds of the way down the stairs. Zeke saw everything about him, and young White knew that he saw. White said with composure but with no expression: "I'm sorry. I thought you'd gone."

"I had. I came back for my Bible." There was no chance for anything but impulse, and before his sympathy for the man should get the better of him, he turned away, saw before him the door to his room, and had gone into the room after his Bible. He picked it up and came out again. White was still there—same place on the stairs. The things that had seemed tragic about him now seemed commonplace—and then, because of that, more tragic.

Zeke said: "Well—I'll see you later."

"I guess so."

And he came out and shut the door. Compared to young White, he was so well off that young White had every reason to be scornful of him. And he probably was, too.

He came up with the others, who were waiting for him.

"Find it all right?" White asked amusedly.

248

"All safe!"—and he exhibited it.

"Good!"

Zeke apologized to the ladies, and the march was resumed.

He was afraid White might be going to ask him about the sermon. "I meant to speak of it before," Zeke said. "I suppose I should have written to you about hymns. Not that it really matters of course, but . . . oh, well, I guess it'll be all right."

White said, yes, he thought it would be. "Unless there was something special you wanted . . . ?"

"Mmmno, I don't know that there is."

"Well, if there is, just speak to the choir about it before service. You'd better make sure that they know it, though. We have as willing a choir as I've ever heard."

"Well, I'd thought that if it was all right we might wind up with *O Come, All Ye Faithful.* Do you think that would be all right?"

"*I* like it. Say, mother—"

"Yes?"

"I see Jason's fixed that post of his."

"So I saw. You don't expect me to settle with you today, do you?"

"Oh, no. I just wanted you to see it."

"Thank you. I saw it."

Deacon White explained to the Reverend Mr. Peele: ". . . that hitching post back there on the other side. Jason Embler's a particular friend of mine, but Mrs. White thinks he's a little shiftless sometimes."

Looking past the back of the Deacon's head, Zeke made out the post—braced upright—in front of a dingy little house.

"I told her he'd have it fixed by the first of October."

249

"When was it broken?"

"Oh—a little while ago."

"Last May," Mrs. White said over her shoulder.

Zeke wondered what they'd bet.

"That's the church ahead there," White said, nodding. The store, this side of it, had hidden it before—the store being closer to the road.

It was tiny. It was a dwarf church. It was a shock, it was so small. And there was no steeple—just a cupola. But the elms in front of it were huge, partly the reason it looked small—and the store, spread out and in the foreground, distorted the perspective. They kept it painted, all right!—it gleamed.

"I like it," Zeke said.

"We're going to put a steeple on someday, if we ever get the money."

Zeke was still looking at the church.

White was saying something about they could do it now, if they wanted to put a mortgage on, too, but he wasn't in favor of it.

Zeke was seeing the church with the steeple. "It looks a little like the church we used to have at home."

"Burn down?"

"Oh, no. It's still there. . . ."

"New Hampshire, didn't you say?—southern New Hampshire?"

Zeke, not certain how long the pause had been, turned to him and said: "What?—I'm sorry, I—"

"You said your people came from southern New Hampshire, didn't you?" the old gentleman said kindly.

'Southern New Hampshire'?—yes, of course. "New Boston," Zeke said.

They talked about that until they were there—and they

were there very soon. As they came up into the yard, the people standing talking in front of the church looked at Zeke—and then politely left their curiosity not quite satisfied as they turned their heads back to conversation.

"I'll be with you in a minute, mother," White said; and to Zeke: "I'll take you round to the back door."

Zeke bowed to Mrs. White and Miss Donaldson, and White led him at a nice distance past the groups in the yard. "You can meet any of them after church," White said.

Zeke said, yes, he'd like to.

At the door, White handed him a slip of paper. "I noted down the Order of Worship for you. That Responsive Reading I've noted there is the one that comes next in the book—after last week's, I mean. I thought you'd rather have your own choice of a Scripture Lesson. The hymns are posted up inside, and I'll speak to them about the last one—*O Come, All Ye Faithful*, you said."

Zeke was staring at the piece of paper in his hand: he was going to have to handle the service alone. He ought to have realized this before—but he hadn't. White's handwriting was clear.

White said, "I'll hand the notices up to you when it comes time."

"Yes . . . thank you." He'd got to take the service alone. Anything that he did differently from what they were accustomed would be charged against him. He was in a nightmare now, staring at this piece of white paper in his hand. Why had he come here? Why had he let them play this trick on him?

White had wished him well and left him.

He stopped staring at the writing on the piece of paper, and looked up at the whitewashed door in front of him.

Automatically he took hold of the doorknob and went in.

It wasn't a room precisely—just a thin slice partitioned off for use as a storeroom. It ran the full width of the church, but was no more than four feet thick. There were some broken chairs at one end of it, and on the floor some careening piles of old hymnbooks. And a big box half full of old clothes. The leg of a pair of boy's trousers hung down over the edge. It had been patched and repatched and worn through again at the knee. Zeke stared at it as dully as he had at the other things—and then he recognized it: These were clothes they couldn't even send in a missionary box. It made him feel comfortable and at home.

He looked up and down the opposite wall for the door into the church—there, over on the left. And up beside it a board with pegs on it—obviously for hats, because there was a hat there. He took off his own as he crossed over, and hung it up beside the other one. That hat had been there a long time. It was dusty on top and not underneath. It must have belonged to the man who'd had the church before.

He felt friendly toward the man—and he shrugged his coat straight and went into the church.

The door opened level onto the platform—and there was his chair, high-backed and armed, and a preaching lectern in front of it and to one side. There was a stand beside the chair with the necessary books. He avoided looking at the congregation until after he had taken his place, and until after he had bowed his head for a moment, presumably in prayer. And even then, no more than a glance—as he reached for the thin book that would have the Responsive Readings in it.

But he'd seen a good deal—there were about fifty seated, and every blessed one of them—including White and Mrs.

White and Miss Donaldson, thank you—just as stiff as a ramrod. Not hostile, not tense. But in church. At the Twelfth, no matter at what stage of the service, there had always been at least some motion here and there over the surface of the congregation, a brisk and general motion before the service started, with an audible amount of pleasant, secular whispering going on. During the forepart of the sermon, isolated swirls of motion, with a child usually distinguishable as the nucleus of each swirl, and latterly the dread warning of epidemic uneasiness.

These people sat still.

He missed, too, the soft, blanketing background of the organ prelude. Each person that he saw now coming up the aisle, each single-file family parade, halting at the predetermined pew, and then moving in one by one, these merely emphasized the stillness of the others. Once seated, they froze at once to the general mass, and no man turned and nodded to his neighbor. Church in the country, Zeke thought, was very carelessly said to be a social occasion. After church, maybe; not now.

He could remember; he'd sat in one of those pews himself once. And not so long ago!

He got out his watch and put it on the stand beside him. Two minutes to go. When the bell stopped, he'd go forward. 'Doxology' was the item at the very top of White's list.

The bell missed a stroke—yes, it had stopped. Those who had not been looking at him were looking at him now. Three or four people had stood up. He got up and stepped forward to the lectern—and turned to catch the choir leader's eye. The choir—ranged competently in the front pew at his left—were covertly regarding the man who sat facing them at a cottage organ; and he, in turn, was appraising the readiness of the congregation. Zeke turned again to the congregation—they'd about finished standing up, and weren't looking at anyone. So he looked back at the man at the cottage organ—in time to see his shoulders move as he began to pump. His head came round to the choir—poised—raised . . . and dipped. The choir, unleashed, sprang into full cry—and the congregation swung in behind. Zeke—before starting to sing himself—had some suspicion that the problem was not going to be to conduct this service, but to stay with it.

He managed much better than he'd anticipated. No one seemed to be unduly concerned with him as an imported curiosity, nor did they appear to be waiting to pounce on any small mistake. His impression was that they felt this to be their part of the service, which—like the choir—they were quite competent to handle without any outside interference. But they were also aware that his turn was coming.

Before they'd got down the list as far as 'Notices,' White had come unobtrusively to the edge of the platform and handed him up half a dozen slips of paper. Zeke had time to go through them during the second anthem. The handwriting was decipherable, and there seemed to be nothing of any tremendous moment.

He was still feeling fairly comfortable, and from time to time optimistic.

For the Scripture Lesson he was using First Thessalonians 4: not all of it germane, and they'd probably think he was going to preach from the last verse or two. But he wasn't. The text was back in the middle of the chapter. Reading the whole chapter, it would probably go relatively unnoticed, because there was some Hebrew frankness at the beginning of the chapter, and a dramatic promise of life everlasting at the end. Still, that was the way Paul had written it—almost certainly with an eye to structure—and that was the way he was going to read it. And it had an admirable closing sentence when read aloud! "Wherefore comfort one another with these words."

All through the service, he had kept his sermon safe in his pocket. The list ran '. . . Hymn,' and underneath that: 'Sermon.'

Under cover of the commotion of the congregation's rising for that hymn, he took the sermon out of his pocket and laid it—folded once down through the middle—on the lectern. There were five verses to that hymn—but after the third, he couldn't sing much.

[Chapter 33]

" 'Study to be quiet, and to do your own business, and to work with your own hands . . .' and the twelfth verse 'that ye may walk honestly toward them that are without, and that ye may have lack of nothing.' " As he closed the book and laid it to one side, he saw the room in which he had written—where he had prepared for this.

He looked up at the people in front of him—and he could not see that the text had affected them in any way. And he had just time to reflect—in the pause before he repeated the text—that he certainly was starting from scratch this time.

Then he went to work. He'd reminded himself several times during the service that he'd have to keep his voice down because the place was so small, but he forgot for the first five or six words, and had to adjust. No one noticed, he was sure, and he went ahead without being upset.

He soon felt another effect of the smallness of the church: the people were so close to him that he was going to have to leave out a good deal of oratorical technique. This was more as though he were in a room. He must say to them what he had to say—instead of manipulating them as a congregation spread out below him in the vastness of a great church. The strain was going to fall on his sermon—not on his preaching of it.

The sermon, as he thought of it ahead of him, was fortunately pretty well adapted to the circumstances. Not emotional, not spectacular. In substance it was not even original. In the main, it was a development of the advice that Paul had written—not preached, come to think of it—and written so compactly that it would stand development without being thinned down.

He told them, first, what he knew about the people to whom Paul was writing. He didn't know much, and he didn't try to stretch it. He had hoped, when he wrote it, that it would be enough to make the ancients seem like people, instead of being forever just a long word like 'Thessalonians.'

But he was forced to admit, when he finished the passage, that judging from the faces in front of him, he was still talking about Thessalonians.

Well, it was a minor point anyhow, and he was not discouraged. He discovered that he was a page and a half ahead of his manuscript, and while he thought of it, turned two pages.

" 'Study to be quiet,' " he repeated. "What did Paul mean by that?" It was encouraging to be able to employ the rhetorical question with such complete safety. At the meetings, they'd been liable to be answered. Having given the congregation time enough to wonder what Paul *had* meant, he said dryly: "Well—he meant 'study to be quiet' " —and then he hurried a little into his explanation. There had been a real and special need for quietness among the surrounded members of the little group in Thessalonica, because they lived under the fearsome power of the Roman Empire. To remind men in their position that there was no need to go out looking for trouble was sound advice. And if it should appear at this distance to have been a counsel of cowardice there was not alone Paul's record of individual heroism as proof of the contrary. Paul knew the world of his time . . . and in some ways it had not changed so very much since then. Let each man look to his own virtue. Energies spent in ranting against public evils could be better employed.

It was a part of the sermon which he had written with considerable enthusiasm, and because of that with unguarded expeditions into repetition. These, subsequently, he had cut out. What was left was, he felt, good, straight exposition, well arranged, and closely knit together.

He knew its wording and its structure so intimately, he had spoken phrase after phrase in its place so many times aloud, that no matter how earnestly he preached it now, and in spite of the importance of the occasion, he was open to a thought or two on the side. But that was dangerous, and he let none of them get very far.

He concluded the passage and made his period: " 'Study to be quiet,' Paul wrote, 'and to do your own business,' " . . . and that led directly into the next phase.

The words continued to strike against the faces of the congregation, and to roll off, leaving no mark. 'Study to be quiet'? They had, all right!

And yet he still felt that it was not so much that they lacked sensitivity, as that they were unknowingly resolved not to show it. They couldn't *all* be deaf!

And he felt no doubts about the sermon. It was as good a sermon as he had thought it was.

He was ten minutes along now—well into 'do your own business' as applied to the Thessalonians. 'To work with your own hands' was ahead, waiting and in order—and having in it some human touches on the then state of the arts in Thessalonica, and that followed by a general summing up of the first part. Then to lift the whole thing up and transfer it to the present. It might be that that would be what was going to make the difference.

As he finished the summary of the first part, it was plain that *some*thing was going to have to make the difference!—and that pretty soon. Fifteen minutes had gone, and there were twenty minutes ahead. There was a long pause scheduled here, and he took hold of the lectern with both hands and looked down fixedly at the face of his watch—noting that his pace was about right—and then looked at the familiar, reassuring manuscript. It didn't seem to have quite the power of reassurance that he'd expected—and he tried to avoid recognizing that his doubts had grown larger and had come nearer. It was no time to get panicky now! And neither would it be well to try for some new element that he hadn't planned. He'd have to go through with it with what he had. He understood now that he had been pretty certain all along that it would go well. And it was not going well.

He tried for some feeling of a fresh start—but it would not come. He saw them, now that he had begun to preach again, and saw that nothing had changed at all. Not even White. White, beard and all, had petrified, and a hundred years from now he'd be sitting there in the same place. Miss-Donaldson-and-Miss-Donaldson's-bonnet were of the same piece of stone. And Mrs. White—carven from the stout stump of a tree.

He went ahead . . . preaching. There was an old rooster toward the back there that he'd his eye on, who had a face that would turn a charge of buckshot. It would be a pleasure to try it on him, too, just to make sure. Zeke thought of the poor man who would be standing here next week, going through this same thing. It made him want to smile. He'd like an opportunity to shake him by the hand just before he went in the door, and say to him: "Good luck, brother"—and then he'd like to meet him somewhere a year or two later and they could sit down and talk about it.

None of this had interfered with his accuracy. He hadn't missed a word.

He said to himself, 'All right, if I have to preach to a stone wall, I can preach to a stone wall. After all, the worst that can happen—' and he recollected, then, what the worst that could happen was.

There was a pause that he did not think of as a pause, and that was not indicated on the manuscript.

He swung forward to the attack . . . having at his back the dark and dingy little room in Boston.

But it didn't last long. He was calmer in a moment. There were fifteen minutes left of it.

He knew that these things were true that he had brought here to say. And what if he had come only recently to see the truth of them?—and what if these people in front of him had known them all along! Well—he had his sermon to finish.

And he finished it. There was no climax—nothing but

the small fact that he had finished now. And he went back to his chair to get his hymnbook.

They sang *O Come, All Ye Faithful*, and he enjoyed singing it. He had failed—but he would see that more fully later on. Just now, he had the singing of this hymn, and the knowing that it was over with. Perhaps the reason nothing was happening to him was that he never really had believed he would succeed. Well—he hadn't, anyway. Sometime later on he would have to think how he would tell of it when he got home. That was not yet. That was tomorrow.

He pronounced the benediction.

White had come forward to take him in charge. Zeke, gathering up the unbound sheaf of his sermon and stowing his watch, did not hurry. He was not quite ready to meet the brief, polite little comment that White, all through the hymn, had undoubtedly been shaping. When the watch and sermon could be prolonged no longer, he looked up agreeably. . . .

"Don't forget your Bible," White told him.

Zeke had forgotten it—and by the time they'd wrung out that saving coincidence, they'd caught up with the people ahead of them in the aisle. These turned round to see what the man they'd been staring at for an hour looked like now that he wasn't preaching. And White, seizing them when they were off balance, forced them to be introduced.

For half an hour, Zeke said the same things to different people, and shook hands, and listened to what each one was starting to say, and as soon as he heard what it was going to be, picked out the answer from his stock and in due course applied it. To a good many of the women he said that he was glad they had enjoyed the sermon, and to a good many men the answer was, yes, he'd come over from Boston yesterday and that things there seemed to be about the same.

Most of the people had left by the time Zeke and White started up the street together. The ladies had gone on ahead—drawn home by the responsibilities of Sunday dinner.

White talked all the way home, and Zeke believed himself to be listening. White was talking of some one of the personalities with which Zeke had been confronted a few moments ago. But Zeke, at the beginning, had missed just who they were and was not moved now to try to bring the story alive by asking. He was conscious of the present blessing of an emotional paralysis, and was hoping it would last. And when they turned in the gate, the fact that they were turning in the gate seemed a sufficient thing to be noticing.

Before they sat down to dinner he asked the blessing, and it did not disturb him nor arouse him in any way. From time to time he watched young White, having a disinterested curiosity as to how much the man would be able to eat. White didn't seem to be eating an awful lot, but Zeke, when he had seen this, couldn't remember for a moment why the point should have interested him. Jamie was being noisy some of the time, and sometimes it was just as noticeable that he wasn't. They were having boiled lamb for dinner, Zeke realized after a while; and later, that it tasted the way lamb does. He understood that after dinner he and White would go back to the church. There five or six men would ask him questions about his doctrinary beliefs. They would go through this formality because it would be embarrassing for them to omit it—which would involve telling him right now that it was all over with. They had in mind that he had come a long journey. Soon after he had finished answering the questions he would be on his way home. Beyond that, he didn't care to look just now.

[Chapter 34]

When he and White came into the church, three of the men who were going to examine him were already standing waiting at the rear of the church talking.

They were crudely able to appear cheerful. Like surgeons.

The fourth man came in, and they joked him for being late. He enjoyed that. He said that was all right with him, he wasn't going to hurry his dinner for anybody. "I beg your pardon, Reverend. I didn't mean you." Zeke said he wouldn't have minded if he'd taken a nap, too.

They all laughed at that—and Zeke wondered what they'd thought he meant . . . he hadn't been quite sure himself.

White said he guessed they might as well go up front —more room up there . . . and they moved up the aisle —one of them making it a point that Zeke go ahead of him.

They were a little quieter now, but clinging strenuously to the minute or two of informality that remained. Zeke wondered if it were possible that they were going to ask him to sit in the high-backed armchair in the middle of the platform—and they'd line themselves up like a row of judges in the pews in front of him.

It was exactly what they did do—one of them commenting to another, "Same as before, eh?" Zeke would have liked to ask him what disposition they'd made of the previous victim. Still, there was a chance—although a pretty slim one—that one of them might not be doing this because he enjoyed it. He had an idea that White had made up his mind to regard it as routine, and that having made up his mind he would feel that he did so regard it. But he distrusted the big, heavy man who had come in late. There was a whiff of reminiscence about him that led back to someone he disliked . . . wait a minute—Graveson. Well, he'd think of him as Graveson. And some time during the hour he'd have a chance to say something to him. There was nothing to lose.

Zeke took his place—feeling that the back of the chair was towering three feet above his head.

Three of them were in one pew, on his left, and the other two across the aisle. They were probably not divided into liberals in one pew and conservatives in the other. Five in one pew and the other empty would have indicated that.

He stretched his legs out as straight as he decently could, settled his back against the chair, and inclined his head slightly forward. He wasn't sure but what he was going to enjoy this.

One of them turned to White and said, "Deacon White." White, matter-of-fact and prepared for it, stood up and offered a prayer. He prayed for divine guidance. Zeke kept his mind where it was. On the whole, he thought, it would have been better taste to have omitted the prayer. White meant it, though, and so there could be no criticism of him.

When he had sat down, White said plainly to Zeke:

"Mr. Peele, it's customary here, as I suppose it is everywhere else, for a committee of the Board of Deacons to ask the privilege of questioning a candidate as to his beliefs. Is it agreeable to you that we now proceed to do so?"

"Perfectly," Zeke answered—with a degree of respect and solemnity which he had not expected.

White spoke to the little old gentleman sitting next to the door in the pew across the aisle. "Deacon Abbott—"

Zeke turned to Deacon Abbott—whose precedence, apparently, was by virtue of his age. People were calling him spry now, but someday—soon and suddenly—he would be feeble.

"I'd like to ask, Mr. Peele, how you feel about foreign missions."

Not dodging, Zeke yet was forced to answer: "In what respect, Deacon Abbott?"

"Well, I mean as to money. How much of the money a church takes in, do you think ought to be sent out?"

"That's up to the church. It's not a matter for the pastor to decide—not where I've been, anyway."

"Oh, I'm not saying it's up to him to decide! But what's your opinion?"

"I can't answer you in percentages. Suppose I put it this way: that I believe that those expenses essential to the existence of a church should be met first. Certainly if you don't keep the church alive, the missions can't live."

Mr. Potter, the latecomer, chose to observe that he had "heard of some missionaries were pretty good at supporting themselves."

"Yes," Zeke said, "so have I. But not many. If a man's dishonest he can find more comfortable opportunity at home."

"*That's* true, all right," said Mr. Potter.

"What I'm getting at, is this," Deacon Abbott resumed. "The way I see it—and these gentlemen here know this, because I've said it often enough—there's too much this-and-that in the church. Now, you take this giving to the poor. *I* don't object to giving to the poor. I *like* to give to the poor. *Any* man ought to. And it's in Scripture. But it *ain't* up to the *church*! What's the church for? To save souls. All right. Let it save souls, then. But once it's got a man saved, then he'd hadn't ought to have to go on having money spent on him to *keep* him saved. That's how *I* feel about it." He appeared to have forgotten that he had asked a question. "Steeple!" he muttered disgustedly.

Zeke liked him. Because he did, he said thoughtfully: "I don't know but I agree with you—once he's saved."

Deacon Abbott was in too thorough agreement with Deacon Abbott to pay any attention.

" 'Once he's saved'?" said Mr. Potter suavely.

Zeke turned to him. "Yes."

Mr. Potter said nothing.

Deacon White chose to call on the next man—with perhaps enough hint of peremptoriness so that Zeke understood how matters stood between White and Potter, at any rate. "Deacon Taylor," White said.

Deacon Taylor was in the pew with Abbott. He was not so old a man as Abbott, but he was getting there.

"Congregational singing, Mr. Peele," said Deacon Taylor, almost too easily. "Not a doctrinary matter, perhaps, but with Deacon White's permission I'd like to ask you. What do you think of it?"

"I thought this morning it was very good."

"Do you approve of it in principle?"

"I'm not sure that I regard it as a matter of principle. But I do approve of it." This really was rather pleasant. Nothing to lose—you could say just exactly what you thought. A minister didn't often get the chance.

"Why?" asked Deacon Taylor.

"I suppose because I like to sing. Another reason is that I'm accustomed to it. We had it in Boston. And when I was a boy."

"Well, I *don't* like it," said Deacon Taylor, "and I never did. We never had it at the church in Morris. And we never had it here until a few years ago. I don't approve of it."

"Maybe you don't like to sing," said Mr. Potter—which was what everyone had thought of, and which thus earned Mr. Potter no gratitude whatever. Potter, finding the sally ill-received, spoke to Zeke: "However, Mr. Peele, I take it you would not regard personal enjoyment as a proper—ah—criterion . . . in the selection of a principle?"

"I'd regard it as an inevitably contributing factor, whether *pro* or con."

"I see," said Potter. Zeke felt pretty sure, then, that Potter would always say, "I see," provided he didn't and that you spoke to him with long enough words.

Deacon White proceeded to the next man.

"Where'd you go to school?" Zeke was asked.

"Andover, sir." 'They *must* have known that!' Zeke thought. He took the question as further proof that this whole thing was just a matter of form. And he was tempted to suggest that they might all save time by admitting the fact and going home.

It was Potter's turn.

"Mr. Peele: I read a book recently by a—well, we might say by a neighbor of ours—or we might con*fess*

266

by a neighbor of ours—that is, he was born in Litchfield County—although he is still, I believe, pastor of a church in New Britain. Horace Bushnell."

"Hartford, isn't it?"

"Ah—what's that, Mr. Peele?"

"Dr. Bushnell is pastor of the North Church in Hartford."

"Hartford, yes. As I was saying, while I make no apology for having done so, I did read recently a book of his. I wonder whether you may be familiar with it?"

"The *Editorials?*"

"No—that wasn't it."

"When was it published?"

"Well, I couldn't say as to that, really."

"*God in Christ?*"

"That's not it. You seem very familiar with his works, Mr. Peele."

"I am, moderately. *Discourses on Christian Nurture?*"

"*Discourses on Christian Nature!*" affirmed Mr. Potter.

"What about it?" Zeke asked.

"Merely as a matter of form, since you profess to be a Christian minister, I wished to ask whether you had any sympathy with his views?"

Zeke's fingers drummed on the side of his chair. This was more like it! "I have," he said, "every sympathy."

It was no great shock to Potter, who said "Ah!" with every appearance of satisfaction. "May I ask you another question, Mr. Peele?"

"Certainly."

"You are a family man, Mr. Peele?"

"Not at present."

"Then that, I think," said Mr. Potter, "is the reason."

267

Zeke thought it must be his turn to say 'I see.' "I'm afraid I don't understand," he said. "What's the reason for what?"

"The reason for your being in agreement with this man Bushnell on this question—if it can be called a question."

"What is the question?"

"The question? Why, the necessity for an experience! The whole purpose of the book—if I understood it correctly, and, if not, perhaps you can enlighten me—the whole purpose of the book—er, what is it?"

"*Discourses on Christian Nurture?*"

"Yes, that's it—*Discourses on Christian Nurture*. The whole purpose of the book is to deny any necessity for a change of heart—or 'conversion,' if you prefer. Surely, Mr. Peele, having just preached to a text from St. Paul, you can hardly deny the necessity for conversion!"

"I wouldn't deny that it was necessary in Paul's case, no. Neither does Bushnell."

"I'm not talking about St. Paul. I'm talking about generally."

"Very well. But before we leave Dr. Bushnell, may I point out that Bushnell is not talking about 'generally.' Bushnell's position is that a child brought up in a Christian atmosphere, trained in Christian principles and continuing to attempt to practice them, does not require to be converted—to have an experience—in order to be eligible for salvation. Did you wish me to state whether that is also my own belief?"

"That," said Mr. Potter, "is what I asked."

"Then I am happy to answer you: that it is my belief."

They were all looking at him—and he couldn't look

at Potter any longer. Potter had made him angry—Potter's voice, and Potter's face. Behind that face, Potter was angry, too. But Potter was probably accustomed to being angry, and was not disturbed. It frightened Zeke to be angry; it threatened him with being defeated and ashamed. But there was no use trying to ease off while he looked at Potter. He turned to White.

Potter called him back. "Do I understand, Mr. Peele, that you suggest that a parent is to damn his own child by teaching him that he need not *become* a Christian?"

Instead of becoming angrier, Zeke felt more calm. He looked at Potter, and he thought: 'I have more brains than you have, and it may be that you are making a mistake to keep this up.' He said: "I don't suggest that anyone damn anyone. I've not heard it suggested that it was within the ability of one person to damn another. But I do suggest that Professor Tyler, whom you've more or less quoted, came pretty close to speaking the truth—even though he meant something else. It was Professor Tyler's contention—and I happen to recall correctly because I didn't agree with him—that for a child to grow up a Christian it was necessary for him to become a Christian. Those words—if I may have my own interpretation of them—are true. But what Tyler intended them to mean is not true. Tyler says also that it is God's prerogative to change the heart. Well, anyone will agree with that. Because, if He so elects, there is nothing that is not God's prerogative. And for me it follows that if He chooses to make a child a Christian by having him born into a Christian family, influenced by Christian example—and precept, too!— and to have him develop gradually as he grows up until, through that gradual development, he shall have become a practicing Christian to the full degree of his ability—then I see nothing to prevent. It is God's prerogative to make a Christian. And it is neither yours nor mine, I think, to attempt to limit that prerogative as to when or in what manner it shall be exercised. It is to my mind just as presumptuous of us to say that the work must be done at one fell swoop, as it would be to say that it could *not* be done in that way. I don't deny the validity of conversions. Paul's conversion was valid. So are thousands of others. But neither for that reason—nor for any other that I can conceive of—is it reasonable for us to say that God is limited to that one particular method in the achievement of His ends." He was seeing his father very clearly then, and Potter—not quite so clearly—as trying to come between his father and salvation. He left Potter apparently not at all discomforted, and, shaken, he turned to White: "I beg your pardon—you've had to listen to me preach once today already."

White said: "You have no occasion for apology."

Another man, speaking what was in his mind, said to Zeke: "I don't agree with you."

Zeke was uncertain whether to acknowledge this. He wanted to nod to the man, to say in understanding, 'That's different.'

Abbott said: "Neither do I. Don't agree with a word of it. But I will say this, young man, that that's more what I call religion—whether you're right or wrong!— than what you were preaching this morning. That wasn't religion," he described the sermon with critical distaste, "that was just common sense."

Zeke had been facing him as he spoke . . . and now

he bowed to him—just a nod and because he felt moved to it—and said nothing.

The long-faced man who was a nonsinger—Taylor, that was his name—said contemplatively: "I knew Bushnell when he was a boy. He's a year or two younger than I am. Knew his people, too. Litchfield. Never seemed to be much about him when he was a boy—not that I could see."

"Went to Yale College, didn't he?"—a morose contribution from the man who had inquired as to Zeke's schooling.

"Yes," said Taylor. "Twenty-five years old when he got through there. Never was real rugged, either."

"What's that got to do with it?" inquired Deacon Abbott.

Taylor said: "Nothing, I guess."

"Well, we'll go on," White said. "Mr. Potter, was there anything further you wished to add?"

"No, I think not. I think Mr. Peele has answered my question very fully, and as far as I'm concerned, has left me in no doubt as to his position."

"Deacon Abbott . . . ?"

"Well, there was something—oh, yes. Speaking about your sermon, Mr. Peele. Now what you said about a man ought to be quiet. I've got no objection to that of course. Man can't spend all his time shouting that he's a Christian. Like you said, he's got to get his work done. All the same, there's a lot of people in this world never heard of the Lord. And until they do hear, they got no chance to be saved. Far as I can see, that puts it up to us to see that they do hear. In a case like that, you wouldn't recommend that a man keep quiet."

"No, sir."

"Well," said Deacon Abbott, a little testily, "didn't think you did. There is a limit."

White waited for the proper interval, and then proceeded. "Deacon Taylor?"

"Didn't they tell me you been a revival preacher one time, Mr. Peele?"

"After a fashion, I was."

"What'd you think of 'em?"

"Depends on the preacher."

"Do more harm than good . . . my opinion."

"Possibly. In my own case, I guess I was never effective enough to do much of either."

"Never lasts, does it?—didn't you find?"

"I've heard of cases, yes."

"I never seen any."

Someone said: "Job Waters was one."

"Maybe," said Deacon Taylor. "I always thought what converted him was more his breaking his leg."

No one said anything, and Zeke inferred that the case of Job Waters had been discussed too often to be of interest, even to Deacon Taylor—who was surprised to discover that White was waiting for him to go on. Taylor shook his head, and dismissed the privilege with his hand.

White went on to the fifth man, and Zeke prepared to report on the village school of New Boston, N. H.

"Mr. Peele—" the man said.

"Yes?"

"Didn't I read in the paper somewhere—I don't know—some time ago, I guess it was—but the name just happened to strike me when we were talking about you—a man by your name was an Abolitionist?"

"Very likely."

" 'Twouldn't 'a' been *you* . . ."

"I wouldn't be surprised. Lecturing?"

"That's right!" Mildly triumphant, he turned to White: "What'd I tell you?"

White's nod admitted that he had been told, but no more than that.

"No harm to tell him?" the man asked White.

"Not that I know of."

"Well," he seemed to be enjoying it as he explained to Zeke, "we got a letter back from the Twelfth Congregational Church of Boston—where you used to be, you understand—"

Graveson, Zeke thought.

"Of course, you understand we had to write to them before we asked you to come here to preach. You'd understand we'd do that."

Zeke nodded.

"Well, we got this letter back from them. It was a long letter, too, but it didn't say much—you know how them letters are—but it did say that you . . ." He stopped, trying to recollect the exact words. "How was that now?" He turned round to White.

White shifted uneasily. "Well—"

"I got it!" The man turned to Zeke. "They said that you and the congregation—yes, this is it!—had not always been in harmony as to matters political."

That would be Graveson! That was Graveson!

"Well, I said to White, I said: 'That's a funny thing to put in. Who *is?*' And then the other day I happened to recollect seeing this in the paper. And I said: 'I bet that was it!' Of course, I don't want to—but—well, you know —*was* it?"

"It was."

"Well, now! They didn't like it, eh?"

"Not particularly, no. Indirectly, that was one reason they decided to get somebody else."

"No!"

"I imagine I was spending more time on Abolition than I was on the church."

"You don't say! Do you still—have these lectures?"

"No."

"Well! So that *was* it, eh? I don't know—we don't have much time for Abolition round here. Politics, yes. But I guess Abolition's more in Boston than it is here."

Zeke smiled. There was nothing for him to say. He'd like to tell these men that he was sorry he was not to work with them. Potter was still there, of course. But Potter didn't affect the others. He wondered how much more questioning there would be. He had a feeling that they'd had about enough—since it didn't amount to anything, anyway. Unless something else should come up, they were ready to go home.

White let the silence run on. . . .

Deacon Abbott said: "I got to get back home. Potter, don't say anything. You had your turn. Deacon White, I move we adjourn."

White said: "Well, if no one objects . . ." No one did.

"Mr. Peele," White addressed him: "do you feel that you've had a fair hearing?"

"I do."

"Anyone else wish to say anything?—Deacon Potter?"

"Nothing at all, thank you. I'm quite satisfied."

Deacon White, as he stood up, permitted himself to say, "Good." And to the others: "Well, then, I guess that's all."

As they were standing, Zeke stepped to the edge of the platform. They were not yet in conversation, but they would be in another moment. He spoke loudly—almost called to them: "I want to thank you gentlemen for asking me to come here." They looked up at him blankly—and one or two showed that they thought it a queer thing for him to have said.

Confusion rolled over Zeke and engulfed him—they thought he meant . . . "I mean today," he said. And they still looked blank.

He went back to his chair, dimly realizing that he was pretending to have some errand there. But there was nothing waiting there of his—no Bible—no papers—nothing. And the fact that he had occupied that chair a few moments ago had now disappeared. The chair itself was repellent and had no recognition of him. So that he went again toward the front of the platform, toward the men who were moving into the aisle now and talking.

Abbott spoke to him as he stepped down. "You going back to Boston tonight?"

Zeke could hear himself say, yes, he'd planned to; he'd be there in the morning.

[*Chapter 35*]

VIOLA HAD BEEN AWAKE off and on all night. She expected him back about half past six. Until half past five there would not be any excuse to get up to get his breakfast ready. He was on the train now. But it was not so dark in front of the train as it was here, because they had a searchlight in front of the train. Every night they ran trains. Nobody ever thought anything about it. It was a little after three now; she'd try to go to sleep again.

275

Someone had knocked at the door—and with her eyes wide against the blackness, she lay there. There was no reason to answer. They knocked again. She had not even thought that it could be Zeke—but she thought now that, if it had been, he would have spoken. Whoever it was, was standing outside the door, waiting.

She got up then—and had put on her coat and stood facing the door. They knocked—not heavily, the same as before. If she should scream—if it should turn out that she had to scream—the Pisanellis would hear her.

She said: "What do you want?"

Immediately the knock—quietly, in answer.

She knew, then, who it was. She had been answered in the same way so many times.

Not bothering with a light, she went to the door, thinking—while she unlocked it—that the maid had come to tell her that he was very ill. She opened the door, and could make out the woman standing there.

Viola said, "Come in," and went back into the room to make a light. Yes, he must be ill. He couldn't have died. When she had the lamp lighted and could see the woman's face, she asked: "What is it—is he ill?"

There was a pause long enough so that Viola had time to understand. Then the woman shook her head, slowly and with the whites of her eyes showing in the light.

Viola said: "Why did you come for me? He can't hurt you now."

The woman made no attempt to answer.

"He is dead, isn't he?"

She nodded slowly.

"What do you want me to do? Go back there with you?"

That was it.

"Are you alone in the house?"

Yes.

"No doctor?"

No.

"I suppose you're afraid the Devil will come for him. Where is he—in his bed?"

No.

"In the library?"

Yes.

"Were you with him when he died?"

No.

"You found him, eh?"

Yes.

"Well, I don't wonder you're upset some. All right—I'll go back with you. Wait till I get dressed." She went over to the bed, where her clothes were beside it on a chair, and began to dress. "How did you get here—walk?"

She had.

"Well, we'll walk back, too. Even for this errand, we don't spend money on a cab."

She left a note for Zeke. He had his key with him.

And they went out. She wondered if the Pisanellis were hearing them . . . and what they were variously imagining had happened.

It was very black going down the stairs. But it was lighter in the street than she had thought.

When she got back, it was only a few minutes after six. She had expected that she would be able to go right ahead and get breakfast, but as soon as she stood in their own room . . . she couldn't. She'd have to lie down for a minute.

She had not been able to get up, when she heard Zeke

coming up the stairs. She managed to stand up then.

Zeke looked at her long enough to say, "Hello," and she knew that he had forced himself to do that, and that he had not really seen her. He was hanging up his hat. . . .

"Well," he said, "failed again."

"You're home."

"Oh, I got here."

"But, Zeke, they—you said they'd write—later, after you got back."

"Yes; they will, too. I'm just telling you what the letter will say." He turned to her. "Well, let's have some breakfast." His face was set—and then he stopped. "What's the matter?" he said. "What's happened?"

"I'm all right."

He came over and took her by the shoulders. Even then she was able to feel that she was standing by herself.

"He's dead," she said.

"Who is? You don't—you don't mean your uncle?"

She looked up into his face. "Yes."

[Chapter 36]

IT WAS A RAW, windy day, and Mr. Graveson, reading the burial service, was happy to reflect that his own physical condition was such that he could stand bareheaded and suffer no distress of mind. Peele, Graveson thought, standing there at the foot of the grave with his wife beside him, did not look well at all. He looked rather badly, in fact. And so did she. Mr. Graveson had not been privileged to view the Deacon. No doubt he looked worse than either of them. But, poor man, he'd died of drink, so Graveson had understood—and so what could be expected? Mr. Graveson, feeling himself threatened by a sneeze, began to hurry things a little.

There had been no services at the Deacon's house. Because the Deacon's house had not been in a condition to receive guests. Viola—as it had begun to grow light that other morning—had discovered that every room in the whole house had been stripped bare, right to the walls and floors. Except for the library and his bedroom. And even in his bedroom, the carpet had been taken up. In the library, all the books were gone, and the desk and chairs. Only the couch remained—standing cold in the middle of a bare floor. It had taken a good many questions on Viola's part to find out just what had happened. He had sold the things—not to buy brandy, although his needs were great —but in order to stay in the house. He had been afraid to go out. And he had had to pay money to the bank, or they would have put him out.

He had been burning his papers that night when the maid found him. He had finished burning them before he died. Some time before, because the room had been cold, the maid admitted, when she found him.

Now the undertaker's man, who had been listening for his cue, came forward, and his helper also. The necessary operations were performed. Zeke and Viola stepped back a little from the grave, and the maid, who had been standing back of them, moved to one side. Zeke went round to speak to Graveson, to thank him.

Graveson said that he had been very glad indeed to be of service—very glad indeed. He asked Zeke whether he had a church now, and Zeke said no. Mr. Graveson said, well, he was glad to have seen him. He bowed from a distance to Mrs. Peele, wondered who the other woman was, said good-by to Peele, and departed. He didn't wish to be brusque at all, but he didn't propose to become involved. People always walked so slowly leaving a cemetery!

Zeke took his wife by the arm, and the maid walked behind them. When they reached the gate, Viola turned to the maid and said, "Well—good-by." Zeke said good-by to her too—thinking of the time she had first let him into the house. He'd thought it was queer, then, about her perfume. Well, at any rate, she'd stayed by—right to the end.

They set off in different directions, the maid—and Zeke and Viola.

The maid, they knew, had a good deal more money saved up than they had. Wislon had paid for the funeral. And the Board of Deacons of the Twelfth Congregational Church had sent a wreath.

They got back to the house, and Zeke saw that he had a letter from his father. He carried it upstairs to read. The stairs were a long pull for Viola, coming on top of the walk home from the cemetery, and he made her lie down as soon as she had her hat off, and he spread his coat over her and went to get some tea. While he was waiting for the kettle to boil, he came back and sat down on the arm of the chair to read his letter.

There was another letter inside it, in a small envelope— his mother's handwriting—and addressed to Viola. Oh— about her uncle! He wondered how they could have heard so quickly. It was nice of his mother to write.

He said, "Letter from Mother to you—" and tossed it over to her.

Then he read his father's letter.

He read it through again—and folded it, and laid it on the table, where he looked at it awhile. Finally he said, "Well, I think we'd better go. When did you write to them?"

"While you were away."

"I see. Well, I don't blame you. All right—soon as you're ready." Then he looked at her. "You didn't *suggest* that we go . . ."

"No. I did say about the baby. That was all. Zeke, I couldn't help it! I *had* to tell somebody. You don't know what it's like."

"No, I suppose not."

"Who did I have that I could talk to? Mrs. Pisanelli? You know what she's like. I *had* to tell someone."

"It's all right," he said. "Maybe you saved me from doing it myself. I'd been thinking about it coming back on the train. But I hadn't told you, on account of—well, this last couple of days . . ."

"Yes."

"I got to see to that kettle!"

He brought back the tea, handed it to her, and went over to the window. "It'll ease old what's-his-name's mind about the rent for this place, anyway."

"You've paid him every month."

"So far."

"What did your father say?"

"Not much. He wouldn't."

"Zeke, does it mean—live there?"

"No. Till I get a job."

"Your mother's letter said for the winter."

"I know. So did Father." He half turned from the window—speaking to her directly: "Listen. I'll take you home, and you can stay there as long as necessary. If I can't support you—well, that's all we can do. Mother'll look out for you. I guess she'll enjoy it. But I leave the next morning. Is that clear?"

"But, Zeke—"

He'd turned away.

"Zeke, she says your father wants you to help him."

"He's already carrying more men through the winter than he knows what to do with."

"You mean—leave me there alone?—without you?"

"You won't be alone! What's the matter with you? They'll look out for you!"

"But—but where will you be?"

"I'll be working—if I can find any. I'll get something —now that it doesn't matter what. By next summer we ought to be in shape to start over again."

"Zeke, I *can't* stay there if you're not there. I can't, that's all! Don't ask me why, because I can't do it." She set the tea down on the floor beside the bed.

"Why can't you?"

"I've told you: because I can't."

"Well, it just so happens, my dear, that you've got to. This isn't the first time I've thought about it. What do you think I did all that night on the train? I know what we're up against. So do you, if you'd only see it. All summer we haven't had enough to eat. That's a different proposition in winter. I figure I can get through, if I'm alone. I can get some kind of job, and maybe save something. And then next summer, as I say, we can start again. It's all we *can* do!"

She had raised up on one elbow. She looked frightened, for some reason. It made him angry—partly because he knew he was a little frightened himself. "What are you afraid of!" he said. "I'm not *leaving* you! Great Scott!"

She sat upright, swinging her legs down over the edge of the bed. "You can't do it, do you understand? I won't let you! You can't! I won't stay there!"

"Why do you act this way about it? Is something wrong with my family? Personally, I think it's very decent of them to have offered."

"Oh, it's not that."

"Well, what *is* it, then? It's not very easy on *my* pride, either. Suppose you stop and think a minute. You're not the only one concerned, you know. It isn't just you and myself any more. In your condition, if we tried to live on what I can earn this winter—well, you wouldn't live, that's all. You'd starve."

"No, Zeke! No! I'm not hungry—I'm strong!"

"You are not. And you know it."

"You mustn't leave me!"

"I'm not *going* to leave you, I tell you!"

"No . . ." she said, her eyes looking past him, "you wouldn't, would you? I know that."

"Of course I wouldn't. Good Lord!" Why should she make such a fuss over some weird impossibility that had nothing to do with the case? He returned to his contention: "Look here, I know what I'm talking about. I know what happens to women who are in your condition in a—well, in a place like this, who are cold and who don't get what they ought to, to eat. There are a good many unpleasant things I've found out in the last few years that I haven't felt it necessary to go round talking about. And that happens to be one of them. *I know!*—do you see? I *know* what I'm talking about. And I won't let you do it. I may be an unsuccessful minister, God knows!—but I'm not a murderer. And even if he is dead," he added a little irrelevantly, "I'm thankful there's no money coming from that source. That would have been a little *too* much."

He didn't know how it had come about that he was talking this way . . . nor why she should look the way she did. He turned his back to her—about to be thoroughly ashamed of himself. He stood there at the window, and put his hand, shaking, on the window ledge.

From behind him he heard her say in a strange voice: "How—how long have you known?"

"Known what?"

"That he was my father. That he—that he made her starve. Who told you? Your Mr. Watling? I thought he'd find out."

Zeke was thinking faster than he ever had in his life. He believed it. MacIntosh was her father. And he saw that in this last few minutes, stupidly, he had been beating her until she told him. Oh, God, let him be gentle with her—let him do the right thing. . . . And he would, if he knew what it was.

Hanging on to the window, he said quietly: "Certainly. I've known it for quite a while. What difference does it make?"

"Do you know it—all?"

"Oh, I don't know. Why talk about it now?" He swung suddenly from the window, and came to her as she stood there, took her by the shoulders, and said: "Now, then, you lie down on that bed. We can talk about your father any time. I'm going to get some supper. You lie down there and take it easy."

Under the pressure of his hands, she sat down on the edge of the bed. But she had to go on now—saying the story, as she had been afraid sometime she would say it. "Gowan—made him marry her. I don't know why, but he

284

did. Because Gowan knew her brother. They were poor people—in New Orleans. Then Gowan found out later that she'd died—my mother had. Because he—he's dead now, isn't he?—because he left her without any money. And when I was born, she—she wasn't strong enough, do you see? And Gowan made him take me and bring me up. Or else he'd tell about it."

There was more coming, but Zeke said: "Well, it's all over with now. Don't worry about it."

Someone had knocked at the door. It made no impression on Viola, but Zeke said: "Sit still—I'll get it."

It was Mrs. Pisanelli—so fat that even now he marveled at it—holding before her in two hands a large-sized bowl.

Mrs. Pisanelli said, "Hello. Here—" and pushed the bowl at him. Zeke looked down into it and saw that it was half full of spaghetti. Mrs. Pisanelli said, "Here—" again, and Zeke looked up and said, "For us?"

"Sure!" said Mrs. Pisanelli. "Here—"

Zeke took the bowl in his hands. It was hot. "Well!" he exclaimed. "Thank you! That's very nice of you. Thank you!"

"Sure!" said Mrs. Pisanelli.

"How's all the family?"

"He's fine. You bury d' pop, huh?"

"No," Zeke said loudly, "the uncle!"

"Sure!" said Mrs. Pisanelli, entirely untroubled by her failure to comprehend. "That's right. G'by."

"Good-by, Mrs. Pisanelli," he called after her, "and thank you. I'll bring back the bowl." He watched her waddling down the hall.

The outside of the hot bowl was greasy enough to be slippery. He carried it very carefully back into the room and set it down on the table. And with his mind full of the fact that in the next moment he must be doing something to get Viola straightened out, and that now MacIntosh was going to be the child's grandfather even though Mac-Intosh was dead—and that he must go back and shut the door he'd left open—he bent over the bowl and inhaled once, and then again.

He glanced at Viola as he went to shut the door. She was sitting exactly as she had been—staring terribly straight ahead. What he was going to do for her, he couldn't know. Something—this wasn't her fault, whosoever it was. . . .

Mrs. Pisanelli was standing in the doorway. She'd come back, of course. He'd seen her go down the hall. *His* head was clear anyway.

From some recess in the folds of her spotted black skirt, Mrs. Pisanelli had drawn out an envelope. She held it out to him. " 'S bring 'em up," she explained, and shrugging her shoulders, "I f'got."

Zeke said, "Oh, thank you," and reached out his hand for it. Some Pisanelli was always bringing up mail from downstairs, and if there was no one home, they kept it until there was. "Dis morn'," she said.

Zeke had seen that the letter was from Halleck's Bridge. Just the time for it! He closed the door behind him with his foot, and grimly opened the letter as he went toward Viola. . . .

When he was certain that it was so, he went dazedly to her, and standing before her, took hold of her arms and drew her up to him. Over her head, he said: "We got it!—it says so—in the letter."

She held tightly to him. She was a little hysterical at first, but no more than was natural, and Zeke realized now that perhaps for a moment he himself had not been—well, quite himself. She was just as happy as he was. He could tell that.

"Yes—" he said, nodding, when he looked at her, "it's all right. It says it—in the letter."

Viola hadn't known about the letter before, but she said, "Let's see it—" and Zeke gave it to her, and she read it, and she understood. There was no need for her to explain why she had been so happy a moment ago, because Zeke wouldn't understand that. But inadvertently she did express some surprise over the spaghetti. It developed that she'd missed that entirely—a fact which greatly entertained them both.

After he'd gone to bed, he got to thinking. There'd be a lot of work in that parish. They expected a country minister to do everything. A lot of work. And the preaching only a little part of it. Well, he was ready for it. And in the morning he'd write to his father. It was strange, this feeling that he had—of his life opening out ahead of him— spreading out, fanwise . . . You couldn't tell what anything was going to be like.

He was blest, he knew, beyond anything that he deserved . . .

And he said so.

[*Chapter 37*]

THEY'D BEEN THREE WEEKS in Halleck's Bridge, when Zeke's mother wrote suggesting that they come home for Thanksgiving. Zeke would have liked to go. But because it was his work that prevented, it was pleasant, too, in a

287

way, to know that he couldn't. He had a service Thanksgiving morning for one thing, and the days on either side of it would fill up as they approached. They were not empty now. He had already been told that on the day preceding a holiday it was a routine duty of his office to see that Jonas Wheeler was started off to Litchfield to be locked up—except for Independence Day and Election Day when, it was considered, it was no more than fair that Jonas be allowed to take part.

Scheduled duties were only a small part of the things that kept him busy. And even if there had been none of those, he still would not have been free to leave. He had to be on hand in case anyone should need him.

He told Viola to write back and say: why didn't they come here?

He hadn't any idea they would come, but as he thought about it from time to time he began to see what an intense pleasure it would be if they should. He wouldn't have much to show his father, but what he did have would be his own. And one way and another, between Viola and himself, they could probably make them comfortable. The spare room was cold as a root cellar, but that could be taken care of, and his father wouldn't want to stay more than two or three days anyway. There were some things, now, that Viola could cook pretty well. Not all of them Thanksgiving items maybe, but put them together all at once and they'd make quite a showing. You could always count on Viola, too, when it came to an emergency. Any kind of emergency. He'd worried for several days about telling her that they couldn't possibly take the remaining cabinet of china knick-knacks to Halleck's Bridge with them . . . only to come home one night and discover that she'd sold the cabinet itself to Mrs. Pisanelli for enough to pay the freight on a barrel of china to Beemansville and to leave a little over. To be sure, she'd never had opportunity to cook a turkey, but even confronted with a dead turkey, Viola was not likely to be dismayed. If his father and mother should come, he'd enjoy showing his work to his father. But he'd enjoy, too, having both of them see Viola. There had been a time when they'd thought that he'd guessed wrong on Viola. He thought they'd be able to see now that he hadn't.

He sat up later than usual that night and wrote to them himself.

Abel, when Minna read him the letter, said, well, they couldn't go, of course, but on the other hand he'd admit that he didn't know as right now there was any real good reason why they shouldn't. They wouldn't have to stay long, if they did go.

Mr. Meeker, by arrangement with Zeke, was waiting at the depot. He'd had to put the extra seat on the buckboard, and he was only getting seventy-five cents for the two people. On top of that, young Peele had got the better of him by shrewdly insisting on paying him in advance—matter of only a couple of hours—but enough so that Mr. Meeker, to meet the move, had had to volunteer to take along a robe. Generally, he didn't take the robe until the first of December. Mr. Meeker, waiting now with the robe over his knees, was cheered by the sudden thought that all the way home he would not say anything about the doughnuts.

The train came in, and Mr. Meeker stayed where he was . . . But while he was having a look at the man approaching him across the yard, and at the lady on his

289

arm, Mr. Meeker was moved to get down. And after the lady, too, had spoken to him, Mr. Meeker asked if they'd mind waiting a minute, and he called a boy to hold the horse. Then he dusted into the station, and he hooked out the hot brick that had been warming under the stove for the stationmaster's ride home, and he brought it out, keeping it on the far side of him as he crossed the yard—the stationmaster was up by the engine—and he set it in back for her to keep her feet on.

He helped them in, and he carefully tucked in the robe. She had on a short sealskin coat, and she looked almost too young to have a son as old as the Reverend. Mr. Meeker thought it might be she was Peele's second wife. Peele looked like the Reverend all right, or rather he could see now that the Reverend looked like his father. In most ways, though, this man looked to be *more* so than the Reverend did. The Reverend wasn't a man to fool around with, but you take this man, he was even less of a man to fool around with than what the Reverend was. Mr. Meeker liked him, though—what he'd seen of him.

Once out of the village, Mr. Meeker turned sideways in his seat. He found Mr. Peele not an easy man to talk to. Mr. Meeker didn't hold it against him; some men were that way, and some men weren't. But he had to abandon, finally, a pleasant hope of finding out just how old the Reverend was. He'd decided some time ago not to say anything about how he'd thought the lady must be Mr. Peele's second wife because she looked so young.

On the other hand, Mr. Peele ate four of the doughnuts and said they were good, and he spoke reasonably of the gray.

It was pitch-dark before they were halfway there. Mr. Meeker, deprived of illustrated comment on the countryside, at length drove on in silence. He was not aware that Mr. Peele, for all the severity of his countenance, was, beneath the buffalo robe, holding the lady's hand.

Viola had hoped all day that Zeke would get home first. He had said that he would try to, but he'd also said he had three calls to make—as long as he was over that way—and he couldn't be sure how long they'd take. She'd told him to hurry, anyway. But he'd reminded her that he'd be driving a borrowed horse and it wouldn't do to bring him in too hot.

Nonetheless, she continued to hope.

When it had grown dark outside, she decided that she was going to have to face them alone. Uncertainly calculating, she arranged things on the stove so that she could leave them long enough to change her dress and fix up her hair a little, and when she had done that she hurried back to the kitchen. Everything seemed to be all right. She went into the sitting room and looked out the front window—and against all probability she saw them actually pulling up at the block in front of the house. She stood there watching them, the lantern under the buckboard making them look tall and strange. Zeke's father got down, and she could see him swing his bag down. The horse kept trying to start up, and Meeker, sitting in the front seat, would shout "Whoa!"—and the horse would back a step or two, stand, and then jerk forward again. Zeke's mother was still marooned in the back seat. Viola wondered why Meeker, the idiot, didn't get down and hold the horse's head. Then she saw Zeke's father step up close to the wheel, reach up both hands and lift his wife up and out and set her down beside him as easily and gracefully as though she'd been a child. It dawned on Viola that they were about to look toward the house, and horror-stricken lest they'd seen her already, gaping at them from the window, she hurried out to the door—and then walked out to meet them.

They were coming up the walk, and Mr. Meeker and the horse had disappeared.

Viola had said something or other, and Zeke's mother had kissed her. His father, standing a little back of them holding the carpetbag, spoke to her, when it was his turn, apparently in reply to something Viola had said herself. He said he was very glad to be invited. There was a kind of gentle, easy pleasantness in his voice that made Viola let go what she had remembered of him and start fresh. Before they were inside the house—this meeting, she had repeatedly told herself, would be on her own ground; the other had been on theirs—before they were inside the house, she found that she was wanting to please them for her own sake. Up till now she'd wanted only to force them to admit to Zeke that she did please them. It was between herself and them, now. She found that she was glad that they were here, and that she was looking forward to the rest of the time that they would be here. Having two people in the house would seem to quicken everything. Not that things needed quickening. But all the same . . .

"Zeke's not here," she said. "He had to go over to Litchfield. He ought to be back any minute now."

His mother said, "Is it a long trip?"

"Not very. He had to make some calls on the way back." "Well, if he's late," his father said, "you can make him go without his supper. That's what I used to do."

As a joke, Abel didn't think much of that; he hadn't any gift for this kind of thing.

Minna said to him that he'd never gone without his supper in his life—and then, he was pretty sure, she felt uncomfortable because she'd contradicted him in public. Abel decided not to explain that he hadn't meant that he himself had gone without *his* supper.

"I see you've got the house banked," he said to the girl.

"Yes. Zeke did that himself." She stepped aside for Minna to go in first.

"Looks all right," Abel said.

The girl looked up at him in the light from the doorway. "He hoped you'd say that."

Minna had gone in ahead of them.

"You mind?" Abel asked.

"His saying that? No! Why should I?"

"Some women might."

She shook her head and smiled, and went into the house after Minna. Abel came in and shut the door.

"Now I know you're busy with supper," Minna told her, "so you just go ahead and don't worry about us. After that train, I don't feel as though I'd ever be clean again."

Viola took them upstairs.

The spare room was over Zeke's study, which was the reason it had previously been so cold. The other bedroom was over the kitchen. Yesterday, Zeke had set up a stove in the spare room and run the pipe into a hole originally provided in the chimney but which since then had been papered over. Viola'd found the brass pipe collar to fit round the pipe packed away in a box with a lot of other things in the attic. She'd had the stove going all day. There was a warmth in the room to be proud of. And she'd been over all the other details a dozen times. She left them and went downstairs.

"Hot in here," Abel remarked.

293

"Well, don't say anything about it," Minna warned him.

"Oh, I won't—don't worry." He took off his coat to get ready for supper, and went over to see if there was anything more he could do to the stove. "*She* looks all right . . . didn't you think?"—speaking of the boy's wife.

"Yes," Minna agreed. "Tired, maybe. Of course, you've got to remember . . ."

"Yes, I know."

"Litchfield, she said he'd gone. You don't know where it is . . ."

"No. I've heard of it, though. He'll be in pretty soon, I guess. You aren't worried about his being out after dark, are you?"

"He's not a baby."

"No, I know that."

"Abel, why *did* you eat those doughnuts!"

"Because I was hungry. They were good doughnuts, too—when they were made."

"You spoil your supper. You know, that man was trying to find out how old he was."

"How old is he? I never can think right off."

"Oh, Abel! You know how old he is—he's twenty-four."

"Yes, I guess he is, isn't he? I was thinking he was twenty-four. You mind if I wash first?"

"No. Go ahead. I'm going to take the spread off this bed and lie down a minute."

"You tired?"

"Some."

"Your head ache?"

"No. Not a bit. It's just being in the cars, I guess."

"You want a cup of tea? I can go down and ask her for it. She'd be glad to get it for you."

"No, no. You go ahead and get washed up. We'll be

294

having supper in a minute." She'd finished folding the spread and lay down.

"Too hot in here," Abel said, "that's what's the matter." He poured the water into the bowl. "Ouch, that's hot!"

"Burn you?"

"No. Maybe this other pitcher has cold in it . . . Yes."

"You aren't much at visiting, are you?"

"Boughten soap, too. You do make good soap, Minna. I always said."

"You know, I never seen you away from home before. You're getting set."

" 'Set'? I'm not set! Plain question of which soap does the work best, that's all."

"Abel, does this house strike you it's kind of—well what I mean—*thin*?"

" 'Thin'? How—the way it's built? Keeps the cold out, anyway."

"You know what I mean."

"Where's that towel?" he said.

"It's right there—right beside you."

"Oh—yes—I got it"—and after he'd used it, he held it out toward her: "That's Boston for you! By Godfrey, look at the size of *that* thing!"

"Abel, you mustn't! This is his house. Besides, she might hear you."

Abel had finished drying. "You know, I like her, Minna. She seems different from what she did before. I think she does. Did you think so?"

"She seemed real glad to see us."

"Well, I think maybe she was. You know, I think maybe she may be going to be all right. You remember before. Well, she isn't that way now. Before she seemed to have her eye on you all the time and was figuring which way to jump. Now she's more easy."

"I wish Zeke'd come home. I'm anxious to see him."

"He'll be here. You going down to help her with supper?"

"No. Her kitchen—I don't want to snoop. It's neat enough, I guess. This room is—neat 's a pin. I'd like to help her, but she might think I was trying to pry into things."

"I'm all through there now."

"All right." Minna sat up.

"You feel any better?"

"Oh, yes!"

"You're hungry. I am."

"My ears ring," she said, going toward the washstand.

"That's the cars. Mine always do. It'll stop. You get ready now, before Zeke comes home. If you'd had a doughnut, you'd feel better."

"If I'd had a doughnut," she told him, "I'd be dead."

Because of her voice, Abel stepped suddenly across to her and stood looking down. "What's the matter?"

"No. It's all right."

"I wouldn't say so. What is it? Look up here."

Minna put her face against his coat.

He waited awhile and then said: "You come over here and sit down now." But she wouldn't. She stood where she was. She'd stopped crying, and she looked up at him, smiling. Abel kissed her once and said: "Go on now and get ready for supper." He went over to the other side of the room. "It's what we both wanted for him, Minna," he said with his back to her, "you know that."

"I know."

"He's been married—what is it?—four or five years. You hadn't ought to get upset about it now—I shouldn't think."

Minna had sat down on the edge of the bed. She was looking toward the washstand. "I'm not upset. It's only— it's only that before—well, this is his home now, isn't it? It seemed like before—until we'd seen his home, that—that *home* was his home. It isn't now. Because this is."

"That's right."

"Yes"—her voice small.

"That's how it should be, Minna. It's his turn now. He'll do all right with it."

"Yes—"

Abel turned to look at her. Every now and then it would come over him: what a least mite of a thing she was. He hated her being hurt—but he couldn't help it this time. He wondered if it would do any good if he said something about the boy's wife—something encouraging. He decided against it. He didn't know what to do, so he went over beside her and he put his hand round her head.

She reached up and took hold of his fingers, hard, and then suddenly she looked up at him. "Do I look as if I'd been crying?"

Abel said: "Well . . ."

. . . and she turned away from him and went determinedly to the washstand.

Abel was getting the brush out of the bag to go after his coat. "It isn't so much this house is thin," he said, "it's new. Doesn't look to me as though it'd been built more'n ten or twelve years. They don't build houses the way they used to—any more'n anything else."

"What's that?"

"Nothing. I was talking about the house."

"What house?"

"This one. You put that brush in here, didn't you? I don't see it."

"The brush? It's in there—over in the corner."

"Oh, yes—I got it."

"I'll brush your coat—soon's I get through here."

"I can do it all right."

"You should have done it before you washed up. You'll get all dusty again. Here—get the brush damp and then it won't fly round so."

Abel handed her the brush, and she wet it, and shook it out vigorously. "There—" she handed it back to him.

He went to work on the coat.

"What was it you said about the house?"

"What?" He stopped brushing.

"You said something about the house."

"Oh. No, nothing. . . . All I said was it was new. Give it time . . . be all right. Looks like a pretty good house—to me."

She said it might be. "Looks kind of bare. Maybe when it gets more things in it, it won't look so—well, you know, like—just a house."

Abel said, maybe, and went on with brushing his coat.

When they were ready to go down to supper, Zeke still hadn't come in. Abel said: "Well, we better go down. You ready?"

"Almost." She fastened a cameo brooch he'd given her way back years ago—before Zeke was born.

Abel said, "You look fine!" and he could see she was pleased.

They went downstairs, neither of them saying anything about Zeke's being still somewhere out on the countryside. Although it made it seem strange, after they'd made this trip just to see him—traveling all day—that now that they were here, he wasn't.

Viola met them at the foot of the stairs and took them

into the sitting room, and just as the room was before them they heard Zeke call "Hello" from the kitchen. Abel said, "Hello," and Viola had disappeared. But Zeke's mother stood where she was.

Viola scarcely checked him in the kitchen, and he came in beaming—grinned at his father—and bent over to kiss his mother.

His father said, "Well, son," and Zeke said, "Father," and then explained to them both that he was sorry he was late, but there were some people he'd had to see on the way back. He asked if they'd had a good trip. Abel said: "Yes, had a good trip." He thought himself the boy looked pretty well, but he didn't suppose his mother'd think so.

Zeke asked if supper were ready—and said he'd go and wash up. He started for the kitchen. Viola said: "Oh, Zeke, you can't—not in the kitchen! Everything's in the sink." But Zeke said he guessed he could find room, and went ahead just the same.

Viola wanted to follow him, but she felt she ought not to, so she stayed. She said to his mother: "Don't you think he looks well?"

Minna, when she answered, said, "Yes." She hadn't noticed, really. "He looks so old!"

Abel and the girl both laughed.

"If you'll excuse me," Viola said, "I'll put dinner on the table. I'm afraid Zeke won't want to wait."

Minna said: "Let me help you."

Viola started to say carelessly over her shoulder, 'Oh, no, it's nothing,' but instead she turned and said, "Why—yes, if you'd like to."

Minna went out into the kitchen with her. After a few minutes, Zeke came back into the sitting room. His father was standing by the table, one hand resting on it, and his head lowered reading the paper that lay there. He looked up, and Zeke said: "I wanted to come over to meet you myself, father, but I—well, I had to work—'bout the size of it."

"I understand. Fellow Meeker seemed to know the way all right."

"He ought to."

"Oh—here, I might's well settle with you now. Seventy-five cents, he said. Is that right?"

Zeke said: "Well—yes, that's right. Still, I—"

"Here—"

"Thank you."

"You're welcome. We got our money's worth."

Zeke put the money in his pocket. "I can use it."

"I guess you can."

"Mother looks pretty well, father—I think."

"Yes, I think she is. We seem to get around all right."

"You been all right?"

"Oh, yes. Nothing the matter with me—that I know of. Old age, maybe."

"Your back bother you any now?"

"No."

"How are things home?"

" 'Bout the same. Prices aren't much. What held you up this afternoon? Anything wrong?"

"No, no. People are kind of spread out here, is all, and I have to see them when I can. Made four calls this afternoon, on the way back. You have to stay longer here, too."

"How many you got now, son?"

"In the parish?"

"Yes."

"Well, it sounds small, but—"

"Why shouldn't it?"

300

"Oh, I know! Sure. Well, when it comes to making calls, there are fifty-three families. In separate houses, that is."

"Seems like a good many—to me."

"It's going to grow, though. It is now. Two new members by letter next week, and one on profession of faith. And then of course children coming on. You more or less count on them, I suppose."

"Mmmwell . . ."

"It's much more of a church than I'd thought it was. I'm just beginning to see it. Now you take this afternoon—"

"Supper's all ready!" his mother called—and Zeke turned to see her standing in the doorway to the dining room.

"That sounds familiar," he said, although he knew it didn't. At home she usually said, 'Supper's ready,' and she said it in a different dress.

His father said: "Well, I guess we'd better come in, then. Your mother didn't like my eating Mr. Meeker's doughnuts," he said to Zeke, "I got to show an appetite now."

The best Zeke could do was to say: "Well, we're having ham."

Abel, coming into the dining room, wondered how long Minna had been worrying for fear he was going to tell about the woman who couldn't cook anything except ham. "Ham, eh?" he said. "Well! Oh, that reminds me, Zeke, Mrs. Tarbell asked to be remembered to you."

Zeke hadn't quite heard, because he was looking at Viola to see whether the ham had turned out all right. He said, "What?" and then saw that his mother was looking at his father to remind him of the blessing. So he said to his father: "Who was?"

"Mrs. Tarbell. Friend of your mother's. Were you going to ask the blessing?"

"Yes. Mrs. Tarbell? I don't remember her."

301

"Doesn't matter."

His mother and Viola were both waiting then, so Zeke asked the blessing. He felt he'd like to add something—some expression of gratitude because his father and mother were there—and he didn't believe his father'd mind, so he did so. Then they sat down.

"Who did you say she was?" he asked.

Abel hadn't meant it to go this far, and he thought Minna was probably through being startled to have him mention Mrs. Tarbell, and she would begin to think the joke was on him. "Mrs. Tarbell, lived down in the village. You remember: thin-faced woman—deaf . . . ?"

Zeke said: "Oh, yes, I remember. Yes, I do remember her." He stood up to carve.

"What made ham remind you of her, Abel?" Minna said quietly.

Abel said he couldn't remember.

"Cuts all right," Zeke said, "cuts very well," and he handed his father a filled plate which went round the table and ended up with Viola. When he'd finished carving, he sat down, and the distribution of vegetables took place.

Someone knocking at the door called Zeke away from the table before he'd had a chance to begin to eat.

They could hear him with some man, but they couldn't hear what he said.

When he came back, he reported that it had been Dr. Thomas. Old Mrs. Perrin— ". . . the old lady sits just back of the Whites," he said to Viola—old Mrs. Perrin had had an accident. Spilled some boiling starch on her arm. Zeke had told the doctor he'd go round to see her in the morning. Viola said she thought she could go Friday. Zeke said that Thomas had said the arm wasn't anything serious at all, although of course it did give her more or less pain;

he'd arranged for the niece to go in there and sleep for the next few nights, until Mrs. Perrin could do more for herself. Viola said she'd give Zeke something to take over to her in the morning.

Zeke asked his father about various people at home, and they talked some about the election. Henry Williams had been home for a week in October. He'd been two voyages to China, first mate the last time, and Abel said he'd understood from his father there was some chance of his getting something of his own, although his father'd said he couldn't say what she'd be. Minna told Viola about the lovely shawl and a whole set of dishes Henry had brought back for his mother. Zeke remembered how one time he'd wanted to go to sea himself, but he didn't say anything about it. He asked his father if he'd have some more ham, and his father said he certainly would, it was the best he'd had in a long time. Zeke had another small piece himself. He'd been afraid it was going to be tough, but it wasn't a bit. When he got a chance to see Viola alone, he'd tell her how good it was.

Twice more Zeke had to go to the door. The first time it was a dozen hen's eggs and two duck eggs one of the Pierce children had brought over. The second time, he was gone longer. There were silences in the dining room, but even then they couldn't hear anything, except once when they heard him moving about in the kitchen. He had an odd look when he came back, as though something had happened. As he sat down, he said to Viola: "One of Chalmers' friends." And Viola said, "Oh"—and spoke immediately to his mother about something else.

Abel asked Zeke whether he'd done anything about a horse.

Zeke said, well, he hadn't done anything yet. The church

was supposed to provide him with a horse, and up till now they'd lent him a rig whenever he had some special use for it. Like this afternoon, for instance. White had spoken to him once or twice about it, and had apologized for the delay, and had assured him he'd have a horse for him inside of another ten days. White had rather intimated that he had his eye on something that he thought would be all right.

Abel asked whether White knew anything about a horse.

Zeke said, well, what *he* wished was that they'd let him buy his own horse, but he didn't suppose there was much chance of that, inasmuch as the church was going to pay for it, and they'd all be afraid he'd be done.

That gray of Meeker's wouldn't be a bad horse, Abel said, if you could take about fifteen years off his age.

Zeke said he'd be a good horse. But he was going to have to get something Viola could drive, too.

Abel said, yes, that was true.

Zeke assumed that his father didn't feel much interest in discussing the kind of horse that Viola could drive, too.

Viola took out the things, and brought in the pie and a plate with the cheese on it already cut. His father was fussy about cheese, Zeke knew, but he'd seen to it that this was last year's and he hoped it would be all right.

Abel peered across the table and said: "That's last year's cheese. And it looks good, too."

Zeke had to go to the door again. He made short work of it this time. They heard him say: "All right, Jason. Thanks. Good night!" He was laughing when he came in. "Jason Embler," he said to Viola. "Borrowed a screwdriver three days ago, and just brought it back."

The piecrust was something it was impossible to overlook. It was so tough there was no use pretending otherwise.

Finally Viola turned point-blank to his mother. "What *is* the matter with it? Can *you* tell me?"

Minna'd known what was the matter with it when she'd seen it in the kitchen: too much water. From a long glance at the girl's face she thought probably it was all right to go ahead. "Well, it used to be with me that I put too much water to it"—looking at the pie as it lay on her plate in front of her.

The girl said nothing right away. Minna was afraid she'd been too sure of her. "But it took me an awful long time to find it out." She laughed a little, "Didn't it, Abel?"

"I don't know," Abel said, "did it? Pie's always a gamble—bottom crust, anyway. I don't see but what this' all right"—chewing "—first rate."

"Certainly it is," Zeke said to Viola. "What are you talking about!"

Viola looked—amused—from one to the other, and conscious of a solid loyalty behind her, turned happily to the woman. "It's the working it up that I don't understand," she said. "Tell me about that."

Minna began hesitantly at first: "Well—my mother used to say, 'You can't fight a piecrust, you got to coax it!' "

Minna began to feel a strange enjoyment. Her mother had taught her these things—she could hear her mother's voice now—and see her hands. It was a long time ago that Minna had known that she herself would never in her turn be teaching them to her own daughter. She still knew that. And she knew also—Abel and her son almost forgotten— that this minute or two was only a small happening, and would not likely happen again.

Abel spoke gently and aside to Zeke, more or less cas-

305

ually—and the boy turned to him suddenly, having heard his voice only and not the words.

"I was saying about that field of yours," Abel told him.

"Oh! What about it? I was listening to Mother—I'm sorry."

"I was just thinking—if you say so, might try some buckwheat in there this time."

"Buckwheat," Zeke said. "We never tried that, did we? You got some seed?"

"Well, yes—some. I thought maybe we might buy some. Try to get hold of something real fancy, just for the fun of it. See how it'd turn out."

Zeke said he didn't know much about buckwheat—what was it worth now?

They were still talking about it when Viola got up to clear the table.

Zeke and his father went into the sitting room, and as they were walking into the room, Zeke asked his father if he'd heard anything from Watling. He'd had in mind to ask him before, but each time he'd put it off somehow, thinking he'd rather ask him when they were alone.

"Yes, a couple of weeks ago," his father said. "Had a letter from him came from down East somewhere. I forget the name of the town—over beyond Portland."

"Is he all right?"

"I guess so, yes. Said he was thinking some of going out West this winter. Missouri, or some place."

"Missouri! I don't see what he wants to go out there for."

"I guess he doesn't either—except he's never been there before. Said someone had told him the West was a good place for a young man, so he thought he might go out there."

Zeke sniffed appreciatively. "He isn't going to drive out, is he?"

"I shouldn't think so."

"She'd do it, though, father."

"Who, the mare?"

"Yes, sir. She'd go to California and back."

"You always did like her, didn't you. You know how old she is now?"

"She's not old. How old would she be? Not over ten, would she?"

"All of that. How old was she when you drove her?"

"Three."

"Well . . ."

"Yes, I guess you're right. It doesn't seem that long."

"I wrote and asked him if he wouldn't make us a visit 'fore he left, but I didn't hear anything back from him, so I guess he must have left before he got the letter."

"Hope he doesn't turn up there while you're away," Zeke said.

"No, he won't do that. I told him we were coming here."

"I'd like to see him," Zeke said.

Viola called to him from the dining room—someone to see him.

"Don't seem to give you much peace," his father said.

"Not much—" Zeke admitted as he went out. "Stay still. I'll be right back."

Viola came in again in a minute to tell his father that Zeke had had to go down the street for something and had asked his father to excuse him.

"Oh! Don't worry about me!" Abel said. "They seem to keep him pretty well on the jump."

"Yes, they do. He never complains, though. It's been the same ever since we got here."

"Well, part of the job, I guess."

"I guess so."

"You need any help out there?"

"Gracious, no! I'm not doing anything as it is."

"Well, you stand up for your rights now!"

"Oh, please, I—I didn't mean *that*. You *know* I didn't— don't you?"

She was so distressed Abel was annoyed with himself for having joked her. He managed to make her see that.

She tried to make him understand that she liked being shown things—shown how to do things—by Zeke's mother. "You see, I—well, maybe Zeke told you. My mother died when I was a baby . . . when I was born. It—it makes a difference."

Abel didn't feel uncomfortable, but he didn't know why. "No," he said, "I didn't know that."

"I'd like to tell you about it sometime," she said gravely.

Abel smiled. "All right," he said.

She left him then, and went back to the kitchen.

Abel settled into a chair, and picked up the paper. 'Yes, sir,' he said, 'I'm beginning to think I was wrong about her. He might've done worse.' He tried to read the paper, but he couldn't take any interest in it. He hadn't realized before that he was tired. But now that he was alone he felt it. His head rang some, and his body was tired from being cramped up all day. Minna was tired, too. He'd have to get Minna to bed pretty soon; she'd had a long day.

Someone was knocking at the front door. Abel sat up straight and wondered whether he'd better go and answer it. Thinking, 'Well, I don't know who else is going to . . .' he started for the door, and added, 'Hope they don't keep this up all night.'

He opened the door to a stocky, square-shouldered gentleman with a white beard. The man had expected to recognize whoever opened the door, and, when he didn't, it seemed to surprise him more than it should.

Abel said: "Evening, sir."

"Good evening, sir. My name is White. I called to see Mr. Peele."

Abel knew who he was then. "He's not here right now. Come in. He'll be back pretty soon."

White hesitated, and then said, "Thank you," and stepped in.

Abel led him into the sitting room. "Come in and sit down." He'd rather not have had to talk with him, but Zeke, he remembered, had spoken warmly of him, and he supposed it was up to him to be polite. He said: "Mrs. Peele's here, if you'd like me to get her."

"Oh, no. Don't disturb her. And don't let me keep you, sir, if you were . . ."

"No," Abel said, "I was just trying to keep awake. I'm his father. We're here for Thanksgiving."

"Oh—yes, I—I should have known. Well . . . Traveling's pretty hard work, I find it."

"So do I—anyway, when you're not used to it."

"Yes," White agreed. "I don't know—I always like to get home at night."

Abel said, yes. But he didn't say it heartily. Any bed at all would suit him right now—give him the nearest one.

White, out of some thought, said unexpectedly: "Mr. Peele: I'd like to take this opportunity to tell you that I think we're fortunate to get your son to take this church here. He probably hasn't told you, but he's doing well."

309

Abel looked at him a moment. "Thank you," he said. White said nothing. Abel felt pretty sure, then, that the man had spoken honestly, because if he hadn't he'd have gone on to say something more—to try to lay it on thick. Abel said: "I guess you had more or less to do with his getting the job, didn't you?—from the way he spoke."

White seemed to be thinking. "No, I don't know—"

"If I recollect, he wrote to me that you—well, he stayed at your house, didn't he?"

"Well, yes, but that had nothing to do with it. No—" White hesitated. He seemed then to pull his mind away from what had been holding it, and to try to put it onto what he wanted to speak about. "What we needed here," he said, "was a man who'd do the work. At least that's what it seemed to me. No fault of the last man. I don't mean that for a minute. He just wasn't up to it, his health wasn't. He was a fine man, and I liked him. We all did. Well, I don't know—" he said hopelessly, "that's the way it goes, I guess."

"M, hm."

White was twisting his hands. "Preaching, yes," he said earnestly; he was looking down at his fingers: "you've got to have that. But that's only two or three hours, say, all told, out of the week." He spoke more easily now, as though he'd been over the subject before. "In a place like this—a small place—people get more of a chance to compare the rest of the week with that two or three hours. And if it doesn't stack up right . . . well, then it kind of takes the edge off of it—of the preaching."

"Yes, I suppose it might."

"I don't mean to say he can't preach." White looked up.

"No—I understand."

"Of course, to my mind there isn't anyone who can preach now the way they used to—not the kind of preaching that I used to sit in front of. But I don't know—well—" he looked away again—"it doesn't seem so important to me as it used to. The older I get, the more I guess I'm inclined to go by what a man does instead of what he can say about what he thinks he believes. And I think sometimes it may be all right to give a little weight to *why* he does it, too."

"Well, I guess a good many feel that way, don't they?"

"Maybe. Maybe more'n we think for."

"Yes."

"Yes, that may be. Oh, I admit there were some—one man in particular—didn't agree with all your son said. I'm talking now about the first time he was here. Still, as I said to this man I speak of, you'd be put to it—when it comes to the details of religion—to find two people who *do* agree. Supposing he and your son didn't agree, I told him. Why, he ought to be glad of it! Most candidates, you can't get yes or no out of them to save your neck. They don't want to offend anyone. Oh, I know, you can't blame them. If they answered straight out to every question, it wouldn't be long before they'd offended everyone there, on something or other. Well, we talked it over the next day, after he'd gone—after your son had gone—and most of them seemed to feel the way I did about it, so all I did was put it to a vote. That was all it was. We voted to call him."

"I see."

"I don't know—" White said. "You go to hire a man for a church and it's about like hiring a man for anything else. If you think he *can* work, and on top of that you're prepared to guess that he *will* work—well, there you are. You need a man, and you hire him. And you hope it'll turn out."

Thoughtfully, Abel said, yes, he guessed that was about the way of it.

White suddenly seemed a little uncomfortable. "I—I just didn't want you to feel he was beholden to me at all. I ought not to stay much longer. You said he was coming right back?"

"Said he was—just had to go down the street for something. Why don't you stay? Mrs. Peele will be in in a minute—both Mrs. Peeles, for that matter."

"I'd like to see both of them."

"They're at it out in the kitchen just now."

"Probably talking about tomorrow's dinner. No—I ought to go back." White stood up, and Abel also. White had something on his mind he wanted to say. Turning away to pick up his hat, he said: "You might tell him that I've been thinking of that matter he spoke of in connection with my boy. I think it might work out."

"Yes, sir. I'll tell him." It was something that meant a good deal to the old gentleman.

White faced him, then, and held out his hand. "Good night."

Abel shook hands. "Good night."

White, going to the door, said: "You'll give my apologies to Mrs. Peele, won't you?—and to Mrs. Peele."

"I'll take care of it," Abel said.

Coming back into the room, he thought that probably the explanation for it was that White had come over pretty well worked up to talk about whatever this business was about his son, and then when he couldn't talk about that—and being sort of worked up, anyway—he'd talked more than he meant to about something else. Because the man didn't seem to be the kind of man who was a chatterbox generally.

312

Well, he guessed he'd go out into the kitchen and see how they were coming along. . . .

Abel stepped into the kitchen from the dining room just as Mr. Watling came into the kitchen from the door to outside.

Mr. Watling bowed to Mr. Peele with exaggerated formality, and without quite keeping back a delighted smile.

Abel felt good—just as he did every time he saw him. He'd more than half suspected he'd turn up—and just about this way, too. Minna, he could see, was as glad to see Watling as he was himself.

But the girl looked frightened—well, startled, anyway.

Mr. Watling spoke to the girl—not bowing, but speaking with a humorous earnestness. "Please don't worry," he said, "I'm not going to stay all night. And forgive me for erupting suddenly this way in the midst of your kitchen. I have a sorry flair for the dramatic—or for what I think's the dramatic, and generally turns out to be rudeness."

"It certainly does!" Minna said.

Watling paid no attention. He said pathetically to the girl: "I *may* come in . . . ?"

Viola laughed then. "Yes. Do!"

"Kind of late for permission, isn't it?" Abel said.

Watling turned to Minna. He said, in the very best of humor: "How do you do, Mrs. Peele?"

"Gracious! You scared the life out of me! You didn't even knock! Where'd you come from?"

"Oh, a lot of places," Watling said pleasantly.

Abel thought that was just about the way he looked. He didn't have about him the mark of any particular place—as though he'd been so many places that none of

313

them showed on him. He stood there holding his sweeping, big black hat carelessly at his side. Abel thought that when Watling got out West, somebody'd probably take him for a card gambler.

"Zeke home?" Watling asked.

"Gone up the street," Abel said.

"You had your supper?" Minna asked cheerfully.

"Thank you. Yes, I had supper." And to Viola: "Are you acquainted with your neighbor Mrs. Parsons?"

"In the little brown house?"

"She's putting me up for the night."

"Oh, I wish we could. Zeke will be disappointed. But you will come over here for breakfast."

Watling bowed. "I should be delighted. So will Mrs. Parsons. I paid her in advance for bed and breakfast, and she still thinks I'm a horse thief."

"She seen the horse?" Abel inquired.

Mr. Watling was shaping an answer with swift but loving care, when Zeke burst in the door. Zeke had shouted, "Sheba's out there!" as soon as he got the door open, and then he saw Watling.

"You didn't think she came alone, did you?" Watling said, and then: "How are you?"

Zeke looked from one to the other. "When did he get here? Did you know he was coming?"—and then he went over to Watling and shook hands with him—and nodded his head, just with a single jerk, as he did so. "You're going to stay awhile?" he said hopefully.

"Tomorrow," Watling said.

"Well, you'll—you'll be here for dinner tomorrow noon, won't you?"

"No, Zeke, I'm afraid not. I've got to get away in the morning."

"In the *morning!* You can't stay for Thanksgiving dinner?—here?"

"No, Zeke, I'd like to, but I guess I can't." He smiled. "How have you been?"

"Oh, I've been all right. Well—come in and sit down." He turned to Viola first: "You're all through here, aren't you?"

"Almost. Your mother's done all the work."

"You all go into the sitting room," Minna said. "We'll be in in a minute."

Going through the dining room, Abel said to Zeke, "Your friend Mr. White was here—" and then delivered the message.

Zeke said: "Oh, yes—all right. I certainly hope it does myself. He say anything else about it?"

"No."

Watling, who was ahead, turned round to them as he came into the sitting room and said: "Reason I stopped here, Zeke, was to see if you'd board Sheba for the winter. Free, I mean. That is, except for whatever work you can make her do—which won't be much."

Finally Zeke said, "Where are you going to be?"

"I'm going out to Missouri."

"I guess we could. You mean it?"

"About the horse? Or Missouri?"

"About Sheba."

"Why shouldn't I mean it? I'll be back sometime round April, I guess. I don't know for sure."

"What in thunder you want to go to Missouri for?" Abel asked, sitting down.

"Man out there said he wanted me to come out. I thought I would. You've never been in Missouri, have you? Neither have I."

315

"Let's see—" Abel said. "No, I don't believe I ever have been to Missouri."

"Why don't you put her in the barn tonight?" Zeke said. "Two stalls there, and one of 'em's all cleaned out and empty."

"What's in the other one?"

"Oh, a lot of old broken things—washbowl, and a step-ladder—and an old broken-down bed, for one thing."

"Wish I'd known it. I needn't've hired a room."

"I can go put her up now, if you say so. You got feed in the back, I suppose—same as we used to? I haven't got any."

"Yes, there's some there. Go ahead. I guess I can walk from here to Mrs. Parsons'."

Zeke turned round when he got to the door. He said to Watling: "Thank you."

"You needn't. The way you'll feed her, she'll get so fat she won't be able to work at all."

Zeke said, "Well . . ." and started to go out.

"I can't take that buggy with me on the train, you know," Watling called. "You'll have to find room for that —and the harness."

"We got *room* enough!"—and they heard him go out the front door.

Watling said to Abel: "How do things look?"

"What do you think?"

Watling sat down first. Then he said: "Same as you do, I guess."

"Yes."

"He's got a good chance here. Looks to me so."

"And nothing to hinder him."

"That's what I mean. You ask me, the day they buried that uncle of hers, she started new."

316

"Maybe before that," Abel said.

"Maybe." And after a pause; "Mrs. Peele looks well—"

"She is, thanks."

"You look as though you might last a little while yet yourself."

"I hope to. If I don't work too hard. How'd you come?"

"Right down across. Took me three weeks from Portland. Roads are bad. Dished a wheel the other side of Worcester."

"I wrote you a letter. You ever get it?"

"When?"

"Couple of weeks ago."

"No. Anything special?"

"Not very. Thought you might make us a visit,—before you went out there to Missouri, or wherever it is. You wouldn't change your mind?"

"It's good of you. Mrs. Peele know you wrote it?"

"Yes—she knew."

"It's good of you. I'd like to. Now I got started, though, I guess I'd better go."

"Hard for you to get started."

"Well, I told this fellow I'd come."

"You wouldn't want to say what it is?"

"It is kind of shameful. Newspaper."

"No!"

"Why not? I can spell. I've never been an editor, either."

"Newspaper, eh? You know, you might like that."

"For a while, maybe. I thought I'd try it, anyway. I'll send you a copy—I guess they do have mail out there."

"Tell me—it's none of my business, but—you weren't planning to put any money into this, were you?"

"Any what?"

"I just thought I'd make sure."

317

"No, I'm safe enough on that score."

"You're not *too* safe . . ."

"No, I'm all right. Things haven't been so bad lately—thank you just the same. I can get out there, all right."

"Back?"

"Well, from what I hear about this newspaper business, you get chased out of town every so often, anyway. I'll just head east and keep going. If I can stir them up enough so that they give me a good, inspiring send-off, I ought to get here by May."

"Where you going to be—St. Louis?"

"Yes."

"Well . . . I'm going to make you a bet. By the middle of the second cold spell—if they *have* cold spells in St. Louis—by the middle of the second cold spell, you'll be sitting up in the sunshine on top of a river boat—looking pretty good because that hat'll be over your face—and you'll have your feet up on the railing, and you'll be just about half-way down to the Gulf of Mexico."

"You shouldn't have said that. I hadn't even thought of it—not more than a few times. What did you want to bet?"

"Oh, I don't know . . . say I bet you the best heifer in my barn against one of those hats."

"*One* heifer?"

"One hat."

"If I lose, will you wear it?"

"No."

"Then it's no bet. Here comes your wife, anyway."

Minna and Viola came in, and Mr. Watling accepted and discharged his responsibilities without making it apparent that he was doing so. He did most of the talking, and he relieved Viola's apprehensions by talking mostly about himself. The stories that he told were complete in themselves and they were good enough to justify themselves. And they had no possible application to anything that Viola was remembering from the past.

Viola began to find him less presently fearsome.

It seemed to Abel that Watling was according her about the same sensible treatment that he would a horse—a good horse that had had a lot of ill-treatment. He was kind of puttering round the stall to begin with, talking, and taking things easy. He had sense enough to know you couldn't do a job like that all at once.

Zeke came in, and was surprised to find they'd been talking about anything besides Sheba. When he found Viola hadn't even been told!—he seemed to think she'd want to run right out to the barn right then and there to see her.

Viola asked Zeke if she could go out to the barn now and see her.

Zeke said, yes, he guessed so, if she wanted to—and when she'd stood up, he took her by the arm and hurried her out, talking all the way.

Neither Minna nor Abel nor Mr. Watling made any comment, but Mr. Watling stretched himself comfortably and said he guessed he ought to be getting along back—he didn't know as Mrs. Parsons would let him in after ten o'clock.

Minna was surprised to find that it *was* almost ten o'clock, and when Zeke and Viola came in, Mr. Watling had already stood up to go. Zeke protested, but Mr. Watling pointed out that he'd be back in no time for breakfast —a fact which made it possible for him to leave without having it dragged out too long.

Abel and Minna being on their feet, Abel took advantage of it to say that he thought they'd go along up to bed. It had been quite a day. He made a sign to Zeke that his

319

mother was tired, and Zeke understood and nodded. Minna'd already told Viola, while they were out in the kitchen, that Abel was tired out and she was going to get him to bed just as soon as she could—Watling or no Watling.

Zeke said he had a little work to do in the study, and said good night to his mother. She didn't say anything but "Good night, son," but he understood from the way she pressed his arm that it meant a good deal to her to be there, and that she was glad to see things the way they were.

Viola went upstairs with Minna to see that everything was all right.

And Zeke and his father strolled out to see what kind of night it was, before going to bed.

It was clear out, and the wind—Zeke pointing out to his father about where north lay, and his father saying, yes, there was the Pole Star—the wind seemed to be coming from pretty well to the west. On the whole, it looked as though it ought to be a good day tomorrow.

Zeke seemed to feel that both of them knew it was a good chance for his father to say something fatherly—and when his father chose not to, he thought that that probably was the reason. For some reason, as they came back into the house, the fact that his father hadn't tried to say anything made him feel more comfortable with him, and more free, and perfectly understanding.

His father said, well, he guessed he'd go up. Zeke said, all right, he was going to himself before long—he had just a couple of letters to write and some other things to attend to and then he was going to bed.

Abel started upstairs, and said: "Good night, son."

"Good night, father."

. . . and then, seeing his father going slowly upstairs,

Zeke wanted to say to him something that would mean: thank you for making this trip because you knew I wanted you to be here.

Zeke said, "Thank's for coming . . ."

. . . and Abel said, "Glad to," and went on upstairs.

Viola put her head over the banisters and called down that she was going to bed. "And don't you work too long. You ought to be going to bed, too."

"I shan't. You put out the light. I'll be up in a few minutes."

His father was at the top of the stairs then, and spoke to her. . . .

Zeke went into the study. He had his whole sermon to write for the Thanksgiving service.

It was cold in the study, a still, gray cold that was a presence and a reality. But he could always warm his fingers over the lamp chimney so as to limber them up for writing. The desk was a table, really, with a green baize top, and drawers at either end. Why anyone should have been led to green baize as a desk covering! A pile of old leaves would have made a better surface to write on. The cloth was worn through in places, and spotted in a good many more—some inkspots, and others of less certain origin, but now stiffened—and the whole cloth had a grimy feel, being filled with dust. He used a board to write on that was fairly smooth. And a type of paper that conduced to thinking before writing.

The cold was thickest down nearest the floor—there was a layer of cold there that he could put his hand down into and feel. His predecessor had used a small, worn, wooden box to put his feet on. Zeke had had to pull the desk out from the wall—and the box jammed up against the baseboard—so as to be able to straighten his legs out.

Low in his chair, his feet thrust forward and sticking out on the other side of the desk, he turned up the collar of his coat. The warmth of his body came up from inside his waistcoat, and made the air in the room seem all the colder. But the study door stood open—and the heat from the rest of the house would be coming in after a while.

He thought: all right, now—'Thanksgiving.' For days he'd known what the trouble was. And now, thinking about it, he'd got to find a way to get around it. When he got this done, he could go to bed.

The trouble was, that it was going to be difficult to stand up and tell these people to be thankful, when, of course, he had about ten times as much to be thankful for as they had. *He* was thankful enough—he couldn't help but be. That was what made it embarrassing. Look at White, for instance. It would be awkward to tell White to stand up in his pew and sing a little song of thanks for the local harvest—said to be somewhat under the average—with White's mind all the time filled with the fact of his son. Still, there was some hope for young White. If you could get him to drug himself with work instead of with rye whisky, there was a chance it might tide him over and he'd come out the right end of the horn after all. Argument, reasoning, telling him to face matters, and so on, weren't going to do him any good because he wasn't up to it. He'd got to have some kind of work that would put him to sleep at night for a few months, until he'd got used to living with things the way they were. He wouldn't work for himself, of course, and he knew his children didn't need money. But he just might be moved to work for people worse off than he was himself. Well, they could try it, anyway. It was standard treatment, but it seemed to have worked before. It looked so from the outside, anyhow. You couldn't tell about inside. Still, if you enabled a man to put up a front, maybe that was something. . . .

Well! This wasn't Thanksgiving. Suppose he went at it by pointing out to them the disasters that might have landed on them during the past year—and hadn't. No locusts, anyhow. No fire and pestilence—except old Hagedorn had had his barn burned down, and then there was that thing that had happened to the Websters' little girl last year—just about this time, too. No, it wouldn't be very helpful to talk to the Websters about fire. Or pestilence, either, to some of them. Well, you take the list now,—of things a congregation was usually supposed to be thankful for. All right: fine for a congregation as a whole. Fine. Fairly prosperous, all of them alive, and looking at them as a whole, things not so bad. But in a small place—where you knew each individual and a little something about what he was up against—then it didn't work so well. Too many exceptions—and in the mind of each individual, it was the exception, the thing that he was up against himself and that perhaps the rest of them had escaped, that he had to be helped against. Reminding them that the rest of them *had* escaped—that he alone out of the lot had been singled out by Providence for this particular form of suffering— well, that wasn't going to do him much good.

'We all have *something* to be thankful for, haven't we, my good friends!' How would that go? Oh, that would be fine. 'Mr. White, what you want to do is forget about your son, and praise God because that lovely barn of yours didn't burn down the way Mr. Hagedorn's barn did. And, Mr. Hagedorn, you can be thankful that even though you haven't any barn, still you haven't any son either. So that puts you that much ahead of Mr. White.'

Or for all of them: 'However bad it is now, it'll just

make Heaven seem that much better'—and be run out of the church for blasphemy. Although there were a dozen hymns that said the same thing in different words—more words, and mixing them up to suit the rhyme. So no one noticed. Most people just used the words to check up on the place where they were supposed to be in the music.

It was cold around his feet—and he knocked the edges of his boot soles one against the other.

No—it was the same old thing. If you thought about a sermon too much, you couldn't write it. Because all the thinking did was to show you what a little way—what a sickeningly little way—your thinking could go. It ended in bewilderment. But after that . . . well, there was faith. 'Faith is the evidence of things not seen . . .' 'Faith without works . . .' Make it: 'Faith without work,' because it's only in the weariness that comes after work that you seem to be eligible to feel faith. Any kind of work . . . for a person that's sick, a day of trying to hang on to his courage. That's a pretty genuine kind of work. He'd never had to try that himself—never been sick. Or a man that *couldn't* work—for any reason. Give him a day of trying to keep his mind from going to pieces—he'd have 'weariness after work' all right. And God send him the peace to go to sleep! You could see it after a lifetime of work. His father'd be that way when the time came. He'd have earned it.

Well, this wasn't *his* work; he'd got to turn out a sermon.

He drew his feet in under him, and reached out to thrust the pen into the jar of shot. Along in January, the ink'd be liable to freeze. Break off a piece, then, and write with it like a crayon.

Now, then!—as he hunched himself over the paper—you

people *have* got something to be thankful about—and you know it. And I'm going to make you see it, and think about it. For a while, anyway—and after that you can go home and have a good time—the same as I'm going to do.

And as soon as I get this job done, I can go to bed.

He hadn't written out the last two or three sermons—partly because he didn't have the time to play with the little phrases, and partly because if he knew what he wanted to say, he wasn't afraid of the words any more. But he had to know what he wanted to say, and to put that down. Then when it came time to preach it, what he had to say would seem to be the important thing, and he'd just use the words that came along—sometimes the one's he'd thought in, and sometimes other words—words that seemed to come handier in a church and to be more natural.

So he went at it—the way a man does with a brush scythe clearing out an old road that's all grown up. He knows the general lay of the road, but he only sees a little of it ahead of him at a time, and he works toward that. And he stopped to turn up the lamp now and again as a man stops to freshen up the edge of his scythe. Those are the times when he thinks back over what he's done and measures up what's ahead. The work gets hold of him after a while, and he progresses by the progress of the work, and he pushes aside the reminders from his sense of time.

Coming down the last stretch, Zeke was going pretty fast. He knew he was tired, but it was the finish of the job, coming closer, that held him . . . and now instead of pushing himself forward against the work, he was drawn on toward the finish.

When he'd come to the end, he said, "There, I guess that'll do it," and sat up. His head swayed a little bit, and he rubbed his hands across his eyes and sniffed. He was hungry, too—must be pretty late. Well, that job was done! He guessed he'd go in the kitchen and get something to eat. He picked up the lamp and went out—quietly.

He'd thought first, just a glass of milk—and then the ham looked pretty good, and he took out his own knife and cut himself off a little slice, and then some more, and sat up on the table, swinging his legs, to eat. It was still warm in the kitchen. Now why wouldn't it be all right to write his sermons in here? Be a good place for it.

He heard a noise in the dining room—and Viola put her head in the door. He grinned at her and said: "You ought to be in bed—come in. Have some ham. You didn't want to save it, did you?"

The light made her blink. "I've been in bed," she said. "Do you know what time it is?"

"Time to eat. You been asleep?"

She laughed. "Don't I look it?"

She did, too. She'd put her coat on, and she had on her feet the carriage boots she'd saved from before she was married.

Zeke said: "You look all right."

Viola was peering at the ham. "Where's the knife?"

"Here—" he slid down off the table and reached in his pocket. She let him use his own knife—not saying anything. He knew if it had been in the daytime, she'd have made him use the kitchen knife. It was light and warm in the kitchen—but it was dark in the house surrounding it, and upstairs in the darkness, the two people were asleep.

"Milk?"

"Yes, I think milk. You get your sermon done?"

"All done."

"Good for you! What's it about?"

Zeke resumed his place on the table. "Well, I thought 'Thanksgiving' might be a nice topic tomorrow."

Viola took the other end of the table. They were separated by the ham and Zeke's glass of milk. "Yes," she said, "that might do very well."

"Timely," Zeke said.

"Very."

" 'Apropos,' as they say in Boston."

"Do they? I'd forgotten." She set down his glass. "That's better milk than we used to get in Boston."

"Glad you like it. Don't hesitate to help yourself—any time. Have some more ham." He pulled off a piece for himself. "My wife cooked this ham."

"Did she really! How is she on pie?"

"Not bad, not bad—she's got a little ways to go yet on pie, but she's learning. Can I get you a piece of pie?"

"No, thank you! And it's time you were coming to bed, too."

"Why, is it late?"

"Two o'clock."

"No, it can't be."

"It is, though."

Zeke stretched pleasantly and yawned. "You ought to be proud of me, Viola. Look how hard I work—just to support you, that's all. If it weren't for you, I wouldn't do a lick."

"I'm not proud of you when you work till two o'clock. Come on, now—you've had enough ham to give you the nightmare."

"Not *that* ham!"

"You know, Zeke, it *was* pretty good—wasn't it?"

"Certainly was." He stood down onto the floor—and yawned again. "All right—I'm ready." He helped her down from the table. "You go ahead," he said, "I'll bring the lamp."

"Wait a minute till I put some water in this glass."

It was a big lamp, and he lifted it gingerly.

Viola said: "Oh, blow it out. We don't need it."

"You might fall."

"I can hold onto you."

He cupped his hand round behind the chimney and blew.

It was pitch-black, and the light from the lamp still shone in his eyes. "Where are you?" he said.

"*I'm* right here. Where are you?"

He found her then, and they started out through the door.

"Can you see anything?" she asked.

"Can't see a thing. But you hang onto me." They worked their way along. Then he said: "Wait a minute—yes, here are the stairs. Now we're all right."